**First published in Australia
in 2024 by the author**
Copyright © CE Shorland

Korean translations provided by Senna Hong-Hepworth.

For more information, or to contact the author regarding permission to reproduce or reference material from this book, please visit
www.ceshorland.com

Independently published.
ISBN 9781764251600

DEADWEIGHT

CE SHORLAND

DYSTOPIA SERIES
BOOK ONE

Content Note

If you're looking for a fairytale dystopian story with a gentle path and a guaranteed happy ending, you won't find it here.

This novel explores a harsher vision of survival and contains explicit material that some readers may find confronting or distressing. While care has been taken to approach sensitive themes with respect, the world depicted is intentionally unflinching - reflecting what may emerge when society collapses and survival takes precedence over comfort.

Before continuing, please take a moment to consider whether this story is right for you. Your wellbeing and mental health matters, and it is completely okay to step back if you feel it may not be suitable. If you feel comfortable proceeding, you are welcome to continue reading.

I would like to explicitly state that, despite the dark content, there are moments of love and tenderness, flashes of humanity and humility, and glimpses of joy and laughter. While this story can be challenging, it also contains moments of hope and happiness amidst the struggle.

If you would prefer to know more before continuing, a detailed list of trigger warnings can be found on the following page.

Trigger Warnings

This novel is a dark, dystopian story and contains themes that some readers may find confronting or distressing. The material ranges from physical and psychological violence to sexual content, moral complexity, and survival in extreme circumstances.

As stated on the previous page, great care has been taken to approach sensitive topics with respect, but the world depicted is intentionally unflinching - reflecting a realistic interpretation of how society may fracture when survival takes precedence over comfort.

While the story is dark, there are also moments of connection, compassion, and small acts of hope. Scenes of love, loyalty, and fleeting joy provide glimpses of humanity even in extreme circumstances.

Take a moment to check in with yourself, and consider your comfort before proceeding. If any of the themes here feel like they may be too much, it's perfectly okay to take a step back.

Readers are encouraged to review the following list carefully before continuing.

Violence & Physical Harm

- Graphic violence and injury
- Gun violence and use of weapons
- Execution and murder
- Torture and physical abuse
- Mutilation and disfigurement
- Blood and gore

Sexual Content & Sexual Violence

- Consensual sexual content
- Sexual assault and rape (including one explicit scene)
- Attempted sexual assault
- Coercion and survival-based sexual exchanges
- Sexual exploitation and power imbalance

Harm Involving Minors

- Death of minors
- Abuse and injury involving minors
- Sexual violence involving a minor (not graphically depicted)

Death, Grief & Trauma

- Death of major and minor characters
- Dead bodies and human remains
- Grief, loss, and bereavement
- Emotional distress and trauma responses

Psychological & Emotional Abuse

- Psychological torture and manipulation
- Degradation, humiliation, and coercion
- Verbal abuse and mistreatment

Self-Harm & Suicide

- Assisted suicide
- References to suicide
- Self-inflicted injury

Captivity & Loss of Autonomy

- Kidnapping and imprisonment
- Forced confinement and restraint
- Loss of bodily autonomy

Survival Themes & Moral Complexity

- Starvation and resource deprivation
- Survival-driven violence
- Moral ambiguity and lack of remorse

Substance Use

- Alcohol consumption and intoxication
- Smoking (cigarettes)

Animal Harm

- Hunting and animal death
- Animal processing (skinning)

Language

- Frequent strong language
- Use of explicit and offensive terms
- Derogatory language
- Degrading and misogynistic dialogue
- Threatening and aggressive speech

Additional Themes

- Infidelity and relationship conflict
- Nudity
- Illness and medical conditions
- Confronting or distressing dialogue and themes

If you feel that any of these themes may be distressing but are still interested in reading, a more detailed, chapter-by-chapter list of content warnings can be found at the end of the book.

Real-world locations are referenced throughout the story and may be distressing to some readers, particularly those familiar with them. A full list of these locations can be found at the end of the book.

This page is included in the contents and can be easily located there.

Contents

Chapter One

Beneath a sky painted with hues of a dying autumn sun, in the heart of a forgotten town, the air was thick with the scent of an oncoming storm. Enigmatic figures materialised from the shadows. Their bodies swayed to the beat of her heart pounding against her chest. A solitary drum beat in the silence as they surrounded her like phantoms in a macabre ballet. A spectral figure from a dream - the first person she saw - soothed her aching head with a damp cloth. Another offered her sips of water while she coughed and struggled to swallow. A man peered down at her with a furrowed brow, and another mysterious figure lingered in the doorway with an unsettling glint of desire in his eyes. As they hovered around her, the room buzzed with a muted urgency. Concern etched their faces, and an undercurrent of tension pulsed in time with her racing heart. Fragmented images flickered like scattered puzzle pieces, and she couldn't fully comprehend the reality they created. With the abruptness of a shattering glass, she jolted awake, her world spiralling into chaos as though she had disturbed an age-old equilibrium. The surreal haze that had once been her refuge now turned into a stormy vortex of uncertainty and fear, spinning wildly out of her control. A cry of pain escaped her lips as she tried to sit up, but her back and legs refused to cooperate. From the corner of her eye, she saw the same woman from her fleeting visions hurry into the room with a damp cloth and a glass of water.

"Easy now," the woman spoke gently. Her mild Spanish accent added warmth to her sharp words. "You're weak, rushing won't do you any favours. The sooner you regain strength, the sooner you can move." A man, the one with the unsettling eyes, appeared in the doorway once again.

"And the sooner we can leave this place, I'm sick of it." He grumbled, striding away with urgency and frustration. He walked with heavy, agitated steps, each one echoing down the hallway. His grumbling was like distant thunder, punctuated by the clenching of his jaw and the tightening of his fists.

"Don't mind my brother. It's not you, he hates everyone," the woman interjected sharply. The girl in the bed wondered what she might have done to earn his disdain. "You must be hungry. I'll get you some soup." The woman stood, walking out of the room. She surveyed her surroundings - beige walls, a shattered TV, torn brown curtains. She squinted at the notepad on the side table, revealing the branding - *Mill Village Motel Eatonville*. The coffee machine at the room's far end, covered in dust, hinted at a neglected past.

"You're awake," a deep voice came from the doorway. "How're you feeling?" Startled, she shifted her gaze to find the man with the furrowed brow. He was tall and dark with piercing brown eyes, yet he appeared softer now. She managed a brief smile before adjusting herself, wincing in pain. He rushed to offer a hand, and she took his arm to shift as he adjusted the pillow. "Want to give walking a try?" The man's warm, brown eyes crinkled at the edges as he smiled down at her. In her visions, his face was concerned and his features were like stone. Now his face was smooth and his brown eyes sparkled with an unfamiliar kindness. She shook her head, and the woman returned with soup and water.

"She needs to eat before attempting to walk, Austin." She said, setting the bowl and bottle on the bedside table.

"Then we'll try again tomorrow," Austin expressed, heading towards the door. "The sooner we leave, the better. We've been here for too long." His footsteps echoed with determination and authority, less frustrated than the other man's but equally resolute.

"Sorry it's cold, heating options are limited. Need a hand?" The woman offered. She shook her head, the pounding of her headache resonating through her body. "Well I'll leave you to it then. Shout out if you need anything, if you can talk at all." She glanced down at her bowl of soup, parting her lips as if to speak, but no words escaped. A deep sigh escaped from the woman's mouth as she turned and left the room, leaving her alone with the cold, untouched meal. The silence in the room was deafening, broken only by the sound of muffled chatter outside. As her need for rest decreased, the days became longer. Boredom and confusion settled in, intensifying as the people from her visions became tangible presences, moving in and out of her room. They attended to her needs but seldom engaged in conversation. At night, their muffled voices in the adjoining room became a distant comfort, and the faint echoes of their arguments a source of intrigue.

"We need to leave," a frustrated male voice pierced through the thin walls. "We have to head further south before winter traps us with little supplies and an extra mouth to feed, considering you're all so intent on keeping this girl alive."

"This *woman* needed help," the familiar female voice retorted. "I distinctly remember a time when I wasn't doing well and needed it too."

"You're my sister, of course I wasn't going to leave you behind."

"I'm not talking about *you* Luis," she yelled. "I'm talking about *before* you came back from Minnesota and found me."

"Why can't we just leave her here with some supplies. Why do we need to bring her with us?"

"Jesus Christ Luis, we're not leaving her here alone and you two can have it out later," intervened another man. It was a voice she didn't recognise. "But Luis is right, we need to leave before the snow settles in." The argument faded into muffled voices again, and she strained to catch the words exchanged between them.

"I hope I'm not intrudin'. I thought the yellin' might have woken you so I thought I'd come in and check on you," a young girl had opened the door quietly without her even noticing. Her soft Southern accent flowed like a gentle breeze through a cornfield. She recognised her from her visions. The girl pulled up a chair beside the bed. "I'm Chantelle. Sorry about the noise. Luis can get into it with everybody, but he means well. Actually no, that's a lie, I don't know why I said that. He's as rude as the day is long—"

"I gathered." She whispered and laughed a little, suddenly overtaken by a violent cough. Chantelle rushed to hand her the bottle of water on the bedside table.

"Hey, take it easy. You're regainin' your strength."

"Thanks." She took the water and sipped slowly.

"From the way Austin and Val were talkin', I thought you might have been deaf or somethin'. But you could clearly hear what we're sayin' because you were respondin' well enough."

"I didn't really have anything worth saying," she laughed and took another sip. Chantelle sat down on the wooden chair, her long dark hair cascading down her back in gentle curls.

"Your name might be a good start." Chantelle laughed.

"Beth," she smiled softly. "My name is Beth."

"Nice to meet you properly, Beth," her bright brown eyes sparkled with kindness as she gazed at her in wonderment.

"Your accent, where are you from?" Beth paused, realising she hadn't thought about home for a while.

"Australia."

"Well, you're a long way from home. Now that introductions are over with, I figured you might be bored and needed a little human interaction that didn't make you feel like you were in a hospital," Chantelle smiled as she pulled out a deck of cards. Beth's eyes lit up. "What do you want to play? I've got all day."

"What do you think you are doing?" Austin stormed into the motel room.

"We're leaving," Luis' sharp words cut through the air. "We're leaving today."

"The van's still in bad shape, and we won't survive this winter on foot." Austin's arms were folded tightly across his chest, the muscles in his biceps and forearms bulging with tension. His jaw was clenched, and his brows furrowed in frustration.

"Then fix the fucking van!" Luis yelled, the sound piercing through the walls and resonating outside the motel room.

"Oh, sorry. Should I see if the local mechanic has some free time to look at it today?" Austin threw his hands in the air before laughing at the absurdity.

"If he can fix it faster than Ben can, sure." Luis' tone softened and he joined in the laughter.

"Luis, what's going on with you?" Austin slowly took a seat on the bed. "We've been friends since forever, grew up together in a way, served in the army together. You can be a dick but this isn't you." Luis sat on the second bed and looked over at his friend, rubbing his face with his hands.

"I don't know man, this just isn't—" he paused, throwing his head back and sighing heavily.

"Isn't what?"

"Isn't life." Luis gestured around the room.

"We'll get to the coast, find a boat, just like we planned." There was a slight taste of bitterness in the air, as if Austin's mild frustration was tangible.

"And then what?"

"Do the best we can," Austin stood up, placing a hand on his friend's shoulder. "We all have our dark moments, brother. You helped me get through mine. I'll help you get through yours." Luis nodded before turning his head away. Austin gave him a final pat on the shoulder before walking out of the motel room into the crisp morning breeze. The atmosphere was fresh, with a subtle scent of dew and grass. The sweet aroma of winter's imminent arrival filled the air, mingling with the faint scent of burning oil from their broken down van across the parking lot. Val caught Austin as he was walking outside.

"Ben thinks he can fix the van by tomorrow. He found the parts we need on the other side of town."

"He went scouting alone?" Austin looked across the lot at Ben. He was leaning into the hood of the black church van they had found a while back. Before Val could answer, Chantelle materialised from the shadows and joined them in the sunlight.

"Beth seems much better today. She's eatin' and drinkin' more. I think she could try walkin' today too."

"Who?" Val and Austin remarked in unison.

"The girl in the bed, she actually speaks. She might have a lot more to say if either of you bothered to talk to her instead of just, you know, talkin' at her." With that, she walked off towards Ben, a light air in her hopeful stride.

Austin found Beth sitting on the edge of her bed, her feet bare and hovering just above the floor. Her toes were curled, squeezing them tight as she wiggled them back and forth. Her face was tense with concentration as she attempted to ease the tingling sensation in her feet and calves.

"Beth?" Austin's voice was not particularly warm, even if it was calm.

"You must be Austin," she looked up at him as he nodded, smiling gently. "I've been piecing together who's who. I guess the angry one must be Luis." She smiled in return and looked back at her toes.

"Do you want to try walking today?" He moved toward the chair, settling down. It creaked underneath the weight of him.

"The sooner I can walk, the sooner you can get out of here," she said with a sarcastic air. "Your friend seems pretty keen on getting rid of me."

"I'm sorry you had to hear that," he looked towards the room next door before facing Beth again. "The sooner you can walk, the sooner *we* can all get out of here. Together." He smiled.

"Your friend Luis seems to be very against bringing me along with you."

"I'm not in the business of leaving people behind. Especially in Washington in the middle of October," he sat forward, leaning his elbows on his knees. "You wouldn't survive the winter alone."

"Then maybe you should've just left me to die," she looked at him abruptly. He opened his mouth to speak, but she interjected before he could respond. "Why did you help me? You don't know me, why would you even bother?" He stood up, his wistful tone switching back to cold and dry as he walked over to her slowly.

"I've watched people kill others over a can of soup. I've seen friends leave friends behind to save themselves. I've watched this pandemic turn kind people into monsters, and I refuse to become one of them. Like I said, Beth," he sat down on the end of her bed, his brown eyes slicing through his words like a thunderstorm. "I'm not in the business of leaving people behind." She looked at his face, tired and weathered from sleepless nights with one eye open to ensure his group's safety. She pegged him as their leader - strong and determined with clear military training.

"What happened to you?" She asked softly.

"What happened to *you*?" He raised a questioning eyebrow. "I doubt you survived a pandemic alone for six months in a foreign country. How'd you wind up half-dead in a motel all alone?"

"I—" was the only response she offered before pursing her lips and looking back at her feet. Silence held them for a while before he stood and headed for the door.

"We need to head south before it's too cold, and we don't know how long the van or the car'll last, so I want to prepare you... there'll be *a lot* of walking. We're leaving the day after tomorrow," his tone was stern before a humoured expression briefly washed over him. "I'd really like you to keep up, especially to prove a point to Luis—"

"I'll try walking today," Beth nodded obediently. "I will walk today."

"I'll send Val and Chantelle in to help you." He replied, his voice returning to its cold cadency.

"Thank you," she wriggled her toes as the numbness started to dissipate. Her voice grew quieter as she spoke. "I know you've all done a lot for me, including putting your friendship with Luis on the line. But I have a favour to ask before we leave."

"What is it?" He asked, stern yet surprised at her audacity to ask for a favour. She looked up at him with tears in her eyes. He noticed the green shades glistening with the added layer of acridity and the change in her demeanour.

"Before we leave," she demanded firmly, shaking the sadness and fear from her voice. "I need you to help me bury my husband."

Chapter Two

There was a shift in the breeze as the group stepped onto the Pit River Bridge. The van that had provided a comfortable ride finally gave out somewhere near the Washington and Oregon border, barely lasting two hours. After cramming into the SUV, they lost it shortly after. For two continuous weeks they travelled on foot along the main highway, bypassing major cities. Beth's newfound determination to survive prevented her from succumbing to weakness. Even though she was exhausted, she refused to give Luis any ammunition to use against her in convincing the group to leave her behind. During the day, she shunned casual conversation to conserve what little energy she possessed, preventing collapse. Night time brought solitude as the others engaged in discussions, leaving her alone to rest. Occasionally, she noticed a recurring pattern where Val and Chantelle were also excluded from decision-making conversations. Strategic planning was left to Austin, Ben, Luis and Reece, with Austin having the final say.

"Austin's our leader," Ben had once said to her in passing. "I trust his judgement more than anyone." They stuck to small motels outside the cities, surviving on meagre meals. They looted what they could each time they stopped. Mornings consisted of black coffee and a cereal or bran bar, while evenings often saw them splitting a tin of soup or beans each between two. Luis grumbled when Beth had received extra to maintain her strength, sometimes tempted to refuse so as not to give him ammunition for an argument against keeping her around. Ben occasionally offered her extra in private, claiming he was full and suggesting she finish his dinner. Her thoughts drifted back to a night, roughly halfway through their journey south, as she had prepared for bed. That particular day had proved lengthy, exhausting her both physically and mentally. Luis had swung her door open, his gaze intense - it was evident that he had been drinking. Startled, she faced him in her underwear, instinctively covering herself up.

"You're wasting our time." He leered at her.

"Can I help you with something?" She asked, her voice soft and weak.

"You can leave," he smirked. "You have nothing to contribute."

"Well I think—" she stuttered. "I think... Austin would have something to say about that."

"About *what*? You having nothing to contribute?" He stepped forward, closing the door behind him.

"About me leaving." She whispered as she took a step back, almost tripping over the bed.

"We've added time to our journey, time we don't have, and we have to spend extra time looking for food because of you." He continued slowly advancing towards her.

"I'm sorry." She whispered again. He took two steps toward her, advancing quicker this time.

"What?"

"I'm sorry." She said louder, almost backed against the wall.

"Can you shoot a gun? Can you build a fire or skin an animal?" The air around them was thick with tension as Luis loomed over Beth, his eyes dark with anger and disgust. "From what I've seen you can barely carry the clothes on your back, nevermind the extra weight from the food it takes to keep you going." She couldn't help but feel afraid, his drunken state making him unpredictable and dangerous. All she could muster was to shake her head and stammer a few words in protest.

"I can—, I—"

"You can what?" He interrupted angrily, looking her up and down. "You can barely string two words together. But you can contribute in other ways." He ran his tongue along his teeth, taking in a deep breath and slowly pulling the sheet down from her hands. "Food wasn't free before, why should it be now?"

"Please," she whispered, her voice cracking beneath the weight of her fear. "Please don't." He ran his hand over the knife hanging from his web belt.

"Then what good are you to us?" He spat, his hand reaching out to grab her arm with a rough, tight grip. "Austin will realise what little use you are if he keeps wasting food on you with nothing to show for it—" Her door suddenly swung open and Austin appeared from the darkness outside. He looked at Luis, and then beyond him at Beth's cowering figure against the wall.

"Luis, I see you had the same idea, coming to wish Beth goodnight."

"Excuse me?" Luis turned to look at him.

"What else would you be doing in here?" Austin's eyebrows furrowed, and he pursed his lips as he stood in the doorway, observing the tense scene before him. Luis sneered at his friend before turning back to Beth, giving her a final look up and down.

"Think about what I said," he leaned in close, breathing the alcohol in her face. "Goodnight, *Beth*." Turning on his heel he stormed out of the room, pushing past Austin. Beth pressed her back against the cool, rough wall as Austin took a few cautious steps into the room. She tried to maintain composure in his presence, but her breaths came in quick gasps and her hands trembled at her sides. Slowly, he closed the distance between them, his eyes locked onto hers with an intensity that sent shivers down her spine. He reached out and gently picked up the shirt she had laid out on the bed to sleep in. With a small, tender smile, he handed it to her and she gratefully accepted it, holding it up against her body for comfort and protection.

"Thank you." She whispered.

"What did he say to you?" Austin asked cautiously as she gazed at him. He expected her eyes to be filled with fear, but instead they reflected a fiery determination and anger that conveyed she wasn't as weak as she may have appeared.

"I'm sorry that I don't contribute as much as I should," she half-answered his question. Beth pulled her shirt over her half-naked body, willing herself to stop trembling with fear. "I can —" Austin raised his hand to stop her mid-sentence.

"I was listening at the door before I came in," he interrupted. "I heard his last comment. You don't know me very well but I can assure you that I'm not interested in exchanging food for sex."

"What are you interested in then?"

"One more person with us is one less person against us. You'll pull your own weight eventually," he turned to leave. "I'll have a chat with him." She warily looked at him as she tugged at her shirt, pulling it down to conceal her underwear.

"You didn't come in here to say goodnight."

"We had an argument about you earlier, as we always do," he offered lightly. "I went to his room to have a chat after he had hopefully cooled down. Noticed an empty bottle on his bed, thought I'd check on you."

"Lucky," she swallowed hard. Her thoughts raced at what might have happened had Austin not intervened. "Thank you."

"Now I will say goodnight." He nodded gently as he showed himself out of her room. Luis had thankfully not tried anything since that night. Whatever Austin had said to him, Luis had maintained his distance. Snide comments still surfaced from time to time, but for the most part Luis left her alone. The distant barks and howls of dogs snapped her out of her trance. Refocusing, she looked ahead, concentrating on the rhythmic march forward. Austin and Ben took the lead, advancing in front of the group, while Luis and another man named Reece stayed at the rear. Val and Chantelle were not far ahead of Luis. Beth found herself walking alone somewhere in the middle, positioned between Val and Chantelle, and Austin and Ben. The wind shifted course, blowing off the river below and carrying their voices directly behind them. Beth could hear them clear as day, as if they were whispering in her ear.

"It's gonna get dark soon," Ben remarked, glancing at the sun well over the midday mark and setting to the west. "We should find a place to stay for the night."

"We can exit after the bridge and camp by the lake." Austin pointed to the exit sign, *Exit 690*.

"Bit dangerous if someone sees a fire from the road." Ben observed.

"No one will be out here at night," Austin replied firmly, set in his plan. "And the treeline should cover us."

"How far do you think she's gonna make it on foot?" Ben quickly changed the conversation, unwilling to argue with his friend. Austin looked back at Beth, who kept her gaze at her feet, attempting not to reveal her eavesdropping. She glanced back at Val and Chantelle, who shot her a reassuring look - if Beth could hear the conversation, they could too.

"She'll be fine," Austin slowed his pace and turned around. "Keep walking, take the exit. I'll talk to Luis and Reece." Austin passed Beth, Val, and Chantelle, instructing them to follow Ben off the freeway. Ben slowed down and fell in line with Beth.

"Haven't had much of a chance to talk to you," Ben matched her gaze down at her own feet. "How are you feeling?" She did her best to conceal her fatigue.

"One step at a time."

"I thought you were dead when I found you."

"You found me?" She looked up at him. He was almost a foot taller than her and she found his dominating presence oddly comforting. The setting sun cast a gentle, golden glow around him, creating a soft silhouette of his scruffy, light brown hair. In the fading light, she could just make out the flecks of green and brown in his hazel eyes. His army jacket hung loose on his broad shoulders, its sleeves torn at the cuffs. The plate carrier he wore showed signs of wear and tear, but it still clung to his body like a second skin. With one hand firmly gripping the stock of his rifle and the other resting casually on the barrel, he exuded a sense of strength and control, a rarity amidst the chaos. The faint scent of sweet perspiration lingered in the air around him.

"Yes, I found you," he replied, smiling. "We were sweeping the town, passing through, and you were curled up on the floor clutching a tin of peas."

"I hate peas," she quipped. "But it was all I had left, and I didn't have anything to open it with."

"There was a knife in your backpack," he paused, and she offered him a blank stare. "You could've used that. I think you gave up—"

"I didn't have the strength to hack into a thick tin with a shitty knife," she shrugged and looked back at her feet. "Besides, I thought if I was going to die, I didn't want my last meal to be *peas*. It's stupid, I know, but I was going to die anyway. I figured I'd leave it for someone who found me and could carry on." He laughed at her logic, and she offered him a reassuring smile.

"Well, I enjoyed them," he smiled, and before she could reply, he pointed at the turnoff. "We'll exit here." She glanced towards the others and noticed they were further behind than she had realised. The conversation with Ben had helped her temporarily forget the aches in her feet, allowing her to move at a faster pace. They stopped at the corner, waiting for the rest of the group to catch up. Val and Chantelle walked in unison, their steps like a march between the two, handguns gently shimmied in their holsters at the side of their hips. Val's dark brown hair glistened and flitted in the fading light, and her light olive skin reflected the sunset like a smooth mirror. The contrast between Chantelle's light brown hair and her darker skin-tone was striking in the evening light. She surveyed the men at the back. Luis' normal towering presence was dwarfed by Austin and Reece, who both stood inches taller than him. The trio appeared as if they were models for a war propaganda poster. They marched across the bridge in their unkempt military attire, clutching their weapons close to their bodies with exhaustion etched on their faces, yet still determined to soldier on.

"Were you all in the army together?" Beth looked back at Ben, the tallest of all of them.

"Austin, Luis, and I," he replied casually. "We all trained together since day one."

"And Reece?" She queried, looking back at the men as they strode casually through the fading light.

"We found him on our way through North Dakota. Shot at us from the top of a barn as we passed through his field, hollering something crazy about us being infected and he was gonna call the police if we didn't get off his property." Ben laughed and shook his head. Beth raised her eyebrows and smiled.

"The police?"

"Drunk as anything," Ben looked down at her. "He fell off the roof and we ran over. Thought he must've hit his head the way he got up and stumbled towards us. Turns out, that's just Reece."

"Well, he doesn't seem like a drunken, stumbling idiot now." Beth smiled at Val and Chantelle as they caught up.

"He ran out of booze a long time ago," Val stopped and turned around to face the three men. "Now he's just a loud, sober, stumbling idiot." She turned and continued down the turn, out of sight from the others.

"She doesn't like him?" Beth asked Ben, looking back between the men and where Val had disappeared.

"When the guys got to me and Val, the first thing Reece did was raid our cupboards for somethin' to drink." Chantelle remarked casually with a hint of amusement in her tone, almost as if she found the memory more entertaining than Val did.

"He'd been sober for a few days by that point and was in pretty bad withdrawal." Ben continued, observing Reece as he was now - strong and determined to stay sober.

"Did he find anything?"

"Oh, he found everythin'," Chantelle laughed. "The weeks after that were a tirade of alcohol withdrawal, bar raids, and drunken fights."

"But he pulled through," Ben retorted. "We all have our issues, but we pull through." He turned on his heel to follow Val.

"Should we wait?" Beth looked back between Ben and the others, who were almost within earshot. Chantelle was already off after Ben and Val, and Beth thought it best to follow.

Just a few metres from the tranquil water of Shasta Lake, the group gathered closely, enveloped in a solemn silence by a campfire on the beach. Ben, Austin, Reece, and Luis had meticulously inspected the rooms, while Val, Chantelle, and Beth scoured for any useful items. The alcohol they had discovered was discreetly stashed away, ensuring Reece remained unaffected until he retired to a room for the night. Val extracted two half-filled whiskey bottles from her bag, taking a sip from one before offering it to Chantelle, who declined.

"You know I don't touch that stuff anymore." She murmured, wrapping her arms around her knees. Beth observed her newfound companions, their fatigued and defeated expressions accentuated by the flickering firelight. Austin, the leader of this tight-knit group, seemed to share a pre-pandemic connection with everyone except for Reece and herself.

"Why me?" Beth questioned softly, breaking the quietude while all eyes turned to her. It was as though she had disrupted a collective trance focused on the fire. "You all knew each other before, so why am I here? Why am I alive?"

"I'm calling it a night." Val announced, handing the whiskey bottles to Austin, who sat opposite Beth. She departed for the rooms, and Chantelle silently followed. Beth remained fixated on the fire, with Ben sitting next to her, staring at her gaunt face. Austin stared at her too, taking a mouthful of the whiskey and handing it to Luis, who took it silently but maintained his gaze into the fire.

"It wasn't my choice," Luis said after a while. "But my vote was outnumbered." He stood up, walking towards the rooms and taking a bottle with him. Austin stood up and walked over to the other side of Beth, taking a seat next to her. He faced her, holding out the bottle. Taking a mouthful and swallowing, the strong, aged liquor hit her throat hard as she coughed and shook her head. The two men laughed. Ben took the bottle from her and took a long drink, sighing and closing his eyes.

"Did I say something to offend Val?" Beth asked cautiously.

"Don't take it personally," Austin said. "Val was insistent on nursing you back to health and it caused a bit of strain on their relationship."

"Luis is—" Ben began slowly, only to be interrupted by Austin.

"Stubborn. Don't take offence to anything he says."

"We don't." Ben laughed, taking another swig as Beth scrutinised them both.

"You didn't answer my question," she persisted. "Why am I alive?"

"How are you alive?" Austin inquired, searching her face for any subtle shifts in expression. Ever since they had left the motel in Eatonville, Beth had kept her past guarded and her emotions in check. In this new reality, time seemed to both speed up and slow down at the same time. The only time Austin saw a change in her was when she asked him to help bury her husband, recalling the look on her face and the tears in her eyes.

"You and your husband," Ben broke their reflective silence. "What happened?" Beth sighed, finally allowing a crack in her guarded exterior. She relaxed, chin on her knees, and recounted.

"There isn't much to tell. We were on a cruise for our honeymoon, and halfway back to Seattle, we began receiving updates about an outbreak. We stopped just off the coast, waiting for more updates, which became less and less frequent, until they stopped altogether," she continued, recounting the chaos that ensued - raiding, fighting, and looting on the ship. "Eventually, we disembarked, found a car with some petrol, and headed inland." Beth paused, staring into the fire.

"How did he die?" Ben asked, observing her face glistening in the firelight.

"Your turn." She deflected as Ben and Austin exchanged glances, brushing off the awkward tension between them. Ben finished his drink before passing the bottle to Austin, who also took a long sip.

"We were in Minnesota when the pandemic started," Ben shared after a long silence. "Luis was determined to get back home to Val and Chantelle."

"He might be a jerk, but he loves his family." Austin added nonchalantly.

"His one redeeming quality." Beth smirked. The two exchanged glances and chose not to dwell on her disdain before continuing. "We gathered up what we could - masks, food, guns - and finally headed west through North Dakota where we met Reece."

"Redneck ex-military with an arsenal in an underground bunker on a farm." Austin laughed.

"I know part of that story," Beth smiled, laughing lightly. "How did he survive falling off the roof?"

"The barn was very tall but he was *very* drunk," Austin took another drink and looked at the bottle. "That and sheer dumb luck."

"He's probably been hurt more than any of us combined and has walked away every time," Ben took the bottle from Austin. "Luckiest son of a bitch I've ever met."

"And one of the toughest," Austin commented. "Only person I've met who actually contracted the virus and survived."

"But it killed his wife though," Ben adjusted his position and stretched his back. "See, apparently she nursed him as best she could. Took all the precautions - wore a mask, cleaned with bleach - but one day Reece got so violent with a coughing fit that he knocked her to the ground and her mask came off."

"She died a week later." Austin cocked his head and stared into the fire.

"Is that why he was hollering about you guys having the virus when he saw you in his field?" Beth looked at Ben, and he nodded reflectively.

"After that we continued through to Montana where we found Val and Chantelle hunkered down at home." Ben sighed, scrutinising their long journey.

"And your families," Beth wondered aloud. "You didn't look for them?"

"My girlfriend was stationed with me in Minnesota." Austin continued gazing into the dying embers of the fire. Beth glanced at him, noting the sadness that had washed over his expression.

"Was?"

"She was a medic. Being around everyone sick like that—" He paused, taking another drink.

"She didn't make it." Ben intervened quietly.

"I'm sorry," Beth looked back at the fire. "What about your parents?"

"Car accident when I was eighteen. Joined the army not long after that." Austin took another drink. The alcohol hit him a little harder than he had anticipated, as it had been a while since he'd had so much to drink on an empty stomach. He laid back on the sand and closed his eyes reflectively. Beth laid back too, followed by Ben. The three of them gazed upward, the absence of city lights making the winter sky shimmer with silver glitter. The sky above them was a vast expanse of midnight blue, dotted with twinkling stars and a bright full moon that permitted the dark expanse to look like a blanket of silver glitter. The air was crisp and cold, carrying the faint scent of wood smoke from their campfire and the subtle aroma of pine trees. The only sounds were the gentle crackle of their dying fire and the occasional rustle of leaves from the nearby trees. Otherwise, the night was eerily quiet, as if the world was holding its breath. The soft sand beneath them shifted and moulded to their bodies as they laid back, creating a comfortable bed. Beth rolled her head on the sand to look at Ben.

"And you?"

"My dad is off on a navy ship somewhere," he maintained his gaze upward. "Though I'd like to think he's still alive, none of us have little hope for anything anymore."

"And your mum?" Beth persisted lightly, not wanting to offend him by asking too many personal questions, but her curiosity took over her will.

"In Italy with her boyfriend," he smirked. "Probably dead too. No great loss there."

"The cheating bitch left while his dad was deployed." Austin laughed loudly.

"Good riddance." Ben offered his fist to Austin who bumped it and passed him the bottle. Beth intervened and took another mouthful, the alcohol seeming to go down smoother than before.

"Atta girl." Austin laughed, joined by Beth and Ben. She savoured the moment, a little tipsy with two strangers who seemed to be friends.

"You still haven't answered my question." She persevered, eager to know what compelled them to help her when they found her dying alone on the motel room floor.

"Mmm?" Ben rolled his head towards her a little while she sat up. As she gazed down at him, she noticed how the deep, dark hues of the night sky were mirrored in his exhausted expression. Choosing her words differently than before, she pressed them once more.

"Why did you help me recover?"

"Honestly," Austin started, and she turned to look at him instead. "You're the first person we've come across who hasn't tried to kill us."

"I was half-dead on the floor." Beth laughed. Austin and Ben sat up, and Austin shrugged.

"Still, figured you might be worth saving—" Their serene moment was shattered by gunshots echoing in the distance, snapping them back to the harsh reality. The trio turned their gaze towards the next town - the direction they had planned to head in the next morning.

Chapter Three

"You're not joining us," Luis declared as he loaded his pistol, securing an extra clip in his pouch. "Val, you're staying put."

"Like hell we are." Val bristled at his command, seizing a shotgun from his bag and standing her ground.

"I said no!" Luis took an aggressive step towards her, his eyes brimming with fury. Val's immediate reaction was to step back, but she forced herself to stand her ground.

"And I am telling you that we are coming with you." She couldn't bear the thought of backing down, even in the face of her brother's anger. Part of her wanted to escape, but another part refused to let him intimidate her.

"We've been through this before." Luis growled, taking another step towards her.

"I can handle myself, and if it weren't for me in Spokane, you'd be dead!" Val argued.

"I was doing just fine in Spokane," Luis snapped. "Before *you* needed saving. You shouldn't have been there!" Outside, the others observed the heated argument through the window. Beth's inquisitive eyes darted between Ben and Chantelle.

"What happened in Spokane?"

"We don't talk about Spokane." Ben's jaw tightened and his eyes narrowed, his arms crossing over his chest in a defensive stance. His brow furrowed and his lips pressed into a thin line. The unmistakable scent of tension hung in the air, a mix of sweat and anger from the argument brewing between Luis and Val. The air was filled with the sounds of raised voices and shuffling feet as their argument grew more intense. Beth's quiet question had broken through the tension, but the words seemed to hang in the air unanswered. Austin barged through the group, gun bag slung over one arm and his rifle in the other.

"Would everyone *please* stop saying Spokane?"

"Here we go." Ben shook his head, eyeing Austin as he stormed into the hotel room, interrupting Luis and Val's dispute and leaving the door open for all to hear.

"Reece and I are going on ahead," Austin declared, throwing his bag on the bed. *"Alone."* Luis glared at him, throwing his hands into the air.

"Austin!—"

"No, absolutely not," Austin interrupted. "We do this quietly, and we find out what that gunfire was last night."

"I am your best sharpshooter, and you know it." Luis's face was flushed, his jaw set in a hard line as he argued. His eyes were narrowed and his hands were clenched into fists at his sides.

"Yes, you are, but you go in guns blazing, and you can't keep it together," Austin fired back. "Not right now, not in this scenario, not after Spokane."

"What happened in Spokane?" Beth asked Chantelle, hoping she would provide the answer that Ben wouldn't.

"We don't talk 'bout Spokane." Chantelle shook her head heavily, her face expressionless as Beth let out an exasperated sigh and rolled her eyes.

"Reece and I are going in quietly," Austin stated bluntly,

taking rifles from the gun bag. "He's our best sniper, and unlike you he's quiet."

"I thought Val said he was a loud idiot." Beth whispered to Ben.

"He can be, but in situations like this, he's the guy you want covering you with a sniper rifle." Ben replied, his face stern and concerned as he stared ahead at the unfolding argument.

"I thought he missed the three of you standing out in a field." She quipped lightly, smiling at him and nudging his arm with hers. Ben replied dryly.

"He's been sober four months. He's fine—"

"Five," Reece countered, startling Beth as he appeared suddenly behind her. "Yesterday made five." Reece unfolded his arms and walked towards his room.

"Like I said," Ben shrugged. "He's been sober five months. He's fine—" Beth observed the way he walked, a callous march of obedience to gather his things and follow Austin into combat. Reece's shoulders were squared and his arms were tense at his sides, his steps measured and precise as he walked. There was a determined set to his jaw and a steely glint in his eye, the smell of sweat and adrenaline clung to Reece's body as he passed by her. Beth looked across the lake as the early dawn sun rising from the other side of the treeline cast a shadow of dancing silhouettes on the calm water. Another gunshot echoed across the lake as birds scattered from the trees. She looked back at the group sombrely. The night before, Ben and Austin had hurriedly put the fire out and taken Beth to her room. More shots had been fired before Ben, Austin, Luis and Reece had finished arguing about heading to town then and there, or waiting until the morning. Ultimately, Austin's demands had been met and the group had gone to bed, but no one had really gone to sleep.

"Are we doing this?" Reece emerged from his room,

covered in his tactical gear, the worn bullet proof vest further bulking out his already muscular frame.

"It'll take us at least ninety minutes to get to Mountain Gate." Austin stormed out of his room, holding out rifles to Reece as he walked over to him.

"As if it's even a choice." Reece replied, smirking as he grabbed a gun without hesitation.

"What are those?" Beth asked, not moving from her spot next to Ben. They had both been observing the chaos unfolding in front of them, unmoving from their positions.

"Reece won't go anywhere without his M110A1." Ben explained, keeping his arms folded. He was seemingly unperturbed by the gunfire in the distance, and Beth found that unsettling.

"His *what*?" She asked. Her tone was filled with curiosity and a touch of confusion. He looked down at her, raising one eyebrow and letting a small smirk form at the corner of his mouth.

"It's a semi-automatic sniper rifle with an eight-hundred-metre range," Ben clarified, looking at her. "And this is going way over your head, isn't it."

"Gun laws are pretty strict back home," Beth remarked, looking back at Reece and Austin. "I honestly wouldn't know where to start—"

"Ahh yes, I forgot that your country took away your gun freedom." Ben stood with his arms folded and a slight smirk on his lips, his eyes bright with amusement.

"We had one mass shooting twenty-four years ago and our government reformed our gun control. How many have you had since then?" Beth's tone was playful but her face remained stoic as she quipped at Ben in return. "Because we've had zero." He raised an eyebrow at her inquisitively.

"That might be true," he remarked, changing his playful tone back to a stern lecture. "But with the situation we're all in now, I'll take my gun laws over yours any day—"

"Ben, I need you," Austin walked back to Luis' room. "If you're done teasing the poor girl."

"He's done," Beth smiled at the two men, nodding at Ben lightly. "But I'm the one doing the teasing." Ben observed her, the way her mood had changed in the last few days, the way she had perked up and how the conversation around the campfire had seemed to bring her out of her shell. Beth's smile was warm and genuine, radiating all the way to her bright green eyes which caused them to crinkle at the corners. Her nod was gentle with a slight movement of her head, her light laughter added a bright spark to her gaunt face. Ben and Reece followed Austin into the room, forcing Val out with a gentle hand and closing the door. Val joined Beth and Chantelle, glancing back angrily at the closed door. The three of them lined up together, startled by another gunshot echoing through the trees. Chantelle's face twisted with worry as she flinched at the sound.

"It doesn't sound like a shootout."

"No," Val sighed. "It sounds like an execution."

"What do you mean?" Beth asked.

"One shot at a time with a long pause in between," Val furrowed her brow at Beth. "They're not firing wildly at each other, they're not fighting, they're shooting something one at a time. Probably people."

"Or they have 'em lined up and torturin' 'em. Just like those bodies at Spokane." Chantelle inhaled deeply before making her way towards her room. Beth positioned herself between Val and the hotel, her eyes meeting Val's directly as she addressed her.

"What happened in Spokane?"

"We don't talk about Spokane." Val repressed her dismissively, following after Chantelle. Beth walked away from the rooms and sat on a bench by the lake, her eyes fixed on the water as she watched the shadows of the trees change with the breeze. The sounds of intermittent gunshots filled the air, making her heart race and her palms sweat. The air was tinged with the earthy scent of pine trees, the crisp smell of the lake, and damp earth all mingled in the atmosphere. There was a faint taste of salt on her tongue from the sweat that had accumulated on her upper lip. She absentmindedly licked them, trying to calm her nerves as she listened to the distant gunfire. They occasionally echoed through the trees, punctuated by the occasional rustling of leaves as the wind blew through them. The rough, weathered wood of the bench pressed against Beth's palms as she gripped it tightly, her knuckles turning white. The lake was a mirror, reflecting the dramatic dance of light and darkness in the trees as the breeze rustled through their leaves. Beth's eyes were fixed on this mesmerising display as she tried to take her mind far away from the chaos and danger that surrounded her. Taking a deep breath and closing her eyes, she tried to block out the mayhem, but she couldn't ignore it. She couldn't ignore any of it. This was their reality now - a world filled with fear, violence, and uncertainty. She had barely realised how long she had been sitting there when Austin and Reece emerged from the room, Luis and Ben following behind them.

"Reece and I are headed out," Austin looked between everyone, holstering his handgun and shouldering his rifle. "Ben and Luis know what the plan is." He looked at Luis, still infuriated and refusing to meet Austin's gaze. Austin walked towards Val and took her by the arm, leading her away from the group.

"Luis'll take Val and Chantelle up ahead in thirty minutes. There's a motel about halfway to Mountain Gate," Ben looked at Chantelle, and then set his eyes on Beth. "We'll follow thirty minutes after that. Everyone get your shit together." Chantelle and Luis walked to their rooms while Ben slowly approached Beth, settling next to her while she turned and looked out towards the lake. Ben kept his eyes on Luis and Chantelle through their windows. Luis took a long, intimidating look at Ben, and shut his curtains.

"What's Austin doing?" Beth looked out at the water.

"Telling Val what Luis *should* be doing, so he doesn't go off the rails." Ben turned to look at the water with her.

"Seems valid," she remarked. "Why's he so on edge?" Ben's lips turned up into a mischievous grin, his eyes sparkling with humour and a hint of sarcasm.

"Haven't the faintest idea what you're talking about—"

"Don't be silly," she turned to him. "I heard Austin and Luis arguing one day through the walls back in Eatonville. Austin said he was going through something and he'll get through it. What's he trying to get through?"

"Look," he turned to face her, eyes piercing through hers and a brooding demeanour settled over his body. "Luis is rough around the edges. He's rude and dismissive and he will do *anything* to protect his family, which includes me and Austin, and to some extent Reece because he's military too. He'll take a little longer to warm up to you—"

"That doesn't explain why he's arguing with Austin so much." She retorted.

"Stay here, I'll be right back." Ben rose from his seat and hurried after Val and Austin as they made their way to their respective rooms. Before Beth could respond, the sound of another gunshot pierced through the air, causing her body to tense up. She realised that she had been growing increasingly on edge, anticipating the distant sounds like watching a display of fireworks and waiting for the explosion.

"We're going," Austin looked at Ben stoically, before softening his expression and embracing his friend in a hug. "Daybreak tomorrow, we'll meet you at the rally point. If we're not there—"

"I know." Ben interrupted, his embrace tightening as they silently acknowledged the potential goodbye. Used to dangerous situations together in the army, neither of them had been apart for long since the outbreak. They knew what to expect on tour - their training had taught them that. While human beings were unpredictable, those disciplined for combat had all been trained in a very specific way, making certain aspects of warfare foreseeable at times. But the pandemic was a different game, one filled with players whose training had stemmed from video games or the basic instinct to survive, making each new adversary they came across all the more dangerous.

"Let's go." Reece entered the doorway and then disappeared just as quickly as he had emerged. Austin glanced at Luis.

"I know you wanted to be the one to—"

"Just go," Luis gave him a small nod. "I wouldn't be level headed if I wasn't with Val and Chantelle anyway."

"Thanks brother." They clasped arms in camaraderie before Austin exited the room to catch up with Reece. Beth observed from a distance as they walked up the driveway together, Austin a few steps behind. Without warning, she bolted after them, her feet pounding on the gravel as she ran. Austin pivoted around at the noise of her approach.

"Austin—" She came to a sudden halt, stopping right in front of him. His stoic demeanour remained as she paused, noticing his impassive expression once again.

"Beth?"

"I—" She felt suddenly overwhelmed by his stoic conduct and the intense focus he seemed intent on directing towards her.

"Beth, I have to go—"

"Thank you," she said firmly. "For not leaving me behind." A loud gunshot pierced the cold morning air, causing her to bundle her coat tighter around her neck. She exhaled deeply, the vapour from her breath visible in the chilly atmosphere.

"I'll see you tomorrow morning." He said and turned on his heel to follow Reece up the driveway.

Chapter Four

Perched upon the rickety wooden bench, Beth gazed out from the edge of the tranquil lake. She observed as Luis, Val, and Chantelle began their ascent up the hill. The morning sun rose higher in the sky, casting warm rays of light that caressed her skin and brought colour to her cheeks. Despite the rising temperature, there was still a crispness in the air that allowed Beth to see her every breath. The serene atmosphere was interrupted only by the gentle lapping of water against the shore and the occasional chirping of birds in the nearby trees. It was a picturesque scene, one that Beth could have stayed lost in for hours.

"Packed?" Ben walked towards her, breaking her concentration and interrupting her peaceful state of mind.

"Never really unpacked," she smiled and looked back at the lake. "It's so tranquil here." Another gunshot in the air disturbed her serene thoughts. Ben sat down next to her.

"Until *that* reminds you that it's not really tranquil anywhere—"

"Tell me what happened," she pleaded, turning her impassive face to him and gazing directly into his eyes. "Why is everyone so on edge? What happened in Spokane?

"Straight to the point." He shook his head and let out a deep sigh. The two of them sat in silence, listening to the peaceful sound of the water gently lapping against the shore. The lake's surface rippled in harmony with the morning sun's bright rays as the trees surrounding the bank remained motionless, the only movement coming from the calm waters. They could taste the freshness of the morning dew on their lips as they breathed in the crisp air.

"We've got the time," Beth couldn't resist her curiosity and pressed on, despite her reluctance to pry. "Before we have to head out." Ben let out a deep sigh. He braced himself to retell the story as if it had happened moments ago, living fresh in his memory.

"Two months before we hit Eatonville," Ben said, sighing heavily. "We were about a mile out of downtown Spokane when we heard gunshots. It was like a war-zone out of nowhere. Val and Chantelle were taking a break on the side of the road, changing their socks."

"Changing their socks?" Beth smiled.

"Yeah," Ben laughed, then his face changed back in an instant. "It'd rained all morning and when it finally stopped they wanted to change. They had these huge raincoats on but their feet were soaked. Luis took off towards the gunfire that was ringing out at this park by the river, and Austin just took off after him. The girls, they frantically tried to get their boots back on but their feet were swollen from the rain and they rushed to pull their boots on and lace them up and by that point Reece and I had taken off after Luis, and we got to Spokane and Luis was already deep in this fight. We didn't know who or what we were shooting at but we were sleep deprived and starving and soaking wet and in *way* over our heads." The words spilled out of Ben's mouth, the memories rushing back like a flood. His movements became frenzied as he mentally relived the chaos and turmoil of that day. His hands trembled and his eyes darted around, as if he could still see the pandemonium unfolding. A bitter taste filled his mouth, a combination of fear and regret lingering from the chaos and violence. "I was at the rear and looked back but I couldn't see the girls. Then I turned around and a boy ran out from an alleyway and had his gun pointed at Austin. Would've clocked him right in the back of the head—" Ben paused, closing his eyes and taking in a deep breath. Beth sensed the fear and pain within him, but couldn't help to press for details.

"What happened?"

"I took him down," Ben's statement was so direct that it landed like a heavy stone. "One straight to the head. He couldn't have been more than fifteen years old and I just—" he paused, and Beth reached out to place a gentle hand on his forearm.

"You were protecting your friend—"

"I killed a *kid*, Beth," he stiffened at her touch and pursed his lips. "You don't come back from that."

"To protect *your friend*—"

"I killed a fucking kid," he said once more with a mixture of conviction and remorse. They were both quiet for a few minutes, and Beth watched him re-live the moment. Although Ben was gazing out at the water, his thoughts were clearly elsewhere. She hesitated to speak, unsure whether to press him further or reassure him. Before she could make up her mind, he continued of his own volition. "At this point, I had no idea where the girls were. Luis was in the middle of it, and he had no idea who was on what side or what they were fighting against, but he was just looking for a fight. Reece had raced up a fire escape and was taking point, firing at whoever he could to protect Luis and Austin, who by this point was pinned behind a statue in the middle of the park, firing at guys coming out of buildings while Luis fired at people headed for Austin. It was chaos, completely and utterly *fucked up* chaos," he looked at Beth, his pensive expression turning to anger. "And Luis, he just ran in there and got all of us into this mess like he was gonna save someone who didn't need saving. We didn't know what these people were fighting over. He just heard the gunshots and was in the mood for a fight."

"Why is he always angry though?" She looked at him and shook her head. "Surely there's a reason he thinks he needs to be a saviour. He clearly thinks he should be the one in charge—"

"He couldn't save his wife." Ben said. His face was cold and impassive, his tone dry and devoid of emotion.

"Wife?" The shock on Beth's face was as evident in her expression as it was in the tone of her voice.

"That's another story for another time." Ben said. Beth stared at him, unblinking. Driven by her insatiable curiosity, she wanted to probe deeper, eager to understand how a man who appeared distant and aloof towards outsiders could open up enough to marry someone. As if Ben could read her mind, he sighed and rolled his eyes. "A carjacking, about a year before the pandemic. He ran inside to pay for gas and in an instant she'd been shot and their car was gone. His hot-headed instincts had him running after the car instead of staying by her side to put pressure on her gunshot. It might've saved her life—"

"It might've not." Beth offered lightly.

"He doesn't see it that way." Ben shifted his stiff body on the uncomfortable wooden bench, stretching his back from slouching. The air was thick with silence and tension, almost suffocating. His breathing was deep and paced, visible in little puffs of air escaping his mouth as he exhaled. Beth couldn't help but notice how smooth and controlled his breaths were, almost like he was smoking a cigar. As he stretched, his biceps bulged against his t-shirt, causing the hairs on his arms to rise and goosebumps to form. She noticed his body soften and shiver as the adrenaline decreased from his pause in telling his story.

"Are you cold?"

"A little." Straightening up, he folded his arms and tensed his body. She hesitated, unsure if she should ask, not wanting to cause him any more pain but determined to find out the rest of the story.

"So, what happened next?"

"The gunfire stopped, bodies were everywhere, Reece had taken down quite a few running from a distance but everything stopped as suddenly as it'd started," Ben's body sank as he remembered the scene. "I stood there for so long after killing that kid that I hadn't even noticed I'd just been a sitting duck in the middle of the street. Reece had been backing me the whole time."

"You were in shock—"

"I was in shock, but not from the kid. A man pulled Val out from behind a building with a gun to her head," he looked at her, meeting her gaze unblinking. "And she stared at Luis, and then Austin, and then me. The look of fear in her eyes was like nothing I'd seen from her before."

"I mean," Beth assessed slowly as she processed his words carefully. "In that situation anyone would be terrified—"

"No, Beth," he interrupted. "Valentina Mendez is one of the toughest, hardest women I know. She grew up on the streets of Puerto Rico stealing food for her little brother while Luis ran drugs for the Puerto Rican cartel. They murdered her little brother and her parents because Luis fucked up, and they narrowly escaped the same fate before they immigrated here when they were teenagers with absolutely nothing in their pockets. She has been held at gunpoint *twice* working as a nurse in a clinic by drug seeking patients she'd cared for previously, people she'd cared for and trusted. She's a hard soul so when I tell you the look she gave us when that man had a gun to her head, her shirt torn and her pants—" Ben's words came to an abrupt halt, his eyes searching back and forth frantically. It was a look that Beth had not seen in him before - a combination of fear and bewilderment that hung heavy in the air, almost tangible enough for her to feel it as well. They sat there in silence, with emotions cascading through Ben's eyes as he re-lived the traumatic experience all over again.

"What happened to her?" Beth's question hung heavy in the air, though she was already aware of the answer.

"A few of them—" he stopped himself, unable to bring himself to say the words out loud. "They'd attacked her before bringing her outside." Ben observed how Beth had reacted, her body tensing as if she was familiar with the sensation. She tightened her thighs and shrugged her shoulders, shuddering. "Her underwear were stained with blood, but she won't talk about it beyond what we saw." Ben said. He studied her face, observing her reaction.

"Where was Chantelle?" Beth spoke softly, trying to mask her fear of the glaring truth that neither of them wanted to acknowledge aloud.

"We found her after, hiding in this book store about a block back. No idea how they got separated, they won't talk about it," they were silent again for a moment before another gunshot broke their reverie. Ben abruptly rose to his feet, causing the bench to jolt and startle her. "We should get going."

"Do you want to finish your story?"

"Not particularly," he shifted his body to face her, gazing down into her pleading eyes. "But if you insist and we can be done with it, then I'll tell you." Her gaze met his, a clear sign of affirmation despite the anger and frustration etched on his face. He threw his arms in the air as he paced back and forth, unsure how to control his body. Ben's movements were frantic, fuelled by adrenaline once again. His arms tensed and his hands turned into fists, his feet scuffing against the damp grass as he moved around in front of her. Beth watched as he spoke, noticing the tense muscles in his back and the way his jaw was set with frustration. The lines on his forehead showed just how much tension he was carrying. "Luis was so still. It was the calmest I'd ever seen him. I thought he would be full of anger and fury but he was calm and impassive and he just stared at his sister like he couldn't believe that he'd gotten her into this situation, and it's so fresh in my mind like I can see him just crouching there with his gun lowered and his gaze just unblinking and just *staring* at her," he paused and turned towards Beth, his voice getting louder as he spoke. "And Val, she just stared back and her face was flushed and bruised and she looked like she was just angry at him for it, for all of it, and Austin just raised his gun and held his sights at this guy who darted his eyes from Luis to Austin, back and forth, and in that instant Luis just *reacted*. That anger I'd expected from the beginning just consumed him and he ran out and shot at this guy who pushed Val in the way of his bullet and Luis shot her."

"Luis shot her?"

"Luis shot Val and Austin shot the guy and Reece shot another guy and it all happened so fast and then it was over and we just thought Val was gone."

"But she was clearly okay—"

"Was she?" He yelled, but it was more for effect than an actual question. His fists were tightly clenched, and his expression showed a mix of anger and frustration as he struggled to keep his emotions in check. He appeared to be on the verge of exploding from the intense inner turmoil he was struggling to keep under control.

"She's alive." Beth said calmly, attempting to defuse his anger.

"Luis grazed her shoulder, but the way she went down—" he stopped pacing and took in a deep breath. "The way she went down, we just thought she was gone."

"But she's alive." Beth repeated.

"We took her into this bar where they had come from and we took down another guy who was hiding in there, and there were broken bottles everywhere and we found her jeans on the floor next to—" He took a moment to collect himself, his icy gaze fixated on the ground as if he were standing in that very spot, witnessing the scene firsthand.

"Next to what?" Pressing, Beth stared at him as he changed and shifted his body uncomfortably.

"It doesn't matter. There was blood all over her. We gave her some painkillers and poured alcohol on her wounds and stitched her up, and in her delirious, drug induced state she told us what they did."

"What did they do?"

"The fuck d'you think they did?" He shot her a look of warning. "I'm not gonna go into detail, and don't you dare ask Val about it. Leave it alone." She swallowed hard and nodded obediently, looking down at her feet.

"Sorry."

"It took us half a day to find Chantelle. She'd pulled a bookshelf on top of herself and was curled up in the foetal position."

"Did they touch her?"

"No, thank God," he began to relax, recalling the sense of relief that had washed over him as he shook his head. "Not in that way, but she said one of them hit her pretty hard before she managed to shoot him." Beth shot him a look of disbelief and he smirked. "She's a better shot than you might think," a light laugh escaped his lips as a smile spread across his face. "She can take care of herself."

"I don't doubt that." Beth grinned, admiring Chantelle's composure in such a tense setting. She wondered if she could be as levelheaded in a similar situation.

"We fixed ourselves up and got the hell outta there." He said finally, taking a deep breath as if he had just re-lived the entire scene and was now relieved to be away from it once again. She ran her fingers through her hair, attempting to comprehend the heaviness of the story.

"How'd it take you two months to hit Eatonville? I didn't think it was that far."

"We stayed just outside of Spokane for a month," he said, shifting his weight and toying with the dirt with his feet. "Luis carried her for hours, without a break, without water or food. He just powered through until we found a house and hunkered down. Val stayed in bed for weeks, curled up and unresponsive." Beth said nothing, unsure what to feel as Ben took in a deep breath and threw his head back. "She finally started to come out of it when she got her period." Beth looked up at him quickly.

"Her period?"

"She wasn't pregnant," he turned to face her, angry and frustrated and visibly pained. "She was worried, and then she wasn't."

"Oh." Beth glanced down at her stomach, unconsciously placing her hand over it. She pondered the thought of bringing a child into this unforgiving world they lived in.

"So we finally made a move a few weeks after, when she began to recover. But she didn't say a word for months, and she wasn't very fast on her feet."

"She's okay now, though." Beth observed lightly.

"None of us are okay, but we don't have the luxury of remorse or regret. We have to move on—"

"Move on?" Beth spat coldly, clearly insulted by his indifference. "You didn't actually say it but I assume she was raped. Am I wrong?"

"Beth—"

"Am I wrong?" She repeated slowly, anger evident in her tone.

"No," he shook his head. "You're not wrong."

"Would you move on?"

"Excuse me?"

"I assume you've never been... otherwise you wouldn't be so—" she stood, glaring at him. "It isn't something you move on from—"

"I've been to war, Beth. I've been in situations—"

"Don't you dare compare the two." She stood firm, clenching her jaw and curling her fists. He observed her - the way she held her body, the way she retracted at the thought. Her visceral response wasn't something he had expected, and he finally realised why she was so insulted.

"You—"

"Yes," she said. "I *promise* you, you don't just move on."

"I'm sorry. I didn't mean to—" he struggled to articulate his thoughts, searching for the proper words to make amends. "Not move on. Just... move forward. This isn't a world where you can curl up in bed and watch TV or check yourself into a mental hospital. You move forward or you die, that's it."

"That's it." She repeated, pausing.

"If that *is* it, and you're satisfied, we can leave," he approached her, towering above and staring down with a clear expression of frustration in his eyes. "Unless you have any more questions." She lifted her head and looked up at him with determination, even though he loomed over her. Despite the difference in size, she exuded an unyielding aura, determined to appear as strong-willed as he did. Ben looked into her eyes, their faces close as his tone lightened and his body relaxed a little. "You know, the first words she said were 'we're not leaving her'." Squinting curiously, she met his stare with confusion.

"We're not leaving her?"

"When I found you, and Luis said we should go, Val pushed through us and knelt down beside you and said 'we're not leaving her', and Luis knew he couldn't argue with the first words out of her mouth for two whole months."

"Right," Beth nodded. "Was that when you stole my peas?"

She joked lightly and he offered her a half smile. As he looked down, the adrenaline from his intense story faded away. All of his pent-up anger, rage, and frustration dissipated from his body, leaving him feeling softer. His face relaxed, his arms loosened - everything about him seemed to calm down. In turn, her anger faded, and she too relaxed. "How long have you been holding that in?" She asked softly, cautiously placing her hand on his arm.

"A while," staring down at his arm, he didn't recoil from her touch this time, instead seeming to relax more from it. "I'm sorry I insulted you."

"I'm okay," as she removed her hand and gently tilted his chin upwards, she gazed into his eyes. "You're okay, and they're okay." Hesitating, she slowly placed her hands on his broad shoulders, sliding them onto his upper back and pulling him towards her, embracing him in a soft hug. His body stiffened, and then a wave of relief washed over him as he hugged her back - a human interaction he had seemingly missed, and craved. Another blast of gunfire abruptly cut their hug short, causing them to separate quickly.

"We should leave," he said, starting back towards the hotel rooms to grab their gear. "We're already running behind."

"One more thing." She said, taking a few tentative steps towards Ben. He stopped suddenly and turned to face her.

"Come on, Beth," frustrated, he looked at her sternly. "I thought we were done—"

"Val said before that if it weren't for her in Spokane, Luis would've been killed, but she was the one who was held at gunpoint. I don't get it."

"Ever since Eatonville, after she started speaking again, they've been arguing non-stop, in case you hadn't noticed," he said sarcastically and shrugged. "Val maintains that if she hadn't been brought out at gunpoint, Luis would've just kept fighting until he would've been killed. Her needing to be saved, in turn, saved him." Ben cocked his head and squinted at her. Beth took in a long, deep breath, and let it out slowly, watching it dance in the cold morning air.

"That is one hell of a story, Ben."

"I know," he said in a dry tone before walking back towards the hotel rooms. "And this is why we don't talk about Spokane."

Chapter Five

Luis, Val, and Chantelle advanced along the highway with determination. They walked in precise sync, their footfalls resonating in the eerie quiet that enveloped them. Val took the lead, her keen gaze sweeping their surroundings for any possible hazards. Luis trailed at the rear, his firearm poised and ready to defend against any potential dangers. Chantelle marched between them, her petite stature shielded by their larger frames. Their journey had been never-ending, but they couldn't afford to pause. The sounds of gunshots nearby only fuelled their determination to keep moving, to reach their goal as swiftly as possible. So they marched on in silence, their footsteps echoing in a steady beat against the ground. Even in the midst of tension and constant danger, there was a strong sense of connection between the three of them. They worked together seamlessly, without needing to communicate through words. Their bond had been formed through difficult experiences and fighting for survival, and it only grew stronger with each passing moment. As Luis walked on, the fresh air helped to calm his initial anger. His time spent on long treks during deployment had taught him to find peace and comfort in the wide open spaces around him. Memories of deployment flickered through his mind like an old film reel. He could see himself and his fellow soldiers in the dry heat, carrying their heavy packs and weapons. The sound of a passing plane caught his attention, and he looked up briefly before shifting his gaze to the right as a truck drove by, kicking up a cloud of dust that covered his face, hidden beneath his shemagh. Chantelle's voice interrupted his train of thought as they collided and she steadied him with her gentle hands, her face filled with concern.

"Luis, are you okay? Do you need a break?—"

"I'm fine." He grunted and pushed through the group, stopping to take a swig from his canteen. As they continued on their journey, Val stayed close to Luis while Chantelle trailed behind. Through the hushed trees above them, they listened intently for any sounds of gunfire in the distance. Val watched her brother's movements closely, noticing his determined and almost mechanical demeanour. She remembered how he was when he returned from deployment - initially humbled by his time overseas until he transformed into a seething vessel of anger. Their relationship fractured after Santos was born. Their father's blindness and their mother's struggles to provide for the five of them put a strain on Val and Luis' bond. Desperate to feed their family, Val turned to stealing food, often risking her life in the dangerous streets of La Perla. Luis couldn't understand why she would put herself in danger, unable to protect her at the young age of ten. But Val did it out of love for her family - especially their little brother, Santos. Despite their hardships, Santos remained the glue that held them together. He was always smiling and laughing, bringing light into their dark world. Luis was not only angry with Val, but also with himself for not being able to protect their family when they needed him most. Impulsively, at just twelve years old, he got involved with the cartel. Thinking it would provide easy money and protection for his loved ones, he quickly realised how wrong he had been. His hasty decision resulted in the deaths of his parents and Santos. Years later, they were still struggling to survive in this harsh environment. The loss of Santos still weighed heavily on them, causing constant grief and guilt. Suddenly, a gunshot interrupted Val's thoughts and she looked back at her brother. Chantelle let out a sigh of exhaustion as she felt her energy dwindling.

"How long d'you think we've been walkin'?"

"We're almost there." Val called back, not turning around to face her.

"Be quiet," Luis demanded. "Anyone could be around here. We don't know who was ahead of us shooting, or where they've gone."

"Well if they're still shooting they're clearly still at the town." Val argued in response.

"And we do know who was ahead of us," Chantelle chimed in. "Austin and Reece would've come across anyone through here first."

"They told us to stay left of the highway to retrace their steps." Val added mindlessly. Luis stopped and turned around.

"And how would *you* know that?" He asked rhetorically, as he already knew the answer to his redundant question.

"Come on, you know Austin told me exactly what he told you," she smirked. "To make sure you don't stray from his orders. Speaking of, you should be at the rear." Their conversation was abruptly halted by the sound of a twig snapping. Luis's eyes shifted to Chantelle, and it became clear that the sound was not from a twig breaking at all, but from the cocking of a gun. His heart sank as he saw the weapon pointed at Chantelle's head.

Austin and Reece glided through the dense foliage, their movements calculated and in perfect unison. With years of practice on their side, they effortlessly traversed the rugged terrain as if it were a choreographed dance routine. The sound of gunshots reverberated through the forest, signalling their proximity to Mountain Gate. Both soldiers halted abruptly as another gunshot pierced the air.

"See any vantage points?" Austin asked.

"Nothing useful," Reece replied, scanning the surroundings. "But if we can get up this hill, I'll get a better view."

"Up *there*?" Austin remarked, eyes fixed on the ascending slope before them. "It looks pretty steep—"

"Then we'd better get going." Reece and Austin quickly began ascending the hill with a calculated urgency. When they reached a clearing halfway up, they took their positions and surveyed the landscape through their scopes.

"There, the trailer park," Austin observed. "Twelve o'clock, 730 metres out."

"I see it," Reece affirmed, moving his sights left to a clearing near the park. "Jesus Christ, Austin. Eleven o'clock, 650 metres."

"I see it," Austin echoed as they witnessed a grim scene - lifeless bodies, hands bound and blindfolded, scattered across the clearing. "They executed them. I count 13, no, 14 dead."

"One o'clock." Reece and Austin turned their attention to the source of the commotion. A man was dragging a woman out of a trailer by her hair. He tossed her onto the ground, out of their line of sight behind another trailer, and pointed a gun at her.

"Jesus." Austin's heart pounded in his chest as he watched the scene play out before them.

"I can take him." Reece shifted his shoulder and flexed his hand before placing his finger on the trigger.

"Hold your fire." Austin commanded.

"Sir?"

"I said hold your fire, soldier," Austin affirmed his order sternly. "You'll give away our position. We don't know what else is going on down there, or who else could be out here in these hills." Reece reluctantly obeyed, taking his eyes from his sights and looking at his friend in frustration. Austin shifted his eyes back to Reece, mirroring his actions and meeting his gaze.

"Austin—"

"I gave you an order." Austin said, staring him down.

"Yes, *sir.*" Reece said reluctantly through gritted teeth, a gunshot ringing in the distance. They looked through their sights again and watched the man walking away.

"I could've saved her." Reece observed in an angry whisper.

"Maybe I should've brought Luis with me." Austin commented snidely. Reece said nothing in retaliation as they lay in observation for a while, surveying the area. Another gunshot rang out as they searched for the source, unable to find it.

"I need a better position." Reece finally discerned.

"A better position isn't gonna help us see into those trailers," Austin noted. "I mark three targets on trailer-tops, handguns, no tactical gear."

"Confirmed." Reece responded dryly.

"Red hat at your ten o'clock, 720 metres." Austin gazed down his sights, scanning his eyes swiftly through the trailer park. Reece followed Austin's visual path through the mess of white trailers and scattered bodies.

"Confirmed."

"Purple jeans, twelve o'clock, 750 metres."

"*Purple jeans,*" Reece exclaimed with a smirk. "Bold choice."

"Reece, focus," Austin said authoritatively, bringing his friend back in check. "Denim jacket, three o'clock, 650 metres."

"Confirmed." They watched their movements for a while,

observing their patterns and habits. Another gunshot rang out, but between the mess of trailers they were unable to find the source once more. "How long are we gonna sit here and watch them *murder* people," Reece asked curiously, a hint of spitefulness in his tone. "Just so I'm clear." Austin shifted his shoulders and stretched out his hands, trying to alleviate the cramping. Laying prone in the grass with his neck stretched awkwardly was a position he had not been in for some time, and the reconnaissance was taking a toll.

"If we clear those trailers, we don't know who's inside to hear those bodies drop. What happens when we get a hundred more people killed? We don't know how many people they have in there."

"A hundred?" Reece said with a hint of sarcasm. "It's a trailer park, not the Ritz. They've already killed a dozen, I'd be surprised if there's a dozen left to save."

"You're cranky, soldier. I'll take point while you get some rest," Austin commanded. "And then you'll cover me at dusk." Reece rubbed his exhausted eyes, realising that arguing with Austin would only lead to him following through anyway, with the added consequence of them harbouring resentment towards each other.

"Wake me if anything changes." Reece said. A deafening shot broke the silence, echoing from the direction they had just come from down the highway. They shared an uneasy look before turning back to face the ominous sight in front of them.

"Fuck." Austin whispered.

Beth walked ahead of Ben, the cold breeze gently rustling through the trees, their orange leaves catching the sunlight on the morning dew. Ben, lost in thought, had been contemplative since their departure from the lake. He had shared one of the most challenging situations he had faced since the pandemic began, revealing a rare vulnerability to someone who was essentially still a stranger to him. Beth exuded a distinct aura, evident in the way she gazed up at the trees or in her smile when she reflected in the enjoyment of the fresh air. When she spoke, even in moments of his anger, her words seemed like a comforting embrace. The warmth of her actual embrace only strengthened this impression. He observed her with the fascination one might have when watching a baby animal discover something new. Occasionally, she playfully kicked at the leaves, or extended her hand to delicately touch a drop of dew nestled at the bottom of a leaf. Sometimes she closed her eyes and took in a long, deep breath of fresh air while a satisfied smile crept across her bright face. Suddenly she stopped and turned to face him.

"I have to go to the bathroom," she announced, snapping him out of his trance. He pointed towards the trees. She followed suit, quickly removing her backpack and gently setting it on the ground before stepping carefully into the woods. "I'm not gonna get eaten by a bear, am I?"

"No." He called back, not entertaining her jest.

"You'd better be looking away." She called out from a distant area too far for him to see through the thick trees. He said nothing, listening to the sound of her soft laughter and the rustling of leaves under her feet as she clumsily attempted to find a spot to relieve herself in the woods. Waiting a moment, he shuffled uncomfortably on the ground, looking out onto the highway.

"Beth, are you done yet?"

"Performance anxiety," she called back, a slight apprehensiveness hinted in her voice. "Give me a moment."

"How about now?"

"Stop talking," she laughed awkwardly. "You're making me

uncomfortable and I... can't go." Ben walked a few more paces towards the highway, giving her some space as she finished. After another minute, she emerged from the trees.

"You finally done?"

"Sorry, I'm not used to peeing in the middle of the woods like you lumberjacks."

"Lumberjacks don't—" he rolled his eyes at her and sighed. "I'm not a lumberjack." She gestured with her hands, circling the air in jest.

"You've got this whole lumberjack vibe going on, Ben."

"If you're done teasing me, can we leave?"

"Don't get your panties in a twist," she pulled her backpack back onto her shoulders, adjusting to the weight once again. "You need to lighten up."

"Lighten up?" He took a step towards her, stopping as another gunshot rang out overhead which made both of them jump. "Does that sound like something I need to lighten up to? Do you take anything seriously?"

"I didn't mean to offend you," she reeled back, her voice softening. "I guess I'm just—" her voice trailed off quietly.

"Just *what*." A mild anger lingered in his voice that sent shivers down her spine.

"Just happy to be alive right now," her tone was hurried and devoid of emotion. "That's all." They stood silent for a moment, staring at one another. Beth offered Ben a slight smile and furrowed her brows as he took in a deep breath and shook his head.

"I'm sorry if I killed your mood." He said.

"You didn't," Beth smiled. "It'll take a lot more than a grumpy lumberjack to make me sad." Turning on her heel, another gunshot rang out. Ben shouldered his assault rifle and took a drink from his canteen.

"Hold on princess," he joked mildly, handing her his canteen. "I have to pee."

"See," she laughed. "Lumberjacks do pee in the woods."

"I'm not a lumberjack." He called out as he continued through the trees, reappearing in less than a minute.

"That was fast."

"I don't get performance anxiety," he stepped towards her, standing close enough for her to feel the warmth radiating from his body. Every time he breathed in, his body brushed against hers lightly. As he exhaled, his breath lingered in the air between them before diffusing away. "My canteen?" His voice was soft as he held out his hand, palm facing upward in front of her chest.

"Oh." Looking down at his hand, she placed it gingerly into his open palm.

"Have some," taking it from her and unscrewing the lid, he handed it back to her. "You need to stay hydrated." She took a long drink, wiping her mouth with her sleeve.

"Thank you," she watched him re-attach the canteen to his web belt as she noticed beads of sweat dripping down his forehead. "How are you that hot?"

"Beth, I am carrying an M4 carbine assault rifle, an M16A2 assault rifle, an SIG M17 handgun, a Gerber machete, a Ka-Bar USMC knife, a canteen, an ammunition pouch, a grenade pouch, a swag, a water purification kit, a radio, food for the both of us to last a few days if needed and I am wearing full tactical gear plus I have half of Austin's gear on me as well. I am *easily* carrying your body weight on my person, if not more," he took a step towards her, assessing her as looked her up and down as he raised an eyebrow. "What's in *your* backpack?"

"You lost me at Gerber," she gazed at him with a blank expression, her eyes flitting around his body at all the items he had just mentioned. "I really have no idea what any of that stuff is."

"Well, it weighs a lot," he nodded down the highway. "And if you don't mind, I'd like to continue so I can get this shit off. Carrying my gear is one thing, but carting around Austin's as well is another." Beth turned and continued down the treeline.

"Why do you have half of Austin's gear?"

"They needed to move quickly," he called ahead. "Luis, Val, Chantelle and I all split Reece and Austin's gear they didn't need to take with them."

"Why didn't you give any of it to me?"

"You're only just back up on your feet. You're malnourished and probably weigh a hundred pounds soaking wet. We decided not to give you any extra weight."

"Thank you." Beth became filled with a sense of awe and admiration as she slowly realised how much they cared for her well-being. After walking monotonously for a long while, she continued taking in the country air, touching leaves as she walked quietly through the treeline.

"Why do you do that?"

"Do what?"

"Touch the leaves, smell the air as if it's the best smell in the world, kick at the ground like a kid." He smiled adoringly, though she couldn't see it.

"I suppose it's a sensory thing," she observed, smiling. "I spent so long in that room alone, maybe my brain needs to be overstimulated. I suppose I have a new zest for life."

"How long was it?"

"How long was what?"

"Being alone," he stated bluntly. "When did your husband die?"

"Well that lasted long." As she continued walking, she turned her head to glance at him with disapproval before facing forward once more.

"I'm sorry, I didn't mean to—".

"Don't be," interrupting casually, she turned to look back at him. "I pressed you when you didn't want to talk about what you didn't want to talk about. I think it was six weeks before you found me, but I could be wrong. Time seems to pass weird when you're starving to death." Ben let out a quick laugh before clearing his throat.

"Sorry. I shouldn't laugh."

"No, please," she smiled. "Feel free to laugh at my dire situation."

"Not so dire anymore?"

"Things are looking up." She joked, looking at him demurely before facing forward again.

"So how did he die?"

"You have a way of ruining a good moment."

"So I'm told." Ben whispered, almost inaudibly as they trudged on through the treeline, a light morning fog creeping in from the hills. They walked in silence for a while longer, the occasional gunshot slicing through the air. Other than that, the silence was filled by their footsteps on the soft ground and the wind whistling gently through the trees. Beth thought for a moment, contemplating how Ben had opened himself up to her. She thought it only fair that she let her guard down and allow him in.

"He was stabbed." She called over her shoulder. Before he could respond, another gunshot rang above them like a gong, startling them both. Beth stopped abruptly, and Ben walked right into her backpack, causing him to reach out and grip her arm. "Damn that was loud. We must be close—"

"*Too* close," he stood directly behind her, the grip on her arm tightening. "That didn't come from Mountain Gate. It was much closer than that."

Chapter Six

"Drop your guns," the man barked. The looming threat pressed his gun harder against the back of Chantelle's head and she flinches slightly. *"Now!"* His presence exuded both menace and desperation as Luis, reacting with caution, lowered his rifle to the ground and raised his arms in surrender. Val, paralysed by fear and haunted by her own past traumas, stood frozen in place.

"Hey, we don't want any trouble." Luis said softly. His surprisingly calm response snapped Val out of her paralysed state. She hastily dropped her gun, the sudden movement causing the man to flinch.

"Neither do we." He said, gesturing at the trees. Luis barely moved his head as his gaze drifted slightly to the right, surveying the wooded area. He couldn't see anyone else, but that didn't mean the man was alone. He listened for movement, changes in the wind, anything that could indicate this man had allies hiding, waiting for an ambush.

"Tell us what you want." Val pleaded desperately.

"Shut up, Val." Luis commanded.

"Well, *Val*," the man shifted his weight unnervingly. "I'll take your guns for a start—"

"That's not gonna happen." Luis clenched his jaw.

"This isn't a negotiation," he pressed the gun firmly against the back of Chantelle's head. "Guns first, then your food." Val watched Chantelle carefully, taking note of her unnaturally calm demeanour. Despite her outward appearance, Val could see the fear in her eyes and the silent plea for help. Chantelle refused to show any sign of discomfort or flinch, denying her assailant the satisfaction of seeing her in distress. But from Val and Luis's point of view, a dark spot began to soak through her jeans - a clear indication of her intense fear. Despite this, she stood strong, maintaining an eerie composure. Val took a small step forward.

"Please—"

"Kick your guns to me," the man requested calmly. Luis did as instructed, the rifle getting caught in the autumn leaves and mud halfway between the two. "Pick it up, *slowly*." Luis approached the rifle, almost looming over it as he took a step closer. He swiftly retrieved the tangled gun while simultaneously unsheathing a machete from his shin in one smooth movement. With skilled dexterity, he tripped Chantelle and sliced upward through the assailant's arm. The attacker barely had time to react and the gun fell to the ground still gripped by the severed limb. The gunshot rang out around them, the bullet narrowly missing Val as the hunk of flesh and bone and blood thudded onto the damp leaves. Chantelle quickly got up and ran to Val, falling into her arms as they both crumpled onto the ground in a tight hug. Luis, taking charge of the situation, quickly grabbed his rifle and scanned the trees around them with intense focus. Their attacker squirmed, moaning in pain and holding his injured arm close to his body. His clothes were stained with blood, and he remained eerily silent, likely in shock from losing so much blood. After ensuring that the man was alone, Luis grabbed his rifle and machete. He positioned himself over the man's body, standing with his feet on either side of his chest.

"I, I just... I wanted to—" gasping in shock, he mumbled while his wide eyes remained fixed on the canopy above them. "To protect my family." Luis turned to look at both his sister and foster daughter. He maintained a steady gaze at Val, who protected Chantelle from the gruesome scene with her hand.

"Same," he crouched down next to the injured man and quickly drew his machete across his throat. A stream of warm blood spilled onto his plaid flannel shirt, staining it an even deeper shade of red. Luis wiped his weapon clean on the man's clothing before putting it back in its sheath. He rummaged through the man's pockets, removing a wallet but nothing else. "No extra ammo, he only had one fucking bullet." He then flipped the wallet open and studied the driver's license inside. "Craig Cole, what a fucking idiot. Rest in pieces." He said sarcastically as he tossed the wallet into the woods. Val rocked Chantelle in her arms, staring at her brother.

"Luis—"

"We need to move," he walked back over to Val and Chantelle, who still hadn't made a sound. "The rally point should be just around the bend." Luis pulled Chantelle from the ground and dragged her through the trees as her heavy feet shuffled along with them. They cut through the woods, avoiding the highway to shorten their final trek. Emerging from behind a long building, they spotted a swimming pool filled with fallen leaves and some deck chairs, seemingly having been blown in by the wind.

"We need to stop." Val said. Chantelle leaned against the side of the building, her posture slumping in defeat as she slid down to the ground.

"I'll clear the area," Luis drew his handgun from his holster. "You two stay here." Val nodded and crouched down beside Chantelle, who was staring blankly in front of her. Luis swept quickly from room to room at the front of the motel, checking every inch of them in his heightened state of wariness. He came back quickly for Val and Chantelle, who was almost catatonic.

"She's in shock," Val observed, the medical professional in her taking over, removing her personal attachment as best she could. "Help me get her up." Luis assisted Chantelle, draping her arm over his shoulder and guiding them to the central room at the front, laying her down on the bed furthest from the front door.

"Lock the door behind me. I'll sweep the rest of the place."

"We're not supposed to do a final sweep until Ben gets here to back you up." Val protested.

"Do you wanna take the chance that someone else is here after what just happened? Right on the doorstep of our rally point?" He barked. She said nothing, but stood up and gestured for him to leave, locking the door behind him. Val moved back to Chantelle, who sat upright on the bed.

"I didn't even hear you sit up. You startled me," Val placed her hand over her chest, then reached forward for Chantelle's arm. "Let's get you cleaned up." Chantelle snatched her arm away from Val's grip, looking forward again with a blank gaze. Val stared at her, almost defeated as she reached down slowly and unbuttoned Chantelle's jeans with caution. Chantelle leaned back, staring at the ceiling. Val took the jeans into the bathroom and placed them in the bathtub. Grabbing a bottle of water, she soaked a cloth in the sink and came back to wash the urine from Chantelle's skin. Chantelle had curled up under the blanket, completely covering her face, and Val knew her daughter well enough not to disturb her now. She quietly pulled a chair to the end of the room by the bathroom, facing the door. Sitting, she placed her rifle firmly under her armpit and waited for Luis to return.

Beth and Ben hurried through the woods, their footsteps crunching loudly on the forest floor. They were no longer concerned with stealth, their main priority was reaching the rally point as quickly as possible. At first, Beth had been fascinated by the peaceful atmosphere of the woods, but now she had stopped touching the leaves as they walked. Ben, trained in the same tactical manner as Austin and Reece, had put more distance between them. Beth struggled to keep up, not having the same level of training. Suddenly, Ben halted and turned to Beth, his ears picking up the sound of a vehicle approaching from behind. She froze, her gaze darting between him and the road ahead. In a flash, he grabbed her and pulled her further into the trees before tossing their backpacks deeper into the woods. He pressed her down onto the ground, covering themselves with leaves. Beth winced in pain as she landed on a fallen branch.

"Steady your breathing, Beth." Ben placed his hand over her mouth and whispered urgently for her to be quiet. As her adrenaline surged, she struggled to breathe with a blocked nose from the cold air. He slowly released his hand and placed it on the side of her face. She nodded obediently, trying to steady her breathing without revealing the pain in her back. A vehicle rolled past them slowly. The mist from the hills added to their camouflage as they lay in silence, listening to the sound fading into the distance. Beth looked up at the clouds through the trees, watching the leaves move in blissful unison with the wind, trying to distract her mind. Startled by the creaking of a tree behind them, she turned her head sharply towards Ben. For what seemed like an eternity, they lay there in silence as they stared, studying each other's faces. She placed her hand on her chest to feel her racing heart against her palm as Ben placed his hand on top of hers.

"Ben—"

"You're okay," he whispered. She closed her eyes softly and tried to maintain a steady breath as he noted the look of concern across her face. He waited a few more moments before shifting his weight, the only sound now was the quiet wind in the tree canopy and Beth's soft breathing. "I think it's clear. We should leave."

"What if they come back?" She whispered, her voice catching in her throat, which betrayed her fear.

"They're probably searching for the source of the gunshots," he observed. "They ring through these mountains like a dinner bell."

"Yeah if you're a cannibal."

"Always with the jokes, Beth." He stood up and helped her to her feet. She winced as she clutched at her back.

"Oh, I'm hilarious—"

"Did you hurt yourself? Let me see." Ben turned her around, lifting her shirt and running his hands down the sides of her torso, placing his thumbs into the crevices above her hips.

"Ow." She flinched as he ran his hand over the small of her back.

"Nice bruise," he observed. "No broken skin though. Just grazed, and it's already purple." Her gaze fell upon the branch, and she noticed just how close she had come to hitting a small protrusion that jutted out, directly upward.

"Lucky," she remarked lightly. "That could've been worse." She nodded toward the branch and Ben followed her gaze.

"Much worse," he lowered her shirt down and placed his hand on the small of her back. "Does it hurt?"

"A bit," she turned to him. "But I'll be fine." They searched through the dense forest to retrieve their backpacks, then quickly resumed their journey through the mist-covered trees. Ben made a mental note to stay close behind her - he promised himself he wouldn't make the same mistake of leaving her behind again.

Austin slowly flexed his right hand, taking each finger in turn before firmly gripping his rifle. He then repeated the process with his left hand before returning it to its place. With his right hand securely back on the rifle, he positioned it next to the trigger, ready for action. His eyes were tired and unblinking as they remained fixed on the men moving around the trailer park. Red hat, denim jacket, and purple jeans stayed atop the trailers as they shouted and tossed cans of beer to one another. Austin watched on attentively, maintaining his vigilant observation of the unfolding scene despite the dryness in his eyes and his throbbing head.

"Bit early in the day for drinking." He remarked.

"It's five o'clock somewhere." Reece muttered from under his shemagh.

"Yeah, well time doesn't seem to exist in the apocalypse."

"Neither does a moral compass," Reece mused. "For some at least." Before Austin could reply, he noticed an SUV cruising down the road parallel to the highway.

"Reece, two o'clock, 500 metres."

"Confirmed," Reece had his rifle out faster than Austin could finish his sentence. "Silver SUV headed west."

"Confirmed." Austin's response was immediate. They watched as the car pulled into the trailer park, and two men stepped out of the front seats. They walked forward with confidence, eventually met by another man exiting one of the trailers. It was the same man they had seen before, the one who had heartlessly shot the woman that Reece had desperately wanted to rescue.

"You reckon he's their leader?" Reece queried.

"I'd put money on it," Austin replied. "Potential leader confirmed. SUV driver, black trench coat." Their reconnaissance was like a rehearsed dance they had done a thousand times before, but never with one another. Still, it seemed without flaw, akin to a routine.

"Confirmed."

"SUV passenger, brown visor."

"Confirmed." Reece readjusted his position, keeping a close eye on the two men as they made their way back to their SUV. They opened the back doors and pulled out two women who were thrown forcefully to the ground. The leader of the group clapped and praised the men before taking charge of the women. The men returned to their car and drove off, leaving behind a tense scene that conveyed the seriousness of the situation they were witnessing.

"I'm going after them." Austin decided impulsively. Reece kept his sights on the trailer park.

"What?"

"We can't see the highway exit from here," he placed his rifle on the ground and detached his sight. "I want to see which way they go. Take point." He rushed down the open trail, pushing his body to its limits in an attempt to reach the highway before the vehicle disappeared. After sitting still for an hour, the cold air filled his lungs quickly as he sprinted. Three hundred meters downhill, he reached a sharp turn and slid to a stop when he saw the highway railing ahead. The sudden obstacle only added to the urgency and tension of the situation, causing him to quickly adjust his movements. Reece watched as his friend disappeared down the hill, then shifted his attention back to what was happening in front of him. He observed as the men circled around the women on the ground. One woman with black hair pleaded with him as he hit her with his gun and she fell to the ground. He approached her and forcefully tore off the light blue shirt from her body. The other was already lying there, struggling in the mud as her blonde hair began to darken. Reece aimed his gun at the supposed leader and carefully placed his finger on the trigger, running it along the slick metal surface while biting down on his lip to control his rage. Reece inhaled deeply, his fury bubbling just below the surface. He lined up his target in the crosshairs of his scope and gently positioned his finger on the smooth trigger. Clenching his jaw to regain control of his emotions, he readied himself for the pivotal moment ahead. The enormity of the situation rested heavily on his shoulders as he contemplated his next moves. Austin steadied himself against the railing of the highway, paying close attention to his breath and listening for any sounds of an approaching car. He pulled out his sights and quickly assessed the area in front of him. Thankfully, there were buildings and trees providing cover, making it less likely for the men from the nearby trailer park to spot him. He leaned forward, taking deep breaths in an effort to steady himself. With a focused gaze, he looked down the highway towards the south, trying to control the trembling in his hand. The tension in the air was thick as he steeled himself for potential action. Frustration and anger surged through him, causing him to push himself harder. He concentrated on steadying his trembling hand as he heard the all too familiar sound of an SUV racing towards him. Acting quickly, he flung himself behind a nearby bush, wincing as his shoulder hit a rock. After waiting a few tense moments to ensure that the vehicle was gone, he sprinted back up the hill towards his lookout point, every move carefully calculated as he tried to blend back in with his surroundings without drawing attention to himself. Reece exerted every muscle in his body to follow the commands of his superior. He carefully positioned his finger on the trigger and a soft click sounded in his ear but no gunshot followed. He grumbled in frustration at the lack of necessary tools for maintenance of his weapons, he quickly removed the cartridge and ejected the bullet from the gun's chamber. With precise attention, he examined the striker and firing pin before reloading and keeping a steady focus. Reece glanced through his sights again, flexing his shoulder and hand in anticipation of firing. But just as he was about to pull the trigger, he stopped. A man stepped out of a nearby trailer, appearing older and radiating a sense of authority. He approached the women, gesturing between them and then at the other man again, injecting a layer of intrigue into the situation. Austin caught up to him and collapsed beside him, gasping for air and trying to calm his heavy breathing.

"Did you see which way the SUV went?" Reece asked, not looking over from his sight. He grunted in confirmation, unable to speak. "Austin, you need to see this. There's another guy, I think *he's* the leader."

"Yeah," he breathed in heavily. "Reece, listen—"

"They're choosing women, and the other guy seems to be choosing first. Like he's picking which one he gets and the other guy gets the other one," Reece observed them taking the woman to their trailers as he moved his sights back over to the clearing near the trailer park. "Austin, all the people executed, they're all men." He removed his eyes from his sights and looked at his friend laying on the ground next to him.

"Reece—"

"Austin I think they're taking survivors, killing the men, and, well... they kill the women when they're done with them too—"

"Reece," Austin finally caught his breath. "They're headed north, towards the rally point." Reece snapped his head towards Austin suddenly.

"Do we head back?"

"No time," Austin handed him his radio. "Break radio silence."

Chapter Seven

Beth suddenly stopped in her tracks and let out a muffled scream as Ben reached her side, immediately placing his hand over her mouth. He pulled her close as they peered down at the motionless figure of a man, buried beneath the rust-coloured leaves and blood that blended with their surroundings. Beth hadn't seen him until she was almost right on top of him, only a few steps away. The man's body was drenched in blood, covering him like a grotesque shawl and staining the vibrant autumn leaves with a deep red hue. The sunlight made it glisten, creating a jarring contrast to the peaceful surroundings. The metallic scent of iron and copper overpowered the fresh, dewy air. It was a cloyingly sweet smell, reminiscent of rotting fruit mixed with metal, combining with the earthy aroma of fallen leaves to create an unsettling atmosphere. Beth could feel the metallic tang of blood in her mouth, even with Ben's hand covering it. The taste made her nauseous, and she tried hard to swallow and get rid of it. Ben also wrinkled his nose at the smell, causing his stomach to churn and his throat to tighten. He held onto Beth tighter in response, trying to keep her safe. Beth shifted uncomfortably as he released his grip on her, realising that he had been squeezing her much harder than needed. Ben quickly positioned himself in front of Beth and crouched down to examine the man. His throat had been cleanly cut and his arm lay detached next to him. As Ben stepped forward, his foot sank into a mixture of blood, leaves, and mud, creating a sickening squelching noise that only made the moment worse. Beth fought back the urge to vomit as she held her nose and mouth with her hand. Ben approached the body cautiously, feeling the warm, sticky blood clinging to his shoes. Beth followed behind, stopped only by Ben's raised hand signalling her not to come any closer. As her initial panic subsided, she could now see the deep red colour of the blood, resembling freshly crushed berries as it stained and splattered across the man's body and the ground in chaotic patterns. In the dim light, it somehow both blended in and stood out against the colourful autumn leaves, creating a morbid contrast. Beth's hand fell from her mouth as she forced herself to swallow the lump in her throat.

"Queasy?" Ben teased, his tone dry as he looked up at her. The attempt to lighten the situation fell flat. The scent twirled through the air and drifted into her nostrils and mouth on the changing breeze.

"I'm not used to this much blood, Ben."

"The smell," he took another quick look at the lifeless figure on the ground before standing up and turning to face her. "It takes some getting used to." Her forehead creased in a frown and she gulped, locking eyes with him.

"How do you get used to this?"

"I grew up on a farm."

"So you are a lumberjack," she joked casually, but her tone remained flat and emotionless. "Do you think the others came across him?"

"The blood's pretty fresh," Ben placed a gentle hand on the man's skin. "And he's warm. His arm was also cut clean off. Takes something long and sharp to do something like that—"

"Like a machete?" Beth looked down at the arm, strangely settling into the scene that moments before had made her sick. "You all have one—"

"Yeah, something like that," Ben rolled the body from side to side before standing up. "No gunshot wound though." Beth looked at Ben before shifting her gaze down the highway, her eyes drifting with thoughts of the worst-case scenario.

"So, that means... someone else—"

"Come on," he turned to look at her, an impassive look on his face. "The rally point is just around the corner."

"*Eagle to cobra team, eagle to tiger team, come in.*" Reece's voice crackled with urgency as it came through the shortwave radio. Ben's hand shot towards his backpack strap, pressing the button and speaking quickly.

"Cobra team here, over."

"Turn it down," Beth said, shooting him a look filled with irritation. "What if that'd gone off when we were hiding from that car?"

"Then we would've been fucked," Ben smirked as he adjusted the volume on the radio. "The volume was low. It must've been knocked when I threw the packs—"

"*Tiger team here,*" Luis' voice crackled through. "*Go ahead eagle.*"

"*Rally point A is compromised.*" Reece's voice sputtered.

"Don't worry, I threw my backpack far enough into the woods that they wouldn't've heard it from the highway anyway," he replied to Beth, then lifted his radio back up. "*Cobra team is less than half a click out.*" Ben spoke through the radio to Reece while trying to hide his concern, his gaze fixed on her.

"They would've if they'd gotten out of the car and come into the woods." She rebuffed, folding her arms. She silently cursed the pain in her lower back that had worsened with running.

"*Negative,*" Reece replied. "*Proceed to rally point B.*"

"Then they would've found us anyway before they even heard the radio," he looked at her in disbelief. "Why are we even arguing about this right now?"

"*Negative*," Luis crackled through. "*Juliet is down.*" Confusion and concern etched Beth's tired face as she looked at Ben.

"Who's Juliet?"

"Chantelle Jones. Jones. Juliet. It's a codename based on surnames and phonetic alphabet," he raised the radio back up. "*Cobra is less than half a click away. We can be there with assistance in less than five minutes.*"

"*Negative, cobra,*" Reece repeated. "*Proceed to rally point B.*"

"Chantelle's down?" Beth took a few steps forward. "What if she was shot? What if what was—" Before she could continue, she felt a tight grip on her arm and she spun around.

"Beth, stop," Ben pulled her closer to him, his grasp firmer than necessary. "Austin and Reece broke radio silence for a reason, and do not use real names while I'm talking into the radio." She glared at him, her arm still firmly held in his grip as he scolded her.

"*Define down, tiger.*" Austin's voice came through now, a blend of concern and static.

"*Down and red.*" Luis replied. Despite the anger evident on her face, Beth's tone was filled with an odd mixture of fascination and unease.

"Down and red?"

"Down means immobile, out means hurt, down and out means dead," Ben gazed down the highway towards the designated meeting spot. "Green, orange, red, all indicators of those. I'm assuming you understand red means bad?" His voice was gravelly, and the more he spoke, the angrier his tone grew. Beth shrugged in an attempt to release her arm from his hand.

"Well you couldn't be down and out and red—"

"Beth." His gaze hardened as he released her, his eyes drilling into hers with an air of disapproval. He lifted the radio again and pressed the button. *"I repeat, cobra can be there in less than five minutes."* Nothing but static and wind filled the air as Beth and Ben exchanged concerned glances, Beth's mixed with confusion while Ben's mixed with frustration. It seemed like hours passed when in reality it would have been only minutes, until Austin's stern voice finally broke through the silence.

"Proceed to rally point B. That's an order."

"Whiskey," Ben's voice, previously commanding and strict in its military tone, now took on a desperate quality as he spoke into the radio. "We are 350 metres away from them. Let us go."

"Whiskey?" Beth looked at him.

"Austin Williams—"

"Mike." The radio crackled with Austin's angry voice. Ben stopped and glanced at Beth, bracing himself for her inevitable question.

"Ben Molina."

"Beth Taylor, for what it's worth." She shrugged nonchalantly and turned to face the rally point.

"Tango," Ben said, a half smile gracing his lips. She met his gaze and pressed her lips together. "It suits you—"

"Sinnersss," a long, lingering voice crackled over the short wave as Beth looked at Ben fearfully. *"There's no need for these codenames, this isn't a war-zone."* Ben pressed the radio close to his chest and shared a look with Beth, reflecting the fear that was visible in her eyes.

"Unknown subject, identify yourself." Austin's voice demanded through the radio, the crackling indicating that the unidentified man was still holding down the button but remaining silent. There was a long, unsettling silence before the man finally spoke up.

"You first." The voice said, its cadence cold and playful.

Beth and Ben exchanged worried glances, both hesitant to abandon the rally point. Beth ran her dirty fingers through her hair, a failed attempt to calm herself before she looked down the highway once more.

"We could've made it to the motel by now." She turned to face the direction of the compromised rally point.

"Beth, stop—"

"During all this we could've been in and out—"

"We don't know what Chantelle's condition is like," Ben's tone was firm and filled with indignation. "She is down and red. She could be unconscious for all we know and we don't know who or where these guys are. Luis'll protect them and Val's a nurse. I promise you she's—"

"She's *what*?" Beth's voice rose as she spoke. "Austin said we don't leave people behind!—" Ben took two strides before he was in front of her, staring down at her before raising his hands in frustration.

"You've known us for *what*, five minutes? I've known him for *years*, Beth," he said her name with such a distasteful tone that it made her recoil. "If Austin's telling us to leave people behind, *we leave people behind*."

"But—"

"No, enough! Do you think I hate this any less than you do? We have our orders," he yelled, before quieting down into an angry whisper. "They could be the ones at Mountain Gate, or they could be the ones Mountain Gate were shooting at, or they could be *anyone else* looking for someone to fuck around with. We've been careful while trying to get to the coast for *months* because we'd heard shit across the radios. Stories of sadistic, *insane* people who patrol the coast preying on innocent, defenceless people to rape, and maim, and murder, and I absolutely refuse to be responsible for any one of those things happening to you. So for a brief moment, could you please let me do what I've been trained to do and *shut the fuck up*." Ben's hands shook as he spoke, his voice grating against the air and his eyes unblinking. Beth took a small step back, glaring at him with a mixture of anger and pain evident in her tearful eyes. She held up both of her hands in front of her and took a deep breath before walking into the woods, putting some distance between them but still remaining within his view. Ben watched her walk away, regret washing over his body instantly. He hated talking to her like that, but it had served its purpose - he finally had the silence to think straight without worrying about her impulsively running off down the highway. With shaky hands, Ben raised his radio slowly and pressed the button.

"Whiskey?" His voice was soft and hesitant.

"*Rally point B, now,*" Austin repeated. The tone of his voice held a definitive weight that Ben couldn't ignore. "*Cobra, radio off until you arrive.*"

"Copy," Ben replied obediently. "Cobra out."

"*Tiger,*" Reece had taken over the radio once more. "*We're coming to you. Switch to secondary channel. Eagle out.*"

"*Copy eagle,*" Luis said. "*Switching to secondary channel. Tiger out.*" Ben approached Beth, gently resting his hand on her shoulder. She brushed it off without hesitation and turned to face him, determined to hide any signs of emotion that threatened to surface.

"Come on," he said softly as he pointed up the hill. "B is this way."

"*Sinnersss—*" The menacing, crackled voice echoed through the radio as Ben quickly turned it off. Beth shot him a final look of concern and anger before they made their way deeper into the woods.

"Why would Austin break radio silence?" Val looked at Luis.

"You know why."

"What if he's wrong?—"

"Val, you didn't hear him. You didn't hear the concern in his voice. You didn't hear the other guys who came through," Luis marched back and forth, seething with frustration as he evaluated their predicament. "And they must've been close, Val. Their voices were clearer than Reece and Austin's."

"But not clearer than Ben's?"

"No," he replied confidently. "But Austin told them to go to B anyway."

"So no one's coming to help for a while," she looked out the window, straight onto the highway. "We need to move rooms."

"That we can agree on," Luis walked over to Chantelle and shook her gently. "But she's out cold." Val stood up and walked to her backpack as Luis watched her intently from across the room.

"I'll grab her things—"

"You'll need to take mine too," Luis cut off any objections from Val before she could even open her mouth. "I can't carry all that *and* her. I'll take your backpack, you can take mine and hers."

"You carried me for half a day," she grabbed his bag and threw it onto her back. "Or so I was told."

"The guys took turns carrying my bag the whole time I ran holding you," he looked at her dismissively. "And I didn't have to carry you over my shoulder with one arm and a handgun in another. They were there to back me up."

"I didn't know that—"

"No," he replied dryly. "Because you never want to talk about that day. You never asked about it." Val handed him Chantelle's lighter backpack, which he hurriedly put on and adjusted the straps. She added her own to the front of her body, doubling up on either side. It was heavy, almost too heavy, but she knew it was their only chance at a quick move. Luis picked Chantelle up and threw her over his shoulder. He took his handgun out of the holster as Val collected her rifle and walked to the door. She looked back at him and he nodded in affirmation. Opening the door cautiously, she waited for Luis to file out before closing it behind her. They ran behind the first building and across the rear parking lot to the rooms at the rear of the motel. Val paused against a wall before looking back at Luis, already struggling with the added weight.

"Think you can make it to B? We could try—"

"Don't be fucking stupid. That's an eight click trek through the woods, carrying her up and down hills," Luis shot her a look of frustration. "Could *you* make it with those backpacks?"

"I'm sorry." She whispered before looking around the corner. Luis groaned before taking a few cautious steps towards his sister.

"Look, I know you just wanna get her out of here but it's not gonna happen. So we hang tight and wait for Austin and Reece. Okay? I won't let anything bad happen to either of you."

"Okay," she nodded. "Pick a room."

"That one, far left," he raised his head towards the building. "Best vantage point out the window to see who might come in from the driveway." They ran into the end room and locked the door behind them. Luis quickly placed Chantelle in the bathtub and threw the backpacks on the beds, opening them with urgency. He began removing every weapon of his, Austin's, and Reece's that they had carried with them. Luis took stock, assessing their ammunition and, if it came to it, explosives. The room, now a makeshift arsenal, held the tools they might need for whatever challenge lay ahead. The atmosphere was charged with urgency and a sense of impending danger. He set out the guns on the bed closest to the door, and dragged a chair over to the back bed against the wall.

"Tell me what do to." Val said, eyeing the stockpile and hiding her fear.

"Help me with this side table," he instructed as they threw the lamp and alarm clock onto the floor. They lifted it onto the bed while Luis sat in the chair and propped his sniper on the table, looking through his scope and shaking his head. "Hand me that phone book." Val scoffed as she picked it up and handed it to him.

"What motel has a phone book these days?"

"This one luckily," Luis placed it on the chair and sat back down, adjusting his posture and peering through the scope. He was just in time to catch the tail end of a silver SUV disappear up the highway. "Silver SUV, headed north."

"Is it them?"

"How would I—" he shot her a frustrated look and paused, observing the fearful expression on her face. "I'm sorry. It could be, Val. There's no way to tell."

"Can you see inside the car?" Val's voice was soft and gravelly. Luis looked back down the scope.

"They're gone."

"They might come back." Val approached the bed with caution and surveyed the hastily assembled array of weapons before them.

"They might," he said calmly. "And if they do, we'll be ready."

Austin and Reece dashed through the forest towards rally point A, the *Fawndale Resort*. They kept a steady pace, ready for any potential confrontation, but moved with a sense of urgency nonetheless. They avoided the highway, sticking inside the treeline, but some obstacles made it impossible at times and their desire to reach the rally point often took over their sense of stealth. Reece paused by a tree and glanced back at Austin, who was slightly behind and still catching his breath from his earlier sprint up and down the hill.

"How far?"

"A mile, give or take." Austin took a moment to collect himself, then stood up straight and prepared to continue running. Reece reached out and grabbed his arm, stopping him in his tracks.

"Take a minute."

"A minute could kill them."

"You're no good arriving winded and useless Austin," Reece said. "Take a minute."

"Fawndale RV park," Austin paused, breathing in slowly and pointing behind some trees. "We're less than a click away."

"Then we can be there in five minutes, so take a breather." Reece let go of Austin's arm, and Austin looked out at the highway.

"I can rest when we're there," Austin said. "We should keep going—"

"And what if someone's been following us? We'll arrive out of breath and unprepared for a fight. Just... give yourself a minute," Reece looked through the trees at the highway observantly. "I don't see the SUV." Austin leaned against a tree and sank to the ground, grabbing his canteen and taking a long drink.

"We don't know if that was them. It could've been anyone within a few clicks with a short wave—"

"Irrespective of who it was, we know the stories of the people along the coast. The trailer park guys, or anyone else, they're all a little fucked up."

"Irrespective?" A small grin spread across Austin's face as he looked up at Reece, amusement clear in his expression. Reece kept his gaze fixed on the highway, his expression impassive.

"I've been reading at night."

"Reading what?" Austin laughed. "A dictionary?"

"Occasionally," Reece smiled. "It was in a book and I had to look it up 'cause I didn't know what it meant. I found a dictionary back at Eatonville and I kept it on me so I could read all my books properly."

"Holy shit," Austin laughed again. "No wonder your pack's always so heavy. You are the smartest, dumbest redneck I know."

"I'm the only redneck you know. Everyone else is dead," his gaze turned back towards the highway. "Besides, reading at night distracts me from being sober." Before Austin could reply, Reece crouched down beside him suddenly. "Silver SUV, coming from the north." He whispered.

"That means they're circling the area," Austin rose to his feet once they were out of view. "We have to move, *now*."

Chapter Eight

Beth and Ben hiked in silence, their footsteps echoing through the woods as they navigated fallen tree branches and rocks. As they steadily made their way up to the east, Ben would sometimes pass Beth when the terrain became steeper to offer a helping hand, guiding her over larger rocks and up steep inclines. However, most of the time he followed behind her, ensuring she maintained a steady pace. His frustration with her slower speed occasionally showed on his face, especially when she double-checked her footing or cautiously held onto rocks and trees for support. Despite moments where he tried to assist her, Beth was able to navigate the terrain on her own majority of the time. Even when Ben walked in front of her to offer help, she resisted until faced with an obstacle she couldn't handle alone. It was during these moments that Ben noticed the exhaustion etched on her face. They continued walking in silence for hours, neither one complaining or questioning their journey. Finally reaching the top of the tallest peak, they both paused and stood in the clearing of the hiking path. Ben took off his backpack and placed it on the ground, pulling out a map from the side pocket and laying it out.

"I took this from the reception at Shasta Lake. They had all these maps for hikers and stuff. See those two mountains ahead," he gestured in front of them. "Rally point B's behind them, but we won't get over them easily so we'll head north. At the rate we're going, we'll probably stop at the creek for the night. It'd be quicker to continue straight, but you won't make the journey easily, and we need more water." He placed his finger on their location on the map and traced it down to a creek bed and around the side of the mountain. She gazed in the direction of the creek, following the mountain base with her eyes, tracing the route around and back up to their final destination. Ben folded the map and returned it to his backpack before slinging it over his shoulders. "Can you say something, please?" He said, and she regarded him cautiously, studying his movements. The rhythm of his breathing, the way he gestured when he spoke. She observed the nuances in his body language, noting the contrast between the way he interacted with her now as civilians compared to the authoritative manner he had when he ordered her as a soldier. "Beth, I'm sorry for the way I spoke to you before, but it was a stressful situation, and I needed to be clear-headed. The panic didn't help me think. You made me panic. I know you wanted to go help Chantelle, but my commanding officer gave me an order, and I had to follow it, and you made me—" he stopped himself from saying something he would regret. She maintained her silence while he looked at her apologetically, choosing his words carefully before continuing. "You made me want to disobey my orders, and I'm not like that."

"I'm not a soldier," she muttered dryly. "I didn't have to follow his orders."

"Austin told me to protect you, and we split up for a reason. Smaller groups are harder to track and harder to spot. You running in guns blazing," he took a step towards her. "It wasn't the smartest move."

"I don't have any guns to blaze," she remarked, glancing

down at his rifle. She noticed his expression softening as he smiled. "You don't have to be a soldier, Ben. This isn't—"

"Isn't *what*?" He interrupted, his indignation bubbling back up to the surface. "A war-zone? Look around you, *everything* is a war-zone." His anger simmered beneath the surface as he spoke, his tone laced with resentment and exasperation. Beth looked around them, over the cascading mountainside and blurry trees in the distance.

"Looks like mountains." Beth's lips curled into a slight smirk as she spoke, but the rest of her face remained neutral and unreadable.

"Why do you always do that?"

"Do what?"

"Make jokes!" He raised his voice again, the echo floating in the air and into the trees. Silence surrounded them as she turned to face him, her face impassive.

"It wasn't a joke," she said. "It was an observation." The mountains languished in an eerie silence left by the halt in their argument. As the wind picked up through the trees, it caused them to creak and carry the sounds of deer and birds through the air. The peaks shrouded in mist and shadow, each one a magnificent display of nature's power and beauty, with rugged faces and jagged edges carved by time and weather. Fresh and crisp, the air around the mountains carried scents of pine and earth through the peaks and valleys. The further up the mountainside they had climbed, the cooler and cleaner the scent became, invigorating their senses and slowly allowing Beth to forget the metallic stench of blood she had smelled earlier that day. Pine and earth lingered on her tongue as Beth took in her surroundings, observing Ben out of the corner of her eye as he continued to glare at her in anger. The peak of the hiking trail they stood on was filled with the sound of nature - the rustling of leaves, the chirping of birds, and the occasional roar of a distant wild predator, all of which cut through Beth and Ben's unpleasant silence. The rocky terrain of the mountains had been rough and unforgiving, and Beth was thankful of the refuge despite the tension which hung in the air. She took a few steps towards the edge of the trail where the decline began again. The terrain rose like jagged teeth from the earth, standing sentry over the landscape as if guarding some ancient secret buried within their depths. The dark shadows of the trees cast eerie shapes on their rough, weathered faces, while the wind whispered through their peaks, carrying the sounds of nature's secrets with it. They seemed to hold a power and mystery beyond human comprehension, vast and unforgiving but also strangely alluring. In this moment of stillness, as the world around them seemed to hold its breath, the mountains exuded a quiet strength that commanded respect and reverence.

"I don't think you have fully grasped the situation. You've probably been isolated in one place since this all started," Ben said suddenly. His voice was flat, and she turned from the edge to look at him, maintaining her silence. He adjusted his stance as he looked down at his feet, shuffling his weight from side to side. "I have walked through cities filled with dead bodies piled onto one another and survivors killing each other for food. I don't wear this stuff because I like the style. I don't speak the way I do in critical situations because it's fun. This is literally life or death. I wear my uniform because it's protective and practical. We talk to each other like that because it's organised and safe." Beth hesitated, her mind racing with conflicting thoughts as she stood with her arms crossed and her gaze fixed firmly on the ground.

"You don't know what I've been through to get here," Beth said. "You walked through cities filled with dead bodies and wear your uniform with a sense of pride. You do it to protect the people you love. I did what I had to do to protect the person I loved, and I watched him die in front of me while I starved to death." Her voice was calm, calmer than it should have been. Ben sighed and shook his head.

"Beth—"

"Can we just agree on one thing for a change?" Beth interrupted him, disinterested in hearing anything further he had to say on the topic. "You got stuck with me by default, I get that. Austin took Reece, and he couldn't leave me with Luis, so you're stuck taking care of me. I know you hate that. You *hate* the way I seem indifferent to the way the world is now, and I hate the way you're so cold to what it used to be, so can we just agree that we're stuck with each other until the rest of them get here and then we can avoid each other?" Ben paused, bewildered by her nonchalance before looking out over to the mountains.

"Alright," he said finally. "We should get going. Hopefully they arrive tomorrow, so we can start ignoring each other." Ben started down the path, and Beth took in a deep breath before following a few steps behind him.

"I don't think that voice on the radio was from the guys at Mountain Gate," Austin said as he surveyed the room. "The guys at the trailers and the guys in the SUV, they all seemed ill-prepared for a proper gunfight."

"What do you mean?" Val asked.

"The way we were communicating," Reece said. "We sound like military, organised and efficient. They don't know what we had packing, and I didn't see any rifles or proper reinforcements at that trailer park. If they'd heard us on the radio they wouldn't've responded." Austin nodded, staring down at the ground deep in thought.

"It looked like they were just having fun at the end of the world."

"Having *fun* at the end of the world?" Val repeated, her tone laced with offence.

"I only meant—" he paused, choosing his words carefully. "I'm sorry. They just seemed like they didn't care what they were doing." Austin and Reece had arrived at the motel without any trouble, but locating the room where Luis, Val, and Chantelle had taken shelter proved to be a challenge. Austin knocked gently on the door before opening it and announcing their presence. He lowered his gun when he saw his friends inside. Luis quickly followed suit and welcomed them in, locking the door behind them for added security. Val was more hesitant than her brother, keeping her rifle pointed at Austin for a moment before realising they were not a threat and lowering her weapon. Austin and Reece had relayed what they'd seen, a story he now regretted telling them. Austin released a low moan, holding onto his shoulder with his other hand. As the adrenaline from earlier began to wear off, he finally started to feel the throbbing pain caused by crushing it on a rock during the earlier chaos. Val walked over to Austin, standing behind him.

"Let me look at it."

"I'm fine—"

"It could be dislocated," she gently placed her hands on his shoulder and upper arm. "You're no use to us if you can't keep up—"

"It's not, believe me," he laughed lightly. "I know what that feels like." She walked to her bag and removed a small bottle, holding it out to him.

"Here, take some—"

"I need to stay alert—"

"It's Tylenol, idiot," she threw the bottle into his lap. "You think I'd waste the good shit on you?" Luis kept his eyes fixed on his scope, peering through the window at the opposite bed. He was barely listening to the conversation happening around him. As the sky darkened, he switched his scope to night vision mode, frustrated at the limited view he had of the highway.

"That voice on the radio was taunting," Reece commented. "Menacing even."

"Yeah," Austin agreed. "We don't know how many people are scattered along the coast." Val looked over towards the bathroom where Chantelle still lay in the tub.

"The coast was a bad idea."

"We agreed it was the best plan," Austin replied, still nursing his shoulder. "Get a boat big enough for all of us, and get the hell off the west coast."

"Where though? Somewhere safe? I don't think any of us have really considered that *nowhere* is safe." Val said. Caution and concern laced her tone as she continued staring at the bathroom door.

"There has to be something somewhere," Austin looked at her, a mix of hope and defeat on his face. "There has to be —" A piercing scream from the bathroom jolted Val from her thoughts. Reacting quickly, she ran towards the door and barged in to find Chantelle sitting up in the tub, eyes fixed on the ceiling. Val hurried over and sat on the edge, gently wiping Chantelle's face with a damp cloth to calm her down.

"You're safe," she whispered. "You're with me and everything's okay." Austin suddenly appeared at the doorway.

"Can you shut her up?"

"She's traumatised," Val glared at him. "When was the last time *you* felt the cold barrel of a gun pressed to the back of your head?"

"About six months ago." He stared at her with a blank expression. She opened her mouth to say something, but chose to stay silent. Reece sat forward in his chair, his tone stern when he spoke.

"Austin, don't." Reece said. Austin snapped his head around to look at him.

"We've all been through shit, and right now she needs to stay quiet—"

"She's sixteen," Reece's eyes softened, empathy etched into his expression. He looked at Austin with a mix of pity and understanding. "What were you like at sixteen? Eating pizza with your friends, kissing girls, going to the movies? That girl in there doesn't get to do that. She gets to eat a can of cold soup for dinner and trek through treacherous woods and have guns held to her head, and she's gonna have nightmares about it." Austin paused and looked back at the bathroom before heading over to the doorway.

"We're all sleeping in one room tonight," he double-checked the locks before turning around. "I'll take point from Luis. Val and Chantelle can sleep in the bathroom tonight in case anything happens out front. We'll bring the bedding in for you." He said louder so Val could hear.

"Thank you." Val called from the bathroom, her tone icy.

"I'll take point tonight," Reece said from across the room. "You need to rest your shoulder." Austin's eyes darted back and forth, contemplating Reece's demand with a furrowed brow.

"Wake me at 3am," he eventually conceded. "You need your sleep too."

Sitting by the campfire, Beth drank slowly from her bottle, finishing the freshly filled supply. Ben watched her, tempted to make a joke but not wanting to antagonise her. Their long walk from the peak had been in silence, filled with the occasional sound from an animal and the wind rustling through the trees. They hadn't said a word while they made camp.

"That hike was rough." She finally broke their long silence, pulling her jacket up to her chin. Ben watched her as he took a tin from the side of the fire with a damp cloth, opening it and handing it to her.

"You're cold," he said. "This'll warm you up."

"I hate beans—"

"Fuck you're picky for someone who nearly starved to death," he snapped, removing another tin from the fire for himself. "At least it's not peas." She tilted her head as she pushed some beans around with her fork.

"No," she pursed her lips together. "At least it's not peas. I'm sorry—" They sat in silence for a while longer, enjoying their meal as the fire crackled and danced before them. The ever-changing flames cast shadows on the ground, creating a mesmerising display of light and movement. The scent of burning wood and pine filled the air, mixed with the faint hint of smoke that hung over them. Beth felt the chill leaving her body - not from the fire or the food, but from the tension that had seemed to ease with each passing second.

"Beth," Ben said softly, breaking her from her reverie. "I'm sorry about today."

"You don't have to apologise—"

"I think I do." He said, and she nodded in acknowledgement before shuffling her body closer to him. The closer she sat to the fire, the more it enveloped her in its warm embrace, relieving her from the coolness of the night. It was like a living creature, its insatiable hunger fueling its constant licking at the logs with blazing tongues of orange and red. But despite its power and ferocity, it also provided comfort and protection for Beth and Ben as they huddled beside it. Beth couldn't shake off the weight of his earlier statement, words that had crushed her spirit with a heavy burden and threatened to consume her. Cities that were once full of life now lay in eerie silence, their streets lined with dead bodies, decaying buildings, and overgrown vegetation. Among the few remaining survivors, adorned in tattered scraps of civilisation, there existed only a bleak existence plagued by loss and isolation. Metropolises that were once symbols of progress and innovation now reduced to lifeless ghost towns. Amidst it all, a government that had abandoned its people to face these horrors alone. Every day was a battle for scarce resources, fuelling a deep-seated mistrust among the struggling inhabitants as they clawed for survival in this brutal new world.

"Ben," she glanced over at him, huddled next to her. "I do understand the situation."

"I didn't mean to imply that you're ignorant," he said softly. "Naive maybe, but not ignorant."

"Just because I haven't been in a gunfight for my life doesn't mean my journey has been any less difficult."

"I didn't mean to imply that either—"

"We came across a group," she said suddenly and hugged her knees tighter. She placed her chin gingerly on top of them. "Just before Eatonville. It was small and kind enough, but I couldn't contribute much and my husband wasn't exactly a survivalist."

"What did he do before all this?" He asked hesitantly.

"He was a real estate agent," Beth laughed. "So not a necessary skill set for this situation. Their leader was happy to offer supplies in exchange for—" Her eyes were distant, lost in thought as the flickering light reflected off her features.

"In exchange for what?" He pressed.

"Me." She looked at him with a neutral expression, a mild glint of fire in her eyes that Ben couldn't ignore.

"What happened?"

"My husband and I were well taken care of for months." Beth looked back at the fire. Ben, understanding the implication of her words, gulped nervously at the thought.

"If the fire and hot food don't warm you up, this certainly will," he reached into his backpack and handed her the near empty bottle of whiskey. "Finish it." She took a mouthful and smiled, offering it back to him. Shaking his head, he pulled an unopened bottle from his backpack.

"Oh, a secret stash," she laughed. "How convenient."

"I looted it from a liquor store in Eatonville," he pulled out a packet of cigarettes. "Along with these."

"You smoke?"

"Not usually," he opened the new pack of cigarettes and tossed the plastic wrapper into the fire, extending the packet towards her. "But tonight, I think we both need it." She hesitated, thinking about the struggles she had gone through to quit. "I doubt smoking is the biggest issue we have to worry about anymore." He smirked. She nodded hesitantly and he leaned over to light a cigarette in the fire, handing it to her before taking one for himself and repeating the process.

"It took me so long to quit." She took a quick inhale and then coughed a few times, before catching her breath and taking a deeper drag. Ben took a long drag and blew the smoke towards the darkening sky, watching it disappear into the darkness. Beth finished the bottle of whiskey while Ben cracked open another one.

"I never had one before this." He said, taking a drink and handing the bottle to her.

"Never?"

"Nope," he took another drag. "I was a pretty healthy guy. No drinking or smoking, always at the gym."

"Not surprising." She commented, making a conscious effort not to let her gaze wander towards his well-defined muscles and athletic build. They sat in silence for a while, finishing their cigarettes and tossing the butts into the flames. After another drink each, Ben stowed the whiskey back into his backpack. They both glanced at the makeshift campsite they had set up.

"It's big enough for two," he paused, realising the implication of his words and speaking quickly. "But I can sleep outside if you'd be more comfortable—"

"It's too cold," Beth's expression changed as she replied, her eyes meeting Ben's with a look of comfort. "And I trust you." After setting their backpacks down near the end of the swag, he held the flap open for her. Beth took a deep breath before entering, and Ben strolled over to the dying fire, carefully covering the embers with dirt. As he watched the wisps of smoke dance in the chilly evening air, he found himself captivated by the ever-changing patterns. After a brief moment, he tore his gaze away and headed back towards the swag, ready to embrace the peacefulness of the night.

Chapter Nine

Austin's exhausted eyes took in the world outside as dawn broke and another chilly late autumn morning began. He shifted his gaze away from his surroundings to check the time on his watch. The group expected him to wake them at seven so they could start their journey at first light. He waited with restless anticipation, eagerly watching the seconds tick away on his watch before they could finally leave and head east. In the darkness, the watch glowed, its green light illuminating the hands and numbers on its scratched face. Despite its wear and tear from years of use, the numbers were still legible and the steady change of seconds was a comforting reminder for Austin that time was passing, even in the quiet early morning. As he looked at the cool watch on his wrist, he couldn't help but feel grounded and connected to the world around him. It represented a bygone era, where knowledge and control were encapsulated in such a simple object, its ticking syncopation like a universal heartbeat. Lost in its trance-like rhythm, Austin had ironically lost track of time itself, neglecting to observe the world outside for what felt like hours.

"Any movement?" Chantelle's whisper caught him off

guard. She had emerged from the bathroom, draped in a blanket and looking well-rested. Her footsteps were quiet and graceful as she approached him. Austin looked up at her with a mix of surprise and indignation.

"*Please* don't sneak up on me like that," he whispered. "Not while I have my finger on the trigger with very little sleep."

"I'm sorry." Her voice grew louder, causing Luis to stir from his slumber. He rolled over on the floor and rubbed his eyes, trying to wake himself up.

"What time is it?"

"Almost seven," Austin replied firmly. "Time to leave." As they began to wake and gather their things, Val took out an unopened box of cereal bars from her bag and distributed double portions to everyone.

"No arguments," she said sternly to Austin. "None of us've eaten since yesterday morning. We'll need the energy for the hike." He accepted the food without protest, realising that any argument would be pointless - it was clear that they were all in need of nourishment. They silently made their way out of the room and slipped around the back of the building, vanishing into the thick morning fog. Eventually, they came upon a small path on the other side of the trees that led to a lane behind the motel. The air was hauntingly quiet, except for the occasional gunshot from the direction of Mountain Gate which seemed to bother them less as time passed. Chantelle was the first to stop, her feet cemented to the ground as Val bumped into her.

"What?" Val's gaze swept from Chantelle's face toward the direction she was looking, her eyes widening at the sight. Austin sensed their lack of movement and turned quickly to face them.

"Keep moving." Austin called from the front, before he too shifted his gaze to their left. Luis and Reece stood behind Val and Chantelle, the five of them staring in a silent unison.

Three decaying bodies were hanging from the rafters of a house on Gardner Lane. Each with a bag over their head and tattered clothing, the word *'SINNERS'* scrawled in bold red letters across the white weatherboard walls. The decaying corpses swayed back and forth in the gentle morning breeze, their clothes torn and stained with blood and dirt. Flies buzzed around their faces. The smell of death was overpowering, a putrid odour of decomposing flesh that hung heavy in the air. They hung like puppets, suspended in an eerie stillness. A strong gust of wind shifted their bodies, causing one of them to snap at the neck. Its head drooped further as its shoulders slumped from the sudden movement.

"What the fuck?" Reece whispered as he exchanged an awkward glance with Austin and Luis. Chantelle covered her mouth with her hand, hurrying past Austin as she walked further towards the woods. The others followed suit, moving in silence, passing through the trees and vanishing among the foliage. After they were deep enough into the forest, Austin faced them and they assembled in a circle.

"Rally point B is eight clicks, but we won't be able to walk straight through. We need to move quickly and efficiently. It should take eight hours, depending on how we track, and I want to avoid camping in the woods overnight. So if anyone has anything to say, say it now before we head off. Conserve your breath, and no unnecessary banter," he said. The group remained quiet, nodding in acknowledgement as his forehead creased with concern. "We haven't done a trek like this. It's been mostly roads and flat terrain so far, but we can do this."

"Standard formation?" Reece prepared his rifle in expectation of the response he was already aware of.

"It's been a while," Austin nodded slowly. "Reece, take the rear and keep your sights on your M16. Check our six. I'll take point at the front, Chantelle behind me and Luis in the middle, Val in fourth. Ten paces behind, maintain the view of the person in front of you at all times. Any objections?"

Austin asked rhetorically as they remained silent in their obedience. Nodding, he turned and walked east towards their final destination. Chantelle smiled at Val quickly.

"Thank you for taking care of me."

"Don't I always?" Val rested her gentle palm against her cheek. Chantelle trailed behind Austin as he walked away. Luis followed quietly behind them, while Val turned to face Reece.

"She seems better." Reece gave her a slight smile, gesturing towards Chantelle.

"We'll see," Val responded with apprehension. "Are you rested enough?"

"Do we have a choice?" He shook his head in frustration, quickly checking the clip and reloading his rifle. Val placed another cereal bar into his pocket while his hands were occupied.

"You need this, no arguing. I know you've got our backs."

"Don't I always?" He flashed her a playful smile, and Val couldn't help but return it before she followed after Luis. Reece then turned his attention back to his rifle, scanning their surroundings one last time before following behind Val.

Ben awoke to Beth stirring as the distant noise of a bobcat growled in the distance. He checked his watch, just past seven o'clock. Somewhere in the night, he had enveloped her in his arms, her head pressed against his chest. He watched her head rise and fall in tandem with his gentle breathing, noting the way her long, dirty blonde hair rustled as she nuzzled her face into his chest. Placing his fingers on the side of her forehead near her hairline, he observed with a tender gaze as she smiled in her sleep. Her lips curled, dimples forming at the sides, revealing a tranquil serenity in the peaceful embrace. His breathing intensified as his hand slid down the side of her torso, settling on the crevice of her hip. Staring at the top of the swag, he swallowed softly. Gradually, he brought his other arm over to her, holding her tight as she slept. In that fleeting moment, a sense of peace washed over him, amplified by the distant rustle of trees and the awakening sounds of birds heralding the new day. Loosening his grip, he felt her head slowly shift upward towards his face. Bringing his arm up, he propped his head onto it so he could look down at her properly. She opened her eyes and stared at him, a delicate smile forming across her lips. The dim light filtering through the seams of his worn swag offered a soft illumination on her bright green eyes. He stared at the delicate and ethereal shades, reminiscent of fresh spring leaves or the gentle hues found in a meadow bathed in sunlight - in the soft light they exuded a subtle and enchanting glow. Without uttering a word, he continued to gaze at her, savouring the quiet tranquillity that enveloped them after the chaos from the day before. Beth maintained her gaze on his gentle, hazel eyes. The warm mix of the brown and gold was deep and rich, a mixture of earthy tones that mirrored the rugged landscape around them. They were warm and inviting, yet held a steady and determined gaze.

"Did you sleep well?" He whispered. Beth nodded and smiled, making a soft moan as she woke. His heart skipped a beat, and she flinched as if she felt it, her head still pressed against his chest. He shifted his gaze to the top of the swag, feeling her heart beating quickly through her chest and the heat radiating from her body. He lowered his chin slightly, placing a gentle kiss on the top of her head. Sliding out from underneath her, he unzipped the swag with deliberate slowness. Stepping outside, he zipped it back up and stretched his back. He welcomed the cold air that washed over him, soothing the adrenaline that had been pumping through his core just moments before.

"Ben—" Beth extended her hand across the foam mat, opening her eyes and propping herself up on her elbow. Unsure of how long she had been alone for - whether he had just left her or if she had drifted back to sleep - she glanced around, allowing her eyes to adjust to the soft morning light. The realisation that she was now alone prompted her to run her hand down the side of her face and then along the contour of her body to her hip, retracing the path of Ben's touch. She could still feel the lingering sensation of his hands on her, convincing herself that it wasn't merely a dream. She unzipped the swag and stepped out, gazing out over the water. Ben stood in the lake, the water reaching his chest as he ran it over his hair and arms. Moving towards the bank, she halted where he had left his clothes. Bending down, she picked up his watch and checked the time. It was almost eight o'clock. Beth wondered when the last time was that she'd had a proper shower. As if he could read her mind, Ben looked back at her from a distance. She began to unbutton her jeans, sliding them down her legs. He watched her, still and unmoving, as she shed her long-sleeved thermal top and singlet, dropping them next to Ben's clothes, her gaze lingering on his underwear in the pile. For a moment, she questioned whether to shed her underwear and bra as well, eventually deciding against it. Hesitant, she walked into the water. The cold water mirrored the crisp morning air, sending a shock through her body. Undeterred, she continued into the water, making her way towards him. The water lapped at her neck as she stood inches shorter than him. Lowering herself further, she tilted her head back, running her hands through her hair as it waved through the water like silk. She could feel the dirt and mud and dust loosening from her scalp as she shifted her hands through the tangles. Bringing her head back up, she squeezed the moisture from her hair. Water droplets cascaded down her arms as she did so, reflecting the morning light. Her body, once hidden beneath layers of clothing, was now exposed and Ben couldn't help but take notice of how emaciated she truly was. The sound of water being squeezed from her hair and dripping onto the water, coupled by their disruption of the lake's surface, was like soft rain. Ben's own breaths were heavy and laboured as he took in the harsh morning air. Beth could feel the water beads sliding down her skin as she raised her head, her hair now slick and smooth to the touch. Each drop seemed to magnify the sharp angles of her bones, shining like diamonds against her pale skin. Ben's eyes traced the path of the water, taking in every delicate curve and hollow, his heart aching at the sight of her fragile form.

"I'm surprised." He commented softly.

"By what?"

"You." Ben couldn't help but look at her from top to bottom. He tried his best not to stare at her, but his eyes wandered over her body nonetheless. She cocked her head and looked at him with curiosity.

"Why?"

"You kept up with me yesterday," he looked at her softly, his face filled with concern and admiration. "You were near death when I found you, and you've managed to keep up every step of the way—"

"Like I said," she washed her arms and neck gently, letting the water drip down and dance on the surface like soft rain. "New zest for life."

"Why?"

"I haven't felt this safe in a long time," she shrugged. "And I didn't have a choice. I didn't want to be left behind."

"I wouldn't've left you behind," he took a small step towards her. "I will never leave you behind." She took in a deep breath as he stepped closer, placing his hands on her hips, drawing her into him slowly. She felt his body press against her as she ran her hands from his elbows up to his biceps, looking up at him. He lingered for a moment, bringing his face closer to hers. He stopped short, and she placed her forehead against his lips, bringing her hands to his chest like a wall. Ben brought his face around the side of hers, taking in a deep breath as he settled his chin on the top of her head. He wanted her, that much was clear, but there was a time and a place for everything and her vulnerability in the calm morning water was not the moment to satiate his need for physical intimacy. If she had felt more comfortable, he concluded that she would have taken her underwear off as well before entering the lake. Beth felt his head rest softly on hers as she relaxed her body into his embrace. She saw the sun reflecting off the water around them, casting a warm golden glow. Their figures were silhouetted against the bright light, creating a peaceful and intimate moment. She felt the gentle rise and fall of his chest as he breathed. She felt the warmth of his skin, the softness of his chest hair against her face, and the strength of his arms as they held her close. The gentle pressure of his embrace seemed to hold her upright and grounded in the moment.

"Ben—" With each exhale, she melted into his touch, feeling safe and desired in his arms. His head resting on hers was a sign of comfort and trust, a physical manifestation of the emotional connection between them.

"I'll make coffee." He whispered, and he felt her head nod against his chest. She pulled away and turned around, walking a little further into the water to wash her face as he turned towards the bank and walked over to their campsite. She turned her head as he exited the water, watching him from afar as he stood naked, the sunlight glistening off the water on his body. He grabbed his shirt from the ground and used it to dry himself off as she continued watching. A sudden, fleeting anxiety washed over her as she cursed herself. She watched as he gathered his clothes and entered the swag. Beth started for the bank as well, washing her legs as she made her way into the crisp air as it washed over her and created a wave of goose-bumps. She gathered her clothes, using her singlet to dry herself. Ben emerged from the swag, freshly dressed in his same military gear. He picked up his backpack and gestured for her to enter the swag to change, observing the black and yellow bruise that had formed on her lower back as she entered. She stepped in, leaving the zip open, pulling out fresh underwear and wringing her wet ones outside the swag as Ben turned his back. She dressed quickly, braided her wet hair into two messy plaits, and emerged from the swag to find Ben with a black coffee ready for her on a little camping gas canister.

"Thank you." She said as he handed it to her, then made himself one.

"You're welcome," he said softly. They stood in silence for a moment, taking in the morning air and savouring the coffee as if they both knew it would be their last moments of peace before they regrouped with the others. He packed up the foam mat and swag with an urgent efficiency. The rest of the morning flittered by quickly as they packed up the rest of their gear, washing the mugs in the lake before shaking them out and packing them away too. He pulled three cereal bars from his backpack, handing her two. Ben pulled out the map from the side pocket of his backpack. "We have about a two hour walk to the rally point, if we're quick. The others should make it there by four or five, if they left at first light."

"If they're okay—"

"They'll be okay," he said dryly as she noted the shift in his tone towards her. Ben dragged his finger over the map around the creek bed, weaving through the mountain base, over small hills to a hiking trail. "We follow this south and we'll be at the campsite." He pointed to a sign with an arrow - *Jones Valley Campground*.

"Sure," she replied, mirroring his now emotionless tone and following his eyes towards the sign. "What if Chantelle needed a few days to recover? We don't know what her condition was like—"

"They'll be fine," Ben snapped with an exasperated sigh. He quickly slung his backpack over his shoulders and tightened the straps. "Let's go." As they climbed the gradual hill, Beth and Ben fell into an uncomfortable silence. The morning air was gentle against her skin, and despite the sudden tension, Beth couldn't help but smile. They walked alongside each other, with Ben holding his rifle in his hands with a firm grip. She noticed how he held onto it, as if ready for an attack at any given moment.

"Will you teach me to shoot?" She asked him suddenly. He stopped in his tracks as she turned to face him. "You can't protect me all the time." He looked down at his rifle, and then back at Beth.

"I will teach you to shoot. But we'll start with something smaller, and somewhere safer—"

"Where's safe?" She looked around. "This place seems pretty desolate."

"Gunfire would ring out in these hills and valleys like a bell," he started walking again, and she fell in line with him. "I'll teach you to shoot Beth, just not today." As they neared the campsite, their pace slowed as they took in their surroundings. Suddenly, a little girl let out a small shriek and dropped her stuffed bear before bolting towards an RV. The door flew open, and a woman emerged with a shotgun aimed at them. The little girl clung to the woman's leg, hiding her face behind her knees. With his rifle in hand, Ben instinctively stepped in front of Beth and raised the weapon. Beth shifted her stance so she could see past Ben, raising her hands up in defence. She observed a young man emerge from behind the trailer, holding a bat, while standing alongside the woman and small girl. The tense atmosphere was filled with an eerie silence as they faced each other in a standoff.

Chapter Ten

Austin came to a sudden stop at the faint sound of a whistle coming from behind them. Chantelle motioned for him to halt and held up her hand. She removed her backpack and set it down on the ground.

"Gotta pee."

"My eyeline at all times," Austin said abruptly. Chantelle nodded and walked a little further into the woods. He turned to call back to the others. "Five minute break."

"Watch our six." Reece passed his rifle to Val, who immediately looked through the scope behind them but found nothing in sight except for trees. She turned to face Luis, lowering the rifle as she noticed his backpack on the ground and his figure disappearing into the woods to utilise the bathroom break. With vibrant orange leaves and sunlight peeking through the canopy, the thick forest loomed over them and created a serene atmosphere. The towering trees exuded a sense of safety and resilience while the air carried a hint of sweetness, reminiscent of fresh rain and sunshine. There was no sound except for the gentle rustling of the leaves filling the air, accompanied by the harmonious chirping of birds. Their surroundings seemed to emit a calming energy, although Val's concerned expression directed Austin's attention towards Chantelle who was slowly walking backward towards them. Val's gaze followed Chantelle's movements as she emerged from the dense woods, making it difficult for her to see anything clearly beyond her through the thick trees. As Austin raised his hand in caution, an unusual sound cut through the peaceful symphony - a sharp, forceful exhale. Reece approached Val carefully from behind and took hold of the rifle, shouldering it with ease and aiming it towards their surroundings.

"What is it?" She whispered.

"Black bear." Reece rounded on Val, stepping in front of her for her protection. Val leaned in close, taking a small step forward before Reece grabbed her arm in a tight grip.

"Chantelle." She whispered, looking at him nervously, and he gave her a cautionary shake of his head.

"That huff is a warning," he urged. "No sudden movements." Chantelle backed away slowly, her gaze fixed on the black bear as it started to clack its teeth together. Austin moved closer, taking small, careful steps towards her with his rifle pointed at the bear. Luis appeared on the other side of Chantelle, mimicking Austin's stance with his own rifle aimed at the bear. With silent and elegant grace, the bear traversed through the forest, its movements deliberate and smooth. Its strong and agile figure was concealed by its lustrous coat that hugged its sturdy legs and robust physique. As it made its way towards Chantelle, its deep eyes portrayed both curiosity and caution, a fierce wildness reflected in its stare that matched its untamed spirit. Chantelle's movement came to an abrupt halt as she backed into a sturdy tree. Her attention remained fixed on the creature in front of her. Luis stood on one side of her, his rifle aimed steadily at the bear's chest, while Austin stood on the other side with his gun pointed directly at its head. A tiny cub bounded towards the bear, playfully hopping over leaves and twigs. The majestic black bear let out a gentle groan, patiently waiting for its little one to catch up as they continued their regal stroll through the forest. Austin and Luis held their rifles at the ready, waiting for the creatures to disappear from view. As the bears ventured deeper into the woods, they lowered their weapons. Turning to Chantelle, they were met with a serene expression and a small smile playing on her lips.

"They were beautiful," she observed softly, looking between the two. "Weren't they beautiful?"

"Yep," Luis replied sternly. "When they aren't a threat."

"How close were you?" Austin asked.

"I finished goin' to the bathroom and walked past it without even noticin' it until it made a noise. It must've been six feet from me before I started backin' away—"

"Mustn't've thought you were a threat." Austin placed a reassuring hand on her shoulder. Val pushed past Reece with determination, the sound of crunching leaves filling the air with each heavy step.

"Are you okay?"

"Did you see 'em? They were so beautiful. I've never seen a bear before—"

"No, I didn't see them." Val's face contorted in disbelief, her eyebrows furrowed and her mouth slightly open as she stood in shock. Chantelle's composure in the face of such a dangerous situation bewildered her, especially after the events from the day before. "Why didn't they attack?" Val turned to face Austin, who was already itching to leave.

"Does it matter?" Luis scoffed, bending down to grab his backpack from the ground.

"They're naturally timid," Reece said as he approached. "They prefer to run or climb trees to escape a threat—"

"I thought they were aggressive," Val breathed a sigh of relief. "Especially with their cubs—"

"You're thinkin' of grizzlies," Chantelle smiled. "If it's black, fight back. If it's brown, lay down. They prefer to avoid danger. We learned that in school." Val scoffed before looking over at Luis.

"A good lesson for all of us—"

"Enough," Austin turned around. "We need to get moving." They resumed their positions, maintaining the same formation they had held for the past four hours, each walking in silence and troubled by their own thoughts. Austin cautiously led the way, glancing to his right every so often, on high alert for any signs of the bears' return while Chantelle followed close behind, wearing an intrigued smile and utterly mesmerised by the enduring beauty that surrounded them. Luis watched her as she walked in front of him, growing increasingly concerned for her emotional state. Val marvelled at the stark contrast between Chantelle's seemingly catatonic state a mere twelve hours prior, and her current calm presence when faced with a potentially dangerous animal she had never encountered before. Reece gripped his rifle, periodically scanning behind them for any possible threats - whether it be from wild animals, or something else entirely. Entirely different thoughts crossed each of their minds yet they were all equally alert to their surrounds, for one reason or another.

"We have nothing," the woman said steadily. "So keep walking." Ben remained silent, his eyes locked on the woman as he aimed his weapon at her.

"Ma'am, we—" Beth paused as the young man took a few steps forward.

"*Meomchwo*," with a fierce command, she ordered him to stop. He tightened his grip on the bat as the little girl sobbed into her mother's leg. "Please, keep walking." The woman's voice trembled with desperation as she repeated her words.

The young man and the woman both appeared exhausted and anxious, their faces reflecting the strain of their situation. The woman's arms shook under the heaviness of the shotgun she was holding.

"Ben," Beth placed her hand on his arm gently. "She's a little girl. You're scaring her." Ben's eyes remained fixed on the family, not allowing his gaze to waver. She stepped in front of him, carefully removing her backpack and setting it down gently. She lifted her arms once more, then cautiously took a step closer towards them.

"Beth—" He whispered, anger lacing his tone. She wilfully ignored him, slowly approaching the family.

"I'm unarmed," she said. "I don't even know how to fire a gun." Smiling, she looked down at the little girl who had turned her face out from behind the woman's leg.

"Beth." Ben cautioned her once more with a stern tone. Beth's response was not in words, but a frustrated glance back at him.

"You must be hungry," Beth slowly turned her body to show the back of her jeans. She steadily pulled out a half-eaten cereal bar, lowering herself into a crouch and holding it out to the little girl. "It's okay, look, I promise there's nothing wrong with it." Beth took a small bite and smiled softly as the little girl looked up at the woman.

"*Gwaen-chana*," she gestured, nodding towards Beth. "*Cheon-cheon-hee*." The small child walked towards Beth with hesitation, reaching for the cereal bar. Beth remained in a crouched position, her hands still raised in a gesture of peace. The child took a slow bite, chewing with a displeased expression on her face.

"I don't like it."

"Neither do I," Beth laughed and looked back at Ben. "But he gave it to me and I didn't wanna be rude so I pretended I liked it."

"Is he your friend?" The little girl asked.

"He's one of the good guys," Beth nodded. "We mean you no harm, really." As she watched the little girl reluctantly take another bite of the cereal bar, Beth's gaze shifted past her to the woman standing behind her. Her face was stoic, her eyes dark and unreadable.

"So-min?" An elderly female voice called from inside the RV. "*Bakke museun iri-ya?*" The woman holding the shotgun motioned for the young man to go inside.

"Are you just passing through?" She addressed them, her shotgun still aimed but her arms shaking from the strain of holding it up for so long.

"No," Beth stood up, looking back at Ben. "I'm afraid we're not." The little girl stood between them, looking at each person as they spoke. She continued to munch on the cereal bar she didn't like, but was clearly hungry.

"Beth." Ben called out in warning.

"We're waiting for some friends," Beth took another few steps closer to the woman, ignoring Ben's protest. "There was a situation and we got separated. We're supposed to be meeting them here—"

"Well you'll have to meet them somewhere else." The woman's arms were trembling, the shotgun held in a tight grip as she pointed it towards Beth and Ben. Sweat dripped down her face, her eyes darting back and forth between the two intruders.

"I can't exactly call them to tell them," Beth smiled reassuringly. "The service up here is terrible." The woman's expression changed, her stern features softening as she let out a small laugh. She lowered her weapon and the little girl came back over to her, offering the remaining piece of the cereal bar.

"Mama I don't like this, you can have it." She said. The woman glanced at Beth, who gave a slight nod in return. With anticipation, she took a bite and savoured it as she chewed slowly, her eyes glistening as they threatened to fill with tears.

"*An-e ga-seo Halmeoni-kke deuryeo,*" she returned the

cereal bar to the little girl, who eagerly took it and ran back into the RV. The woman turned her attention back to Beth. "Thank you." She spoke in a weak voice, her legs giving way as Beth hurried to her side and caught her before she hit the ground. They fell together with a soft thump. Ben quickly ran over, setting down his backpack and kneeling beside the woman.

"She's probably famished." Beth delicately brushed a lock of hair away from the woman's face, taking notice of her delicate and weak frame.

"She looks worse than you did when we found you—"

"We've barely eaten for days," the young man appeared at the door. "And she has low blood pressure. She ran out of her fludrocortisone a month ago and we haven't been able to find anything for her." Beth turned to look at him.

"Her what?"

"Her medication," the young man replied. "For her blood pressure."

"Val might have something," Ben's gaze shifted from the woman to Beth and then back again. "When they get here we can check."

"She needs food first." Beth's expression was one of concern as she gazed at Ben, silently pleading with him. He let out a deep sigh, clearly frustrated, before reaching into his backpack and pulling out a tin.

"We don't have much water left either," he said, handing her the can of soup. "But water it down and we'll make it work for them."

"We have a bit inside, but I can get more water," the young man exclaimed with sudden enthusiasm. "I can get to the creek and back in no time." Before either of them could protest, he ran around the side of the RV and came back with a mountain bike equipped with two metal cages on either side, jerry cans nestled inside.

"It's too dangerous." Beth protested.

"I do it all the time. It's only forty minutes on foot, and I'm quicker on my bike," he said. Before she could protest any further, he had mounted his bike and was already off down the hill. "Even quicker if you cut through the trees!" He called back as his voice trailed off. Beth gently shook her head before turning back to the woman.

"He's excited," she whispered. "We haven't come across anyone for, well, I don't know how long."

"Go inside and see if their stove works to heat it up," Ben said, handing Beth the canteen. "Use this to water it down for now and whatever else is in there." Beth carefully entered the RV and inspected the stove, turning on a burner.

"*Nun nugu-nya,*" an elderly woman called from the other side of the RV, startling Beth. "*Yeogiseo mwo haneun geoya!*"

"*Halmeoni,*" the little girl said, stroking the woman's arm. "It's okay. She's my friend." Beth flashed a warm smile at the little girl, then turned her attention back to the stove. After opening the tin of soup and pouring it into a pot, she added water from her canteen. As she reached for a half-full bottle of water on the counter, she looked over at the little girl and elderly woman with a kind expression, trying not to startle either of them further.

"Do you drink from this?" Beth asked. The little girl nodded in response and Beth poured the water into the pot. She stirred, watching as the soup began to thin out. Her forehead creased with worry as she prayed that it would be enough food for them to eat.

"Easy." Using a jacket from Beth's backpack, Ben propped up the woman's head. Beth walked outside with a bowl of soup and crouched down beside them.

"Can you try to get her to sit up?"

"I don't want to do that too quickly," he took the soup from her. "In case her pressure drops."

"There's an old woman inside," Beth looked back towards the RV door. "She needs to eat too." Ben nodded as Beth stood and retreated back into the RV. Dipping the spoon into the soup, he carefully brought it up to the woman's mouth. She licked at it slowly, struggling to swallow and managing a small smile of gratitude.

"Thank you." She whispered as he held another lightly coated spoon to her.

"Do you think you can sit up?" He asked.

"In a minute," her tone carried a hint of optimism, her light Korean accent more noticeable now that there was some hope in her voice. "Thank you for doing this. Others wouldn't be so kind."

"No," Ben replied sternly. "Other people aren't kind these days."

"My mother, she's very frail—"

"Beth is inside taking care of her," he interrupted softly, feeding the woman another spoonful. "She'll make sure she has some food."

"She seems like a sweet girl," she smiled at him. "Can you help me sit up?" He leaned her against the side of the RV, spooning a larger portion into her mouth now that she was sitting up. Inside, Beth approached the elderly woman in the bed, carrying a bowl of watery soup. The woman eyed her with suspicion and scepticism in her expression. Despite her age, she sat upright against the headboard, clutching a walking stick and ready to strike with unsuspecting agility.

"*Jeo-ri gah*," she exclaimed. "Min-ji, *jeo michin miguk-in-i oji mot-ha-ge hae*!"

"*Halmeoni*," the little girl put her hand on her cane. "The crazy American is trying to help you—"

"Well, it's your lucky day," cautiously, Beth sat on the side of the bed. "I'm not American." Holding a spoonful of soup in front of her, Beth gestured as the elderly woman observed her. Beth pursed her lips and reluctantly took a mouthful for herself before scooping more with the spoon and holding it out to the woman. "If I was going to kill you, I wouldn't waste food doing it." Beth tilted her head and raised her eyebrows. With hesitation, the woman opened her mouth as Beth carefully guided the spoon inside. As she relished the flavour of the food, her features relaxed. She opened her mouth eagerly for another spoonful, and Beth observed in quiet contentment as she fed her until the bowl was completely empty.

"See?" The little girl said. "She's my friend."

"Do you feel better?" Beth placed the bowl onto the nightstand as the elderly woman gave a small nod and closed her eyes gently, resting her head back onto the headboard.

"My daughter—"

"Is just fine," Beth interrupted. "My friend is helping her eat."

"Good. She is very sick and very hungry. She gives all her food to everyone else," her thick Korean accent added a sharp tone to her resentful words. "She married a crazy American. I do not like him."

"Well, like I said I'm not American," Beth let out a soft laugh and pursed her lips into a gentle pout. "And I hope I'm not crazy."

"You are sharing your food with people you do not know," she replied slowly, looking at Beth before closing her eyes again. "You must be crazy." Beth's lips curved into a smile before she turned her gaze to the little girl.

"Are you Min-ji?"

"Mama calls me MJ." She said with a smile.

"How old are you Min-ji?"

"This many." The little girl held up three fingers.

"Three!" Beth feigned surprise. "I thought you must've been so much older because you are very brave."

"You can call me MJ," the little girl said as she caressed her grandmother's face. "She's sleeping now." Beth rose from the bed and walked back to the stove.

"Come on MJ, we'll let her rest. It's your turn to eat."

Chapter Eleven

"They're both fed and fast asleep." Beth said as she emerged from the RV, slowly approaching Ben and the woman who were both seated on the ground.

"Thank you." The woman said.

"There's plenty more," Beth reached down for the bowl. "I'll get you some—"

"No," the woman's brows furrowed as she tightly gripped the empty bowl against her chest. "Save some for So-min when he gets back, and more for my daughter and *eomeoni* when they wake up."

"There's *plenty* more." Beth repeated with determination as she grabbed the bowl and headed into the RV. When she returned, she sat down next to her on the ground and handed her the bowl. The woman hesitated before taking another spoonful but eventually gave in, letting out a grateful sigh after swallowing.

"Thank you."

"Your mother said you make sure everyone else eats more than you," Beth said quietly. "You need to make sure you eat."

"There's barely anything," she said. "My husband and sister

and her husband walked to town to find food and medication but they haven't been back for days." Ben's eyes darted back and forth between the woman and Beth, his brow furrowed and his mouth slightly open.

"The closest town is Mountain Gate—"

"No," she said, shaking her head. "They went further south, to Redding."

"What's in Redding?" Beth queried. Before responding she savoured the warmth of the soup on her tongue, a fleeting moment of comfort in the midst of chaos and uncertainty.

"Pharmacies for my medication," she said. "I have orthostatic hypotension and need fludrocortisone, or midodrine if we can't find that." The spoon clinked against the bowl as she lifted it to her lips, her eyes closed in relief as she swallowed the sustenance that her body desperately needed.

"The young man, the one who went to get the water—" Beth said, trailing off as she looked down the path where he had disappeared.

"My brother."

"Your brother said you hadn't had your medication for a month," Ben pursed his lips. "Is there anything you can do?"

"Increase my salt intake, stay hydrated," she smiled softly. "Quite hard to do here, without any food. We have no car and I won't let him go to Redding on his bike. If my family hasn't returned, something must've happened—"

"Eat." Beth interrupted in an attempt to calm her. The woman's voice quickened as she became visibly distressed.

"Did you come from Redding? Maybe you saw them. My sister and her husband, they are both Korean. She was wearing a light blue shirt and he had a, uhh," she paused as she struggled to remember. "What was he wearing?" Asking herself rhetorically in frustration, the woman took in another mouthful of soup.

"It's okay." Beth comforted her, noticing her rapid

breathing and worried that she would faint again from the surge of adrenaline in her system.

"And my husband, he's American," she spoke quickly. Her accent and worried tone made her words difficult for Beth and Ben to comprehend. "And he has brown hair and had a red tartan shirt on. What are those shirts called? The ones with the squares?"

"A flannelette," Beth said flatly, looking at Ben. "A red tartan flannelette."

"Yes, that's it," she said. "Did you see them?"

"We didn't come from Redding," Ben responded with an icy tone, evading the question without outright lying to her. "We need to get you inside so you can rest."

"I sleep in the blue tent," she gestured to the right. "With my husband."

"You need to rest comfortably." Ben echoed the statement as Beth relinquished the half-eaten bowl of soup from her hands. With his assistance, she stood up and he guided her towards the RV.

"Is there a bench in there?" He addressed his question to Beth, who responded with a quiet nod. Ben led the woman by placing her arm on his shoulder and guiding her into the RV. Beth searched for a blanket and found one to cover the woman as they both carefully manoeuvred her onto the cushioned bench, making sure she was comfortable before covering her. They stepped out of the door and gently shut it behind them. Beth made her way to a tree located on the opposite side of the campsite, sinking down onto the ground with her back leaning against the trunk.

"A red tartan flannelette—"

"I know," Ben glanced over his shoulder at the RV and swallowed hard, shaking his head in disbelief. "Do we tell her?" She shut her eyes as he slowly walked back and forth in front of her, taking in every detail of the campsite.

"I don't know."

"We can think about that later," he stopped a few paces away and turned to face her. "I need to get food." Beth looked up at him pleadingly.

"You can't go into town, not now—"

"Not town," he stepped closer and sat down next to her. "There're deer, elk, rabbits, a bear if we're lucky. I'll go hunting." Her brow furrowed and her eyes widened as she tilted her head slightly to the side, studying his expression intently.

"A *bear* if we're lucky?"

"Bear meat goes a long way," he nudged her shoulder with his. "It's just harder to skin."

"Gross." She revolted.

"Hey," he looked at her with a stern expression. "You need to learn this stuff. You can't just go to Walmart and shop for groceries."

"I know," she complained softly as she rested her head on his shoulder. "Can't we just order a pizza?"

"Sure," Ben leaned in towards Beth, resting his head on top of hers. "Your shout." Their heads fit perfectly together, creating a peaceful picture amidst the chaos of the campsite. His eyes were closed, his lips curved upwards in a small smile. Beth savoured the moment of peace between them, surrounded by the desolate campsite and vast woods beyond it.

"Why were you so mad at me this morning?" She asked.

"Honestly?" He sighed before raising his head and looking out at nothing in particular. "When we're moving it feels like work, like when I was in the military."

"So you change?"

"I guess I do," he said. "You just kinda turn into work mode. I'm sorry if I snapped at you, it's just hard when I'm not used to people asking questions when I'm giving orders—"

"I'm not a soldier Ben," she lifted her head and looked at him. "Sometimes I'm gonna ask questions. Sometimes I'm gonna have an opinion—"

"And I'll try to remember that," he turned his head to face her. "As long as you try to remember that sometimes I won't be able to answer you if we're in a sticky situation."

"But this morning—"

"I know," he interrupted. "This morning we weren't in a sticky situation. I was frustrated. I don't want to think about the others not arriving here on time. If it gets to five, or even six, I'll start worrying. And I won't be mad at you for worrying too."

"Okay," she conceded. "I promise I'll try to frustrate you less while you're in work mode." She placed her forehead gently on his shoulder.

"Thank you." He said, resting his head against hers once more. They sat in silence for a while, listening to the birds and the wind echo in tandem through the trees. Ben found himself almost nodding off - despite having a good night's sleep, running on rations and instant coffee paired with the events of the morning had knocked the energy out of him.

"I thought you said shooting around here was dangerous." Beth whispered, and he startled from his meditative trance.

"What?"

"You said you were gonna go hunting," she whispered, slightly louder this time. "You won't teach me to shoot because it's too dangerous but you want to go hunting?"

"It *is* dangerous," Ben said. "But necessary if we need to eat. Hopefully the echo makes it hard for anyone nearby to pinpoint where we are."

"Then you have no reason not to teach me how to shoot," she pressed. "Like you said, it's not like I can walk to Walmart for groceries. And I can't call the police when I'm in trouble. You said I need to learn to hunt and skin animals to survive. Shooting comes with the territory—"

"Fine," he sighed, closing his eyes and taking in a deep breath. "You win." They fell into a comfortable silence for a long while, pressed against each other for what seemed like hours, until the young man slowly rode back up the hill. When he reached the top, Ben stood up and helped Beth to her feet. Ben walked over to assist the young man with the heavy containers while Beth took a leisurely stroll around the campsite. The three tents were set up at the edge of the tree-line, with a blue one placed in the centre. Clotheslines strung between the RV and trees were adorned with dry clothes, seemingly left there for days with little energy from any of the group to retrieve them from where they hung.

"Thank you," the young man said as Ben carried both jerry cans to the side of the RV. "They're a bit heavy for me. My brother-in-laws usually do it but they haven't been back for days." He seemed exhausted from the journey.

"Your sister mentioned that they're missing?" Beth shifted her gaze from Ben to the RV, then back to the young man who gave a solemn nod in reply. Ben's stance shifted, his muscles tense as his fingers tapped nervously against the side of his leg.

"I'm Ben, and this is Beth." He said, changing the topic quickly.

"So-min, or Sam if that's easier," he smiled. "Is there any water that's drinkable? We can't drink this yet." He gestured to the jerry cans.

"Here." Ben grabbed his water purifier and used it to filter some water into his canteen, then handed it to Sam. Thirsty and in a hurry, he drank hastily, accidentally spilling some down his shirt.

"How old are you?" Beth asked.

"Seventeen." He smiled at them, taking another drink.

"You should eat, and get some rest," Beth commanded, concern etched in her brow. "There's some food on the stove, and space on the other bench in your RV. Just go in quietly, everyone else is asleep."

"Better rest with the thicker walls than the tent." Ben added before Sam could object.

"I guess you're right," Sam let out a heavy sigh, his fatigue clearly written on his face. "Will you wake us if my family comes back?"

"Of course," Beth said solemnly, swallowing hard and trying not to allow her voice to break. "Eat, get some rest, and you'll feel better." Sam softly opened the door and stepped into the RV, closing it carefully behind him. Beth walked towards Ben and leaned into him, placing her forehead against his chest without hesitation as he enveloped her in his arms.

"I'm exhausted." She exhaled heavily. Gently, he stroked her back, careful not to touch her bruises.

"You should eat too."

"It's pea and ham," she wretched sarcastically. "Let them have it. I'll eat later when you bring me back a black bear or something."

"Once you go black—"

"Well I'm hugging the wrong man then." Beth's blonde hair, tangled and disheveled from the day's events, fell across her face as she tilted her head to look at Ben. Her green eyes were tired with dark circles visible underneath.

"Hey," he smirked, kissing her forehead lightly. "Not funny."

"Oh, I'm hilarious." She wiggled away from his embrace and made her way to where her backpack was lying on the ground. He retrieved his own backpack from where he had abandoned it on the ground and leaned it against the RV. He picked up his rifle and some rope, scanning the woods ahead.

"I'll be back soon. I'm gonna go find you a bear." He said, smiling, and disappearing into the trees. Beth's eyes darted around the campsite, taking in the peaceful scenery. But underneath the surface, she felt a growing sense of unease and isolation that reminded her of the terrifying days before Ben had rescued her. In her solitude, she came to conclude that it was the first time since that day that she truly felt alone.

Looking down at the steep hill ahead, Austin knew this was their last push through the third and final peak. He halted at the top of the mountain, surveying the distance through his scope. Pulling out the hiking map from his pocket, which Ben had given him days earlier, he quickly examined it, ensuring they were on the right path. Standing in the clearing of what seemed like a thin hiking path, he scrutinised the map closely - Bear Mountain Lookout Road. Continuing left would take them on a path through a steady decline but add an hour to their trek. Cutting directly east through the trees would have them there in half an hour. Folding his map back up and tucking it into his pocket, he peered through his scope once more in the direction of the rally point. Seeing no obvious signs of danger, he lowered his rifle.

"Thirty minutes," he turned to Chantelle. "Give or take." She nodded and turned to tell Luis and send the message down the line. Austin pushed forward through the trees, eager to get to their final destination and rest his shoulder. The terrain was steeper than he had anticipated, and he unintentionally quickened his stride with the pull of the mountainside, navigating rocks and fallen branches, ensuring the others kept up with him. Chantelle and Val both felt the struggle, while Luis and Reece made sure they weren't left behind, maintaining the ordered line. An unexpected gunshot rang through the woods, piercing their ears like hot needles. Austin, Luis, and Reece swiftly drew their rifles, ready for action, as Val and Chantelle instinctively pulled their hands to their ears. All five of them dropped to the ground in a unified crouch.

"The fuck was that." Luis looked back at Reece, gesturing for him to stay put. He then turned and moved forward to join Austin's position.

"Cover the front," Austin whispered. "I'll push forward." He stood up, moving through the trees carefully and quietly. Hiding behind a large tree, Ben held his rifle to his chest, watching as his friend walked past him. A sudden wave of comfort and relief washed over his body.

"You need to brush up on your stealth." He emerged, holding his hands up in a mock gesture of surrender. Austin swiftly turned and aimed his rifle at Ben, pausing for a moment, and then lowering his rifle. He walked quickly to his friend, embracing him with a heavy thud as their bodies collided.

"Man, am I happy to see you."

"Likewise, brother." Breathing a sign of relief, Ben looked past Austin at the others who slowly began to emerge from the trees. Luis approached him angrily, pushing past Austin.

"What the fuck're you doing out here, shooting up the joint?"

"Dinner." Ben gestured further into the woods, ignoring Luis' obvious contempt. Luis opened his mouth to argue, but Austin interjected quickly in order to change the subject.

"How far to the rally point?"

"Ten minutes," Ben shrugged. "Give or take. I'll take you once I've tied her up." Austin gathered the rest of the group, who were relieved at the news on all fronts - they were close to the camp and a hot, fresh meal awaited them that night.

"No bear then?" Beth turned to the treeline as she heard rustling, seeing Ben emerge with a deer slung over his back.

"No," he smiled. "But I brought you something much better." Austin pushed through the foliage, looking over at her. She started walking towards them as the rest followed Austin out of the treeline. Beth was quick to embrace Chantelle, holding her face in her hands.

"I'm glad you're okay." She said. Ben placed the deer on the ground, looked around the group, and finally set his eyes on

Beth, nodding. She looked back at the RV before subconsciously stepping between Luis and the RV door.

"We need to tell you something." Ben looked at each of them evenly as he spoke. Reece placed his bag on the ground and stretched his shoulders.

"Can it wait? We're exhausted—"

"Not really," Ben remarked quickly. "There's a family inside that RV." Luis' grip on his rifle tightened, his body stiffening. Beth quickly put her hands up in defence and moved closer to the RV door.

"They're no threat—"

"How can *you* guarantee that?" Luis's tone was laced with anger, exhaustion and frustration both evident on his dirty face.

"Because there's a sick woman, her three year old daughter, a malnourished teenager, and an elderly woman," Beth retorted sternly. "They are no threat to *you*." Luis looked at Austin pointedly, awaiting his validation of his apprehension. Austin looked at Luis and shook his head.

"If Beth says they aren't a threat, they aren't a threat."

"Austin—"

"*Enough*, Luis," he interrupted. "I've had enough for one day." Luis trudged over to a tree, visibly frustrated and exhausted, and laid down underneath it. Austin gestured for Val to check on him, which she did obediently. Ben showed the others where they could set up their swags, explaining the sleeping situations of the tents, omitting the fact that half of the family were missing, while Chantelle set hers up next to Val as usual. Fuming with frustration, Luis walked away and chose a spot far from the rest of the group. Austin didn't acknowledge this decision, but if he was truthful with himself, he was relieved about it. Reece dropped his bag onto the lawn, marking his territory for where he planned to sleep beneath the stars later that night. Austin and Ben selected spots under some nearby trees, giving each other at least ten meters of distance between their swags.

"There's a lake about forty minutes walk that way," Ben gestured down the trail. "You can all wash up."

"Later," Austin replied. "I want to know what's going on here." Austin was taken aback when Ben summoned Beth to join him in narrating their day. Together, they recounted every detail except for one minor aspect - the mysterious woman's missing family, particularly her deceased husband who they had encountered earlier. That story could wait for another time.

"I'll leave you to it." With a smile, Beth headed towards the washing line to begin tackling the laundry that the family had neglected.

"If anyone feels like washing up before nightfall, now's the time," Austin called to the group. "It's an eighty minute round trip, plus bathing time."

"I'm exhausted." Chantelle exclaimed warily.

"But if we do it now, you can go to sleep and wake up refreshed," Val rubbed her back affectionately. "Come on."

"You two as well." Austin pointed to Luis and Reece, who both said little in protest knowing they needed it.

"And you," Ben nodded at Austin. "You look like shit."

"Thanks," Austin laughed. "You look fresh."

"Beth and I washed this morning," Ben commented as Austin raised a questioning eyebrow at him. "No, nothing like that—" He stumbled over his words, trying to correct himself. The two men glanced at Beth, who was peacefully folding laundry. She could feel their gazes on her, but she gave no indication that she could hear them.

"Ben—"

"Go wash up," Ben's expression was tense, his eyes darting nervously as he tried to avert his gaze from Austin's questioning stare. "We can talk later."

"Sure." Austin gave a final warning look at Ben before

gathering a fresh change of clothes from his backpack. Ben walked over to Beth casually as the others departed for the lake.

"Enjoying yourself?"

"As a matter of fact, yes," she laughed. "I'm enjoying this very peaceful frame of mind doing a menial task like folding laundry."

"Good. Enjoy it while it lasts," he replied. "Because when you're done I'm gonna teach you how to skin a deer."

Chapter Twelve

Mildly traumatised but eager to learn, Beth watched with a mix of awe and slight disgust as Ben expertly skinned the deer in a little over an hour, his knife slicing through the animal's tough hide with precision. The carcass was laid out before them, bloody and glistening in the sun.

"You make it look so easy." She gently pressed her hand against her mouth, attempting to acclimate herself to the strong scent of fresh blood.

"Would've been quicker if I wasn't going through the process with you," he smiled. "But you need to learn and I'm a little out of practice. Any questions?"

"Yes," taking in a deep breath, she attempted to steady her queasiness. "Will I ever get the sound of you ripping the skin from its body out of my head?"

"Hopefully," he teased. "Anything else?"

"Nope, I'm good." A flicker of jest and nausea danced across her face as she smiled. After changing out of his bloody clothes, Ben constructed a larger fire in the same area where the family had previously cooked, making sure to improve its structure for cooking the deer meat. Ben poked at the kindling as he stared at the RV.

"I don't think they'll wake tonight."

"They'll probably sleep all the way through after eating for the first time in days." Beth hugged her knees, resting her chin on them as she sat in contemplation.

"Then we'll save them some food for tomorrow, and we'll go hunting again," he stared at the fire as it started to take hold. "And I'll teach you how to shoot." Her excitement was evident as she leaned forward and perked up, her eyebrows raising in anticipation.

"Really?"

"Really." He said, smiling.

"What are we gonna do about them?" Beth glanced towards the RV and swiftly redirected the conversation to the topic of the family.

"Ultimately, it's up to Austin," Ben raised an eyebrow. "To be honest, I don't think he'd intended to find this many people."

"But he won't leave anyone behind," she took in a deep breath. "I'm glad. They really need help, but Luis isn't gonna like it—"

"Oh, fuck Luis. I get that he wants to take care of his family but he needs to get in line. He's aggressive and dismissive and it just doesn't help the situation," pre-empting her question, he turned to face her and rolled his eyes. "And yes, I feel better getting that off my chest."

"Good," she smiled at him as she looked back towards the tents, and beyond that to the swags while they both had the same lingering thought. "I can sleep in the empty tent tonight if you'd prefer." He remained silent, pondering how Austin would react if they shared a bed, what his friend would say if he knew what had occurred earlier that day. The thought of sleeping next to her again and reliving the memory of waking up to her nestled in his embrace, gazing at him with her captivating green eyes, filled him with longing. The memory of their morning together flooded his thoughts, but he couldn't push away the doubts that remained. He used to be captivated by her emerald eyes, yet now they held a hint of doubt that matched his own conflicted emotions. Part of him yearned for her touch, but he couldn't ignore the opposing thoughts swirling in his mind. Beth misinterpreted his silence as hesitation. As he was lost in thought, he barely registered the approach of the others, who were returning from the lake after washing up and changing into regular clothes. Seeing all four of them out of their uniforms created a strange and surreal image.

"That smells incredible," Chantelle sang as she took in the aroma. "It's the first proper meal we've had in ages." The group gathered around the campfire, with Val and Chantelle occupying the only two chairs they could find. Beth sat apart from the others, preferring to eat her meal in solitude. The fire crackled and flickered as the flames danced, casting a warm light over the faces of those huddled around it. In the centre of the flames lay a large portion of roasted deer meat, cooked perfectly on thin yet sturdy branches. The smell of sizzling fat and charred meat filled the air, accompanied by occasional drips onto hot coals, causing everyone's mouths to water as they ate in contented silence. The distinct scent of smoke that mingled with the rich, savoury aroma of venison was both comforting and enticing. As they shared stories from their day, Austin and Reece took turns describing what they saw at the trailer park. A sense of unease hung in the air as Val, Chantelle, and Beth contemplated the possibility that they could have been taken by the men in the SUV if they had been caught on the highway. Luis recounted their encounter with the man wearing red tartan flannel, causing Ben and Beth to exchange awkward glances, but they both chose to remain silent for the time being. They were unsure how Luis would react towards their family in the morning, so sharing this information with him wasn't a risk they wanted to take. Austin stood up from his spot on the ground feeling satisfied and safe in their temporary sanctuary.

"We've all had a big few days," he addressed the group, looking around at each of them. "So we need to rest. I want everyone in bed soon so we can sort this out tomorrow." He nodded towards the RV. Chantelle and Val stood up in unison. As they walked, Chantelle turned back quickly.

"Beth! I didn't even think 'bout the fact that we don't have a swag for you. You can share with me if you want. It's small but two people can fit—"

"I'll sleep in one of the empty tents." Beth declared quickly, glancing out of the corner of her eye between Ben and Austin.

"Alright then," Chantelle smiled naively. "Goodnight everyone." Ben's expression shifted to one of resignation as he suddenly announced his intention to call it a night. Beth made her way towards the RV, planning to store the spare food in the fridge for the family the next morning. She quietly entered the vehicle and discovered the family still fast asleep where she and Ben had left them. Upon exiting, she found that everyone else had already retired to their beds. Slowly, she strolled towards the tents, catching snippets of conversation between Austin and Ben in the distance near where they had set up their swags.

"So where did she sleep last night?" Austin pressed.

"It was cold," Ben replied. "I offered her the swag."

"So you slept outside then," there was an eerie, awkward silence for a few moments, before Austin pressed on. "Don't complicate things, Ben. You see how Luis is protecting Val and Chantelle. I can't have your judgement clouded too." She heard the familiar sound of zippers being unzipped, but only one being closed. As the fire slowly died out, she looked over at the three tents in front of her, watching the flames light them up in the darkness. She couldn't help but wonder if it was

Ben's swag that was still open, an invitation for her to join him. After much deliberation, she chose to enter one of the tents and made sure to zip it closed tightly behind her. In the darkness, she strained her ears and heard the faint noise of a swag zipper slowly closing nearby.

Barely sleeping at all during the night in anticipation for the day's events, Beth was up at the crack of dawn. She unzipped the tent as quietly as she could and stepped out into the soft, crisp morning air.

"Morning." Reece's voice broke the silence, surprising her. He was busy brewing coffee in a large pot over a newly kindled fire. Holding up a fresh cup, he offered it to her as she approached, and she graciously accepted.

"Good morning." She greeted him lethargically, taking a slow sip and scanning the campsite for signs of others who might be stirring.

"I'm usually the first one awake." Reece remarked, a hint of humour in his tone.

"Because you don't sleep in a swag?"

"Because I don't sleep," he quipped. "And I suspect, neither do you?"

"I am anticipating the day," she replied slowly, her gaze drifting to the trees, a subtle contemplation in her eyes. "Can I ask you something?" She looked down at him suddenly, a slight kick of energy in her tone from the coffee.

"I don't know you very well, Beth, but you strike me as the kind of person who would ask anyway, even if I said no." He gazed up at her, gesturing for her to sit next to him on the ground as she complied, but left a few feet between them to maintain her personal space.

"You're perceptive," she smiled, diving head first into her inquisitiveness. "When you all found me, what was the conversation?"

"It wasn't really a conversation," he responded slowly. "It was an argument."

"Between Luis and Austin?"

"Between Luis and all of us," he replied bluntly. "Luis has had a tough life and his number one goal is to look after his family. He's failed in that task before and he doesn't intend to do it again."

"So I've been told," she looked at the fire as he poked at it with a stick. "So what happened?"

"Luis demanded that we leave you behind, Austin gave him a command, and that was it," he maintained his gaze on the fire. "He didn't think you'd offer much to the group, that you'd be a burden we'd have to take care of." Beth paused her inquisition, reflecting on that night at the motel where Austin had prevented Luis's discovery concerning Beth's potential.

"I'll pull my weight eventually," she said. "When I have my strength back and I've learned a thing or two. What's Luis gonna make of them?" Beth turned her attention towards the RV, and Reece's eyes followed her line of sight.

"Two kids, an old lady and a sick woman?" Reece scoffed light-heartedly. "What do you think?" Beth turned her attention back to Reece, gazing at him, unblinking.

"One of the kids is a year older than Chantelle," she pointed out. "He could hold his own eventually."

"Fair enough—"

"And what do you think?"

"Of them?"

"Of me."

"I think that I haven't spent enough time with you to know what you'd contribute," he said with a blunt honesty. "But you *are* another mouth to feed, speaking of—" Reece looked up at the RV as the door opened slowly. The woman appeared on the steps, appearing rested and alert, a stark contrast to her state from the previous day. Beth walked over to her, offering her the rest of her coffee. The woman looked at her, taking a moment to adjust and realise that she recognised her.

"How're you feeling?" Beth asked.

"You are here," she said, taking the cup. "I thought I might have imagined you."

"Very real I'm afraid," Beth smiled, creasing her eyebrows. "What's your name? We never got to that part yesterday."

"Su-ho Cole," she responded, taking a slow sip of the lukewarm coffee. "Please, call me Su."

"I'm Beth, if you remember," Beth placed a hand on her chest, and then gestured towards the fire. "And this is Reece, one of the friends Ben and I told you about." Reece stood up and offered her a small bow.

"*Mannaseo bangapseumnida.*"

"*Jeodo bangapseumnida.*" Su responded, bowing in return. Beth looked between Reece and Su in astonishment, her gaze settling on Reece with unequivocal surprise and bewilderment in her eyes.

"You speak Korean?"

"Apparently." He sat down again, turning his attention back to stoking the fire.

"Okay," Beth turned her attention back to Su, her eyes briefly lingering on Reece before focusing solely on her. "We left some meat in the fridge for you and your family. Please eat as much as you need. We'll go hunting again today."

"Thank you." Su walked into the RV and closed the door behind her as Beth headed back to her tent to collect her backpack.

"Full of surprises," she said lightly as she walked past Reece, who smiled at her mischievously. Beth shook her head at him. "I'm going to the lake."

As the last rays of dawn painted the sky with hues of pink and gold just as the sun began to fully rise, Ben and Austin decided to start their day with a morning jog - partly for exercise but mostly to make a sweep of the surrounding areas. The air was crisp, carrying the earthy scents of pine and damp soil. The quietude of the early morning was occasionally interrupted by the distant calls of waking birds.

"I met one of your new friends," Reece glanced up at Ben as they approached him on their way to start their jog. "Su-ho." Ben raised his eyebrow at him.

"Who?"

"The sick woman," he replied. "Beth asked for her name so I assume you didn't get it yesterday." Ben scanned the campsite quickly.

"Beth's awake?"

"She went down to the lake to wash up." Reece's eyes followed Ben as he moved towards the trail, but his progress was halted by the unexpected touch of Austin's hand on his shoulder.

"Give her some privacy. She'll be fine." Austin encouraged and Ben glanced at him, then returned his gaze to the trail with a worried expression. With a nod between them, they set off, their footsteps creating a rhythmic beat on the forest floor. Their trail meandered through tall trees, their shadows playing on the ground as they moved beneath the canopy. The chill in the air contrasted with the warmth generated by their increasing pace. As they navigated the trail, the camaraderie between Ben and Austin was evident. Their breaths synchronised as the path led them through varied terrain - soft pine needle-covered sections, rocky stretches that demanded careful foot placement, and open clearings where the rising sun filtered through the branches. Their breaths formed visible puffs in the cold air as they pushed themselves further. They turned a corner and came to a halt at the intersection of what seemed like a small town. A white truck with Hidden Valley Market branding sat outside a blue wooden-clad corner store. They entered with caution, handguns drawn from their holsters. They surveyed the store, completely empty and void of any food or drinks.

"That family must've taken everything." Ben observed as he re-holstered his gun.

"Hopefully it was them," Austin did the same, cautiously snapping the strap in place. "And not someone else in the area." Both men returned outside and sat at the picnic table, removing their canteens from their web belts, taking in the silence, the tension palpable.

"Ask me," Ben urged suddenly, his gaze steady. "Ask me what you want to—"

"Did you sleep with her?"

"No," Ben responded quickly, then paused as he looked down at his canteen. "But we could've. The opportunity was there, and I wanted—"

"We don't need the complication, Ben." Austin stated firmly.

"I'm not interested in creating complications, *Austin*," Ben dismissed. "I'm not Luis."

"You know what I mean," Austin continued, offering a half-smile. "It's a different complication, and you know it."

"He's really pushing you."

"He is *really* pushing me." Austin echoed, acknowledging the struggle with his long-time friend.

"He doesn't think you should be in command." Ben pointed out brutally.

"I was his commanding officer before," Austin said, a touch of frustration in his voice. "Why is he pushing me now?"

"Is that rhetorical? Everything's different. Now he's trying to protect his family, and you're making those decisions for him that he doesn't like—"

"Exactly my point," Austin looked deep into Ben's eyes, searching for any signs of wavering loyalties. "What happens when you care so much about her that you start disagreeing with my decisions to keep everyone safe?"

"I'll only stop agreeing with your decisions when they put us in danger," Ben asserted, taking a drink from his canteen. "And I would've done that whether she was here or not, but I don't see that happening."

"As long as we're on the same page." Austin declared, raising his canteen.

"Always," Ben agreed, pressing his canteen against Austin's. "*Sir.*" He quipped, injecting a moment of humour in an attempt to alleviate Austin's obvious stress. Austin let out a hearty laugh, taking a swig from his canteen.

"Shut up." He smiled and shook his head. The forest was alive with the soft glow of morning sunlight filtering through the leaves, warmth breaking through the lingering chill. The air was cool and clean, laced with pine, damp earth, and something faintly sweet beneath it all. Birds called overhead, branches creaked, leaves whispered together in the breeze. For a moment, it almost felt untouched, like the world hadn't fallen apart just beyond the trees.

"Don't you miss it?" Ben inquired dejectedly, following a lengthy pause between them.

"Miss what?"

"Just—" he paused, choosing his next word carefully. "Interaction."

"We're interacting now—"

"No, Austin. I mean," Ben looked up at him. "Human interaction. *Female* interaction."

"Female interaction—"

"Having options—"

"Options?" Austin repeated, side-eyeing him now. "That what you're calling it?"

"You're being deliberately difficult."

"Well Christ, Ben. You don't have to sound so fucking delicate—"

"I miss sex." Ben let out a small, humourless laugh. That earned a proper reaction. Austin snorted, shaking his head.

"There it is—"

"I'm serious," Ben insisted, though he was half-grinning now. "I didn't realise how much of my personality was built around it until it just... vanished."

"Tragic," Austin muttered. "Truly, a devastating loss—"

"Don't pretend you're above it."

"I'm not," Austin said easily. "I just don't dress it up like I'm writing a love letter to society." Ben studied him for a moment.

"You're insufferable—"

"Yeah," Austin shrugged. "But I'm right." A beat passed, the quiet forest filling the space again.

"I miss it too, though," Austin added, a little quieter. "The normal stuff." Ben glanced at him.

"Yeah?"

"Yeah," Austin exhaled. "But we have bigger things to think about." Ben nodded, the humour fading again as quickly as it had come. Austin wanted to end the conversation as quickly as it had escalated, not wanting to think about Samantha, not wanting to think about Ben and Beth, or even the idea of Beth altogether. "We should head back." He had avoided thinking about what they were missing out on, about lives that should have been lived or futures that would never arrive. But now that Ben was pining for a possibility that he thought was long behind them, Austin too wondered what they were surviving for if not for a little sense of normalcy. They both stood and secured their canteens to their web belts. Despite the physical exertion, their morning run was more than just exercise. It became a shared experience, a moment of connection between two friends navigating the uncertainties of their situation. The rhythmic sound of their footsteps echoed the pulse of survival in the untouched beauty around them. As they neared their campsite on the final stretch of their run, the sun had fully risen and enveloped everything in a warm glow. They were relieved they hadn't encountered anyone else during their run, having passed through other empty campsites. For the first time in a while, they felt a sense of peace and normalcy in their surroundings.

Chapter Thirteen

Beth reached the campsite just as Austin and Ben did, slowing as the tension ahead came into focus. She lingered at the treeline, half-hidden among the trees, unwilling to step into the middle of whatever was about to erupt. Austin was already on Luis, his voice sharp with a mix of concern and rising frustration. Luis didn't look at him. He tore through the three abandoned tents with restless urgency, yanking open bags, rifling through supplies, keeping what mattered and tossing the rest aside without hesitation. Fabric snapped, zippers rasped, gear hit the ground in careless bursts. He moved like time was against him - like stopping, even for a second, would cost them something. Beth's backpack came next. Luis flung it over his shoulder without checking, sending it skidding across the dirt until it thudded to a stop near the edge of the clearing. Dust kicked up around it, settling slowly as Beth watched from a distance, her jaw tightening, still not moving to claim it.

"What the fuck are you doing?" Austin demanded.

"We can't afford the dead weight," Luis glanced upwards, his eyes a mix of determination and exasperation as he continued his search without pause. "I'm searching for supplies we might need and then we're leaving. We need to travel light, only carry what's essential. Only take *who's* essential—"

"I don't know how many times I have to say this, Luis," Austin's brows furrowed as he watched Luis dismantle their camp. "We're not leaving anyone behind, and we're sure as hell not robbing these people."

"It's about survival, Austin," Luis shot him a challenging look. "We need to be efficient. We can't afford to slow down."

"We're a team," Austin took a deep breath, attempting to maintain his composure. "We stick together."

"What *team*? Get your shit together! We need to be realistic. We're not running a charity here," Luis spat. Beth approached with caution, retrieving her backpack from the ground and retreating to stand between Ben and Reece. Luis looked towards her menacingly as she moved. "Ahh, here she is. The *dead weight*."

"What the hell does that mean?" Ben took a step forward, and Austin held up a cautionary hand.

"Luis, stop," Austin warned. He ignored the command and continued to rifle through the tents. "I gave you an order! Stop!" Austin shouted, grabbing his friend and swiftly bringing him down to the ground in front of the campfire. Ben, Reece, and Beth stepped back in shock at the sight of Luis tumbling towards them. A cloud of dust billowed up as Luis frantically tried to regain his footing, while Val and Chantelle peeked out from their swags, watching from a safe distance.

"What the fuck, Austin?" Luis hit the ground hard, the cloud of dust dancing around him in the morning breeze. Austin stood over him, frustration and anger etched on his face.

"Enough, Luis! I'm getting sick of this!—"

"You're letting emotions cloud your judgement, *sir*," Luis

pushed himself off the ground, his gaze locked on Austin. "We need to make tough choices."

"We are not sacrificing our principles for the sake of efficiency," Austin remained stoic and shook his head, trying to keep his emotions in check. "We're a team, and that includes everyone—"

"No!" Luis clenched his fists, his frustration boiling over. "You're putting everyone at risk with this sentimental bullshit! We're not equipped to take care of others!"

"Enough, Luis," Val stepped forward, her voice stern. "Austin's right." Luis's eyes flashed with anger as he glared at Val, but he kept his mouth shut. The atmosphere was tense, and everyone held their breath in anticipation of what would unfold. Luis brushed off his clothes and gave Austin one last scornful look before turning on his heel and marching off towards the trees. After a brief hesitation, Ben hurried after him.

"Ben, leave it." Val begged.

"No!" Ben yelled. "Everyone lets him have his outbursts and then lets him walk it off as if it'll fix the problem but enough is enough! What the fuck is wrong with you?" Ben's face was twisted in fury, his muscles tense as he pushed Luis from behind with a forceful shove. It was like a tsunami crashing into a fragile shoreline, and Luis stumbled and flailed like a marionette with its strings cut. They were barely through the treeline, and the others hurried towards them to intervene, or observe.

"Defending your *girlfriend*?" Luis turned to him. Beth shifted uncomfortably on her feet. "She's dead weight and you know it—" Ben's fist collided with Luis's cheek, the force of the blow sending him reeling backwards.

"Say that again!" Ben roared, but Luis quickly regained his footing and retaliated, charging at Ben like a raging bull. They grappled fiercely, their bodies slamming against each other as they exchanged brutal blows with no regard for their surroundings. The sound of fists hitting flesh echoed through the air, creating a cacophony of violence. Blood dripped from their split knuckles and sweat poured down their faces as they fought with savage intensity. The atmosphere crackled with vigorous energy as Austin stood frozen, unable to comprehend the savagery before him. As Ben hesitated, torn between following orders or unleashing his rage on Luis, he noticed Austin watching passively from the sidelines. With a primal roar, Ben lunged at Luis once more, determined to bring him down for good. Their bodies thrashed about in a fit of violence, limbs entangled and muscles straining as they fought relentlessly. The sounds of grunting and fists flying intensified the chaos around them, drowning out all other noise. Neither man showed any signs of slowing down as they fought for dominance over the other with unrelenting determination. Austin could only watch in disbelief as the two men continued their savage struggle without any sign of backing down. Beth took a step forward and placed her hand on Austin's arm.

"Stop them," she pleaded. "Do something!" Austin eventually erupted and his voice boomed, the authority in it cutting through the tension.

"Enough! Both of you!"

"Fuck you both!" Luis pushed Ben backward with a force that had him reeling to the ground next to Austin, who looked down at Ben as he seethed with anger. He then turned his gaze back to Luis, who wore a defiant expression.

"We can't afford this kind of division." Austin remarked sternly. Ben nodded and propped himself up onto his elbows, his anger still evident while Luis glared at him, wiping a trickle of blood from his split lip. Ben growled, his fists clenched.

"You're lucky Austin stepped in—"

"You're the one on the ground, brother." Luis scoffed, licking the blood from his lips and spitting a pool of it onto the ground. Austin sighed at them, the weight of leadership heavy on his shoulders.

"We're going to have disagreements, but we can't let it tear us apart," Austin's eyes darted between the two, but his message was clearly directed at Luis. "We're stronger together." The three maintained an uneasy silence until Luis turned on his heel and vanished into the trees with Val close behind him. Chantelle hesitated, as if torn between following her family and staying with the group. Val gently gestured for Chantelle to remain, and Austin ushered Ben back to the campfire as the aftermath of their clash lingered, casting a shadow over the campsite. Su emerged from the RV with Sam and MJ, the group looking at them in collective shock - for a moment they had forgotten that they were there, why the arguments had started in the first place. Ben clutched at his side as Beth placed a gentle hand on his shoulder.

"Let me look at you—"

"I'm fine." He shrugged off her hand and stormed over to his swag, snatching up his backpack before marching off towards the lake. She ran her tongue along her bottom lip and bit down on it in frustration.

"*RV da-reun jjogeuro de-ryeo-gaseo nolge haera*," Su looked at Sam, ushering MJ to go with him. "Now, please." Sam's nod was a small, yet respectful gesture towards Su. He then turned to his niece, taking her hand in his and giving it a reassuring squeeze before leading her away.

"Come on, MJ," he took off towards the other side of the RV. "We're going to go play." She trudged alongside him, following without question. She turned to take one last look at Beth, giving a small wave before continuing on. Beth waved back and tried to smile reassuringly, despite her forehead being creased with worry. Austin walked confidently towards Su, his tall frame looming over her. Despite his slightly messy dark hair, his piercing brown eyes radiated determination as he refused to let the fight consume him with rage. He extended his hand towards her, his fingers outstretched.

"You must be Su-ho."

"Su, please," she shook it cautiously. "I thought you were all friends." Austin's gaze shifted to her with a curious expression, and she subtly nodded towards the ground where the altercation had just occurred. Austin glanced over his shoulder towards where the fight had erupted on the outskirts of the campsite before turning back to face her.

"I'm sorry about that—"

"You scared my daughter."

"I am sorry about that too. We're not—" Austin smiled at her guardedly, pausing for a brief moment. "We're not... usually like this." Su's face was cold, as if she somehow didn't believe him.

"You have been through a lot." Her words lingered somewhere between a statement and a question.

"So have you," Austin's intense gaze scanned the abandoned tents. His eyes absorbed every detail as if he could see the anecdote written in the dirt and forgotten belongings. "Why don't we have some coffee and you can tell us your story?" Su nodded cautiously as she stepped down from the RV. Reece gathered more cups and carefully poured coffee into each one, passing them around to the group as they sat around the campfire.

"There isn't much to tell," she spoke softly as she settled into one of the folding chairs by the campfire. "My family live in London. My parents, brother, sister, and her husband were here visiting when the virus broke out. My neighbour had this old RV they loaned us because my husband wanted to take them camping, which they did not want to do." She raised her cup of coffee to her lips and took a small sip, all while keeping her stoic expression trained on the flickering flames of the campfire.

"Your parents?" Beth pressed, confusion etched on her face. "You haven't mentioned your dad until now—"

"No," Su looked over at her remorsefully, "He died quite early during the outbreak. My husband isolated him in a tent on the other side of the campsite, but he did not survive long. I have no idea how he even got the virus—" Su's voice trailed off, deep in thought.

"Sam-ga goin-ui myungbok-eul bibnida." Reece whispered as his hand moved slowly, poking at the campfire with a stick. The flames flickered and danced around it, creating a mesmerising display of red, orange, and yellow. The stick glowed red hot as it was pushed deeper into the fire.

"Gamsahabnida." Su expressed her gratitude with a subtle nod, taking another sip of her coffee. Austin raised a questioning eyebrow at Reece while Beth tried to suppress a knowing smile.

"Where're you from?" Austin's brows were furrowed as he hesitantly spoke, his gaze shifting between Reece, Su, and the campfire.

"Sacramento," she smiled nostalgically. "But my husband grew up in Portland and has been camping most of his life. I moved here for a semester of university and he worked at the local cafe, where we met. My parents wanted me to come home but I never left America." The group fell into a hush, anticipating Su's next words as she reflected sadly on her family's absence. "He must have got it when we stopped for the bathroom. He was the only one who left the RV—"

"Who?" Beth scrunched her eyes.

"My father," Su whispered. "Someone must have had it at the gas station, someone in the bathroom." She trailed off again, staring into the flames.

"So how did you get stuck up here?" Austin pressed slowly.

"We knew we'd be gone for a while so we had packed a lot of food and water. Craig, my husband, he wanted to go for about a month, so naturally he packed for two," her laughter slowly faded, and her sullen expression was replaced by a sudden wave of sadness. "He was not prepared for a lot of things but he liked to make sure we had more than enough whenever we went camping. We had been up here for about a week when we heard over the radio that a virus had broken out. Didn't believe it at first, but my father was already showing symptoms, and here we are." Su concluded quietly.

"How did y'all survive up here for so long?" Chantelle's eyes were wide with curiosity as she leaned forward, her dark hair falling in waves around her face. "It's been more than two months."

"We didn't leave for a while until my medication ran out, and then food began to dwindle," Su thought pensively. "So my husband and my sister and her husband went on drives to the local market, and then further and further as we needed because there was nothing left."

"Drives in what, that?" Austin looked towards the RV. "With everyone in it?"

"No, no," amused, she shook her head. "We had an SUV but it broke down on the highway. Stupid thing was brand new too." Beth, Austin, Reece and Chantelle exchanged awkward glances. Su continued, oblivious to their unspoken communication.

"What happened to them?" Austin asked.

"They went on a run to Redding about a week or two ago for medication for me," she replied morosely. "I haven't seen them since. I don't even know how long it's been. I am so ill, the days... they seem to all blend together."

"Su-ho," the elderly woman called from inside the RV. "*Dowa-jyo.*"

"My mother needs me," Su stood up without hesitation and handed Reece the cup. "Thank you for the coffee, and for listening to my story. I hope to soon hear all of yours." She bowed quickly before disappearing into the RV. Austin took a brief moment to absorb Su's words before turning his gaze towards Beth, Reece and Chantelle. He then glanced over to where Ben, Val and Luis had all separately disappeared into the trees.

"Chantelle, why don't you go inside and see if they need any help." He suggested.

"Sure." Without question, Chantelle made her way over to the RV and gently closed the door behind her. Once he was certain she wouldn't come back, Austin redirected his focus towards Beth.

"You should go and check on Ben."

"I don't think he wants me to check on him." Beth sat with her chin resting on the fabric of her jeans. Her expression was sombre, her eyes downcast as she stared at the ground.

"That was Austin's polite way of asking you to leave," Reece smiled, raising an eyebrow at her. "Besides, I think you're the only person he'll talk to right now." With an awkward sigh, she rose to her feet and made her way towards the start of the trail. Austin's gaze stayed fixed on Beth as she walked away, observing her every step and movement. His face was serious, his eyes focused and intent.

"That girl is a complication."

"Then don't let her be one."

"What do you mean?"

"We should be showing her how to take care of herself," Reece argued quickly, his tone filled with mild frustration. "Not doing it for her."

Val chased Luis along the path and eventually up the main road, scrambling to keep pace with him. He was determined to lose her on the incline, knowing she would struggle to maintain his speed and strides. It took her a solid twenty minutes just to catch up and be within a safe distance to call out to him, nevermind the uphill battle she now literally faced.

"Luis," she yelled, but he continued walking with an air of defiance. "Luis, please! Stop!—"

"Leave me alone." He called out into the open air.

"Luis, what's wrong with you?" She gained some distance between them as the terrain evened out, her thighs burning from the slow incline.

"Perfect," he smirked, walking into a bar on the corner of the intersection. She looked up at the sign on the power pole - *Idle Hour*. Catching her breath, she stormed into the bar after him. Luis was behind the counter, raiding the untouched bar shelf behind it. "This'll do." He popped the top off a bottle of rum and took a long, lingering drink, spilling it down the side of his mouth.

"Really," she looked at him disbelievingly, checking her watch. "It's nine o'clock in the morning—"

"Oh, wake up Val!" Luis looked at her defiantly. "It doesn't fucking matter. There's no time in the apocalypse!" He extended his arms in a mocking gesture, laughing. She took a seat at a table in the middle of the room, crossing her arms and leaning back in the chair. Val's face was flushed with anger, her eyebrows furrowed and her lips pursed tightly.

"Talk to me." She demanded.

"We don't *need* them," he grabbed a bottle of tequila and looked at the label. "Gran Patron, *nice*—"

"Talk to me." Val repeated, her jaw clenched as she stared at Luis, her eyes clear with frustration and determination.

"Top-shelf." He shook the bottle at Val, ignoring her demand. He unscrewed the cap and tossed it carelessly into the ether before making his way to a stool on the other side of the bar. He sat and spun around to face her. Val observed Luis, her eyes reflecting a mix of frustration, concern, and the weariness of the difficulties they had faced both pre and post pandemic.

She knew why her brother was the way that he was, but it still aggravated her to the end of the earth that he was treating everyone like his emotional, and now physical, punching bag. She took a deep breath, trying to find the right words to reach her brother.

"We need everyone in this group," Val spoke slowly and firmly, her voice cutting through the heavy air of the musty bar. "We're stronger together. You can't just decide to cut people out because you're upset—"

"*Upset?*" Luis scoffed, taking another swig from the tequila bottle. "Val, you don't understand. It's about survival. Every extra person slows us down. We can't afford that."

"Survival doesn't mean abandoning our humanity, Luis, or our humility," Val leaned forward, her gaze intense. "We're not just trying to stay alive, we're trying to live, and that means caring about each other, even when it's hard—"

"Fuck you, Val," Luis looked away, his expression conflicted. "You don't know what you're talking about." The weight of responsibility and the fear for his family's safety battled against the bonds of camaraderie he had with Austin and Ben, and even Reece to an extent.

"I might not've been to war with you but you forget, we grew up on the same streets," Val added, her tone hardening. "We can't sacrifice everything that makes us human in the process. *Tu eres mi hermano*, and I love you, but I can't support you when you're like this—"

"We're leaving," he looked at her sternly. "I'm done with this. We are taking that RV and we are leaving with Chantelle—"

"No," she said, an air of authority lacing her tone that he had not heard from her in a long time. "We're not stealing from that family and we certainly are not leaving—"

"Yes we are!" He stood up, taking a step towards her. The unexpected sound of a bottle rolling across the floor from a room behind the bar startled both of them, Val jolting briefly with apprehension. Luis stormed over to it and yanked the door open. A man stood up, raising his hands as Luis grabbed him and dragged him out to the middle of the room.

"Please," he said, startled. Luis threw him onto the ground and the man propelled forward, landing in front of Val with a thud. "I'm alone, and unarmed."

"That's unlucky." Luis raised his eyebrow as he took a drink, keeping one eye on the man.

"Luis." Val took a cautionary step towards him, and he raised his hand to her in warning.

"Where'd you come from? I haven't seen anyone in weeks —" the man's voice trembled with hesitation as he noticed the anger radiating from Luis and the nervousness emanating from Val. "I thought the area was deserted." It had been a while since Luis had consumed this much alcohol, and the strong concentration of the drinks quickly left him heavily intoxicated.

"There've been people at the campsite nearby for months, twenty minutes from here," Val raised an inquisitive eyebrow. "And you never came across them?"

"Like he said," the man nodded towards Luis. "Unlucky." Luis shot an angry look at Val.

"Now why would you go and tell him that?"

"I'm sorry, I didn't think—"

"No, you don't *think*," he spat. "This is why we need to leave. You, me and Chantelle—"

"You have a camp nearby? I could really use some help," the man said, swaying on his feet. "I've been holed up in this bar for months and—"

"Sorry buddy," Luis's hand shook as he aimed his handgun at the man's head, his eyes narrowed in anger and determination. "Bar's closed." The man's face was still and expressionless as the gunshot hit its target right between his eyes. With a loud thud, he fell to the floor, lifeless. Val gasped in shock and covered her mouth with her hands to stifle a scream as Luis calmly lowered his pistol and took a swig from the bottle.

"Luis—"

"Search him." He commanded coldly, beads of sweat glistening on his forehead. His eyes were narrowed with anger and his face was flushed with intoxication.

"You've fucking lost it," her head shook with fury as she moved closer to the door, refusing to back down even as he aimed his gun at her. "You won't shoot me, but you're on your own with this battle. Fight it yourself, here, alone. Come back when you've got your shit together." Luis' hand steadied the handgun as its cold, metal frame glinted in the dim light of the bar.

"Val, stop—"

"I won't tell the others about this," she said, heading for the door. She paused at the threshold, turning back to face him before opening it. "Lord only knows what Austin will do to you." Val left him to face his demons alone, providing him the solitude to drown his sorrows and either come to a cathartic realisation or succumb to a slow death. At that point, she didn't care which outcome he would face.

Chapter Fourteen

The cool breeze swept over the lake, causing ripples in the water. Ben, still catching his breath, gazed out across the calm surface. His hands, however, betrayed the turbulence within him, trembling despite his attempts to steady them. The trees around him exuded a serene atmosphere, a stark contrast to the inner turmoil he grappled with. The rhythmic lapping of the water against the shore provided a soothing backdrop, but his mind remained occupied by the events of the morning. Closing his eyes, he took a deep breath, trying to regain control over his body's involuntary response to his heightened emotions. Beth emerged from the treeline, stopping and staring at him as he shook.

"What're you doing here?" His voice was filled with anger as he spoke, his rapid breaths visible in the crisp, cold air. She walked over to him determinedly.

"Are you okay?"

"I don't want you here!" Ben yelled, and she stopped in her tracks. He turned to face the water. "Please, just go away." Without warning, he felt a gentle touch on his arm, causing him to flinch. He hadn't realised she had silently approached him from behind.

"Ben—"

"Why do you care?" He turned to her and looked at the ground.

"Thought you could use a friend," she smiled at him softly. "Let me see." She pulled up his shirt, examining the bruises that were starting to appear on his stomach. Her thumbs moved gently over the ridges of his abdominal muscles as she tried to hold back a lump forming in her throat.

"It's nothing." His words were short and dismissive, and she reached out to gently brush her hand against the bruise under his eye.

"It's not nothing," she assured him. "You could've left it alone."

"He called you dead weight—"

"I *am* dead weight," she observed candidly as she smiled. "I can't contribute much and I am just another mouth to feed."

"You're eager to learn," he replied. "Luis can't expect you to figure out how your role fits within this group in just a few weeks."

"My point exactly," she took a step back. "It's been just a few weeks and you're fighting your friend because of me—"

"Someone has to fight for the underdogs." As he smiled at her, his lips turned up in a gentle curve, revealing dimples beneath his beard that added to his charm.

"Then you can teach me not to be the underdog."

"You already know how to skin a deer." He said, his eyes crinkling at the corners.

"Don't remind me," she quipped, gagging in jest. "Now, if you've pulled yourself together, we're going back." Ben raised an eyebrow at her.

"You're ordering me about now?"

"I'd like to get back before Luis does," she turned to walk away. "In case we need to defend Austin's decision about Su and her family. You know, fight for the underdog." He grinned, matching her strides as they made their way up the hill. Their relaxed stroll was suddenly disturbed by a far-off gunshot that reverberated through the surrounding woods. They stopped and exchanged a worried look before quickly picking up speed and running back up the hill together.

"What're we gonna do about this family?" Reece's features were creased with concern, eyebrows knitted together in a worried frown.

"We're not leaving them here," Austin said, his face impassive and deep in thought. "They won't survive." Reece stared at the ground, his eyes flicking back and forth as if searching for a solution he was unable to find in the dirt.

"We won't survive if we keep picking up stragglers."

"I get it, okay," Austin said. "But we can't just turn a blind eye. They need help, and we can provide it. We can't abandon them here."

"I'm not heartless, Austin," Reece shook his head, a mix of frustration and perturbation on his face. "But we've been pushing ourselves to the limit. Every new addition to our group slows us down, increases the risk. I hate to sound like Luis, and you know I've got your back, but we need to prioritise our own survival. Beth already cost us weeks—"

"She didn't cost us *weeks*," Austin interrupted. "She cost us days at most. The van was already fucked before we found her. It was just a matter of time—"

"I'm not arguing with you, Austin," Reece raised his hand in defence, his voice soft. "You and I both know that the only reason we needed to fix the van was because we had one extra person who couldn't make the journey on foot. If Beth was out of the equation then we would've abandoned it a lot sooner and covered more ground *a lot* quicker."

"She's kept up with us so far—"

"Yes, she has," Reece was quick to respond. "But even on foot she's still slowed us down. Beth is one thing, but these people? Austin, be realistic—"

"I hear you, but these are people in need," Austin nodded, acknowledging the validity of Reece's point. "Maybe we can guide them to the next safe spot, share some supplies, and then part ways. We can't just leave them stranded here—"

"There is no next safe spot," Reece locked eyes with him. "I'm not gonna argue with you and Lord knows I'm not fit to be the leader here, so I'll listen to whatever commands you give but I want you to seriously think about this. Beth was one thing, but she seems like she could eventually hold her own. We're talking about a sick woman, her elderly mother, and two kids." Austin's face softened as he paused, deep lines around his eyes and mouth showing the weight of their situation.

"Heavy is the head that wears the crown."

"What?" Reece strained to catch the faint words Austin muttered under his breath.

"We can't just leave them stranded," he repeated loudly. "Do you want their deaths on your conscience?"

"Alright," Reece ran a hand through his hair, visibly conflicted. "But we can't afford to keep doing this."

"I'm sorry you had to hear that," Chantelle sat at the end of the bed with the elderly woman, listening to the conversation outside as she looked at Su. "You must've heard everythin' this mornin'—"

"These walls are thin," Su's lips began to quiver as she spoke, her eyes darting back and forth between Chantelle's face and her mother asleep on the bed. "Your friend does not want waste resources."

"Luis," Chantelle said, pursing her lips together. "He's my foster-dad, kinda. More like a foster-uncle."

"He does not want to put his family in danger. I under-stand that," Su looked at her mother. "I might offer your friends outside some tea. I think I have a bag or two laying around."

"I think they'd like that." Chantelle smiled at her and Su walked out, leaving the door slightly open. Chantelle's attention turned to the kitchen, cluttered and unused.

"My daughter is a good girl." The elderly woman startled Chantelle, who turned abruptly in her direction, placing her hand on her chest.

"You frightened me!" Chantelle's eyes widened with surprise, her face contorted into an expression of shock as she laughed nervously. "Can I get you something?"

"You seem like a good girl too." The elderly woman said.

"I wasn't always," Chantelle smiled. "But I'm tryin'." Their peaceful moment was abruptly shattered by the loud bang of a gunshot, causing Su to quickly seek shelter inside the RV and slam the door shut behind her.

Val arrived at the campsite in just ten minutes, jogging downhill with urgency. She knew that they would have heard the gunshot and she would need to come up with an explanation for it. Austin ran towards her as he saw her coming down the path.

"What was that? Are you okay?"

"It's nothing," Val reassured him. "Luis started drinking in a bar he found and tripped. The gun went off accidentally."

"Luis was drinking and tripped," Reece echoed her words. "Doesn't surprise me."

"Why was the gun out of his holster?" He asked, his lips pursed and eyes narrowed.

"You know Luis," Val walked past him, avoiding any potential for eye contact. "We were arguing and he was waving it around." Austin's expression shifted from concern to suspicion, his jaw clenched as he took a step closer to Val.

"At you?"

"Nothing serious," she continued towards her swag quickly, wanting to avoid their questions and doubtful eyes. "Everything's fine."

"Everything is *not* fine," Reece turned his gaze to Val, just as Beth and Ben appeared from the woods, hurrying towards them. "Val's lying." Austin shook his head, rubbing his temple with one hand in frustration.

"I know."

The remainder of the day dissolved into casual chatter and chores. Beth consciously avoided requesting Ben's guidance on hunting, deciding today was not the right time. Instead, she joined Su in tackling laundry and tidying up their campsite, even taking a stroll with her to the lake to wash neglected dirty clothes and sheets. Chantelle lent a hand to Sam in entertaining MJ, engaging in games and basking in the sun. Val, nestled in her swag, passed the hours absorbed in a book, punctuated by the occasional nap and invasive thought of the morning's events. Meanwhile, Austin, Ben, and Reece immersed themselves in a private conversation, mapping out their next steps.

"If we continue to head south, we can make it to LA in less than a day, with all of us in the RV." Austin spoke with confidence, his broad shoulders and upright posture giving off an air of authority.

"That's assuming we don't run into complications," Ben

crossed his arms over his chest. "Did anyone actually bother to ask Su if the RV still works?" Reece's dark, curly hair fell slightly into his eyes as he leaned in towards the group, his expression thoughtful.

"Assuming they haven't turned it over for months—"

"Then we go as far as we can, if the RV works," Austin considered their options pensively. "And if it doesn't, could you fix it?"

"Depends on the issues," Ben replied despondently. "An engine that size is prone to all kinds of problems if left idle. Battery issues, flat spots on the tyres, fuel system. Any one of those or any combination, among others." Austin shook his head, running his hand through his hair.

"We'll find out and go from there."

"And if it doesn't?" Reece asked, concerned.

"We'll go from there." Austin repeated with a hint of impatience. Reece disappeared into the woods to search for their next meal, while Austin and Ben examined the RV. Su watched them as they inspected the engine, sustaining them with cups of coffee.

"I occasionally started it," she said. "In case we needed to make a run for it. But my husband took some petrol from the RV for the car so we could keep going into town. I got sicker and forgot to start the engine, and I don't know how much petrol is left—"

"Then we'll need to make a run for some gas." Austin declared.

"I'll look at the engine properly tomorrow, and we can plan a run in the next few days," Ben looked at the jerry cans on the ground next to Sam's bike. "But it's a risk leaving you without water. Maybe we can fill some tubs and take those with us."

"Why?" Su asked.

"If we get to a gas station and there isn't anything to bring gas back with us, it'd be pointless. We need those jerry cans," Austin said. "A few days?"

"Look around, Austin," Ben gestured around the campsite. "It's a safe place to rest for a bit. Gather our thoughts, and resources. Let everyone rest." Austin gave a nod in affirmation as Reece proudly emerged from the forest carrying a deer over his shoulder. He dropped it onto the ground next to the campfire with a heavy thud.

"I didn't even hear a shot go off." Beth commented as she walked over.

"I've got the silencer," he smiled. "Who wants to do the honours?"

"Come on, Beth," Ben walked over to the deer. "Walk me through what I showed you yesterday."

The campsite transformed into an impromptu dinner gathering with everyone congregating around the crackling campfire - all except Luis, Su's mother in the RV, and the already-sleeping MJ. They enjoyed a hearty meal as dusk draped itself over them, casting a dim glow through the trees. Beth settled beside Ben, both of them choosing to ignore Austin's intermittent concerned glances. Ben's bottle of whiskey circulated amongst the group, fostering a jovial atmosphere filled with light-hearted stories and occasional reflections on things missed from days past.

"I miss bowlin'," Chantelle's lips stretched into a wide smile. "Stupid thing to miss but it was really fun." Val's dark eyes sparkled with amusement.

"I miss working. Never thought I'd say that."

"I miss poker night at the base." Austin interjected, glancing at Ben who raised his bottle in a silent toast before taking a swig and handing it to Austin. Beth's lips twisted into a rueful smile.

"Didn't even get to find out how Game of Thrones ended—"

"Yes we did," Ben's face contorted into a small grin, his eyes crinkling at the corners. "And it was—" Beth nudged Ben's shoulder with a rough push.

"Don't you dare finish that sentence," she laughed. "And I'm talking about the books, not the show."

"You actually read those? Much, much too long." Su joined in with their laughter, but it quickly faded into an unsettling stillness. Sam cocked his head, looking into the fire as the eerie silence fell over the group.

"I miss my friends." He said, his face impassive.

"I miss my dog." Beth fought back tears, biting her bottom lip in an attempt to maintain her composure.

"My wife." Reece added, nodding.

"My girlfriend." Austin took in a low, deep breath.

"My husband." Whispered Su, who put her arm around Sam as he placed his head on her shoulder. As the group reflected on the people they'd lost, a drunken, stumbling figure walked into view from the road. Luis threw an empty bottle into the bushes as he approached the group.

"*Friends*!" He exclaimed, extending his arms outward.

"Luis," Austin greeted him sternly. "Nice of you to join us."

"Come on, time for bed," Su nudged Sam's shoulder with hers, standing up. "This isn't our business." Luis glared at them with anger.

"This most definitely *is* your business—"

"Luis." Austin warned him as Su and Sam walked into the RV and closed the door behind them. The distinct sound of the door locking rang out through the awkward silence.

"Well, now that *most* of the dead weight is gone, we can chat," Luis stumbled over to the campfire. "Beth, you can join them too." They all watched as he took in a deep breath and laughed. Ben stood up suddenly, with Austin in tow to stand between his friends.

"Both of you, calm down." He commanded.

"Now, now, *sir*," Luis slurred his spitefully-laced words. "Call off your guard dog." Austin struggled to restrain Ben from advancing on Luis. The entire group had risen to witness the unfolding confrontation and positioned themselves to swiftly step aside should another altercation erupt. Ben calmed down, but Austin maintained a hold on his arm.

"He's drunk," Austin whispered. "Let it go."

"Val, Chantelle, and I are getting out of here," Luis declared, locking eyes with Austin. "And we're taking the RV." He stumbled towards it, grabbing the door handle and shaking it wildly in frustration as it resisted his efforts. The screams from MJ inside the RV only added to the already heightened tension.

"Luis, stop!" Austin marched over to him, but he continued to pull at the door. MJ's screams grew louder, and Su's voice was audible enough that they could hear her trying to sooth her daughter. Su's mother yelled something, and Beth looked at Reece.

"She's telling Sam to stay away from the door." He said softly.

"Luis, I said *stop!*" Austin yelled, his voice almost primal. He unsheathed his handgun, pointing it directly at Luis' head. As Luis turned to face him, the fiery light from the campfire created a menacing shadow on his features. He had already retrieved his own handgun and held it firmly by his side.

Chapter Fifteen

"**Y**ou're gonna have to shoot me." Luis smirked, a foreboding and taunting tone escaping his lips, like he was almost singing a derisive tune. Austin's face contorted in anger, the tension escalating.

"Enough." He said.

"Or *what*?" Luis sneered. Austin's hand wavered slightly before lowering his handgun, discarding it on the ground.

"I'm not gonna shoot you." He said in a quiet anger as Luis circled him, walking towards the rest of the group. Ben instinctively took a step in front of Beth, and she placed her hand on his forearm.

"That's right," Luis gestured towards them, rolling his eyes at Ben's defence of her. "I did mention there were other ways for you to contribute, I just didn't think you'd take my advice." Luis' face contorted with amusement as he laughed, his lips stretching into a wicked grin.

"What're you talking about?" Ben's face turned a deep shade of red, his eyes narrowed in anger, and his jaw clenched tightly. His fists were balled up at his sides, ready to strike at any moment.

"I just didn't think you had the *balls*, Ben," Luis said

dismissively, sidestepping the question. "She's easy on the eyes though, I can see why you like her. And that body—" Ben took an angry step towards Luis as Beth urgently grabbed his arm.

"Please Ben," she pleaded. "Don't."

"Just ask Austin," Luis glanced back at him, then turned and looked towards Beth, licking his lips. "We both saw it one night in that motel near Chemult. I mean, if they don't have anything else to offer, what are they gonna contribute? What are they *good* for?" Ben ripped his arm from Beth's grip and lunged at Luis, tackling him to the ground. The impact sent both men sprawling, their struggle intensifying in a chaotic tangle. Tense moments hung in the air as the group grappled with the reality of the situation. The only sounds that broke the silence were the muffled grunts and strained breaths of the two locked in combat, echoing the inner turmoil that gripped the entire group. Austin threw himself at Luis, ripping him off Ben and throwing him backward. Luis lay on the ground laughing maniacally as Ben sat up, staring at Austin.

"Stand down," Austin commanded, knowing Ben wouldn't defy his directive. "That's an order." Ben nodded, his jaw clenched and teeth grinding as he willed every fibre of his being not to rip Luis limb from limb. Luis slowly brought himself to his feet. The night air hung heavy with tension as Austin and Luis stood facing each other near the flickering remnants of the dying campfire. The glow highlighted the exhaustion etched on their faces, but the animosity between them crackled in the charged atmosphere. Chantelle's eyes were wide with fear and desperation, tears glistening in the dim light of the campfire.

"Come on," Val wrapped a comforting arm around her shoulder and took her towards their swags. "We need to let them work their shit out." Reece fixed his gaze on the dying embers of the campfire. The crackling flames cast flickering shadows on his face, reflecting the weariness that weighed on their shoulders. Standing next to him, Beth and Ben observed the heavy suspense which lingered between Austin and Luis, the tension palpable in the air. Beth exchanged a concerned glance with Ben, silently acknowledging the strain that had surfaced between the two friends. The subtle glow of the campfire highlighted the lines of fatigue on their faces as they locked eyes in a silent standoff. The crackling fire seemed to mimic the simmering tension, casting an uncertain ambiance over the campsite. As the embers dimmed, the shadows played tricks on their expressions, amplifying the gravity of the unspoken conflict unfolding before them. Austin's eyes bore into Luis's, frustration and fatigue evident in the lines on his forehead. The weight of leadership burdened his shoulders, and the recent events had taken a toll on his patience. Luis, on the other hand, held a simmering anger, fuelled by the recent encounters with danger and the unease about the safety of those he cared about. The obvious difference between the two was Austin's need to care for everyone equally, while Luis' interests were more self-serving. Without a word, Austin threw the first punch, a burst of emotion propelling his fist forward. Luis deftly dodged the blow, his instincts honed by survival in the unforgiving world they now navigated. He countered with a swift jab to Austin's side, the impact reverberating through the quiet night. Ben stopped himself from taking a step forward to defend his friend - this was a fight Austin needed to have with Luis, two alphas fighting for authority. The two men circled each other, fists clenched, as the sounds of their scuffle echoed through the stillness. Each punch and block conveyed unspoken frustrations and fears, the physicality an outlet for the pent-up tension that had been building within the group. Ben remained stoic as Beth's fingers dug into his arm, refusing to flinch despite the tight grip. Their fists collided, a symphony of blows punctuating the silence of the night. Austin's military training clashed with Luis's raw determination, creating a dance of aggression beneath the moonlit canopy of the trees. The air crackled with energy as the two grappled, neither willing to yield. Austin landed a solid blow to Luis' ribs, causing him to recoil in pain but recover swiftly, his alcohol-induced state aiding his lack of acknowledgement of his anguish. Luis swung at Austin, missing him slightly as Austin managed to dodge the swing and wrap his arms around Luis' neck, holding him in a head-lock. The alcohol had made Luis invulnerable to pain, but clumsy in his movements. Luis stomped on Austin's toes, elbowing him in the stomach as he did, which caused Austin to relinquish his hold and reel backward. Before Luis could turn back towards him, Austin swiftly darted towards Luis, throwing his pained shoulder into Luis' torso as they both fell to the ground in a gasping heap. As the confrontation reached its peak, Austin and Luis lay in the dust and dirt, their breaths heavy and laboured. The surrounding silence seemed to echo the intensity of their physical confrontation. Both men had delivered and received significant blows, their exhaustion evident in the way they sprawled on the floor, battered and bruised in a conceding draw. Austin brought his hand up to his shoulder he had used to tackle Luis - the one he had smashed into a rock just days prior - as he winced in pain. The flickering remnants of the campfire cast intermittent shadows on their weary faces, capturing the aftermath of a drawn-out struggle. The forest around them bore witness to the toll exacted by the unspoken tensions that had erupted into a physical confrontation between two friends, bound by their trials of survival. Despite the mutual weariness, a sense of respect lingered in the air. Austin and Luis, having fought each other to a standstill, turned their heads towards one another and glared in the dark night. The surrounding stillness seemed to magnify the gravity of the moment, as if nature itself held its breath in the wake of the conflict. In the dim light, the bruises and blood on their faces told a story of the challenges they faced and the burdens they carried. The forest, once again enveloped in an uneasy quiet, bore witness to the complexities of their journey, where camaraderie and conflict coexisted in delicate balance.

"If you're done," Reece kicked dirt at the fire. "I'm going to bed." He walked over to his sleeping bag, disappearing into the darkness. Beth walked slowly over to the two men who still lay on the ground in mutual defeat, standing between them and looking down at them nonchalantly. Austin had been fighting for Ben, but in a way had been fighting to protect her too. Beth pulled a small medical kit from her backpack and crouched by Austin.

"Let me look at you." She said. Austin turned to face her, and then looked over at Luis.

"He needs it more than I do—"

"Fuck you," Luis spat, standing abruptly. "Both of you. All of you." He walked over to his swag, limping and cursing into the air as he spat blood onto the ground. Austin sat up and looked into the fire, propping his elbows on his knees and spitting blood at his side. Beth sat next to him, facing him with her legs crossed. She gingerly held some gauze coated with antiseptic to his face, applying it to his open wounds. Despite the stinging sensation that followed, Austin didn't flinch, his stoic expression barely registering the discomfort. Austin spat on the ground again, the red of the blood mixing with the dark dirt. The dim light of the campfire flickered, casting dancing shadows on their faces as Beth tended to the aftermath of the physical altercation. The forest retained an air of hushed solemnity, a backdrop to the shared moments of vulnerability and resilience that defined their journey. Beth's hands hovered delicately over Austin's skin, her touch light and gentle. He could feel the sting of the antiseptic seeping into his cuts, but he remained still, refusing to flinch. The scene was like a painting, with Beth's graceful movements and gentle touch contrasted against Austin's rugged and wounded appearance, yet both figures exuded a sense of strength and resilience in the face of pain. Silence hung in the air, the crackling of the dying campfire punctuating the quiet exchange between Beth and Austin. The forest seemed to bear witness to the intricate tapestry of their interconnected lives, marked by wounds both physical and emotional. As Beth continued her careful ministrations, her eyes met Austin's, conveying a silent understanding that transcended the need for words. In that intimate moment, amidst the fading glow of the campfire, they navigated the complex terrain of their shared experiences, finding solace in the quiet companionship of the forest night.

"What did he mean?" Ben asked, his expression a mix of confusion and anger as he gazed at Beth and Austin. Beth and Austin exchanged an uncomfortable look.

"Luis," Beth hesitated, choosing her next words carefully. "He tried to—" Pausing, she stopped tending to Austin's wounds and looked up at Ben solemnly.

"Enough of the vague bullshit, Beth," Ben growled. "What did he do?"

"He cornered me in a hotel room—"

"He assaulted you." Austin's eyes slowly drifted from the fire to Beth, meeting her gaze.

"He barely touched me," she said, pouring antiseptic onto some gauze. "I don't know what he would've—"

"You know *exactly* what he was gonna do." Austin said softly. Ben threw his hands in the air, his tone filled with frustration.

"You didn't tell me?—"

"Nothing happened." She interrupted, looking at Austin.

"I handled it." Austin added, maintaining his gaze on Beth before looking back at the dying embers of the campfire.

"Clearly you haven't handled it!" Ben yelled. "Why didn't you tell me?"

"It wasn't your business," Austin looked up at him slowly, a scornful gaze in his eyes. "She isn't yours to protect." Beth returned to tending Austin's wounds silently, letting them talk as if she weren't there.

"Fuck this." Ben walked to his swag in anger, leaving the two of them alone in the dwindling firelight.

"Ben!" Beth protested as he continued walking, ignoring her.

"Let him go." Austin said impassively.

"You didn't have to do that for me." She said, subconsciously pressing the antiseptic harder into his skin.

"I didn't fight Luis for you," he spat more blood to the ground and finally winced at the pain from the antiseptic. "I did it for Ben. He would've killed Luis if I'd let him."

"All the same," she shook her head. "Ben told me you've known him since high school. I gather you two haven't always been this way?—"

"No," he replied despondently. "We haven't always been this way."

"I'm sorry I've caused all this tension." She said gingerly.

"Don't be," he said, his eyes drifting from the fire to look at her. "You shouldn't have to put up with it."

"I've met worse." She offered a half smile, lowering her head to the ground.

"What do you mean?"

"It doesn't matter—"

"What do you mean?" He pressed, narrowing his eyes. Beth sighed and looked at the fire.

"Luis is menacing and cold, but he's not clever or calculating. He's simple and emotionless. It's manageable, more susceptible to influence. Those with intelligence, the *adept* manipulators, they demand a higher level of manipulation in return. Relying solely on manipulation falls short, you have to craft an idea favourably aligned with their interests, *persuade* them it originated from their own mind. You tell them it was the best idea they have ever had, and then make sure that subtly over time, the idea works to their detriment. You have to *convince* them to create their own downfall," Beth's words were short and sharp, spiteful and full of hate. Her breath caught in her throat as a torrent of vivid memories came rushing back, threatening to drown her. "Luis created his own downfall, Austin. He doesn't need anyone's help doing so." She met his gaze with wide eyes, her face contorting with pain and anguish as she relived the past. He studied her closely, his brows furrowed in confusion as he struggled to comprehend the intensity of her reaction. His lips twitched upwards, forming a small, sarcastic smile.

"You surprise me."

"Why?"

"I just—"

"Didn't think I was clever?" Her lips stretched into a mischievous smirk, her eyes sparkling with amusement.

"Yeah," he nodded. "I'm sorry I underestimated you."

"Don't be," she said. Adrenaline filled the air, the tension between them palpable as she challenged him with a playful smile. "I've been underestimated my whole life." Austin turned to face the fire. The flames danced and flickered in front of him, casting an orange glow on his features.

"Well maybe this world is your chance to prove them wrong."

"I don't *need* to prove them wrong," she spoke with confidence. He looked back at her, and she shrugged nonchalantly. "Odds are they're all dead, and I'm not. I've already won."

As dawn broke, Beth was the first to stir. She gathered her things and headed towards the lake through the trail. The water's stillness and radiance in the gentle morning light brought her a sense of satisfaction. The trees around her rustled softly with the breeze, and birds chirped in the distance, adding to the peaceful atmosphere. Beth walked along the shoreline for a while, making sure she was alone before she undressed completely, relishing the cool air against her skin. The sound of sand crunching beneath her feet and the distant lapping of water provided a soothing soundtrack as she stood naked by the edge of the lake, taking in its tranquillity. Looking at her body, she could see that some weight had returned after the few days of cereal bars and tinned food and deer meat. Stepping into the lake, she shivered as the cool water enveloped her body, immersing herself fully in its refreshing embrace. She cupped water in her hands and splashed it onto her face, feeling a sense of renewal with each gentle movement. As she floated on the water's surface, letting go of all worries and focusing on nature's beauty, she sensed someone else entering the lake. Startled, she looked up to see Austin wading into the water from a nearby path. Beth submerged herself up to her chin, watching him wash his face and hands where his skin had been split open. Her heart raced as she observed him from afar, admiring how the water droplets glistened on his dark skin and how his wet hair clung to his forehead. She could feel the slight chill of the water against her body mixed with a warm tingling sensation in her chest as she crouched within its depths. Austin continued to cleanse himself peacefully as Beth remained still, hoping he wouldn't notice her presence. Almost as if he read her mind, he looked up around the water, locking eyes with her. Caught off guard, Beth held his gaze, a subtle exchange of acknowledgment passing between them. The quiet understanding seemed to bridge the unspoken gaps that had formed within the group as the water around them echoed the tranquillity of the moment. After a minute that felt both simultaneously fleeting and timeless, Austin offered a faint but genuine smile.

"I'm sorry, I thought I was alone." Austin's voice was like a pebble skipping across the surface of the lake, gently breaking the calmness of the water as it reached Beth's ears. She made her way slowly towards him through the water.

"I didn't think anyone else would be up this early." She said, apprehension washing over her face as she sank lower to cover her naked body.

"It's okay," he said. "I'm not interested." He became aware of his tightly clenched fists, a physical manifestation of his nervousness.

"Didn't think you would be," she teased, relaxing her body slightly. "Doesn't mean I'm comfortable with you seeing me naked." He laughed, and Beth realised it was the first time she had seen him differently. She stared for a moment, watching his eyes crinkle and his cheeks dimple.

"What?" He asked, breaking her from her reverie. She creased her eyebrows.

"What?"

"You're staring—"

"First time I've seen you laugh," she said, tilting her head. "I wasn't sure you knew how—"

"Haven't really had anything to laugh at," he pursed his lips. "Until now. Can I ask you something?" Beth stopped a few meters away from him, making sure to keep her distance. She was acutely aware of the lake's translucency and hoped that the ripples in the water would act as a shield, preventing him from seeing her clearly.

"Sure."

"Last night, you said you missed your dog, but not your husband," after a long pause, he looked at her with a questioning expression. She remained quiet and motionless in the water, gradually sinking deeper beneath the surface. He waded a little closer. "Why?"

"I loved my husband," she said with a detached and insincere tone that didn't align with her words. "But he changed."

"When?"

"When he let someone fuck me for food." Her eyes were

empty, devoid of any emotion or recognition. She looked straight at him, unblinking and almost lifeless.

"Fuck, Beth," he said, surprised by her indelicacy. "I'm so sorry—"

"Don't be. You didn't do it." Pursing her lips, she closed her eyes softly as she tried to push out the memory.

"What happened?" He pressed. She let out a heavy sigh, unwilling to re-live the memory but urging herself to be open and honest with him.

"When we were making our way out of Seattle, we met a group at this lake resort near Eatonville. Their leader offered to help us in exchange for my... *personalised* services." Her tone was dripping with sarcasm as she rolled her eyes and gazed out at the lake, fixating on nothing in particular.

"So he let them rape you?" Austin's voice was like a sharp and jagged blade, slicing through the air with the force of his disgust and disbelief. She shuddered at the word.

"Not entirely," she said. Her eyes scanned the water, taking in the peaceful ripples and the reflection of the trees on its surface. Her gaze was distant, detached from the present moment. "They said it was our choice, and we were free to leave at any point. They had already given us some food and the taste made my husband determined not to go hungry again. I was obviously against the idea but he had convinced me that this was the only way to survive, so I complied." Beth looked back at Austin, and he was staring at her. A mix of disbelief and empathy washed over his features and she realised the soft current had brought him closer to her. "He crafted an idea favourably aligned with his own interests, persuaded me that not going hungry again was my own idea, convinced me that it was the best idea I'd have ever had, to let them use me so we could eat, and then he made sure over time that it worked to my detriment. He convinced me to create my own downfall." Austin remained silent for a moment while his face twisted into a mask of revulsion.

"You don't seem to have created your own downfall." He spoke in a gentle whisper, his voice filled with understanding and compassion.

"I escaped, and ran to Eatonville where he'd followed me to bring me back," she said. Her gaze swept over the water like a gentle rain, lingering on every ripple and glimmer on the surface before looking back at Austin. "We fought, and I stabbed him, and he died, and I nearly starved to death alone in a motel room—"

"So that's your downfall," he said, laughing awkwardly at her perception of herself and the way she compartmentalised the memory. "Why tell me all of this?"

"I figured the best way for me to survive is to be honest with all of you," she replied. "There's no way we survive this mess if we keep secrets from each other." Austin tilted his head.

"So Ben knows?"

"No," she shook her head. "And I'm realising now that it makes me a hypocrite, but I get the feeling Ben is more interested in keeping me safe than teaching me how to keep myself safe. You saw the way he reacted about Luis in the hotel room. How do you think he'd react to *this*?"

"I think he'd just be glad to know more about your journey—"

"He knows all he needs to know," she said. "I killed my husband, Austin. There's no coming back from that."

"Beth," he said, his voice low and soft. His expression was one of pure remorse, no hint of judgement or disdain evident on his features. "He deserved it." Her eyes were like a cold, glassy pool reflecting nothing but the harsh light of reality, her face a mask of blankness hiding a river of grief and pain.

"I know."

Chapter Sixteen

Ben watched as Beth and Austin emerged from the edge of the trees, their faces bright with conversation. Ben poked at the fire before grabbing his mug and walking abruptly to his swag. They watched him retreat, walking slower as they entered the space. Austin's words were like a sword thrust, sharp and pointed, cutting through the air with precision and purpose.

"I think he owes us an apology—"

"I think he owes *you* an apology," Beth argued. "You kept my privacy of your own volition. After that night, you made sure I wasn't alone with Luis for a moment, and you paired me with Ben when we split before Mountain Gate so I'd be safe."

"I knew Luis wouldn't protect you over his family," he justified coldly. "Given the opportunity, he'd probably throw you under a literal bus."

"Probably," she agreed, laughing to herself. "If there was a bus to throw me under—"

"Why didn't you tell him?" He asked, stopping in his tracks. The sudden halt created a gap between them, Austin standing a few steps back from Beth, his body turned slightly away from hers. Her eyes, normally bright and alive, now looked downcast and heavy with burden as she turned to face him.

"What Luis did?"

"Yes." His face was tense and serious as his eyes focused on nothing but her.

"I told you," she said. "Back there at the lake—"

"No," he interrupted. "You dodged the question."

"We got to know each other a fair bit over the few days we were alone," she said, They both looked over at Ben who had now emerged from his swag, mulling around as if he was pretending to look for something to do. "He seems to care about me." The air around Austin seemed to thicken and freeze.

"He does."

"They don't strike me as close. I thought he'd probably kill him," Beth replied candidly. "I don't want to become the kind of girl you kill for." Austin thought for a moment, walking closer to her and placing a gentle hand on Beth's arm before looking over at Ben.

"Truthfully, he didn't like Luis before all this," he paused. "But he tolerated him." Beth looked down at Austin's hand on her arm and he removed it quickly.

"Because you were all in the army together?" Her question was more of a statement than an actual inquiry, and he silently nodded in agreement.

"I should go and talk to him," Austin said before holding out his hand. "I want you to take this." Grabbing the bundle he offered, she opened it cautiously.

"What is it?"

"A sheath, and a hunting knife. Assuming you're right handed?" He asked and she nodded slowly. "Buckle it around your left thigh." She looked up from her hands.

"Why my left?"

"Because when you get a handgun you'll want to keep it by your dominant hand," he looked back over to Ben. "So you should get used to unsheathing it from your left." Wrapping the bundle up, she tucked it under her arm.

"Are you gonna go talk to him?"

"There's something I want to do first." He headed towards the RV, leaving Beth alone with her thoughts. Beth made her way over to Val, who was laying on the grass, basking in the sun.

"Where's Luis' swag?"

"After you and Austin went to the lake he sulked off to the lower campsite." Val's eyelids remained closed, her expression distant and unchanging.

"Like a thief in the night." Beth commented, mirroring her flat tone.

"Hey," Val sat up quickly, her elbows supporting her weight as she protested. "He's an asshole, but he's still my brother—"

"Why don't you tell Val what her asshole brother did." Ben stormed over, glaring at Beth. Her voice was filled with desperation as she protested.

"Ben—"

"I think she has the right to know what kind of person her brother is."

"I know what kind of person my brother is," Val said, sitting up properly and looking up between the two. "Besides, you guys weren't exactly quiet last night while you were arguing, but I didn't think it was my place to ask until she was ready to share, *if* you were ready to share." Val gazed at Beth with a regretful expression, her face conveying a sense of apology for her brother's behaviour. Beth glared angrily at Ben.

"I wasn't."

"That wasn't exactly your story to tell, Ben." Val said, standing and glaring at him. Her face conveyed a hint of frustration as Beth shook her head and disappeared into the trees.

"Beth—"

"Let her go," Val said, grabbing Ben's arm as he took a step in Beth's direction. "Give her space to cool down. Besides, I think I should probably tell you something."

Beth angrily stormed through the dense trees, her footsteps punctuating the quiet of the forest. She pushed through the underbrush until she reached a clearing and stood in the middle, surrounded by the towering vegetation. In the relative openness, she took a moment to catch her breath, her chest rising and falling with each frustrated inhale. She looked around at the treeline, the shadows dancing in the mid-morning light filtering through the leaves. The distant rustling of leaves and the soft murmur of the wind created an eerie backdrop to her simmering anger. Frustration etched across her face, Beth stared up into the sky as if seeking answers from the vast expanse above. The wind rustled through the fallen leaves on the ground and the canopy above, lending an unsettling undertone to the scene as Luis approached her with an arrogant swagger, his usual haughtiness evident in every step.

"Tell me something, Beth," he sneered as she turned to face him, her expression impassive to his sudden presence. "How did you survive for so long?"

"Because so far the only terrible people I've come across are idiots," she replied with a dismissive tone. "Present company included." Looking him up and down, she leered at him with a challenging glint in her eyes. The tension in the air heightened as the wind continued to carry the rustling whispers of the forest, amplifying the unease surrounding their exchange. Luis' arrogant facade wavered for a moment, replaced by a flash of annoyance.

"Idiots, huh? Maybe you're just lucky, or maybe you've

been *riding* on someone else's coattails." He said. Proud of his own clever wordplay and with a lecherous grin, he inched closer to her.

"Luck has nothing to do with it," Beth's eyes narrowed, disgusted by the implication. "And I don't need anyone to carry me—"

"So far all you've done is have others fight your battles for you," smirking, Luis took a step closer as Beth stood her ground. "So maybe all you have to do is bat your eyelids and watch while everyone else does the hard work." The wind continued to whip through the clearing, heightening the tension. She stiffened her body, prepared for any sudden movement he might make. Her fight or flight response was telling her to stand her ground for a change, and she firmly planted her feet in the dirt and clenched her fists.

"What's your problem, Luis? Why are you so determined to pick a fight?"

"This isn't a fight, Beth. This is a reality check," he laughed. "Survival of the fittest."

"You don't know anything about me," she moved past him, leaning in closely as she walked. "And from what I can see, maybe survival of the fittest also means cutting loose dead weight like *you*." Continuing her stride, with her back turned to him, Luis abruptly lunged at her and forcefully tackled her to the ground. Beth fought to reorient herself as he pinned her down, the lingering scent of alcohol from the previous night still emanating from his breath. Much too determined to remove herself from the situation, she cursed herself for turning her back to him as she tried to maintain focus on fighting him off. Beth gritted her teeth, the forest floor beneath her offering a cold resistance. She squirmed, attempting to break free from his overpowering hold, the wind now a silent witness which carried echoes of their scuffle through the rustling leaves and the dancing shadows. She tried to scream, but the wind had been knocked out of her. Luis, fuelled by a volatile mix of aggression and arrogance, maintained his grip, his intentions clear and undeniably threatening. Beth's laughter started off as a light giggle, but quickly escalated into a near-manic state, teetering on the edge of being menacing yet maintaining an oddly upbeat tone. Luis's eyes widened in surprise and confusion as Beth's face contorted into a manic grin while she laughed.

"What's so fucking funny?—"

"Ben and Austin are going to kill you." She whispered as she smiled, the words ringing with an unsettling certainty. The expression on Beth's face was unsettling, her lips curved into a maniacal smile, her eyes wild with a mix of fear and defiance. His momentary confusion caused Luis to loosen his grip, unwittingly providing Beth with her only opportunity to escape. With one swift movement, she pushed herself sideways, employing her knee to create a leverage point that sent the two of them into an odd, uncoordinated tumble. As they rolled and twisted, Beth seized the chance to free herself from Luis's grasp, each movement fuelled by a fierce determination to break away from his threatening hold. Fuelled by a surge of adrenaline, she managed to break free from his grip. Rolling away, she reached for the sheathed hunter's knife strapped to her left thigh, fumbling with her lack of skill and coordination with her non-dominant hand.

"Bitch." Luis smirked, crouching down to reach for his machete at his shin. Placing a steady hand, he felt around for the missing blade, cursing as he realised he had left everything in his swag.

"Guess it's a fair fight then." She smirked as she rose to her feet, putting some distance between them. Luis, recovering quickly from his confusion, pursued her with a renewed determination. Unperturbed, Beth raised the gleaming knife, its blade capturing the mid-morning sunlight filtering through the dense canopy. Unyielding to the threat, he continued to charge at her. Spotting a vulnerability in his hungover stumble, she swiftly brought down the knife, driving it into his shoulder. The two of them tumbled to the forest floor as he clutched at the wound. Seizing the moment, Beth swiftly rose, extracting the knife as she did, and bolted back towards the campsite. The forest floor resonated with the echoes of her rapid footsteps, the crunching leaves beneath her boots amplifying the urgency of her escape. With her heart pounding, Beth's adrenaline-fuelled flight blurred the boundaries between friendships and the primal instinct for survival.

Val and Ben strolled leisurely through the trees, Ben's hands constantly moving through his hair and rubbing his face as he struggled to comprehend the information he had just been given. As Ben spoke, his voice was filled with erratic energy and mania, a stark contrast to Val's flat, emotionless tone. She seemed detached from the situation, devoid of emotion.

"Okay, so let me get this straight," he let out a disgruntled huff as he threw his hands up. "You followed Luis to a bar where he got hammered and shot a man, point blank."

"About sums it up—"

"And on top of that, we find out he tried to—" He stopped himself from saying the word, staring into the forest with a mixture of anger and disgust as the visions appeared in his mind.

"Apparently."

"You have to tell Austin." Ben came to a halt and turned towards her, his sudden demand seemingly rooted and unshakeable.

"I know," her gaze fell to the ground as she started lightly kicking at the dirt below. "And Austin won't let him stay, which means—"

"Hey, no," he approached her, gently resting his hand on her arm. "You and Chantelle aren't going anywhere."

"He's my brother—"

"I don't care," Ben interrupted. "No one is safe with him and if you follow him, you're putting yourself and Chantelle at risk."

"What if I left with Luis, and Chantelle stayed with you?"

"She wouldn't," he shook his head. "There is no way that girl is leaving your side." The eerie pause cast a dark shadow through the canopy. Ben leaned against a tree, his back pressed against the rough bark, and looked down at his feet. The silence lingered, heavy with unspoken concerns and the weight of impending decisions. The rustle of leaves in the gentle breeze added a sombre note to the atmosphere, as if nature itself held its breath.

"Say it." She pressed. The sunlight filtered through the thick canopy above, creating a mosaic of light and shadows on the forest floor, mirroring the complexities of the thoughts racing through his mind.

"What?"

"Say what you want to say."

"I want to kill him," his gaze was intense, unyielding and filled with anger as he locked eyes with Val. "All the shit he's pulled. Spokane, that guy at the bar... when I think about what he *could* do to her, I want to fucking kill him."

"I know." Her face was a mask of resignation as she nodded, her gaze flickering to the ground before meeting his once more.

Beth raced through the trees, her footsteps pounding against the forest floor, until she burst into the clearing of the campsite. Skidding to a halt on the rough surface, she took a moment to catch her breath. The campsite appeared eerily deserted, with no sign of the others. For a moment, a pang of isolation gripped her, and she felt as though she were entirely alone. As the dust settled, Austin emerged from the RV, his gaze immediately drawn to Beth standing in the middle of the empty space as he walked over to her quickly.

"Hey, I just told Su about her husband and sister, but left out a lot of the details. She's pretty upset if you want to—" he stopped in his tracks a metre from where she stood. His eyes immediately locked onto the bloody knife in her shaking hand. "Whose blood is that?" A gut-wrenching realisation washed over him as he observed the detached look of fear in her eyes, a look that screamed at him with a haunting intensity. As the adrenaline began to wear off, fear crept into her as the thoughts of what could have happened raced through her mind. All the potential outcomes of the situation played in her head over and over again before she tried to speak.

"Luis—" Beth's lips barely moved as she whispered. Her face was still, and her eyes were glassy and unblinking, as if she were in a trance. "He—"

"Did he touch you?" Austin took a step towards her and reached out his hand as she retracted and pulled the knife close to her.

"I—"

"Hey," he took another forceful step towards her. "I'm not gonna hurt you, but I need to know what happened." She shook her head, attempting to clear the confusion from her thoughts.

"I know—"

"What happened?" He continued to press.

"He tried... he tried to—" she stumbled over her words, glancing up at him with tears in her eyes. "I got away." Ben and Val emerged from the trees, catching their attention suddenly as they looked over in surprise.

"Come on," Austin ushered Beth out of sight behind some of the hanging laundry. "He can't see you like this. He'll kill him." Beth's eyes, still glassy and unblinking, met Austin's with an unyielding gaze.

"Would that be the worst thing?"

"You need to let me handle this," he hissed, looking down at her shirt. "You have blood on you. Take that off." He instructed, and she unbuttoned her flannelette shirt and handed it to him. He took the knife from her hands, wiped it clean on the shirt, and sheathed it.

"What are you gonna do?" She whispered softly. Ignoring her, he dusted the dirt from her legs and picked leaves from her hair, placing a reassuring hand on her cheek.

"You good?"

"I'm good." She nodded slowly, gazing up back at him.

"Okay. Now, tell me where he is."

Chapter Seventeen

Beth had been cold towards Ben for most of the day, creating a distance between them which was filled with insurmountable tension. Though he kept his distance, assuming it was what she wanted, the reality was that Beth desperately wanted to tell him everything. The conflicting forces within her waged a silent battle - the urge to uphold Austin's trust fighting against her desperate need to confide in Ben. Throughout the day, the unspoken tension between them had cast a shadow over their interactions. Beth's guarded demeanour masked the internal struggle she grappled with, torn between loyalty to Austin and the need to unburden herself to Ben, someone she considered a pillar of support. As they moved through the motions of the day, the weight of her unshared truth lingered like a heavy fog. The forest, once a place of refuge, now seemed to echo the complexities of her emotions, mirroring the tangled web of alliances and secrets that threatened to unravel in the face of her internal turmoil. Val had pulled Austin away, with Ben by her side, to disclose what had happened in the bar. Understandably, and to no one's surprise, he took the revelation hard. The weight of the news bore down on Austin, and the lines etched across his face spoke of a mix of disbelief, anger, and a profound sense of betrayal. In the shadow of the trees, Val and Ben exchanged uneasy glances as they observed Austin grappling with the harsh truth. The camaraderie that had once bound the group now faced the threat of unravelling, and the gravity of the situation seemed to settle over them like a heavy shroud. As the trio navigated the difficult conversation, the forest remained eerily quiet, absorbing the weight of their words. The once-solid foundation of trust within the group trembled, and the fate of their makeshift family hung in the balance as they confronted the harsh realities that had unfolded in the depths of their conversation. Austin's face was drawn and tense, his eyes fixed on Val.

"If I cast Luis out, will you and Chantelle stay? You aren't safe with him."

"I lost faith in my brother a long time ago," she confided in them quietly. "What I saw at the bar, what he did in Spokane... you're my family now." Austin later pulled Reece and Ben into a private huddle, sharing his next plans with them. The sombreness of the situation reflected in his eyes as he outlined the tasks ahead. He had a specific mission for Ben and Reece - to head to Redding and gather essential supplies.

"We need to fix the RV, find medication for Su, and scavenge for anything else that'll aid our trek south. You two'll take Val with you," he commanded sternly. "She's a good scout and a good shot, and she'll be able to find the right meds."

"Why can't you go with Reece and Val, and I'll stay at the camp." Ben's face was furrowed in concern, his brow creased and his eyes pleading while he tried to convince Austin to let him stay. Austin shot him a stern look.

"Are you questioning my orders?"

"Austin, please," Ben urged. "Let me stay—"

"Enough Ben," Austin raised a cautionary hand. "We spoke about this."

"Yes, sir," Ben replied obediently, a hint of disdain lacing his tone. "May I be dismissed?" He asked with a mocking tone and Austin silently nodded. Angered by the situation, Ben stormed towards his swag.

"I need a favour." Austin directed at Reece as he watched his friend storm off. As Reece raised his eyebrow, the muscles in his forehead tensed and shifted under the skin.

"A favour, or a command?"

"Both," Austin's expression was grim as he turned to Reece, his jaw set in a determined line and his eyes hard with a sense of responsibility. "My command is that I need you to keep an eye out for Beth. Make sure she's okay, and don't leave her alone with Ben. Just for today, until you head to Redding tomorrow."

"Sure," Reece's eyes narrowed in confusion as he pursed his lips together. "And the favour?"

"You can't ask me why."

The cold night passed with surreal speed - days shortened, and the air became thin, signalling the approaching winter. Luis remained unseen at the lower campground where he was licking his wounds, leaving an unsettling void within the group. Su, consumed by grief, sobbed in her cabin, and Chantelle and Sam focused on keeping MJ occupied, shielding her from the sombre atmosphere around camp. Amidst the heavy emotional currents, Ben, Reece, and Val found them-selves packing and preparing for their assigned mission. The weight of the impending tasks hung in the air as they readied themselves for the journey to Redding, unsure of the situation at Mountain Gate. The forest, now adorned with the first signs of winter, bore witness to their preparations, the chill in the air mirroring the solemnity that gripped the group. In the face of uncertainty, the three of them shared a determined resolve, each step in their preparations echoing the unspoken commitment to survival and the bonds that held them together in the midst of adversity. The forest, now touched by the delicate fingers of frost, seemed to breathe a quiet acknowledgment of the challenges that awaited them beyond the safety of their makeshift home. As the night wore on with a fresh deer on the fire, they ate in silence. Beth sat with Su and Sam as MJ slept in her mother's arms.

"Do you want me to help you put her to bed?" Beth whispered. Su shook her head solemnly.

"Not yet," she tenderly stroked her daughter's black hair. "Sam can help me carry her in."

"I lost my husband too." Beth's voice was barely audible as she rested her chin on her knees and hugged her legs tightly.

"So you grieve as well?"

"In my own way, yes." Beth said, staring into the dying light of the fire. Sam cautiously held out his arms for his niece and lifted her up, walking over to the RV.

"You shouldn't talk about it in front of her." He whispered with an undertone of anger, and Beth nodded apologetically. The flames danced in the fire pit, casting flickering shadows on Su and Beth's faces as they sat in the silent embrace of the night. Sam disappeared into the RV with MJ, leaving a sombre air between the two women.

"Grief, it's a heavy burden to bear." Su broke the silence, her gaze distant yet filled with understanding. Beth took a deep breath, exhaling slowly as she contemplated her response.

"I'm not sure I've entirely figured it out," she said. "Sometimes, it's just about surviving one day at a time. Finding small moments of peace, even in the chaos." Su nodded, the pain in her eyes mirroring her internal anguish.

"I never expected this kind of life for my family."

"Life has a way of throwing unexpected challenges our way," Beth reached out, placing a comforting hand on Su's knee. "All we can do is face them together, lean on each other when needed." Su sighed, her breath hitching with the weight of sorrow.

"How do you keep going?"

"I just... do." Beth glanced into the fire, the embers glowing like fading memories. Their shared silence held the unspoken truth of the hardships they faced, bound together by grief and the fragile threads of camaraderie in their makeshift family. The night lingered, offering solace in the quiet companionship as they navigated the intricacies of their loss. Ben observed them whispering from the other side of the fire, his gaze fixed on the dance of shadows that occasionally lit up Beth's face. The flames played tricks on her features, revealing fleeting contradicting glimpses of hope and sorrow amidst the darkness. Her face became an unpredictable puppet show, each emotion emerging like an unexpected character on the other side of each dark interval. As Beth and Su shared their private conversation, Ben couldn't help but feel like an outsider peering into the complex tapestry of their emotions. The warmth of the fire contrasted with the cool breeze of the night, echoing the ebb and flow of the emotions that flickered across Beth's face. Ben pondered the weight of their shared grief, the unspoken connections formed in the crucible of their experiences. The fire crackled and popped, a symphony of sounds accompanying the delicate ballet of shadows that painted the night. For a moment, Ben felt his body shiver and contract with a wave of anxiety at the thought of leaving her alone for even a single day. The realisation hit him that they would be gone for more than that, a truth reflected in the meticulous preparations between himself, Reece, and Val. The weight of the impending separation from Beth gnawed at him, and the gravity of the situation was written on his face. Austin, keenly observant, noted the anger and trepidation etched on Ben's features. The unspoken concern lingered in the air, mirroring the internal struggle Ben faced between the urgency of their mission and the protective instincts urging him to stay by Beth's side.

"Ben," Austin whispered. His soft voice cut through the crackling of the fire. "You'll be back as soon as possible. You know why I need you to go. No one else can fix that RV and you know what you're looking for."

"I know." Ben nodded, trying to convey trust despite the knot of worry in his stomach. As they exchanged a silent acknowledgement, the firelight danced on their faces, casting shadows that whispered of the challenges they faced, both internal and external.

"I promise she'll be okay." Austin offered, his tone reassuring. Ben, his concern unabated, shot his friend a stern glance.

"Don't let Luis touch her." He said, the gravity of the warning cutting through the air. The unspoken understanding between them held the weight of shared protectiveness over Beth, a silent agreement in the face of potential threat. Austin met Ben's gaze, conveying a sense of determination.

"I won't." He said, recognising the unspoken pledge to safeguard Beth in his absence. The fire crackled, casting a glow on their faces as the weight of responsibility settled over the campsite. In the dance of shadows, the bonds that held their makeshift family together were tested, their collective resilience facing the challenges that lay beyond the safety of the fire's warmth. One by one, they slowly made their way to their beds. The solace of the campsite had been bittersweet - Austin, Ben, Reece, Val, Chantelle, and Beth all found relief in the rest they were able to have after weeks of walking, however, this respite was countered by the weight of the events from the last few days. It was as if they were finally able to ignore their physical feats, allowing the emotional and mental challenges to take their place. The relentless physicality of their journey so far had, in a way, masked the underlying turmoil between everyone. Now, as they rested in the quietude of the campsite, those dormant conflicts had come to light, unravelling like shadows in the glow of the fire. The forest, usually a silent witness to their struggles, seemed to hold its breath in the face of the emotional storm that had been unleashed. Each member of the group, lost in their thoughts, grappled with the complexities that had surfaced - their journey became more than a physical odyssey, it had become a test of endurance for their relationships, resilience, and their strength. The last two remaining members around the campfire, Beth and Austin, stared at each other across the dying flames. Between them lingered a silent exchange, a mixture of remorse for the challenges faced and gratitude for the shared strength that had carried them through. The embers cast a soft, warm glow on their faces, illuminating the weariness etched in their expressions. Each flicker of the fire seemed to weave an unspoken narrative of the days to come. In the quietude of the night, Beth's eyes reflected the dance of the flames, holding a depth of appreciation for his actions. Austin, in turn, conveyed a silent acknowledgment of her trust in him. As Beth finally found herself alone, Austin's retreating figure disappeared into the shadows, leaving her to contemplate the events of the day. The fading glow of the fire cast elongated shadows across the ground, weaving a tapestry of darkness that enveloped her in a cloak of solitude. In the quiet of the night, the forest stood as a silent confidant, absorbing the weight of her thoughts. The echoes of the day's challenges lingered in the air as Beth became enveloped by the night, her mind a canvas painted with the emotions stirred by the events that had unfolded. The rustle of leaves and the distant sounds of the wilderness provided a natural symphony, accompanying Beth's reflections in the darkness. The campsite, once alive with shared laughter and camaraderie nights before, had transformed into a sanctuary for introspection, where emotions flowed freely in the stillness of the night.

By the time the early light of dawn broke through the trees, Reece, Ben, and Val had already traveled halfway to Redding. The sun rose like a golden egg, cracking the sky open and spilling out hues of pink and orange, painting the horizon with a vibrant tapestry of colour and illuminating the scenery around them. The landscape was bathed in its warm glow, casting long shadows that danced across the open road and inspiring a sense of determination and hope in those who travelled under its stirring rays. It stretched ahead, a path of uncertainty and promise under the awakening sky. The air was crisp and clean, carrying the scent of winter morning as the sun rose higher. The warm scent of pine and cedar permeated the air, reminding them of the forest they were leaving behind. The birds sang their morning songs, filling the air with a symphony of light and happy chirps which contrasted their morose body language. The morning breeze brushed against their skin, carrying the coolness of the night mixed with the warmth of the rising sun. The four-day journey had been meticulously planned out by Austin, with Reece and Ben offering occasional input, but ultimately following their captain's orders.

"Does everyone remember the plan?" Ben called from ahead.

"Confirmed." Reece called from the rear as Val, locked safely in between the two, nodded despondently. Ben turned to her.

"Val?"

"Sorry, yes." She responded, her thoughts on her brother and the complexities that the days ahead would involve for him. Austin's plan had been clear - they would make the 24-kilometre journey in one morning and base themselves at a hotel near the Sundial Bridge. After dark, they would scout the downtown area, ensuring there weren't any major threats. Ben was reassured by the fact that most major cities had been abandoned during the initial outbreak due to the infected masses. In the aftermath of the virus disappearing, violent survivalists had looted cities and pillaged their way along the coastal highways. Austin had calculated that there would not be too many conflicting groups so near to each other, and that Mountain Gate posed the only threat in the area. Ben had tried to argue about the unknown group on the radio, but Austin was convinced that they were transients simply passing through. And if they weren't, he concluded, it didn't matter anyway - they weren't going anywhere without the parts they needed for the RV. In the days following, the three of them would head straight to the medical centres on the north side of town before snaking across to the major hospital and then south to another medical centre. Val had expressed concern about their lack of antibiotics, painkillers, gauze - anything they'd need to get them through whatever crisis they would face. The rest of their day would be spent separately, with Val and Reece searching grocery stores for spare food while Ben would head to various mechanics and auto-body shops, searching for the parts he needed to fix the RV. Their final days would be spent via a detour to a gun range before heading back to the campsite that evening if they could. Otherwise, they would spend the night there before making their final journey forward the following day. As they approached their halfway mark, Ben looked to his right at the stone and cast-iron fence which surrounded the Tierra Oaks Golf Club. The three of them came to a halt and stared at the scene before them - a man strung up with his arms outstretched, clothes ripped from his body, the word 'SINNER' carved into his chest with what seemed like a heated knife, skin burned and seared where the flesh had been torn. Reece and Val shared worried glances, their concern evident. Ben watched their reactions as he made his way towards the body.

"He's been here a long time," he observed. Ben turned back to face them, curious by their apprehensive expressions. "What is it?" Val hesitated as she swallowed the lump forming in her throat.

"We saw—"

"Three bodies," Reece interjected quickly. "Hanged from the rafters of a house behind rally point A. The same message was painted on the side of the house in red paint." Ben hesitated for a moment, weighing the potential threat that might be harboured inside the golf club, or ahead of them in Redding, or behind them at Mountain Gate. Either way, the grim display hinted at a fanatic group with a sinister message. As the sun continued its ascent, casting an eerie glow over the macabre scene, a sense of unease settled over the three of them. They realised they were venturing into uncharted territory, where hidden dangers lurked in the shadows, or, if they were as bold as their threatening message seemed to suggest, prowled in broad daylight.

"Come on," Ben said, finally breaking the eerie silence. He continued down the road. "We're wasting time."

Chapter Eighteen

⸻ ❖ ⸻

Beth pushed herself through the tent flap, shielding her eyes from the high sun, not realising she had slept through most of the morning for a change. A sudden wave of anxiety swept over her as she raced behind the tents to Ben's swag, his backpack and some of his essential gear missing. Austin walked over to her, offering a reassuring look.

"They'll be back in four or five days," he said, his lips curling into a half smile. Her resentment kept her from speaking. "They wanted to leave before sunrise." Austin sighed, a mixture of understanding and empathy etched on his face as he placed a comforting hand on Beth's shoulder.

"I thought, at the very least he'd say goodbye." Though her words were filled with malice and resentment, there was a trace of sadness behind them.

"I know it's tough," he said gently. "They had their orders to leave early, and you weren't exactly friendly yesterday. When would he have had the opportunity to say goodbye?"

"I know," Beth said, nodding. She tried to suppress the emotions that threatened to overwhelm her. "I shouldn't've been so cold—"

"You had a rough morning," Austin said. His features softened as he looked at her. "And I wanted to thank you for not telling him what happened." Her words were like a cool breeze as she turned to face him.

"I know that Ben would've literally killed him, and I didn't want to be the one to put that on his conscience."

"I know it wasn't about me, but you made my job easier by not telling him."

"Because you're sick of trying to keep everyone alive?" Beth's eyes, usually filled with warmth and humour, now held a touch of sadness as she looked at Austin. "Never mind diffusing arguments between the two of them—"

"You're perceptive."

"Anyone could figure that out by looking at the way you all interact."

"Beth," his pause was like a delicate spiderweb, a glistening thread that he carefully spun and examined before speaking again. "I've never seen Ben so irrational." Stepping backwards slightly, Beth's tone revealed her obvious contempt.

"Protecting someone is irrational?"

"That's not what I meant—"

"Then what?" She asked. Her face, etched with frustration and weariness, scowled at him.

"Ben is my voice of reason," he took a cautious step towards her. "He's gentle and kind, has always had my back, never questioned orders—"

"And?" She gazed at him with a neutral expression, attempting to read his face and connect it with the words he was speaking. In an effort to soothe the tension between them, he spoke again in a more composed manner after their briefly heated moment.

"Ben has no one left, and I think you've given him something to live for," he said. "Something to protect other than himself, something to care about. I want to thank you for bringing my friend back to life, but you make him irrational and angry." Beth took a deep breath, attempting to soothe her nerves, appreciating Austin's attempt to ease her irritation. She lifted her hand and placed it softly on his forearm.

"What can I do?" She asked. Austin's body tensed as soon as her fingers made contact with his arm, catching him off guard. He couldn't control the involuntary reaction his body had to her touch, every inch of his skin tingling with intrigue and wonder. His gaze shifted to where her hand rested on his arm, trying to swallow the lump that had formed in his throat.

"You can make sure he continues to follow my orders, and not put yourself in danger."

"Then someone needs to show me how to take care of myself," she said. Her eyebrows rose and a pleading expression washed over her face as she stared at him. "Ben certainly won't do it, no matter how many times I ask." Without fully realising it, Austin instinctively took a small step away from her, shrugging her hand from his arm.

"I think he thinks that if you can protect yourself, you won't need him anymore."

"That's ridiculous." Beth's face scrunched in frustration, her brows furrowed and her jaw clenched as she shook her head.

"I'll teach you some basics," he reassured her. "Over the next few days, so you can start somewhere. I need to start fixing some things around here." Pausing, she looked in the direction of the lower campsite.

"And—"

"Yes," he followed her gaze into the trees. "And I need to take care of that."

As Beth stepped into the cramped RV, her eyes scanned the small space for Su. The outdated furnishings and cluttered shelves gave off a musty smell that made her wrinkle her nose. Noting Su's absence, Beth took a step back towards the door. She heard a gentle voice call out, stopping her in her tracks.

"Stay," Su's mother whispered to Beth. "Sit with me." Beth approached slowly, taking a seat at the edge of the bed and reaching out to rest her hand gently on the covers.

"Is there something you need?"

"No," the elderly woman shook her head. "Closer." It was as if she were approaching a fragile bird, her movements delicate and cautious, as if the slightest touch could break the creature. But as she reached out to take the woman's hand, her touch was gentle yet firm, a gesture of understanding and compassion.

"I'm sorry," Beth's lips curved into a polite smile, her dimples appearing briefly on her cheeks. "I never really asked your name." She clutched Beth's hand tightly, her face twisted in concern as she leaned closer.

"You may call me *eomma*."

"*E-om-ma*," Beth repeated slowly. "What does that mean?"

"You have taken care of my family so carefully, and I thank you for that." The elderly woman's frail body slowly sat up on the bed, her wrinkled hands gripping the edge for support. The faded floral sheets crinkled and creased under her weight.

"Here." Beth reached out a hand to help her, but she politely pushed it away, determined to rise on her own. With a piercing glance, she locked eyes with Beth, her intense stare bearing down on her.

"I have heard your plans to take us south with you, but I want to ask a favour."

"Yes?" Beth said slowly.

"Su-ho will do anything to protect her family, and I cannot be a burden to her. Do you understand?" She tilted her head to the side and Beth slowly nodded, the gravity of her request slowly sinking in.

"I think I understand what you're asking, but—"

"My daughter, her daughter, and my son will be okay with all of you." She said softly as Beth nodded in understanding, the weight of her appeal sinking in further as she listened. It was the ultimate farewell, a desperate and final act of surrender to the overwhelming darkness that had consumed her. It was a sharp blade cutting through the tangled threads of her existence, a haunting echo of what once was. The words loomed ominously in Beth's mind, threatening to swallow her whole. She could see the desperation and pain etched on the elderly woman's face, a stark contrast to the calm exterior she had usually presented in their limited interactions. The air seemed to thicken with the stench of sadness and regret, an almost tangible scent that lingered around the conversation like a dark cloud. As she spoke, Beth's mouth was filled with a bitter taste, like swallowing poison. It left a lingering aftertaste of sorrow and sacrifice. The weight of her words burned on Beth's tongue, heavy and sharp like a piece of broken glass. Beth's hand trembled as she reached up to wipe away the single tear that had rolled down her cheek.

"But I won't be the one to help you—"

"That was not the favour I was going to ask," she looked at her cautiously. "I want you to help me up into my wheelchair so I can sit in the sun for a while. I want to see the water." Beth's shoulders were tense, her body rigid as she stood up.

"Today?"

"She will need time to grieve in a place of solace," she gestured out the window. "While your friends are away."

"I'll need Austin to help me carry you outside."

"I can walk," the elderly woman's wrinkled hands trembled as she reached up to grip the edge of the bed, her knuckles white with exertion. "I just had no strength until you came along." With gentleness and patience, Beth assisted the woman in exiting the RV through the door and down the small steps to the ground. As her feet touched the gravel, she instinctively curled her toes, wincing slightly at the sharp pebbles beneath them. Tilting her head up towards the sky, she let the warmth of the sun wash over her and felt its rays caress her delicate features.

"Are you alright?"

"Yes," she steadied herself on the side of the RV. "The wheelchair is around the back." Beth made her way to the opposite end of the RV, taking out a folding wheelchair and setting it up for her. She helped her sit down gently, and then motioned towards the lake. Beth hesitated at first, but then pushed the chair down the trail, carefully alternating between using the brakes and letting them go. It was a challenge for both of them as they reached the lake, with Beth working hard to push her along the bank. But she remained determined to fulfill this final wish for *eomma*.

"Will this do?"

"Leave me." She commanded, her lips barely moving.

"*Eomma*," Beth muttered softly. "Don't you want to say goodbye?"

"I have already done this," she whispered. "Although I do not think Su-ho understood at the time, but she will." Beth squatted down beside her, supporting herself on the arm of the wheelchair and gazing up at her aged face.

"What you're doing is very brave—"

"Not really," she remarked absentmindedly. "But it is the right thing to do for my family. Don't forget that *sonnyeo*."

"What?" Beth whispered softly.

"That sometimes you must do the right thing for someone else," her voice was soft and gentle, like a soothing melody. "Even if it will hurt them, or even if it will hurt you." Beth thought over the words carefully and nodded. "Don't be sad, *sonnyeo*," she whispered to Beth, placing a gentle hand on her face. "I thought I was going to die in that bed, but you gave an old woman some happy memories to end with. That has been a true gift." Beth watched the lines on her face crinkle as she smiled softly. She wanted to say something, anything to make her change her mind, but deep down Beth knew that this was her last wish and didn't want the final memory to be an argument. Her face was lined with deep wrinkles, each one telling a story of a life well-lived. Some were etched deep, others shallow like ripples on a pond. They formed a map of her experiences, showing where she had laughed, cried, and smiled. Beth could feel the woman's hand on her arm, her grip light but firm.

"It's been an honour meeting you," Beth said. "I'm sorry we couldn't do more to help."

"And I'm sorry I thought you were a crazy American," she smiled. "Now leave me. I want to be alone." Beth walked back up the trail, wondering what to tell Su and Sam when she saw them. Or perhaps they would go to the lake to play with MJ or wash themselves and discover the body on their own. Or they might even discover the empty RV and think she had been kidnapped, an absurd thought which crept into Beth's mind nonetheless. Either way, it was not her concern. She took a final look back before disappearing up the path.

"Hey!" Austin spotted Luis sleeping peacefully next to his swag, basking in the warm sunlight. His anger flared up as he thought about all the things Luis had done earlier that morning, marching over to him with a determined expression on his face, kicking his legs to wake him. Luis grumbled angrily.

"What?—"

"Get up." Austin commanded with an authority Luis had not heard from his friend before. It wasn't his usual authoritative military tone - it was primal and fearless, full of rage and betrayal. Austin began to pack Luis' backpack for him, dismantling the swag in frustration.

"Get out of my stuff!" Luis grasped Austin's shoulder, but was suddenly pushed away with such force that he stumbled backwards.

"You're leaving." Austin commanded again, standing up to face Luis.

"And where am I gonna go?"

"I don't care." Austin walked back towards the campsite, Luis hot on his heels.

"Austin," Luis' face contorted with pleading and fear. "I'm sorry about that night but—"

"That night?" Austin interrupted, turning to him and pushing him backward. "This is not about *that night*. This is about Spokane, *and* that night, and the bar and yesterday, and all of the other shady shit you've done to put us in danger!" He took a step towards Austin, his body trembling in fear.

"You know—"

"Of course I know!" Austin's voice was laced with rage and disappointment. "I know about you wanting to steal the RV, and about the man you shot in cold blood, and about Beth yesterday. What's wrong with you?"

"You're more concerned with saving other people that you've lost the ability to save yourself," the air was thick with the stench of sweat and adrenaline. "You and Ben are so caught up with that girl that you've lost sight of what's important!"

"*Enough*!" Austin's face was flushed with anger, his fists clenched at his sides.

"You aren't fit to provide for anyone," Luis pushed Austin forcefully backward as Austin stumbled, falling to the ground. "You should've pulled Samantha from the medical tents when this all started but you were too weak to take care of her! I should've taken over command when you let your girlfriend get killed in all that chaos!" Austin scrambled to his feet and tackled Luis to the ground, pressing his forearm against his neck. Luis gasped for breath and clutched at Austin's arm, flailing his legs underneath him. Unrelenting, Austin pressed harder into his trachea as Luis struggled to speak. He continued to press as Luis' gasps became raspy and guttural, watching the colour slowly drain from Luis' face. Unable to breathe, Luis felt a wave of panic wash over him. In Austin's eyes, he observed a look of malevolence he had never seen before. It was a cold, detached gaze that sent shivers down his spine. Luis, who was usually confident and unyielding, now found himself genuinely scared. As Austin maintained his grip, Luis' vision began to blur, and the edges of his consciousness faded. Panic intensified, and his body reflexively fought for air. He clawed at Austin's arm, desperately trying to pry it away. The world around Luis started to spin, and he realised that he was truly at Austin's mercy. In that moment, Austin saw the fear in Luis's eyes, something he had never witnessed before. It struck a chord deep within him. The malice in Austin's gaze wavered, and a flash of realisation crossed his face. The weight of what he was doing hit him, and he abruptly relented the weight from his arm, standing up and stumbling back. Luis writhed on the ground, gasping for breath through hoarse wheezes and gasps, his hands clutching his throat. He coughed violently, trying desperately to restore air to his lungs. Austin, wide-eyed and stunned by his own actions, watched as Luis struggled to recover. The reality of what had just transpired hung heavy in the air between them. For a moment, neither of them spoke. The forest seemed eerily silent, as if nature itself was holding its breath.

"Luis—"

"That is the kind of leader we needed." Luis managed to say, his voice hoarse. Austin couldn't find the words to respond immediately as the gravity of his actions sank in, and the lines between ally and adversary blurred in that brief, intense encounter.

"You leave by tonight and if I ever see you again," he looked down at Luis on the floor. "I *will* kill you."

"Yes, *sir*." Luis said mockingly as Austin walked through

the trees towards the campsite. Luis's derisive words hung in the air with a tone of malice that he had hoped was the last time he'd ever hear.

Austin burst through the treeline, observing Beth as she aimlessly wandered around the quiet area. The aftermath of the confrontation with Luis had left a sombre expression on Austin's face. Beth, lost in her thoughts, was startled when he approached her.

"It's done." He breathed slowly, his adrenaline leaving his body as she raised a hand to his upper arm.

"It's for the best," a wave of relief washed over her face as if a gentle breeze had swept through her. "You look a little worse for wear. Are you okay?"

"I nearly killed him." Austin said, his face impassive.

"What?—"

"I had my arm on his throat and I could see the light draining from his eyes," Austin whispered, his voice shaking. Beth could see his body vibrate with adrenaline and fear. "And for a moment, it felt—" He stopped himself from saying the words, from openly admitting how good it felt to watch Luis slowly drift away.

"Austin—"

"It wasn't for you," he said. "He said something and I just —" Beth pulled him to her, embracing him and placing her hand against the back of his head.

"But you didn't kill him," she whispered. "You stopped yourself. If the roles were reversed, he wouldn't have." Austin slowly brought his arms up to hug Beth, and he relaxed his body into hers, burying his face in her hair. When they parted, she offered him a reassuring look, and he lifted his eyes to meet hers. They held a glint of moisture, a sign that tears would spill over if he let them. "I know the timing's awful, but I need to tell you something—"

"You can tell me anything." He smiled. She looked back towards the trail which led down to the lake.

"I did something, and I don't know if it was the right thing to do."

"Tell me." He lifted his hand to her chin and brought her face back to him, looking into her eyes. She recounted her story from the morning, carefully choosing her words, and watched as his expression shifted from sadness to understanding, but not a hint of anger or disgust marred his features.

"Do you think I did the right thing?" She asked, craving validation.

"You did what she asked," he nodded at her approvingly. "You provided an old woman with her final wishes."

"I hope so."

"You'll need a thicker skin to survive in this world, Beth," he pursed his lips together. "And tomorrow I'll start teaching you how to take care of yourself."

"Tomorrow," she mirrored his words. "Right now, I need to tell Su about her mother."

Chapter Nineteen

Beth hesitated for a moment, grappling with the weight of the secret she held. She took a deep breath and began mentally recounting the conversation she had with Su's mother. Beth needed to tell her, sooner rather than later, while it was fresh in her memory - she refused to dishonour the woman's final moments by misremembering her last words. She walked over to Su, a look of despair on her mournful face.

"Su," Beth called out hesitantly. "I need to talk to you—" Hesitating, she mustered the strength to speak the rehearsed speech in her head, but like a drought it felt that every drop of water had been sucked from her soul, leaving her parched and barren. Su looked up from her load of washing that she was scrubbing in a large plastic tub.

"Yes?"

"Your mother asked me for a favour." Beth said. It was all she could muster from the forefront of her mind, as the depths of her psyche went blank.

"She likes you." Su smiled up at her, continuing her washing. Looking down at her feet, Beth scuffed the dirt with the heels of her boots.

"Yeah—"

"What is it, Beth?" Su looked up at her, her expression a little more concerned now that she had noted the shift in Beth's body language. Beth met her gaze, mildly bewildered as she had been lost in her own shallow thoughts.

"What?"

"What was the favour?" Stopping her work and steadying herself on the side of the tub, Su's concerned expression grew. Beth's voice quivered with the gravity of her words.

"I took your mother down to the lake—"

"You left her there alone?" Su stood up suddenly, spilling water from the tub and wiping her hands on her jeans.

"She asked me to—"

"You should have asked me first," Su exclaimed. "We don't know who's down there!" Su's quick movements were a blur as she hurried over to the RV, her long hair flying behind her. She flung open the door and reached for her jacket, pulling it off a hook on the wall.

"I should've asked you first." Beth's eyes seemed to shrink back into her head, avoiding Su's piercing gaze. Her body language became small and submissive, her shoulders hunched and her arms wrapped tightly around her body. Su walked briskly towards the trail, her heavy feet causing the gravel to shift and crush underneath her boots. Beth paused, wondering if she should let her find the body of her mother on her own. She wondered if maybe she hadn't done it yet, that maybe Su would get there just in time to stop her, but she knew deep down that the deed had already been done. Beth ran after her, grabbing her arm to stop her determined march to the lake. Su spun around, glaring at Beth in anger.

"Let me go—"

"She asked me to do her a favour," Beth spoke quickly. "But I said I wouldn't help her, only that I would take her to the lake—"

"What do you mean, Beth?" Su's eyes narrowed in anger,

her body tense and rigid as Beth's gaze shifted downwards, avoiding Su's wrath. "What am I going to find when I go down to the lake?"

"She said she wanted to be alone." Beth whispered. Su's eyes widened, a blend of shock and sorrow flickering across her features, her voice quivering.

"What are you talking about?"

"She said she didn't want to be a burden to you," Beth continued, her words heavy with sorrow. "She asked me to help her fulfil her final wishes—"

"Her *final* wishes?" Su's face twisted with a mixture of emotions - sorrow, fury, and astonishment. Suddenly, she swung her arm through the air and struck Beth's cheek with a loud crack. The sound reverberated throughout the empty campground as Su struggled to come to terms with the harsh truth.

"I'm sorry—"

"You took away my chance to say goodbye," Su's voice cracked with a mixture of pain and anger. "How could you decide that for me?" Beth, her cheek stinging, met Su's gaze with tear-filled eyes.

"I thought I was helping her. I thought it was what she wanted—" Beth said, her tone pleading for understanding. "She said that she had already said goodbye to you and that you'd understand—"

"Understand?" Su took a step backwards, her hand shaking as she tried to process the shocking revelation. The truth hung heavily in the air, and Su couldn't believe she hadn't seen it before. She remembered all the recent conversations with her mother, wondering when they had said their final goodbyes to each other. But deep down, Su knew the exact moment. In their last few days together, they had experienced a surge of happiness and security for the first time in a while, with fresh food and safety among new friends. During this brief respite, Su's mother spoke about life as if it were a story she was imparting wisdom through. Su reflected on their last conversation where her mother had expressed how proud she was of her, a sentiment that had been buried and forgotten for so long.

"You do not get to decide what is right for my family." She whispered with a low, furious mumble and took off down the path to the lake. Sam handed MJ to Chantelle and took off after his sister. Austin approached from behind, standing by Beth as they watched the two of them disappear behind the trees.

"You made the right call, Beth." He said, and she turned to face him.

"I made the right call," Beth scoffed sarcastically. "What if Su decides not to come with us now? I might've condemned them to die up here alone, with Su grieving for her husband, sister, and now her mother. She'll be too consumed by grief to provide for any of them."

"In a way, you might've done her a favour," Austin replied, his expression contorted with frustration. "One less person for her to take care of—"

"That's cold, Austin." Beth's face twisted in a scowl as she shook her head, her eyebrows furrowed and her lips tight in anger.

"It's harsh reality—"

"And what if she doesn't come with us? She certainly won't just give us the RV, so Ben went into town for nothing." Beth's voice was like shattered glass, the pieces falling and breaking into smaller shards as she fought to keep her emotions in check. But the cracks were visible, and the pain in her words was palpable, a heavy weight pressing down on her as she struggled to hold back her tears. Austin placed a reassuring hand on her arm, but she recoiled and reeled backward. She threw both of her hands up in front of her, creating a symbolic barrier between them.

"Beth—"

"This place is a prison," she said. "The sooner we get out of here, the better. I can't go anywhere without wondering if Luis is gonna attack me. I can't find a single place to just... to just—" She paused, breathing heavily and trying desperately to hold back her tears, uncertain of where to turn and unwilling to be alone with Luis potentially lurking around. Austin approached her with caution, raising his hands and placing them on her arms.

"Tomorrow, when Luis is gone," he said. "You can roam around freely without worrying."

"Yeah, and now I have to wonder if Su is gonna slit my throat in my sleep." Beth said, her eyes glistening with unshed tears. Austin's lips curved into a small smile, the corners of his eyes crinkling as he ran his hands down her arms and grabbed the tips of her fingers.

"Su doesn't strike me as the silent assassin type."

"I hope you're right." Beth said, looking down at their hands, noticing how Austin's larger hand enveloped hers. She tentatively licked her dry lips, tasting the salt of her tears mixed with nerves. Her gaze remained on their fingers, taking note of the warm and reassuring feeling of Austin's grasp. His thumb traced gentle circles on the back of her hand, as if trying to comfort her, feeling the slight roughness of his skin against hers. She quickly pulled her fingers away, turning to face the campfire. Austin crossed his arms awkwardly and took a step back.

"Do you want to go check on her?"

"Now?" Beth asked, turning her head to look towards the lake. "I am the last person she'll want to talk to—"

"Then when she's calmed down, I'll go check on her," he offered. "And then I'll help bury her mother."

The afternoon winter sun was high in the sky, casting a bright light that emphasised the briskness of the air. Ben, Reece, and Val arrived at the hotel right on schedule - their bodies ached from the five-hour trek to Redding without a break, their muscles protesting the unaccustomed strain. The three of them approached the hotel with caution, glancing around for any signs of movement. The silence hung in the air, broken only by the occasional rustle of wind through the trees. As they reached the entrance, Ben gestured for Val and Reece to wait outside while he slowly pushed the door open, revealing an empty lobby. He looked over his shoulder, signalling for them to follow. Val and Reece joined him inside, and together they diligently swept through the entire hotel to ensure it was indeed deserted. The quiet halls echoed with their footsteps as they checked each room, confirming that the place was abandoned. Dust-covered furniture and the stale air told a story of long neglect. Dirt and cobwebs clung to every surface, from the light fixtures to the faded wallpaper. Furniture had been overturned and scattered, the carpets were worn and stained, and the once-luxurious decor was now dull and lifeless. A musty, stale odour permeated the air, mixed with the faint scent of mildew and decay. The silence was eerie and oppressive, broken only by their footsteps tapping on the tiles and occasional distant howl of wind. The walls and floors felt grimy and sticky underfoot. Furniture was coated in a layer of dust, and Val ran a soft finger over a side table which left a powdery residue on her fingertip. The building was a ghostly shell, a forgotten relic. Its once grand exterior now shrouded in layers of dirt as if time itself had grown weary of its existence. The deserted halls held remnants of a life long gone, the creaking floorboards and tattered curtains a mournful symphony for the neglect that saturated every inch of the place. Once satisfied that they were alone, they reconvened in the lobby. Val's arms were crossed, her fingers rubbing her sore shoulders with a grimace on her face.

"Looks like we've got the place to ourselves."

"Let's find a room on the bottom floor and take a break," Ben suggested. "We could use some rest before nightfall." The trio made their way down the dimly lit corridor, glancing into rooms along the way. They eventually settled on the room closest to the emergency exit, providing some semblance of security but a quick escape should they need to vacate in haste. Inside, they found a couple of chairs and a small table.

"This'll do." Reece dropped his backpack with a sigh as Val eased herself slowly into one of the chairs. Ben took a moment to scan the views outside the window for any signs of movement before finally allowing himself to relax.

"We'll rest here for a bit, catch our breath, eat something," he said, drawing the curtains closed. "We've got a lot of ground to cover." As they settled into the room, the exhaustion of the journey caught up with them, but the mild sense of security offered by the abandoned hotel brought a temporary respite.

Beth and Chantelle had resigned themselves to playing with MJ, chasing her around the campsite as she giggled and waved her arms. Beth was doing her best to keep herself distracted, but Chantelle was doing a much better job of playing make-believe with the little girl. Beth stopped playing at the sound of determined footsteps approaching them as the steps crunched on the gravel. She spun on her heel to find Su storming up to them, a fire in her eyes.

"Get away from her!" She quickly pushed Beth aside and lifted her daughter into her arms, hurrying inside the RV and swiftly shutting the door behind them.

"What's happened?" Chantelle asked naively, shock sweeping across her innocent face.

"Austin'll fill you in." Beth replied. They watched as he appeared from the treeline, carrying a body wrapped in a sheet. Sam grabbed a shovel from behind the RV, handing it to Beth.

"This *dishonour* should be yours." He said with a soft anger, following his sister and niece inside the RV and locking the door behind them. Chantelle's face was twisted in confusion and concern.

"Beth, what happened? Who's in the sheet?" She asked. Beth ignored her, walking over to Austin as he placed the body beneath a tree.

"She's requested that we bury her next to her husband," he took the shovel from her. "So she has time to mourn her parents before we leave." Beth's face relaxed and her tense shoulders slumped, her expression shifting from worry to relief. She ran a hand through her hair, damp from sweat and dirt.

"They're still coming with us?"

"Yes," walking over to a small clearing between the trees, he planted the shovel into the ground and removed a large patch of dirt. "She didn't think Sam and MJ should be punished for your mistake, though it wasn't easy convincing her—"

"So it *was* a mistake." Beth lowered her gaze to the body.

"She'll see that it wasn't," he shovelled another patch of dirt out of the ground. "In time."

"How did she do it?" Beth asked gingerly, unsure if she wanted to know the answer.

"She slit her wrists." Austin grunted, shovelling another patch of dirt.

"Here," she said, taking a step forward and holding out her hand. "I should be doing this—"

"It'll be *next* winter before you get this done," he said, his face impassive. "But if you want to help you can get me some water." Beth nodded as she walked over to Austin's swag, searching for his canteen, finding it next to his backpack.

Picking it up, she glanced over her shoulder to see him still digging the grave. The rhythmic scrape of the shovel against the soil echoed in the otherwise quiet forest. As she filled the canteen with water from a nearby jug, Beth's thoughts swirled with a mix of emotions. The weight of the day pressed down on her, and she couldn't shake the feeling of responsibility for the choices she had made.

"Here." She said, approaching Austin with the canteen. He wiped sweat from his forehead with the back of his hand and nodded appreciatively before taking a deep drink.

"Thanks." He said, his voice low and tired. Beth watched him for a moment, her eyes reflecting the turmoil within her. She couldn't bring herself to voice the thoughts that circled in her mind, questions about whether the decisions she had made were truly for the best, the fear of unintended consequences, and the uncertainty of the future - the awkward future she faced within the group and the horrible position she had put Austin in.

"I just hope I've done the right thing—"

"Enough, Beth," he said, looking at her through his tired eyes. "I'm not gonna keep validating your decisions. You made it, and it's done. Own it, deal with it, stop seeking my approval—"

"I'm sorry—"

"Don't be sorry," he continued digging. "You made a decision without consulting anyone. A correct decision that has probably made our future journey easier." A sense of exhaustion reflected in her eyes as she stared at him with a blank expression.

"I'm sorry—"

"Fuck's sake, Beth. Stop apologising!" Austin said, his voice raised but not quite yelling at her. The lines on his forehead deepened and his jaw clenched. His fists gripped the shovel tighter as he stopped to look at her. "What do you think would've happened when we're inevitably being shot at, or we're split up, or something happens to the RV? She wasn't gonna make it out there. Su wouldn't've left her behind, or she would've left her behind to save MJ, and then she would've grieved all over again, probably in the wrong place at the wrong time. She can rest here, and grieve in this peaceful place before we're all thrown out into the storm again. Stop second guessing yourself, and stop assuming that everyone is angry at you. The only person angry at you right now is Su, and probably Sam, and they'll get over it—" His string of words began to shorten as he tried to speak between shovelling dirt, his breaths becoming more and more laboured as he spoke. Finally, he planted the shovel in the dirt and walked over to her, removing his gloves and throwing them onto the floor, taking a moment to catch his breath. Beth hesitated, unsure of how to respond. She couldn't quite decipher if he was reprimanding her or praising her, or perhaps a combination of the two.

"I—"

"If you say you're sorry one more fucking time—" he said, pausing to place his hand on her cheek. "You did what anyone would've done, and you did it with humility. She could've asked me, or Chantelle to help her. She asked you. She could've been left to die in the middle of an unfamiliar place surrounded by chaos, but instead you honoured her last wishes and provided her with her own means to take her own life in a place she felt *safe*, surrounded by her family. Su will come around to that." She placed her hand on his and closed her eyes as he tenderly wiped a tear from her cheek. For a moment, he gazed at her, studying the lines and structure of her face. Her sheer determination etched into her features like it had been carved there permanently. She opened her eyes, once filled with sorrow, now carried a certain vivacity. Beneath her fatigue, there was a resilience, a determination that spoke volumes about her character. Austin recognised the burdens she carried and the internal struggle she grappled with. He had thought of her as weak, and despite not vocalising them at the time, he had once shared Luis' concerns. She wasn't an extra mouth to feed, she wasn't going to be dead weight - she was going to be incredibly strong once her potential had come to light. As they stood beside the makeshift grave, the forest absorbed their shared silence. Austin continued to observe Beth, not with the eyes of someone seeking perfection, but with an appreciation for the strength he saw within her. In the midst of the uncertainty, he found a quiet admiration for the woman standing in front of him, and for the first time he thought about how truly beautiful she was.

"Austin—"

"So please," he said, removing his hand suddenly. "Stop seeking my validation, because I'm not gonna entertain it anymore." The sudden movement had snapped Beth out of her trance. As he resumed digging, she lingered for a moment, her gaze shifting between the makeshift grave, the lifeless body of Su's mother, and the surrounding woods. With a deep breath, she turned to walk away from him. The forest held an eerie stillness, absorbing the weight of her choices and her newfound decision to stop being weak, to stop caring about what others thought of her. It was time to grow up. The trail she took through the forest was a mix of familiarity and uncertainty. Her thoughts swirled in the silence, contemplating the recent events that had reshaped her perspective. Each step resonated with a determination to shed the insecurities that had clung to her. The crunch of leaves underfoot echoed in the quiet woods, a stark contrast to the rhythmic digging sounds behind her. Beth's journey through the trees became a metaphorical passage, a symbolic transition from hesitation to resolve. As she emerged into a small clearing, the sunlight filtered through the canopy above, casting scattered beams on the ground. Beth paused, absorbing the warmth on her face, as if seeking solace in the embrace of nature. The decisions made in the shadow of the trees seemed to lift off her shoulders, replaced by a newfound clarity. Taking a moment to collect herself, she acknowledged that growing up in this harsh reality meant making tough choices. It meant confronting the challenges head-on, even when faced with an unsettling weight of responsibility that loomed over her like a dark storm cloud, heavy and oppressive. It cast a shadow over her thoughts and actions, a constant reminder of the weight she carried. It was a heavy cloak, one that draped over her shoulders and seemed to pull her down towards the ground. Yet somehow, with each step, it felt a little lighter, a little more manageable, as if the journey itself was giving her strength to carry its weight. As Beth pondered her reality and the world she lived in, she couldn't help but think about the two people in her life. Ben, who was fiercely protective of her and made sure she was safe, and Austin, who pushed her to be stronger and to stop doubting herself. Ben offered her the opportunity to truly live, while Austin offered her the chance to survive. She wondered if these two paths were incompatible, or if it was possible to have both relationships in her life at once. With a steady resolve, Beth turned back towards the campsite, ready to face whatever lay ahead. The echoes of her footsteps served as a testament to the evolving strength within - a strength she would need to navigate the uncertainties of their new world.

Chapter Twenty

A s night descended, Ben, Reece, and Val geared up for a swift and silent sweep through the town. Under the cloak of dusk, they meticulously manoeuvred through the quiet streets, starting their sweep from the north side. The subtle glow of evening light painted the sidewalks as they checked buildings and alleys, ensuring that their path was clear for the following day. Landmarks and intersections became waypoints as they navigated through the town, their steps deliberate and cautious. The occasional rustle of leaves or a distant hoot of an owl served as the soundtrack to their reconnaissance. Their eyes scanned every corner, alert to any potential signs of danger. The stillness of the night heightened their senses, emphasising the importance of their mission to secure the area. As they neared downtown, their movements continued to be methodical, double-checking each block to confirm that no unforeseen obstacles lay in their path. The city remained silent around them as they continued through the streets to the south end. Val stopped in her tracks, staring up at a street lamp, a body hanging from its armature. Val read the words on the man's chest, her gaze lingering on the dangling body and the street lamp's silhouette against the darkening sky.

"Sinners—"

"They won't be here." Reece observed aloud with a blunt undertone. Val's eyes narrowed as she turned to him.

"Why do you think that?"

"This one's been here a while. They're making a point, leaving their mark along the highway," he looked around. "They'd've been and gone."

"Valid assumption," Ben nodded, but still eager to move on. "Come on, we need to continue and get back to the hotel. We need more rest for tomorrow." In the shroud of increasing darkness, they pressed on with their methodical sweep of the town. The ambient winter moonlight cast elongated shadows along the deserted streets as they maintained their vigilance. The occasional creak of a distant sign or the soft rustle of wind through the trees became the only audible companions to their cautious footsteps. It was an all-encompassing shroud of ebony, a dense and unyielding void that seemed to swallow all light and sound in its path. The night's presence loomed like a foreboding storm, filling them with a sense of trepidation and urgency as they pressed forward. Darkness shrouded the streets, enveloping everything in its inky embrace as the ambient moonlight seemed to cast elongated shadows that crept and crawled along the deserted buildings. The air was musty and stale, mingled with the scent of decay and abandon which intensified the looming black veil. Despite the potential threat that lurked in the unknown, a growing sense of confidence enveloped them. The empty streets and uneventful corners seemed to suggest that, at least for now, they were navigating through the town without immediate danger. They remained alert, yet the prevailing quietness of the night calmed their nerves. As they ventured back to the hotel, the familiar landmarks of the town unfolded before them. With each passing moment, their assessment of the situation leaned towards the belief that they were, indeed, alone in the silent night.

"He's gone," Chantelle emerged from the treeline, holding a plate of food she had prepared. "Luis is gone!"

"Thank god." Beth whispered to herself. Chantelle's silhouette moved through the dark, her figure illuminated by the glow of the campfire as she approached.

"His stuff is missin' and he's packed up his swag and everythin'!"

"I asked him to leave." Austin stared into the fire with a blank expression.

"Why?" Chantelle cried, a wave of sadness crossing her face.

"Because he was a danger to the group."

"But we *need* him!" As Chantelle protested, shadows danced across her features, making her seem almost other-worldly.

"We don't," Austin looked at her firmly. "He's done some incredibly dangerous things and he wasn't fit to be part of this group anymore—"

"When Val hears about this—"

"She knows," Austin stood, interrupting her angrily. "And if you want to know *why*, it's not my place to tell you. You can ask her when she comes back."

"I don't believe you!" Chantelle yelled. "When she comes back, she'll be furious and we'll go after him!"

"Sure Chantelle," he said, sitting back down slowly. "But she's not back yet. You should go to bed."

"But—"

"Go to bed!" Austin's command boomed with anger.

Chantelle stomped away in frustration, her emotions raw and seething. His gaze shifted from the retreating figure to Beth, who sat across from him around the fire. "I'm not in the current frame of mind to argue with a moody teenager." They sat alone, the crackling flames providing a backdrop to the heavy silence that hung between them, each grappling with their own thoughts in the aftermath of the last few days. Beth's face contorted, her eyes red and puffy from lack of sleep.

"I'm exhausted."

"Me too. It feels like we walked for weeks without incident, and then days with so much—"

"Drama?" Finishing his sentence, she flashed him a look of amusement.

"Drama is right," he smiled. "Feels like high school."

"Yes, if everyone was trying to steal your food and shoot at you," she quipped. "Oh wait, I forgot that does happen here —" The smile that had been playing on Austin's lips faded into a hard, unamused line.

"Hey, watch it," he said. "I lost a cousin in a school shooting."

"Austin—" she shook her head, her once relaxed posture now tense and rigid. "I'm sorry. It's a serious issue. I shouldn't joke about that—"

"Was."

"What?" Beth's face twisted in confusion. She looked at Austin, her eyes narrowing.

"*Was* a serious issue." He said, his face impassive. The campfire crackled, casting dancing shadows across the faces of Beth and Austin as they sat in an uncomfortable silence. She fidgeted with a twig, absentmindedly breaking it into smaller pieces. The crunching sounds seemed loud in the quiet night, punctuating the uneasy atmosphere. Austin stared into the flickering flames, his mind undoubtedly racing. As the fire continued to illuminate their faces, the shadows played tricks on the edges of their expressions. Beth took a deep breath.

"I'm sorry," she said, finally breaking the silence. "I have a very dry and dark sense of humour, and I make jokes when I'm uncomfortable. I didn't mean to offend you—"

"You didn't," he took in a low breath. "I think we're both just really tired, and I told you to stop apologising." She opened her mouth to say sorry, but instead bit her lip. In an attempt to lift the sombre atmosphere, she abruptly shifted the subject.

"Tell me a story."

"What?"

"Tell me a bedtime story," she repeated. "First thing that pops into your head."

"What are you, five?" He looked at her, perplexed, and then smiled as if reminiscing.

"Tell me," she pressed. "Something's clearly just crossed your mind." He thought for a moment, his smile reaching his eyes as they crinkled at the corners.

"Alright," Austin began, pausing and closing his eyes for a moment to remember. "We were fresh recruits, just a bunch of greenhorns trying to survive boot camp. Ben, Luis, and I were as green as they come. There was this one time during a field exercise. We were out in the middle of nowhere, and we had these MREs, do you know what MREs are?" He asked. Beth nodded and smiled, and Austin leaned forward, his body relaxing. "Anyway, so they're not exactly gourmet, but they're supposed to keep you going in the field. So Ben, believe it or not, was the prankster of the group—"

"Oh, I believe it—"

"He decides he's had enough of the MREs. I mean, who could blame him? They're like military-grade TV dinners," Austin took a moment to collect himself, his laughter filling the air and bringing a smile to Beth's face. She thought it was refreshing to see him truly happy, showing a side of himself she had yet to experience. "Anyway, he comes up with this *brilliant* plan to spice things up a bit, literally. Ben managed to sneak in a small bottle of hot sauce from the commissary. Nothing too crazy, just like... a little kick to liven up our food. The first night, we're all huddled around, eating our shitty dinners. That's when Ben pulls out the hot sauce. He starts offering a few drops to anyone willing to take the risk. Now, you've gotta understand, our taste buds were practically on life support at this point. These things are loaded with sodium and the only flavours we'd had were meat with salt, chicken with salt, pasta with salt... at this point pepper was too spicy. A tiny drop of hot sauce felt like a five-alarm fire. Luis, being the daredevil he is, takes a massive spoonful. The poor guy turns red, starts sweating, it was like watching a comedy show right there in the middle of nowhere."

"Shit." Beth's face lit up with a wide smile, her eyes squinting in delight as she envisioned the moment.

"But here's the kicker," Austin continued, his eyes crinkling at the corners as he smiled. "Luis, with tears in his eyes, looks at Ben and says, 'I bet you can't do better.' So Ben, without missing a beat, grabs the bottle and practically drowns his food in hot sauce. We thought he was insane. I mean, he practically set his own mouth on fire—"

"I'll bet," Beth's laughter was genuine, a sound she hadn't heard escape her lips in what felt like ages. "Did you get in trouble?"

"Oh yeah, it gets worse," Austin shook his head, laughing and running his hand through his hair. "So Ben blames the whole thing on Luis, tells the sergeant Luis was the one who stole the bottle and put it on his dinner without knowing." They both kept laughing, their volume increasing as they struggled to stifle themselves and avoid waking anyone up. She took a breath to hush her laughter.

"What happened to Luis?"

"He got latrine duty for a month, but because Ben had

eaten so much of it he was in the bathroom for *days*," Austin said. He released a gentle exhale, preventing himself from being overwhelmed with laughter by the memory. "And Luis had to clean it up—"

"Wait, so Ben blamed it on Luis, and Luis got the punishment and had to clean Ben's—"

"Yes!" He couldn't help but interrupt her, quickly covering his mouth to muffle his laughter. Beth's eyes crinkled at the corners as she smiled, her mouth open wide in a genuine expression of joy. Austin's head was thrown back, his chest rising and falling with each laugh, the flickering light from the fire casting shadows on their faces. Their pleasure echoed in the quiet night as they tried to hush themselves, a soothing symphony of joy and friendship. It mingled with the popping of the fire and the rustling of leaves in the winter breeze. It was a warm and contagious breeze that swept through the chilly night air, easing the tensions of their desolate life and reminding them that even amidst the challenges, there was always room for joy. As they shared the amusement, Austin couldn't help but appreciate the lighter moments that bonded them, even amidst the challenges of military life, and their life now. As the laughter died down along with the glowing embers of the fire, they took in a few shallow breaths of the cold winter evening air. Beth looked at him inquisitively.

"Where do you think he'll go?"

"Luis? Don't know. I don't know where there is to go," Austin said. The smoke from the campfire blew into his face, and he wrinkled his nose. "And right now, I don't care."

"I guess that's not our problem." Beth gazed into the crackling flames, her expression thoughtful. The cold night air nipped at their faces, but the warmth of the dwindling fire offered a comforting contrast.

"You know," Austin continued. "Luis always had this way of finding his own path, even back in the army. Sometimes, I think he finds comfort in isolation. It's like he believes he can navigate the world better on his own." Beth nodded, absorbing the insight into Luis' character. The distant hoot of an owl echoed through the night, underscoring the solitude that surrounded them.

"I wonder how someone who prefers to navigate the world alone got married in the first place," Beth said. Her hair shone in the light of the fire, casting a warm glow on her face as her head tilted slightly, her eyes fixed on the dancing flames. "Did you know his wife well?"

"Not really, none of us did," Austin admitted. "Honestly, I never really understood him. Even when we were in service together, he kept a part of himself hidden. He's fiercely protective, especially when it comes to family, but it's like there's this wall he's built around him." As the fire's glow painted shadows on Austin's face, Beth sensed the complexity of Luis' character. She leaned in, her eyes flickering with the warm light of the fire.

"Was he always like this, or only after she died?"

"He's always been like this. He's got his demons," Austin mused. "Just like the rest of us. But sometimes, facing those demons means confronting the things we'd rather leave behind." Beth sighed, her breath visible in the chilly air. The silence settled over them, interrupted only by the occasional crackle of the fire. "They don't talk too much about their pasts. Val mentioned a few things every now and then, but we don't know too much."

"Ben told me some of it," Beth said softly. "They had a brother?"

"They lived in Puerto Rico," he said. "Val blames Luis for his death. They immigrated here when they were teenagers, some distant aunt sponsored them. I don't really know too much beyond that—" Austin's voice trailed off, and he stared across the flames, meeting Beth's gaze. She offered him a light, empathetic smile. Her eyes glistened as she sought to understand his sorrow - Austin's brother in arms, someone he loved and cared about, had caused so much pain and anger. Austin's face had lit up when recounting stories of their training, memories of happier times, and she knew that casting Luis out had put a strain on Austin's emotional state. She knew he wouldn't freely admit it, but it was written across his face as clear as the winter's night sky.

"Guess we all have our journeys." Beth finally spoke, breaking the quiet introspection.

"Yeah," Austin agreed, glancing at the stars above. "Some are just rougher than others." They sat there for a while longer, enveloped by the night, sharing unspoken understanding in the camaraderie that the flickering flames and memories of their past provided.

Chapter Twenty-One

Ben, Reece, and Val left the hotel at the earliest light, heading to their first mission point - the *Shasta Regional Medical Center*. Cautiously, they made their way over the broken glass, stepping through the metal frames of the front doors. They pulled their shemaghs over their noses at the musty stench of decayed bodies and stale air as the dim morning light filtered through the shattered windows, revealing the remnants of a once-busy hospital. They slowly navigated the debris, every sense on high alert for any sign of movement or danger. The air inside was thick with an unsettling mixture of stillness and abandonment. Shafts of morning light cut through the shattered windows, stretching long shadows across the abandoned halls. The silence held thin and brittle, broken only by the creak of metal and the faint scurry of something small across the floor. Once white walls were now stained and crumbling, debris scattered across the floors while broken equipment and furniture lay in disarray, creating an atmosphere of chaos and neglect. The hospital was like a hollow shell, once bustling with life but now decaying and forgotten, swallowed by the earth and filled with the eerie remnants of a distant past. It was a place of ghosts and trapped shadows, where the darkness seeped through the cracks and the air was heavy with the weight of abandonment. The three of them moved methodically through the hospital, checking rooms for medical supplies. Drawers yanked open, cabinets examined, and the occasional murmur of disappointment passed between them when they found nothing but empty shelves.

"We should make our way to the pharmacy." Val whispered with caution, mindful of the echoing footsteps that resonated through the halls, reluctant to contribute to the already eerie atmosphere. Ben and Reece acknowledged Val's suggestion with subtle nods, their eyes scanning the signs that led the way to the pharmacy. The once familiar hospital signage, now discoloured and chipped, directed them through a labyrinth of hallways. As they approached the pharmacy section, the anticipation heightened, knowing that this part of the hospital held the potential key to their needs. They ventured further into the hospital, the gravity of their situation sinking in with every slow footstep. The once sterile and bustling facility had transformed into a haunting shell of its former self. Upon reaching the pharmacy, Val took the lead, carefully pushing one of the swinging double doors open. The squeak of hinges reverberated through the silent space, making them cringe and freeze at the unwelcome noise. Once inside, they were met with rows of shelving units, some overturned and others still standing, though not without signs of looting. Val motioned for the others to spread out and search for Su's medication, as well as anything on their lists Val had made for them - painkillers, antibiotics, gauze, bandages, and adhesive tape, anything antiseptic, thermometers, disposable gloves, sterile dressings and wound closure strips, tourniquets, haemostatic agents, antacids, oral rehydration salts, water purification tablets, N95 masks, respirators, needles, and a stethoscope.

"You don't want much." Ben whispered, smiling at her as he scanned the list once more. Val's lips formed a sly smirk as she looked over her shoulder at Ben, her eyebrows raised in challenge.

"It's shorter than your list when we we're looking for car parts back at Eatonville—" She paused, and spun her head to the sound of rattling. Reece held up a bottle, shaking it in the air.

"Valium." He grinned before placing it in his backpack.

"Great," she smiled sarcastically. "Maybe I can get a decent sleep tonight—"

"No," Ben said. "We need to stay alert."

"I was joking." Val whispered to herself, rolling her eyes as she continued searching the shelves. Ben approached a counter cluttered with scattered prescription papers and pill bottles, while Reece cautiously examined the shelves for any over-looked supplies. Val herself started rifling through cabinets behind the pharmacy counter. Their hands moved with a sense of purpose, yet every rustle of packaging and clink of glass felt intrusive in the otherwise desolate environment. Val's lips parted slightly as she leaned in close to the cabinet, her movements slow and gentle as she closed the doors with a soft click. She turned to face them, bracing her hands on the counter.

"Anything?"

"No." She whispered, an air of defeat lacing her tone. Reece's tall figure leaned against the counter next to her, his hand gently resting on the dusty surface as he nudged her arm with his.

"Don't beat yourself up. We still have a million places to check," he offered her a soft smile. "Should we check the patients rooms?"

"We could," she made a small attempt to smile back at him. The dim light from outside cast shadows on Val's determined expression. "But we won't have time to check each one. We should be fine with what we can get here and move on."

"Anyone find Su's medication?" Ben glanced over the top of a shelf at them, and they both shook their heads in reply.

"Nothing yet." Val attempted to stay positive, but the inflection in her voice betrayed her uncertainty that they would.

"Then let's move on." He said, zipping up his backpack and placing it back onto his shoulders. Their forty-minute walk to the *Vibra Hospital of Northern California* proved uneventful as they slowly traversed the main road, staying on high alert with tensions running high. The hospital loomed ahead, its once sterile and bustling halls now eerily quiet, just as the previous hospital had been.

"These hospitals, they all look so desolate." Val said, a hint of sadness sweeping through her voice as if she were mourning the loss of an old friend. Ben's gaze moved slowly, roaming from the rustling trees to two flags straining against their poles just outside the hospital entrance. The California state flag had choked itself around the rope, long forgotten. The American flag was worse - torn in two, one half wound tight, the other thrashing uselessly against the metal.

"I know we swept the town quickly last night, but I keep waiting for the other shoe to drop."

"Understandable. The last time we walked through a big town we were all nearly killed," Val said, shaking her head to push the memory of Spokane from her mind. Ben and Reece remained silent, not wanting to betray their trust in Austin that Luis would be gone by the time they got back. Sensing their tension, Val looked between the two of them. "I know Austin is making him leave before we return." They stopped in their tracks, and she continued a few steps ahead before stopping and turning to face them. Ben opened his mouth, then paused to rethink his words. Anything said in haste about Luis would be insensitive, and he knew better than to upset Val - especially now, when her composure mattered more than anything. He stepped forward slowly, his words deliberate and measured.

"And you're okay with that?"

"I've given up on him," Val shook her head heavily. "I'm done." As she pivoted to resume her path towards the hospital, a shared look of concern passed between Ben and Reece. With a resolved interest, they followed her, their steps measured and cautious as they carefully approached the entrance, glancing at each other. Val took the lead, her eyes scanning the lobby as they entered. Before them lay a gruesome scene of bodies piled together in an execution-style manner. At their feet, shell casings littered the ground near the entrance.

"What the fuck?" Reece whispered softly as Ben pressed forward, examining the corpses closely, trying to make sense of the decaying scene.

"Looks like some of them were blindfolded." He looked over at the two of them, Reece standing firm by the door while Val had slumped herself against a counter, covering her mouth with her shemagh.

"Can we just get this over with?" Val asked rhetorically. "*Please*." They continued through the dimly lit corridors, their footsteps muffled by the worn-out tiles and discarded gauze, navigating the silence that surrounded them like a shroud. She gestured suddenly towards a sign. "There, cardiology. We might find Su's meds in there."

"Okay," Ben nodded with an air of authority. "We'll split up and get this done quicker. Reece, head to the pharmacy and start searching. Val and I will go to cardiology and then we'll meet you there." Reece's figure disappeared down the dark, dingy corridor, his silhouette growing smaller until it was just a shadow against the dimly lit walls. The journey towards the cardiology wing unfolded with a cautious tread, Ben and Val carefully navigating the grim aftermath that lay before them. Their path demanded careful negotiation, as they sidestepped lifeless bodies, avoided shards of broken glass, passed remnants of medical supplies, and encountered the occasional overturned stretcher or wheelchair. They edged into the cardiology wing, scanning every surface for the medications they were after. The sterile scent of the hospital mixed with the underlying odour of decay tickled Val's nose. She sneezed, sharp and sudden, tearing through the silence. Ben flinched as the noise ricocheted off the walls, bouncing and fading into the shadows. They froze, every muscle taut, every breath held hostage by the echo. For a long moment, nothing moved - not a sound, not a whisper. The quiet pressed down on them, thick and heavy, as if the building itself were holding its breath. Ben felt his heart stutter, then hammer, each beat louder than the last, thudding against his ribs like a warning. She stayed still beside him, eyes wide, every inch of her body coiled and tense. The seconds stretched, dragging out with a cruel slowness, until every rustle of distant air, every faint creak of metal, made them startle again. It felt like an eternity before either of them dared to move, scanning and straining, listening for any hint that the sneeze had betrayed them - that someone, anyone, had heard. And all the while, the silence stretched, endless and suffocating, a void in which even the smallest sound could shatter them.

"Sorry." Val whispered, and Ben said nothing as he willed his heart to still. When they finally dared to move again, the dim light filtered through the partially closed blinds that cast eerie shadows on the walls, making the search even more challenging. They combed through drawers and cabinets with methodical care, hands moving deftly over medical supplies and paperwork, now overly cautious and every motion measured to avoid even the faintest sound. Val, with her nursing background, offered insights into the potential locations for the medication, while Ben, though unfamiliar with the intricacies of a hospital environment, proved resourceful in his determination to assist. After what felt like an eternity, Val's eyes widened as she discovered a partially stocked medication cart. Hope flickered as she identified vials and packages with Midodrine written on the side. Collecting the single packet of medication, she quickly checked the other carts to see if she could find any extra, but had no luck. The relief that washed over them was palpable, knowing that each packet represented a potential lifeline for Su, and with her health being in check she wouldn't be as much of a burden on them. They looked at each other with a glint of triumph, heading back down the corridor towards Reece.

Approaching the pharmacy with caution, the eerie silence which echoed his every step heightened Reece's senses. The automatic sliding doors, now slightly ajar, creaked softly as he pushed them open to squeeze himself through. The interior was dimly lit, with the occasional flicker of light drifting through the window casting intermittent shadows. Carefully, he surveyed the shelves, occasionally double checking the list in his hand. The air inside was stale, the scent of medicines and antiseptics lingering despite the passage of time. The quietness of the space magnified the tension, each footstep echoing through the empty aisles. He checked the labels on various boxes and bottles, his trained eyes discerning the familiar names.

"Bingo." He whispered softly, as he placed two bottles of Fludrocortisone in his backpack. He continued to sort through the shelves as Ben and Val appeared through the doorframe.

"Anything?" Val whispered.

"Two bottles, you?"

"One packet."

"I win." His lips curved upwards, revealing a mischievous

glint in his eyes. Exiting the pharmacy, the three of them moved much quicker through the hospital corridors upon their escape, finally exiting the building. Val breathed an audible sigh of relief as she stepped into the pale sunlight, the anxiety she had held deep within her core escaping through her lungs. The weight of the abandoned hospital shifted as Ben and Reece followed her out, creating a stark contrast between the outside world and the enclosed, sombre atmosphere they had just left behind.

"I think we've determined that the town is pretty empty." Ben commented, relieved to be out of the hospital, noting how strangely harrowing it was being inside such a dark and desolate place.

"So far, so good," Reece commented lightly, raising his rifle to his chest. "But we shouldn't let our guard down—"

"No," Ben looked down the road, scanning the area quickly. "But I think you two should head to the next one and I'll go find the parts we need for the RV—"

"We shouldn't split up," Val shook her head in disagreement, her gaze sweeping across the deserted streets. "We can't afford to get careless." Reece shifted uncomfortably from side to side.

"We have our orders, Ben. Austin said—"

"Austin isn't here. We shave a day off our assignment. Maybe two, if we get what we need today and head out tonight." He retorted, turning to face them. His face was a mask of indifference as his gaze darted between Reece and Val. Reece shook his head, making no attempt to hide his disappointment.

"Ben—"

"I am in charge here," Ben said dryly. "And the sooner we get back to the camp—"

"The sooner you get back to Beth?" Reece interrupted as Ben took an angry step towards him, halting in his frustration.

His jaw tensed before settling and taking a small, shallow breath.

"That is my order," he said sternly. "If you want to break radio silence to ask Austin, by all means, go right ahead. Otherwise, this is what we're doing."

"*Sir.*" Reece's response, spoken through clenched teeth, was laced with sarcasm and disdain. Val said nothing as she looked down at her boots. She shrank beneath their presence - two arguing giants casting long shadows over her as she wrestled with how to tell the one in power that he was completely, undeniably wrong. Ben pursed his lips and began walking down the street before either of them could protest further.

"Three hours, then we rally at the hotel," Ben called over his shoulder. "We leave at dusk." Reece and Val made their way south towards their next destination - the *Mercy Medical Center*, while Ben headed back into the downtown area to look for the fuel filter, a new battery, and some new lubricant. The *NAPA Auto Parts* store stood proud and solitary, its once bright blue and white facade now faded and chipped, the blue and yellow logos grimy and covered in dirt. Broken windows and shattered glass littered the ground, and the door hung off its hinges, giving the appearance of a forgotten relic. The creaking of the shop door as Ben entered cautiously only broke the eerie stillness of the abandoned street. The search for supplies felt like a scavenger hunt in a city frozen in time, but to his surprise, this first building he stepped into was a success. He collected all three items with ease, sighing gratefully that he no longer needed to search the other buildings on his list. A mixture of gasoline, oil, and rust filled the air, creating a pungent and acidic odour. A hint of mould and mildew tinged the air, as nature had slowly taken over the abandoned building, and the taste of dirt and pollution filled his mouth with each inhale. The lingering smell of gasoline gave Ben a faint taste of metal on his tongue. Reece's words hung heavily over his head - it was no secret how he felt about Beth, and his internal struggle not to disobey Austin was greatly outweighed by his need to get back to the campsite to protect her. Unsure of what Luis would do, or how he would react to his commands to leave, he was sure the man would take it out on Beth, and wasn't so sure Austin would protect her the way he could. Content with what he had discovered, Ben cautiously packed the items into his backpack. He turned to the door and froze instantly. Luis' smug grin met him, framed by the barrel of a gun aimed squarely at his head.

As they moved through the trees, the chaos behind them fell away with each careful step. Beth and Austin finally emerged into a clearing, where the ground was blanketed in soft, emerald grass that seemed to spring beneath their feet. The morning sun filtered gently through the canopy, scattering dappled light across leaves and moss, warming their skin with a quiet insistence. A gentle breeze stirred the branches overhead, carrying with it the faint scent of earth and wildflowers. The air was thick with the kind of silence that wasn't empty - it was full, almost sacred, as if the forest itself had taken a slow, deliberate breath. Birds called intermittently from hidden perches, their songs threading through the hush like a delicate melody. Beth paused, letting the scene wash over her. She could feel the tension of the past days uncoil slowly, a solemn weight settling in her chest as she took in the simple perfection of the clearing. Austin watched her silently, each aware of the fragile peace surrounding them, as if stepping here had placed them temporarily outside the reach of every danger they had just left behind. Beth's expression changed as she settled into her surroundings, looking towards Austin and offering him an awkward smile. He threw his bag onto the grass, the rattling of weapons clashed together as it hit the ground with a thud.

"Problem?" He asked.

"This is where Luis attacked me." She commented lightly, scanning the area.

"Well, he's gone now." Frustration laced Austin's tone as he refused to entertain the idea that they should move, hoping she would simply toughen up and get over it. Beth continued to look around for a moment, before almost reading his mind and shaking herself back into reality. This was where Luis had attacked her, but it would also be the place she would learn to defend herself. She turned to face him, placing her hands on her hips and cocking her head to the side.

"I guess the gym was fully booked then?" She struggled to stifle a smile. Austin grinned at her comment, thankful she chose the lighter route than to dwell on her memories of her brief encounter with Luis in the clearing.

"I figured some real life training would be more beneficial."

"So what's first, drill sergeant? You gonna make me run laps?"

"Nope," Austin shook his head, a small smile playing on his lips. "We're going straight into combat training."

"Combat training?" Beth's eyebrows shot up in surprise. "You're not serious—"

"Deadly," Austin replied with a nod, his playful demeanour taking a turn. "We need to make sure you can defend yourself properly."

"But we have guns—"

"Those're good for long range attacks, and you'll learn to shoot eventually. But if someone gets too close, having hand-to-hand skills is always useful," Austin shrugged nonchalantly. "Besides, bullets won't last forever." He raised his fists and took a defensive stance, to which she countered, placing her fists below in front of her chin and levelling her balance. "Nice placement." He commented, smiling at her.

"I took some self defence classes, once upon a time," she shrugged. "But I'm not a boxer."

"Not yet," he laughed lightly. "So you know some basic terms then."

"Vaguely—"

"Good," he narrowed his eyes coyly. "Hit me."

"Now?" She raised her eyebrows in surprise as he stood straight and lifted his hands out to the side, gesturing around the clearing.

"We don't have all day, Beth."

"Actually we kinda do, Austin." She joked as he scoffed and resumed his defensive stance. The morning sun cast long shadows, creating a dance of light and shade in the clearing. She took a deep breath, eyeing him with determination and throwing a few cautious jabs to test the water as he easily dodged them with a playful smirk on his face.

"You're holding back, Beth," he teased. "Come on, give me your best shot." Beth scowled, annoyed by his casual demeanour. She launched a more forceful punch, which Austin effortlessly sidestepped. Frustration etched on her face, she took another swing and missed again.

"I can't hit you if you keep moving—"

"Oh, sorry," he said lightly as he moved around her. "Do you think an enemy is going to stand still for you while you slap at them daintily?"

"But if I worked on my punches, wouldn't the movement come with it?" She countered lightly, mirroring his side-steps and moving around him slowly.

"Keep your guard up and maintain your balance," he raised his fists again. "Don't overthink it. Feel the movement, trust your instincts." Beth nodded, centreing her weight and raising her fists to her chin level, her left foot slightly forward. With a sharp exhale, she extended her left arm straight out, pivoting on her back foot and rotating her hips to generate some power. Her fist snapped forward, connecting with Austin's closed fist. "Good," Austin praised. "Now follow up with a right jab." Beth smoothly retracted her left arm and quickly snapped her right arm forward, ensuring her other hand remained in a protective position near her face. Though he blocked the punch, she still hit his forearm. It was muscle memory coming into play - with a few quick moves it was as if her body was willing her mind into knowing exactly what to do. She threw punch after punch, left then right, her fists cutting through the air with growing confidence.

"Like riding a bike." She said in jest, though her face remained hard and determined. The movements emphasised power and torque, requiring coordination and control she'd forgotten that she had. Instinct took over as Beth drove an upper hook past Austin's defences, her fist smashing into the base of his jaw.

"Fuck—"

"Oh shit," she took a step towards him, lowering her fists. "Austin, I'm so sorry, I just—"

"It's fine," he laughed, shifting his jaw from left to right before smiling at her. "You don't hit *that* hard."

"Yet." She smiled. His gaze swept over her before he shook his head, raising his fists again.

"Come on Rocky, I think you're ready to try some sparring."

"I guess," she said slowly, admiring Austin's strength and agility as he took his defensive stance in front of her. "I don't wanna hurt you again—"

"You didn't, and you won't," he laughed at the thought of her actually landing a punch that would hurt him. "Now come on, hit me." Beth observed his arrogance, taking a mild offence at his teasing. She placed her hands firmly in front of her face - he was either goading her into genuinely trying to hit him again, or conceivably amused at the thought of her actually hurting him. With a slow, purposeful gait she moved slowly towards him, faking a left jab and countering with a right hook to his shoulder as he moved into her fist. "Ouch." He rubbed his arm mockingly, feigning pain.

"Stop making fun of me." Beth gritted her teeth, frustration building. She unleashed a flurry of punches, aiming for Austin's chest. He dodged most of them but allowed a few to connect, exaggerating the impact.

"Is that all you got?" He laughed, continuing to tease her.

"Stop it!" Beth's competitive spirit ignited, and she landed a swift kick to Austin's side, catching him off guard. He winced, playfully clutching his ribs.

"Austin—"

"Okay, I'll admit that was a good one," he said, a grin breaking through. "You might be able to take care of yourself after all. One day."

"Yeah, one day." Beth smirked, feeling a sense of accomplishment. The sun cast a warm glow over the clearing, and the sound of their laughter echoed through the trees, momentarily pushing aside the shadows that lingered in the wake of their recent challenges. Austin threw a jab in Beth's direction and she sidestepped his punch, countering with another swift hit to his shoulder. They laughed, the physical activity proving to be a welcome distraction. Amidst their playful sparring, Austin dropped his guard and let his strength take over and carry a jab. It caught Beth on the lip, sending her stumbling to the ground. Her face twisted in pain, eyes squinting, lips pressed in a sharp grimace.

"Fuck, Beth, I didn't mean to—"

"It's fine," she cut him off with a raised hand, picking herself up off the ground. "I know you didn't mean to."

"Are you okay?" He asked, unable to shake off the guilt, his concern evident in his expression. Beth dusted herself off, offering him an assuring grin.

"I've had worse," she placed herself back into a defensive stance. "Again."

Chapter Twenty-Two

"You seemed pretty on edge back there," Reece said as he and Val walked slowly down the street. "Back at the hospital—"

"I'm fine." Val's response was sharp, but Reece continued to press.

"If you're worried about Luis—"

"I'm not," she stopped and turned to face him. "And I'm getting kinda sick of people assuming I give a shit when I've expressed how I feel about it—"

"Fine," Reece raised his hands in mock surrender. "But I'm not moving another step until you tell me what's wrong."

"You're wasting time. Ben'll be pissed if we're late—"

"Val," Reece raised his eyebrows at her. "Talk to me." With a reluctant sigh, she turned to face the direction of their next hospital.

"I'm just—" she paused, taking in a deep breath. "I didn't sign up to be a combat nurse. Walking through these hallways, seeing everything so... *desolate*. I just miss the clinic." Reece took a cautious step towards her and placed a gentle hand on her shoulder.

"We all miss before," he offered her a small smile. "But hey, silver linings. If the apocalypse hadn't happened, then we wouldn't't've met."

"Your silver lining is very thin," she said as she continued to walk down the street. "Come on, we should get moving. Let's check the pharmacy first, and then we can see if there's anything else useful in there." As they rounded the corner and the hospital came into view, Reece suddenly pulled Val behind an abandoned car, their footsteps muffled against the debris-strewn pavement. Squinting, his eyes narrowed as he observed a group of people loading medical supplies into a truck. Men with guns stood guard, creating an imposing barrier around the valuable cargo.

"We need to get back and find Ben. This isn't a situation we wanna fuck with." Reece murmured, keeping his voice low as Val nodded in agreement. Her eyes remained fixed on the armed men.

"Looks like Ben's plan to get out of here tonight might've been the best idea—"

"Give me a minute." Reece crept forward slowly.

"Reece!" Val exclaimed in a low hush as he pressed further towards the men with the truck, shielding himself with abandoned cars. Moments passed for Reece which felt like an eternity to Val, before he returned to her, grabbing her arm and gesturing back towards the downtown area.

"We have to go."

"Mountain Gate? Or that sinner group?" She questioned as they hurried down the street.

"No idea," Reece said as he hurried his walk, his grip firm on her arm. "But I don't wanna stick around to find out." They retraced their steps, moving away from the hospital with silent urgency, their senses on high alert for any signs of danger coming from any direction. The decision to regroup with Ben and reassess their strategy became the immediate priority, as the unpredictability of the situation hinted at potential risks that could jeopardise their safety, and everyone else.

Austin and Beth trudged back toward the campsite, muscles still aching from their morning training. His eyes flicked to her lips, noticing the faint swelling and the darkening bruise left by his earlier jab. Despite the sting he had caused, she carried herself with steady determination, refusing to let it slow her down. He felt a surge of admiration - her resilience, her focus, the way she refused to let a single misstep define her. For all the chaos of the morning, he couldn't help but respect her even more.

"You've got some serious guts," he said, watching her. "Not everyone would take a hit like that and jump right back in." Beth laughed lightly, a mix of self-deprecation and genuine amusement.

"Well, I figure if you're going to the effort to teach me, then I owe it to you not to be delicate—"

"You don't owe me anything," he said, his heart skipping a beat. "It's just... you surprise me sometimes, Beth."

"Is that your way of saying I'm tougher than I look?" She shot him a sidelong glance, a playful smirk tugging at her lips.

"Something like that," he replied, joining in her laughter until his expression suddenly shifted, a thoughtful look replacing his usual stoic demeanour. "You know, back when we found you, I never would've guessed I'd find myself here, in the middle of nowhere, sparring with you." Beth raised an eyebrow, a curious smile forming on her face.

"Maybe tomorrow we can find ourselves there, in the middle of nowhere, teaching me how to shoot."

"I want you to learn to fight first," he replied. "Understand the basics of defending yourself."

"Thank you for looking out for me," her eyes softened, a genuine warmth in her gaze. "But if I'm gonna protect myself, and others, I doubt knowing how to throw a punch when someone is holding a gun at my head is gonna help."

"That's true, but as I said before, ammunition won't last forever and when it comes down to it, learning how to defend yourself in a fistfight might be the difference between life and death. Don't rush it, you're adapting faster than I thought you would—"

"Adapt or die, right?" Beth shrugged modestly. "Besides, it helps having a patient teacher."

"Am I patient?"

"For the most part." Smirking lightly, she nudged his shoulder with hers as they walked.

"Fine," he relented. "We'll be here for a few days anyway while the others are in Redding. Seeing as we have nothing else to do, we can go through guns and ammunition this afternoon, and train tomorrow."

Ben's heart skipped a beat as he locked eyes with Luis, the shock of the unexpected encounter freezing him in place. The air hung heavy with tension, the silence broken only by the distant howl of the wind through the desolate streets. Luis maintained his smug expression, relishing the power he held in the moment. The gun in his hand spoke of a threat that loomed large over Ben, who was unarmed and vulnerable. The weight of the situation settled in, and Ben's mind raced to calculate his options.

"Fancy seeing you here." Luis sneered, his tone dripping with condescension. Ben cautiously raised his hands to his chest-height, a gesture of surrender.

"Just looking for supplies, Luis," he said softly. "No need

for trouble." Luis snickered menacingly, the sound sending shivers down Ben's spine.

"Supplies, huh? Getting the RV ready for a quick getaway?"

"Look," Ben's eyes darted between Luis' gaze and the end of the barrel of his gun. "It wasn't my idea to ask you to leave—"

"*Ask*? Who *asked*? I was forced to leave."

"Because of what you did," Ben said slowly. "Because of the things you've done—"

"Perhaps you're right," Luis taunted lightly, lowering his rifle while a menacing smile crept across his lips before suddenly raising it again. "But then again—"

"Val is here," Ben offered quickly. "If you want to say good-bye." Luis said nothing, his eyes gazing deep into Ben's. He suddenly turned to leave, and Ben felt a palpable tension in the air, unsure if Luis would turn and shoot him or simply walk away and vanish. "I'm gonna regret this," Ben ran his hand through his hair. "But you've wanted to kill me for days. Why are you walking away?"

"Because," Luis turned to look at him as he held the door open. "There will come a day when that girl dies, and I want you to be there to *watch*."

Val and Reece spotted Ben making his way back toward the hotel, his pace uneven, shoulders tight with whatever Luis had left behind. His focus was turned inward, gaze fixed somewhere ahead that he clearly wasn't seeing. They closed the distance without calling out. It was enough, and Ben reacted instantly. His body snapped taut, a sharp inhale cutting through the quiet as his grip on the rifle tightened hard enough to blanch his knuckles. He pivoted half a step, not fully turning, but enough. Enough that the barrel shifted with him, instinct dragging it up before his mind could catch up. For a split second, it wasn't recognition driving him, it was reflex. The kind that didn't ask questions first, but Ben stilled. Recognition hit a beat later, tension bleeding out of him in a controlled exhale as the rifle dipped back down. His hand flexed against the grip like he was forcing it to remember where it was, loosening his fingers one by one.

"Jesus." He muttered under his breath, more to himself than them. Val stepped forward carefully now, eyes flicking between his face and the rifle, reading the remnants of the reaction he was trying to bury.

"You alright?" She asked, quieter. Ben nodded once, too quick, dragging a hand over his face as if that might reset something. He nodded once, but Reece had already seen it. Not just the flinch, but the way Ben had moved before he'd thought, how close he'd been to following through on it. His gaze lingered a second longer than it should have, something tightening behind his eyes, a flicker of concern he didn't voice. That wasn't just being on edge, that was a man starting to expect the worst before it even arrived.

"You two were quick—"

"There are heavily armed men loading medical supplies into a truck," Val said. "We never made it inside. Ben looked between her and Reece, who nodded in confirmation.

"We need to leave." Ben looked back towards the auto body shop, looking for signs of Luis potentially following them. The three of them hurried back to the hotel, urgently packing their backpacks for a long walk to the gun club.

"Is that still the best idea?" Val queried.

"We have orders to go and see what we can find." Ben's face was set in a determined expression as he quickly forced his backpack onto his shoulders. Now, more than ever, he needed

firepower. Every gun, every bullet, any chance to protect them
- to protect her.

"You didn't seem concerned with orders when you wanted
to change the assignment and shorten our mission by a day."
Reece said, his tone flat. Ignoring him, Ben opened the door
and hurried down the hallway, walking outside and feeling the
sun on his face. As they stepped out into the daylight, tension
lingered in the air, fuelled by the strained conversation. Val's
concern echoed the uncertainties that clouded their mission,
but Ben's stoic determination seemed resolute. The three of
them walked briskly through the silent streets, backpacks tight
over their shoulders. Val caught up to Ben, matching his stride,
frustration evident in her voice.

"We need to consider the risks, Ben. This isn't a simple
errand. We don't know what we'll find at the gun club, and we
can't afford to underestimate the dangers out here." She said
breathlessly as she struggled to keep in time with his long
stride.

"Val," Ben sighed, pausing for a moment to address her.
"We can't afford to waste time debating. We need more ammo
and if what you said is true, these men are probably dangerous,
and we don't know if we're headed in the same direction as
them or not—"

"People don't hoard loads of supplies into trucks
surrounded by armed guards to sit at home and watch the
world burn," Reece interjected. "They're stocking up." Val's
expression changed.

"A camp nearby maybe?"

"I'm not sticking around to find out." Ben continued his
journey forward, Val and Reece stepping in line behind him.
Val's expression tightened with dissatisfaction, but she chose
not to press the matter further. As they continued their journey, the weight of uncertainty hung over them. Their fifteen-
kilometre walk was fuelled by pure adrenaline and Ben's unre-

lenting need to get back to the campsite. What normally would have taken them three and a half hours at a standard pace took them an hour less. They pressed on with determination, their pace brisk with urgency in each step. The dense forest around them blurred as they moved swiftly through the winding roads, their senses heightened and alert to any potential threat. The crunch of leaves beneath their boots and the rhythmic thud of their steps reverberated through the otherwise silent walk. They had forged a focused determination, propelling them forward at a pace that defied the norms of their routine journeys. As they covered ground at an accelerated rate, the gun club loomed closer, a beacon drawing them towards their final destination for the day. Ben stormed through the door without attempting to clear the space first. Val and Reece exchanged glances, a mix of frustration and concern adorning their faces. They looked around the mostly looted front room, noting some rifles still hung on the walls and boxes of ammunition under the counter.

"There's barely anything left—"

"Check the back room. We'll grab what we can, and we leave." Ben commanded as Reece nodded and slowly walked through the door into another room.

"We're not staying?" Val queried, maintaining her concerned expression. Ben remained silent, so she followed his orders without question, her gaze scanning the remaining firearms on the walls. Dust particles danced in the air, and the musty scent of aged weaponry lingered in the room. Rifles, stripped of their magazines, hung as silent relics on the walls, and boxes of ammunition, though sparse, hinted at what once was. Reece had disappeared into the back room, his footsteps muffled by the worn-out carpet. The air grew heavy with anticipation as Ben and Val waited, their senses on high alert. The quiet murmurs of the forest outside seemed to encroach upon the stillness of the gun club, adding an eerie backdrop to their goal. Val's fingers traced over the barrels of the remaining rifles, assessing their condition. As the minutes passed, the three of them silently loaded their spare gun bags with every rifle and box of ammunition they could find.

"Anything?" Ben addressed them once Reece had appeared from the back room, who held up a packed gun bag and shook it gently. Ben nodded in acknowledgement. "Good. We're leaving—"

"That's not a good idea," Reece placed the gun bag on the counter. "It's another four hours on foot." Val stepped forward, placing her bag on the counter.

"We're exhausted—"

"We can make it in three." Ben declared determinedly.

"No, we can't," Reece protested. "It's all uphill and none of us have had a break, never mind the extra weight we're gonna be carrying." Val slumped her shoulders forward.

"Or anything to eat—"

"Then eat a fucking bran bar," Ben threw up his arms. "I'm going. Follow me, or don't." Reece slammed his palm on the counter, startling Val.

"You'd leave us here to get back to the campsite two days earlier than planned?"

"Follow me, or don't," Ben repeated darkly. "But I'm leaving... *now*." Throwing a gun bag over his shoulder and finding his balance between the new-found weight of it along with his backpack, he headed for the door and swung it open, walking outside. It hit the external wall with a loud thud. Val grabbed her gun bag, throwing it over her shoulder and adjusting to the weight.

"I've never seen him like this."

"He's being irrational," Reece observed, doing the same. "But we should stick together."

"If you insist." She said dryly, both mental and physical fatigue evident in her voice. Reece walked over to her and held out his hand.

"Make sure you eat a fucking bran bar." He said in jest, handing one to her while she awkwardly laughed with exhaustion as they walked out the door.

Chapter Twenty-Three

Beth lay prone on the forest floor, the rifle snug beneath her shoulder, her eyes focused through the scope. Austin had meant to keep the afternoon to theory - teaching her about guns without putting any of it into practice - but the moment he said he was heading out to hunt for dinner, Beth insisted on joining him. Aware that her inexperience might spook their potential prey and that hunting would likely take longer, Austin accepted the added challenge. He recognised the importance of Beth acquiring shooting skills, and he had come to realise that he relished having her in his company, a revelation that had hit him like a freight train. Laying side by side, he pressed close to her, whispering instructions into her ear to avoid alerting any nearby animals. The closeness of his body radiated warmth, his breath brushing lightly against her neck as he spoke. A trail of pins and needles followed in its wake, spreading down her neck and into her arm.

"Alright, easy now," he murmured, steadying her nerves. "When you're ready to take the shot, gently squeeze the trigger. No sudden movements."

"Okay." Beth whispered, not daring to divert her gaze. The

surrounding forest seemed to hold its breath in anticipation. In the distance, a deer grazed peacefully, unaware of the two hunters silently watching.

"Deep breath, take your time," Austin instructed. "When you're steady, squeeze... *slowly*." Beth followed his guidance, inhaling slowly, exhaling even slower. The tension in the air was palpable as she focused on the target. After a moment that felt like an eternity, she squeezed the trigger. The shot echoed through the forest, breaking the tranquil silence as the deer dropped, its swift falling movement a testament to the power of the gunshot. Austin grinned, impressed by Beth's first attempt.

"I did it."

"You did it." He whispered, offering her a soft congratulatory pat on the middle of her back.

"It feels like cheating," she whispered back softly. "Having the rifle still on the ground probably makes it easier."

"You need to start somewhere." His hand lingered, moving slightly to her lower back as he looked at her. They held each other's gaze, the quiet triumph settling between them. Adrenaline still hummed between them, sharpened by the closeness and the win they'd just shared. Their breaths mingled in the crisp air, and the sounds of the forest seemed to fade into the background. Austin's hand settled at the small of her back, the warmth of his touch seeping through the fabric. She felt it immediately - steady, grounding, and impossible to ignore. The air shifted. Not silent, not still, just different. Her gaze lifted to his, and for a moment, neither of them moved. Something held there, unspoken but undeniable, pulling tighter with each passing second.

"Austin—" Beth whispered. She became acutely aware of how close he was, of the space between them shrinking without either of them meaning to close it. Their breaths mingled, and her pulse quickened. Then, just as the moment tipped, just as it threatened to become something more, Austin pulled back.

"Let's get this deer back to camp." He said suddenly, clearing his throat, his eyes briefly avoiding hers. The moment broke, fragile as it was, and they both turned away from it. By the time they reached the fallen deer, the silence between them had shifted, the tension still there but left unspoken. Beth slowed, her gaze settling on the animal. A flicker of pride stirred first, then came the weight of it. It was quieter, heavier, settling somewhere deeper in her chest. This was what survival looked like. Not clean, nor simple. And beneath it all, something else lingered - confusion, sharp and unresolved, from the moment they'd just stepped away from too quickly. It had come and gone in a breath, leaving her no space to make sense of it.

In the dim interior of the RV, Su and Sam leaned close, their voices barely above a whisper, careful not to wake MJ. Su's eyes flicked toward the door, her fingers worrying the edge of her jacket, while Sam leaned in, his expression set with quiet determination.

"*Iri wa-seo nae yeop-e an-ja.*" Su said softly, patting the seat next to her on the bench.

"English, please *nuna*," Sam insisted, sitting next to her. "I don't speak Korean as good as you." Su sighed as she shook her head, closing her eyes.

"We need to talk about what happened," she began, her voice tinged with worry. "I know you want to stay away from the group, but we can't take care of ourselves."

"After what *Beth* did," he paused and sighed, running a hand through his thick hair. "It's not a good idea—"

"Where does that leave us? We cannot survive on our own out here," Su shook her head, her lips pressing into a thin line. "We need them just as much as they need the RV. And I need Val in case I get sick again—"

"I can take care of you," Sam reached out to gently grasp his sister's hand. "We'll find a way to make it on our own. I'll find the medication. I'll protect you and MJ—"

"So-min," Su's eyes softened as she looked at him. "I appreciate your determination, but my answer is no." His expression faltered slightly, a hint of frustration flickering across his features.

"What if one day they just decide one of us isn't worth the trouble anymore? What happens when MJ can't keep up, or you run out of your meds again?" Sam said angrily, standing as MJ stirred slightly in her sleep.

"Keep your voice down," she hissed at him. "I am just as angry as you are, but they didn't kill *eomma*. She asked for Beth's help, and she took her to the lake." Su chewed on her lower lip, her brow furrowing with uncertainty. Sam scoffed bitterly.

"Or so she says—"

"Don't be nasty. Beth is not a murderer. Did you see signs of struggle? She didn't kill *eomma*, she honoured her final wishes, of that I am certain. I believe what she says happened." Su stared into his eyes, tears forming slowly as she refrained from blinking them away. Sam sighed, his shoulders slumping in defeat.

"I know you wouldn't put MJ in danger. I know that," he said quietly. "So if you think this is what's best for you both, then... I trust you. I do. But I don't trust them. And I don't get how you can be okay with this—"

"Do not think I am weak because I go along with this," Su snapped. "I don't like any of it. But they keep us alive. I'm not stupid enough to bite the hands that feed us—"

"At least," he smirked coldly. "Not yet." Su stayed silent,

studying her brother. The once-chubby, fumbling boy had grown into a hardened teenager. His eyes held something cold and unfeeling, something that she couldn't read. He had been so docile the last few months, still so innocent, but the last few days had awakened a new temper, one that unsettled her. If this was what just a few days glimpsed of the world outside their cocoon had done, she shivered at what full exposure might do to him.

Beth let out a frustrated low scream as she emerged from the water, the high afternoon sun beamed down on her face as she closed her eyes and ran her hands over her hair. She thought about Austin leaning into her while they hunted deer. She thought about Ben wrapping his arms around her when they were asleep. She thought about the way Ben had continued to protect her while Austin had offered to teach her how to protect herself. A mix of emotions and confusion raced through her mind as she rubbed her temples with her fingers. The complexities of their dynamics weighed on her, creating a tangled web of feelings that seemed to grow more intricate with each passing second. The heat of the sun provided no solace, and the internal turmoil mirrored the intensity of the light bearing down on her. Beth took a deep breath, attempting to clear her mind. Still submerged in the water, she felt a mix of vulnerability and strength, as if the lake offered a refuge from the complex emotions stirring within her. The ripples around her seemed to mirror the turbulence in her mind, and she let herself float, temporarily detached from the uncertainties awaiting her on the shore. With each gentle sway of the water, Beth allowed herself a moment of solitude, contemplating the intricacies of their survival and the relationships entwined in this incredibly complicated situation she had found herself in. Yet, as she remained immersed, a determination grew within her, a resolve to navigate the emotional currents that threatened to pull her under. As she approached the bank, Austin stopped at the base of the hiking trail, holding his blood-stained clothes from skinning the deer. She waded out of the water without hesitation, too focused to care that she was naked, snatching her clothes and dressing quickly. He looked down at the bundle in his hands, fumbling over his words as he spoke quickly.

"I'm sorry. I didn't mean to—, I came to find you to help skin the deer but I didn't know where you'd gone. I didn't know you were here—"

"It's fine." She remarked coldly, walking past him. He turned to look at her as she walked up the path.

"Are you angry at me?"

"No," she whisked around, releasing a slow breath. "No I'm not."

"Then why are you being so cold?"

"I'm not!" Her eyes narrowed and her jaw clenched as she glared at him, lines of frustration etched on her forehead and lips pulled taut in anger.

"Beth," he stepped forward and grabbed her arm. "What's wrong with you?"

"I'm not angry at you," she ripped her arm from his grip, checking her tone and lowering her voice. "I'm angry at myself." Austin furrowed his brow and shook his head.

"Ben."

"Ben." His name sounded cold rolling off Beth's tongue.

"I'm sorry for before," he stared at her, clenching his jaw. "I know how he feels and I shouldn't've done that—"

"*We* shouldn't've done that. This isn't just on you," she bit her lip hard, feeling the split from where he had hit her earlier. "And if you know how he feels then that's great because I don't even think he does."

"And how do *you* feel?" Austin asked her bluntly, and the question wiped the anger from her face, replacing it with concern.

"Confused." She admitted after a brief moment.

"Why?"

"Because you both treat me very differently, and I'm unsure how I feel about that." She swallowed the lump that had formed in her throat. Studying the lines on her face, Austin took a small step closer to her.

"And that makes you confused?"

"I don't like feeling unsure of what I want," she confessed. "This entire world is filled with uncertainty. I just thought I'd at least be able to keep my own mind in check." Beth observed Austin as he rubbed his forehead hard, scrunching up his eyes. She watched him cautiously, noting the way his face contorted when he was frustrated. The lines etched on his forehead spoke of the burdens he carried, and the weariness seemed to seep through the cracks in his determined facade. Concern crept into her expression as she moved closer. "Are you okay?" She asked gently.

"Just a headache." Austin sighed, releasing the tension that had built up within him. His gaze met hers as they locked eyes again, memories from earlier flooding both of their minds as her breath shortened and his jaw clenched.

"The old me," Beth said, stepping closer. "The me *before* all this, I would've needed Ben to survive. Needed someone to take care of me. The person I'm becoming, the person I want to become, needs *you* to teach me how to take care of myself." Their eyes met, and the air between them seemed to thrum. The tension was sharp, almost tangible, pulling them together. Austin dropped the bloody clothes and stepped forward suddenly. Beth's heart raced as he closed the space between them, his hands finding her waist and the back of her neck. Their lips met in a hard, lingering kiss, a moment suspended in time. She wrapped one arm around his neck, the other threading into his hair, and he held her close, grounding them both. The world faded. Nothing existed but the heat, the pull, the connection. Finally, Beth drew a deep breath and gently pulled back, letting space return to the moment.

"We can't do this." She murmured, her voice a mix of regret and arousal. Her hands lingered on his chest, a bitter-sweet reminder of the oversight that had briefly taken hold.

"He's my best friend." He said, letting her go gently, a conflicted expression in his eyes.

"This never happened." She swallowed hard, still tasting him on her lips. The split had reopened, sharp and metallic, mingling with a sour sting of regret. Mercifully, the taste of him began to fade.

"You're right." He conceded, still holding her in his arms. They quickly separated, the tension hanging between them as he stepped back, wiping his bottom lip with his thumb and collecting his clothes to be washed in the lake. She watched him for a moment, her entire being pulsed with anxiety and regret mixed with longing and titillation. She raised her eyes upward before taking in a deep breath and continuing back up the hill.

The afternoon light drifted across the campsite, soft and warm, but it did nothing to ease the weight pressing between Austin and Beth. The smell of cooking meat curled through the air, a mundane comfort that only made the silence sharper. Beth lingered at the edge of the clearing, her feet rooted to the ground. Her heart thudded in her chest as she watched him tend the fire, his back rigid, movements precise. She wanted to speak, to break the tension, but each step forward felt heavier than the last, as if the space between them had grown thicker throughout the day. Finally, she took a tentative step, then another, hands twitching at her sides. Every nerve screamed caution, every instinct told her to stop, but something deeper, stubborn and unrelenting pushed her closer.

"Hey," she said softly, not wanting Chantelle to overhear their conversation from the seclusion of her swag. "Can we just... give ourselves some space? Maybe stay out of each other's way, let the dust settle—"

"Sounds like a good idea." He stood, keeping his distance from her.

"They won't be back for a few days and I'd like to make sure we take that time to get over—" she gestured between the two of them with her hands. "Whatever *this* is."

"Good idea." He repeated, his tone flat, processing the weight of the complication. He had pressed Ben to make sure that she wouldn't be an impediment for him, to make sure she wouldn't cloud his judgement or make him disobey his duties, only to realise he had done exactly the same thing.

"Right," she whispered, eyes flicking toward the treeline. "I'm gonna go for a walk. Clear my head." She rested a light hand on his arm and he flinched, recoiling slightly.

"Beth—"

"I'm sorry." Her hand jerked away, and she vanished into the shadows of the woods, leaving him frozen.

"Beth, wait—" he took a hesitant step after her, then froze. Voices carried from the road, familiar and sharp, pulling him back before he could move any further. He turned to see Ben, then Reece, and finally Val making their way back into the campsite. "What happened? What're you doing here?"

"Give us a minute to catch our breath." Val said, gasping for air and clearly exhausted. She threw her gun bag to the ground and removed her backpack quickly, letting it go with a heavy thud as it hit the ground.

"Did something happen?" Austin pressed.

"There were men loading medical supplies into a truck,"

Reece said, lowering his bags gently to the ground. "Hoarding them, more accurately."

"Where?"

"South-west side of Redding. We didn't get a chance to get to the biggest hospital." Val's dark hair was disheveled and tangled, a look of determination and exhaustion in her eyes as she spoke.

"I listened to some of them talking," Reece continued. "They were talking about hitting Anderson next, then Cottonwood, and then Red Bluff—"

"They're headed south," Austin interjected as Reece nodded in response. "How many were there?" Austin directed his question to Ben, who was shaken out of his trance.

"Too many," Val responded. "And heavily armed." Austin maintained his gaze towards Ben.

"Ben?"

"I didn't see them." He responded flatly, finally removing his gun bag and taking off his backpack, dropping both to the ground. "I got the parts for the RV, we went to the gun club, and got the hell out of there." Their breathing slowly evened out, exhaustion etched into every line of their faces.

"You weren't together?" Austin asked angrily. "I told you to stick together—"

"I made the decision to separate to get the mission done faster," Ben looked at him with a blank expression. "I made a calculated deduction that there was no risk in the area after our initial sweep and thought it best to minimise our time there by splitting up and completing two objectives within the same timeframe." Ben's jaw muscles bulged as he clenched his teeth together, his expression tense and determined. Austin took a step forward.

"Clearly, you were wrong—"

"Where is she?" Ben's eyes were cold and blank. He wavered where he stood, catching his footing. Austin took another step forward to steady him, catching his arm.

"You're exhausted. You should rest—"

"*Where is she?*" He repeated, his voice rising. Austin let go of him and gestured into the trees, as Ben took off after her. Val's eyes narrowed as she took in the scene before her, her brow furrowed in deep thought. She watched Ben as he stormed off, his body language tense and his expression filled with exhaustion.

"Something happened when we were separated."

"What?" Austin whisked around to face her.

"I don't know," she shrugged. "Something."

"We found him idly walking back towards the hotel," Reece said. "We startled him when we came up beside him. If he'd taken any longer to realise it was just us, he might've blown my head clean off." Val swallowed hard. Austin nodded, looking towards the treeline where his friend had disappeared into the dusk light.

"Beth." With relief flooding through his body, Ben quickly made his way to her in the grassy clearing. He had shown determination and energy on his trek to the campsite, but now he approached her with a sense of fire and resolution, grateful that she was unharmed.

"What're you doing back here?" She exclaimed, facing him, her face mixed with surprise and guilt. With a swift motion, he enveloped her in a tight embrace, his scent carrying the traces of a diligent journey, while the undeniable potency of his pheromones permeated her senses like a searing brand. He had spent the entire day repeating Luis' words over and over, imagining her dead in his arms, his exhaustion and weariness weighing heavily on him all day. He replayed the words in his head like a broken record - there will come a day when that girl dies, and I want you to be there to watch. He recoiled at the thought, embracing her tighter. The warmth of his body enveloped her, a reassuring shield against the harsh realities of their existence. The subtle rise and fall of his chest, synchronised with the rhythmic beats of her own heart, created a soothing cadence that temporarily silenced the cacophony of fears echoing in her mind. In that moment, the worries of survival, the weight of loss, and the uncertainty of the future dissolved into the background. Ben's arms provided a sanctuary, a haven where vulnerability and strength coexisted. His heartbeat was steady and strong, transmitted a silent promise - a promise that, for this fleeting interlude, she was shielded from the harshness of their world. As they lingered in the embrace, time seemed to stretch and contract, suspended in the delicate balance of shared comfort. The subtle touch of his fingers against her back carried a tenderness that spoke volumes without uttering a word. The reality of their journey, the perils that awaited, momentarily dissipated, leaving only the present moment, wrapped in the embrace of a friend who had become a pillar of support in the face of adversity.

"Beth," he said again softly, pulling back from her and placing a gentle hand on her face. "You're okay."

"Of course I'm okay, why wouldn't I—" Her words were cut short as his lips met hers in a sudden, light kiss. The brush of his lips against hers was feather-light but sent shivers down her spine. The warmth of his hand cupping her face, his thumb gently stroking her cheek, caused her heart to skip a beat. It was a moment of gentle violence, of tectonic plates shifting in perfect sync, of two bodies finally coming together in a collision that was both soft and electric, shattering the surface tension of their individual existences. She felt his lips leave hers suddenly, opening her eyes just in time to see his strong frame crumble and hit the ground with a jarring thud.

Chapter Twenty-Four

B en shot upright, a sudden realisation hammering through his mind. He startled Val, who was pressed close with her stethoscope, timing his heartbeats on her watch. His hand went to his head as a sharp ache flared from the motion, echoing the shock in his chest.

"How did I get here?"

"Reece and Austin carried you here. Lay down," Val's lips barely moved as she spoke, her expression stoic and unflinching. Luis' words played over and over again in his throbbing head. "What?" Val's dark eyebrows were knitted together tightly, her forehead creased in confusion as she stared at Ben. He stared at the top of his swag with no trace of emotion or understanding evident in his expression.

"What?—"

"What does that mean?" Packing her supplies back into her small first aid bag, her eyes narrowed slightly as she looked at Ben. He thought for a moment as she eyeballed him closely, considering that he had said the words aloud unintentionally.

"What does what mean?"

"Never mind," she shook her head, "You're dehydrated and

exhausted. You need rest. What's the last thing you remember?"

"Leaving the gun club," he swallowed hard, closing his eyes. "Can you get Austin please?" He asked softly as she placed a gentle hand on his arm and stood, fetching his friend for him.

"Hey brother," Austin knelt down next to the swag and smiled. "You had us worried for a minute. How're you feeling?" Ben tried hastily to sit up, struggling to prop himself up on his elbow.

"Luis—"

"Whoa, take it easy. You're exhausted and you hit your head pretty hard," Austin laid a soft hand on his arm, crouching lower at Ben's side. "Luis is gone. I made sure of it—"

"No, Austin," Ben said, breathing a resentful sigh. "Luis was in Redding. He held me at gunpoint at the auto shop." Austin sat back suddenly, tension rising in his body.

"What? Why didn't you say something before?" He asked, and Ben thought for a moment, barely remembering the last stretch of their trek from the gun club, never mind the events of the evening after they had returned.

"He's no threat," Ben shook his head, still feeling the pain as if a metal bat had repeatedly smacked his forehead. "He's gone for good. Well, he's gone for now at least."

"How do you know?" Austin's face was serene, his eyebrows slightly raised in curiosity as he looked at Ben.

"Trust me, I know."

"What happened?"

"He said something to me," Ben paused, the words playing over again and again. "And it just—"

"Got to you," Austin finished the sentence as Ben nodded in silence. "Did it have anything to do with her?" Austin gestured towards Beth who was sitting at the campfire. Ben maintained his silence. "Right. Well, get some rest—"

"No," Ben sat up. "We need to get this RV up and running—"

"*No*, you need rest," Austin's face contorted with authority. "You're no good to anyone today. Rest, and we can get started tomorrow. That's an order."

The following days blurred together in a surreal haze. They cleaned and tidied the campsite, collected belongings, and sorted through the new guns and medications. Su started to feel better as her medicine began to take effect again. Austin took to teaching Sam how to hunt and skin deer, though Sam met each lesson with reluctance and barely disguised disdain. Ben worked quietly on the RV, speaking little as he focused on fixing it. Beth helped Val and Chantelle organise supplies, making sure every backpack had a steady mix of food, medication, blankets, and clothing - everything anyone might need if they got separated. After careful consideration from Austin, with input from Reece and little from Ben, the group had decided to head inland, away from the highway that ran south.

"Why are we strayin' from the original plan? Better the devil you know than the devil you don't, right?" Chantelle quipped, her drawl thick and mocking.

"Not this devil." Val's tone was low, sharp, and cautious as she stared into the campfire. Chantelle knew better than to push - that tone always made her shut up. Beth and Ben sat next to one another, barely speaking a word to each other for days as they had kept their distance.

"Are you feeling okay?" She whispered finally, breaking the long silence between them. Ben's shoulders slumped and his head hung low as he whispered back to Beth, looking defeated and tired.

"I'm fine."

"Don't lie to me," she leaned in. "If it's about the other night—"

"I don't remember," he interrupted dismissively. "Did I say something?" Beth stared at the crackling flames, refusing to meet anyone's gaze as she concealed her disappointment behind a mask of indifference.

"No—"

"I'm sorry, I don't mean to be rude," he sighed. "I just don't remember much past leaving the gun club." A pang of anxiety washed over her as she thought about their embrace, the way he hugged her tightly as if he needed to make sure she never left his arms, and the way it had ended.

"You must've been exhausted—"

"We leave at first light." Austin announced, noticing the look on her face as she and Ben spoke, before retiring to his swag. Beth, resting a gentle hand on Ben's forearm, leaned into him. He stood up and walked to his swag, leaving her around the campfire to be gawked at by Reece, Val and Chantelle, before retiring to bed herself.

The drive down the mountainside was bumpy at best. Eight people crammed into an RV meant for three, each gripping whatever they could to avoid cracking their skulls on a sudden jolt. Reece sat at the wheel, carefully navigating the twisted gravel roads, unsure how the tyres would hold after sitting idle for so long. The suspension groaned with every bump, turning each pothole into a miniature earthquake inside the compact space. Occasional glances were exchanged among the passengers, silent acknowledgments of shared discomfort. Beth, squeezed between Val and Chantelle, tried to make light of the situation, though even she couldn't mask the tension. Despite the chaos, the RV remained their lifeline, carrying them toward an uncertain future. Outside the windows, the scenery shifted from dense forest to open roads as they descended, leaving the mountains' isolation behind. They'd opted to avoid the main highway down to Los Angeles, heading inland toward San Diego, through Reno along Highway 395, east of Yosemite and the Sierra National Forest. At least, that was the plan. Somewhere south of Reno, after two days of slow, careful driving, a tyre finally blew. The RV lurched, throwing its passengers against one another. Su clutched her daughter tightly as they rolled along the double bed at the rear. Val grabbed the bench, steadying herself and catching Chantelle as the RV tilted left and then right. Beth hit the floor with a resounding thud, having stood moments before to secure a partially open gun bag filled with sharp weapons. She had barely managed to keep it from sliding onto anyone else, avoiding further injury amidst the chaos.

"Is everyone okay?" Austin called back, who had taken over driving for the morning. Subtle groans filled the cramped RV as Beth rolled onto her side, pain flaring in her lower back where she'd injured it during the fall near Shasta Lake and Mountain Gate. Ben offered her a cautious hand, helping her to her feet. They both froze, eyes fixed on a machete that had slipped from the gun bag, embedding itself into the floor just inches from where she'd been laying.

"Thank you." She said lightly, swallowing hard and brushing herself off. He nodded in silence, then pushed past her to Austin who sat in the passenger seat, his hand still propped on the dashboard to steady himself. Reece's knuckles were white from gripping the wheel, and he finally let go and flexed his fingers.

"That lasted long." Ben quipped as he rested his hands on the back of the driver's seat. Austin turned to face him, reading his friends' thoughts.

"Not your fault," Austin said. "Can't help a blown tyre."

"I could've—"

"Could've *what*?" Reece interrupted him. "Carried a brand new set all the way back from Redding along with everything else while we were dehydrated and exhausted?" Ben and Reece's clenched jaws and narrowed eyes spoke volumes, the air between them practically crackling.

"Enough," Austin raised a dismissive hand. "I'll get the spare."

"There isn't one," Sam observed solemnly. "We already used it driving up to the campground in the first place." Val stood, grabbing her belongings.

"Perfect—"

"What're you doing?" Austin queried in protest.

"We're not staying in town, stranded in the middle of the road," Val said, refusing to meet his gaze. "Nothing good's ever happened to us in bigger cities."

"She's right." Ben agreed, gesturing for Austin and Reece to follow him outside. The men obliged, leaving the rest to collect themselves inside. The three men looked around, noting the Quality Inn off to the right down a side street.

"Too risky," Austin objected, looking further south down the highway and pulling his map from his pocket. "We'll walk down the 88 for a bit. There's bound to be a farm or ranch we can hold up in."

"We can come back and fix the tyre tomorrow." Reece suggested to Ben, his tone measured and softer than before. As they walked cautiously down the highway, they were silent in their frustration at the once again immobile RV. Reece, as usual, took the rear, observing their once small group now having extra members between Austin taking point at the front, and Ben safeguarding the middle of the line. As they crossed the East Fork Carson River, Austin observed a sign directing his gaze to their right, noting a larger white structure in the distance.

"Historic Dangberg Ranch." Chantelle read aloud as she caught up to him.

"We'll check it out." He observed dryly, taking the lead and walking steadily along the gravel driveway to the ranch house, his eyes scanning for signs of movement through the windows and inside the barn. They stepped inside cautiously, Austin's rifle raised as he swept behind structures and peered into small rooms. Makeshift tabletops rested atop shortened barrels, forming an improvised outdoor dining area. Fairy lights hung between poles, swaying gently in the breeze. At the back, he approached a small room and eased the door open, taking in the abandoned wedding decorations within. The delicate arrangements and faded ribbons felt almost out of place, reminders of a celebration long past in a space that now held only quiet and unease.

"Clear." Reece called from the side of the building, emerging from a stable.

"Clear." Ben echoed, emerging from the other side of the large barn. Austin turned to face the rest of the group.

"Stay here so we can clear the house." He nodded to Ben and Reece, who followed him back outside. They approached the house slowly, eyes scanning windows and doors, rifles at the ready.

"I'll go in front, Reece to the back door," he gestured behind the rear of the house. "Ben, cover the exterior and check through the side windows."

"Copy." Reece and Ben had replied in unison, raising their rifles and moving silently around the structure. Austin slowly opened the door, the creaking leaving an ominous echo through the front room. He carefully scanned the space, noting the furniture and decor that had seemingly transported him back in time. Dust adorned the surfaces like a grey blanket, and he pulled his shemagh over his face to unsuccessfully stifle a sneeze. Reece paused at the back door as the sneeze echoed through the house, tensing his body and holding his breath to listen for further noise. The stillness of the abandoned house seemed to magnify every sound, and the unexpected disturbance set all three men on edge. After a moment of strained silence, Reece relaxed slightly, continuing to press further into the kitchen. Ben carefully scanned the rooms, struggling to see inside from the dust that had built up on the windows. The muted light filtering through the grime created an otherworldly atmosphere. He moved cautiously, his eyes darting from corner to corner, unsure of what he might find. The air felt heavy with the weight of abandonment, and the silence was broken only by the faint sounds of footsteps inside on the creaky floorboards. As Reece entered what appeared to be a living room, he met Austin's gaze who nodded at him apologetically for the sneeze. Startled by a low groan, both men pointed at the direction from which it had come, a small hallway with stairs leading upward. Austin pressed forward a few steps before being met by the barrel end of a rifle at the other end of the hallway.

"Not another step." The deep voice spoke gently. Austin stood firm, keeping his rifle raised towards the stairs but otherwise unmoving. Reece stepped towards Austin cautiously, while Austin looked over at him as his expression changed. Reece gave him an inquisitive look before lowering his rifle slowly as he felt the blade of a pocket knife press into his neck.

"Drop it." Another low voice requested. He lowered his rifle slowly and obediently as Austin backed into the room, the man from the hallway pressed forward slightly. Reece could see the end of the barrel at the doorway but not the man himself. Austin and Reece scanned the room for potential escape routes, but the clutter of antique furniture and strewn decor proved too many hazards for them to make a quick exit. Ben entered the rear door where Reece had moments earlier. He noticed the dust-covered furniture, frozen in time, listening to the threatening commands of unfamiliar voices coming from the other room. A forgotten family portrait hung crookedly on the wall, the faces of those captured in the frame staring into a past that had been abruptly forgotten. He couldn't help but wonder about the lives that had once thrived within the walls. Continuing through the kitchen, empty cans and food wrappers littered the counters, as he pressed further into the lounge room. The remnants of a once-lived-in space now seemed like relics of a bygone era. The eerie stillness of the house made Ben acutely aware of the solitude that surrounded them outside, amplifying the situation in front of him.

"Like you said," he pressed the rifle into the back of the man's skull. "Drop it." The man maintained his position with the knife at Reece's neck. Austin moved further into the room as the man from the hallway appeared at the door, directing both Austin and himself further into the cramped space.

Beth lowered herself onto the small bench beside Su, careful not to crowd her. Su's eyes were fixed on MJ, whispering something quickly into her daughter's ear. The motion was gentle, protective, but there was a distance in Su's posture that made Beth hesitate. She wanted to say something, to bridge the quiet that had settled between them over the past days, but the words caught in her throat. MJ nodded and darted inside the barn, calling for Sam and Chantelle, leaving the two women alone in the stillness. Beth shifted slightly, hands resting tensely on her knees, noticing the tight line of Su's shoulders. For a moment, it felt as though the air between them was thick enough to choke on, full of unsaid apologies, judgements, and the invisible weight of responsibility each carried. Beth's gaze flicked away, studying the horizon rather than meeting Su's eyes. She could feel the strain, a subtle push and pull, as though every thought and gesture might tip their fragile balance. Su's silence was steady, controlled, but it carried an edge, a reminder that trust had to be earned in increments.

"I am truly sorry about your mother." Beth offered finally, breaking the silence between them. Su turned her gaze towards Beth, her eyes reflecting a complex mix of emotions. The lines on her face told stories of pain and loss, etched deeply in the canvas of grief. She took a deep breath, trying to compose herself before responding.

"I know you did what you thought was right, but it's hard for me to understand right now. Everything happened so fast. My husband, my sister, and then—" Su paused, swallowing the lump which had formed in her throat, her voice carrying the weight of sorrow. "I haven't had the chance to process it all."

"I can't imagine what you're going through," Beth nodded empathetically, her eyes fixed on Su's face. "Losing so many loved ones in such a short time... it's unimaginable." Su's gaze remained distant, focused on a point far beyond the visible horizon. "If we're gonna survive, we need to have each other's backs. I just wanted to say I'm sorry, and I won't—"

"Please, Beth. Stop," Su sighed. "I understand that you thought it was the only option for my mother. I'm not saying I won't ever forgive you. But right now, the pain is too fresh. I need time."

"Do you want me to leave you alone?"

"No." Su maintained her gaze on the horizon. A heavy silence settled between them, broken only by the distant sounds of the others inside the barn. Beth swallowed hard, the weight of Su's words sinking in. She respected Su's need for time and understood that forgiveness might be a distant destination in the grieving process. They sat together in shared sorrow, surrounded by the echoes of loss that lingered in the air.

Chapter Twenty-Five

The five men froze, locked in place as if a single wrong move would set everything off. No one spoke, no one dared to move. Austin didn't take his eyes off Reece, his hands raised just enough to show he wasn't reaching, but not low enough to seem compliant. Reece mirrored him perfectly, their stances almost identical, like reflections caught in opposing glass. Between them, the air felt tight, ready to snap. In front of Austin, the man from the hallway kept his weapon trained on him, unwavering. The other stood behind Reece, the blade of his knife pressed firm against his throat, just enough to remind him how quickly things could end. Ben stayed where he was, silent and steady, his rifle pressed to the back of the man's head. He didn't shift, didn't blink. The slightest tremor in his grip could tip the balance, and he knew it. They all did. Eyes moved, quick and calculating. Austin, Reece, and Ben scanned the space without turning their heads, mapping exits, distances, and angles, all while measuring risk, and calculating timing. Searching for something, anything they could use. The strangers weren't still either. Their gazes flicked again and again toward the stairwell, restless, distracted for just a fraction too long. Waiting, listening, and expecting something. The room held its breath. One move, that was all it would take. An elderly man with greying red hair appeared halfway down the stairs, stopping once the lounge room came into his view.

"What's happening?—"

"Go back upstairs." The man from the hallway said slowly, authority mixed with fear lacing his tone.

"Tyler?" The elderly man directed his gaze towards the man with the knife at Reece's throat.

"*Now*, dad." He said firmly. Austin noted the obvious intimate relationships between the three, then glanced out the window towards the barn. The man with the gun on Austin took a quick step towards him.

"I said *don't fucking move*—"

"Hey," Austin turned back to face him. "You're trying to protect your family and that's cool, we're just trying to do the same."

"Shut up." The man with the knife, Tyler, tensed up. Ben shifted his weight slowly, making sure not to make any movement too sudden to start a gunfight.

"Bold words for a man with a gun pressed against his head." He said. The elderly man took another step gingerly down the stairs, staring at his son with the gun against his head.

"Stop, dad—"

"You're outnumbered." Ben said softly.

"Where'd you learn to count? There's three of you and three of us—"

"What?" Ben let out a low, disbelieving laugh. "Your old man gonna join the fight?—"

"Enough, Ben," the quiet authority in Austin's commanding voice spoke volumes. Ben clenched his jaw and tightened his grip on the rifle in his hands. "See those two women out there, on the bench by the barn." Austin gestured outside slowly, shifting his gaze to look through the window.

The man with the gun shifted his gaze slightly through the dust covered panes as Austin took a small step towards them.

"So?—"

"We're just trying to find a place to stay for a few days—"

"Find somewhere else." He suggested forcefully.

"We have a sick woman, and her exhausted three year old," Reece said. His skin scraped against the knife as he swallowed hard. "Two tired teenagers, and two others who need rest. We're not getting far on foot... *you* find somewhere else." Alex began coughing on the stairs, mildly startling the men as they tensed up.

"Looks like they won't get far either," Austin looked at Reece, then back at the man in front of him. "Is he sick?"

"None of your damn business." Tyler responded angrily, tensing the knife at Reece's throat.

"We have a nurse." Reece offered in protest of the tensing knife.

"And medication." Austin extended a gesture of good faith, noting the rare flash of discomfort across Reece's expression. Tyler, and the other man with the gun exchanged cautious glances between them. The man with the gun nodded as Tyler pulled the knife back from Reece's throat. Austin nodded to Ben as he slowly lowered his rifle from Tyler's head.

"Army? Or you steal that?" The man asked, gun still trained on Austin as he looked him over, eyes catching the surname etched into the patch across his chest. Austin didn't move.

"Staff Sergeant Williams. U.S. Army," he paused for a heartbeat. "Austin." The man held his gaze, weighing it.

"Staff Sergeant Matthews," he said after a moment. "National Guard. Chase." Neither of them lowered their weapons straight away. The silence stretched, tight and uncertain, before Austin took a slow step forward, extending his hand, careful and deliberate. Chase hesitated, jaw tightening, then lowered his gun just enough to meet it. Their handshake was brief, firm, and far from friendly.

"Guess we're on the same side." Austin said, though there was no warmth in his tone.

"Depends," Tyler took a step sideways, relinquishing the barrier between Ben and Reece. "Are you with those bastards ransacking the coast?"

"Which ones?" Austin let out a rough scoff and took a step towards the window. He looked out at Beth and Su, still sitting on the bench by the barn. "We came across a few of them—"

"Same," Tyler offered, walking over to his dad. "Why don't you go lay down and I'll bring you something to eat?" His previous low harsh tone had changed into a softer one as he coaxed his father back up the stairs.

"What's wrong with him?" Austin queried.

"Nothing really," Tyler watched his father disappear from sight before turning to face Austin. "He's just exhausted and hungry."

"I'm sure there's some food in town we could—"

"There isn't," Chase interrupted. "We've gone through every supermarket, every corner store, every restaurant."

"They've been picked clean." Tyler's thick red beard was matted and tangled, with bits of dirt and debris caught in it from their travels. His rough, calloused hands scratched at it absentmindedly as he spoke, his beard rustling against his fingers.

"We went through a couple of houses before settling here so Alex could rest." Chase said. Tyler's face was etched with worry, his eyes fixed on the stairs where his father had disappeared.

"Ben," Austin's gaze remained out the window. "Get Val, and tell her to bring her first aid kit to check on him." Ben silently and obediently walked through the room, pushing through the front door. Austin took a seat on the dusty couch, sneezing as a cloud of dust erupted and tickled his nose. Stifling their laughs, Tyler and Chase loosened up slightly, the tension in the room lifting.

"Fucking allergies," Austin said, wiping his nose with his hand. "As if we don't have enough shit to deal with." Chase smiled, taking a rag from his pocket and offering it to him.

"It's clean." He said. Austin slowly took it from his hands, blowing his nose as Chase took a seat opposite him.

"So," Chase relaxed into the chair loosely. "What's *your* story?"

Val's shock faded almost as quickly as it had appeared, replaced by her usual efficiency. She didn't wait for Beth's usual questions or Su's hesitations before she had grabbed her first aid kit and was moving toward the house. Inside, she tended to Alex in the upstairs bedroom, her hands steady even as her mind flicked over the chaos. Beth followed shortly after, carrying some of the leftover deer meat from the RV fridge - a half gesture of goodwill, half curiosity about what she might find inside. Outside, Ben and Sam crouched near a small fire they had built by the barn, stirring the soup and keeping a careful eye on their temporary companions. The air smelled of smoke and simmering tin, a thin comfort in the tense evening. Beth moved between the tables, arranging a makeshift campsite for the night, her hands smoothing blankets, stacking supplies, and trying to impose some order on the uncertainty that surrounded them. The arrangement had been agreed quickly - the barn for Beth, Val, Chantelle, Su, Sam, and MJ. The house for Chase, Tyler, and Alex. Austin and Ben had already set up their swags side by side, and Reece had found a patch of grass to roll out his sleeping bag, opting to sleep under the stars as usual. Even so, despite the divide, all three men had joined them outside for dinner, wary of inviting anyone indoors while nerves were still raw. Their eyes darted often, scanning the tree line and the open fields, ever aware of the possibility of an ambush. Beth couldn't help but notice the imbalance in their group. A frail woman with a gaunt teenage brother and a small, restless child. A stubborn, sharp-edged nurse who moved with practiced efficiency. A scrawny teenage girl shadowing her, picking up tasks without hesitation. Three men - the only ones with any real combat experience - handled the fire and food with quiet competence, keeping the rhythm of the evening steady. They all carried an unspoken awareness of their strengths and weaknesses, and of the power held by the three strangers who had joined them. Beth eyed them as they sat quietly at the table. Two men with combat training, their purpose obvious, and an elderly man. Beth counted the numbers in her head. Her group had strength in quantity, but these strangers had only one life to protect. If it came to a fight, she realised, they stood to lose far more than they would. Despite the tension, the afternoon stretched into evening with cautious conversation. Stories of the coast were shared in low voices, laughter occasionally flickering across faces, a fragile attempt at normalcy. Each glance, each gesture, carried the weight of recent losses, the unspoken calculations of survival, and the tentative bonds that were forming across wary lines.

"We were with another group." Alex offered, already better from having a decent meal in his system. Ben idly poked at his tin of beans with a spoon before sliding it across the table to Alex. Tyler offered him a thankful smile and Ben nodded at him.

"What happened to them?"

"A woman, Katie, she was taken by some men." Alex said, taking the new tin of beans slowly.

"Her husband and the rest of their group took off after her

and we all got separated," Chase said between hearty mouthfuls. "We never actually saw them, but her group did—"

"You said there were more than one group along the highway?" Tyler asked, swallowing a large mouthful of food and wiping his chin with the back of his hand.

"The ones at Mountain Gate, and the hoarders at Redding," Reece shrugged, finishing his food. "My money'd be on Mountain Gate." Alex swallowed his last bite and set the tin down on the table gently, his hand shaking. Austin had pondered the words, curious at the situation and wondering what the world was coming to outside of the temporary safety they had found at the ranch. They all sat in silence for the rest of the night, Alex retiring to the house once he was satisfied he had eaten enough to regain some strength and make the short walk alone in the dark. Beth watched the men talking, itching to join the conversation. Val stepped quietly to her side, startling her.

"What're you doing?"

"Oh, nothing." Beth fumbled, pretending she'd been preoccupied with her food. Val raised a curious eyebrow and slid onto the bench at the opposite corner. They both tugged their jackets tighter around their necks, shielding themselves from the night's chill.

"Observing?" Val asked, rubbing her hands together.

"Always." Beth hesitated, unsure what kind of interaction awaited - she wasn't in the mood for conflict. From the shadows, Su emerged, carefully carrying a pot of tea in her covered hands, a small canvas bag looped through her arm. She set it gently on the table, then pulled a bottle of whiskey from the bag, placing it beside the pot. Beth and Val glanced at the drinks as Su slid onto the bench next to Val. Beth studied Su across the table, tilting her head slightly, eyes narrowing with curiosity. She watched the subtle movements, the way Su carried herself, as if trying to read more than just her face.

"Tonight, maybe a night for truce," Su said, pulling mugs

from the bag and nodding toward the men at the other table.
"If they can, I can too." Val looked from Su to Beth, the weight
of grief easing slightly as Su offered a small, inviting smile.
Beth hesitated, then returned the smile with a slow nod.

"You sure it's not poisoned?" Beth joked, though her
words fell a little flat. Val shot her a sharp look.

"Beth—"

"It's a joke—"

"There are plenty of things out here that could kill us. I am
not one of them," Su said, pouring the hot tea into three
mugs. "At least... not yet." She chuckled lightly. Beth and Val
exchanged uncertain glances, then Su laughed. "It's a joke." She
smiled, taking a long drink from her mug before placing it
down again.

"Where's MJ?" Val asked, sipping cautiously.

"Sleeping in the stable with Sam and Chantelle." Su
glanced at Beth, then back down at her untouched mug. Beth
lifted it, drinking slowly, letting the warmth spread through
her. Su smiled again and refilled their cups. The mix of
whiskey and tea created a comforting contrast to the cold
night. Gradually, the tension lifted. For the first time in weeks,
they allowed themselves light banter, small smiles, and the
quiet relief of companionship. The barn's soft glow made the
world outside feel distant, harsh realities temporarily replaced
by the warmth of shared presence. One by one, they sipped
and lingered, letting the fleeting night offer them a rare
reprieve from everything they had endured.

Austin woke to the first whispers of winter, the ground dusted
with a delicate layer of white as he pushed aside the opening of
his swag. The crisp morning air bit at his cheeks, sharp and

clean, carrying the faint scent of frost. Stepping out, he took in the mountains beyond, their peaks softened under the hush of fresh snow. The world felt quieter, as if the snow had swallowed the usual morning sounds, leaving only a tranquil stillness. He walked a few paces across the gravel, boots crunching lightly, and spotted Ben at the end of the driveway, rubbing his hands together in a futile attempt to chase off the cold. Their eyes met, and they exchanged a nod, a quiet acknowledgment of the morning's bite. Austin exhaled slowly, watching the mist of his own breath curl and fade into the cold air as he moved toward him, taking a moment to appreciate the fleeting serenity that winter had brought to their rugged surroundings.

"Guess we couldn't outrun it," Austin said, a hint of disappointment in his voice. "Once that tyre blew, I knew we weren't gonna beat winter to the south."

"We'll be alright," Ben sighed, then laughed as he looked across the field. "Reminds me of those winter mornings in Minnesota. Remember those frosty morning drills we used to do? If we can survive that, then we'll survive this." Austin grinned, taking in a long deep breath of the fresh, snowy air.

"I swear, Minnesota winters made boot camp seem like a vacation."

"Oh yeah, *those* were the days. Nothing like starting the day with a freezing cold run." The corners of Ben's mouth curled upwards, his cheeks slightly dimpled while his eyes crinkled at the corners with genuine warmth.

"Or the snow camouflage drills," Austin added, shaking his head. "Trying to blend in with the snow while freezing your ass off. Good times."

"And let's not forget the survival training in the snow," Ben laughed. "They made us build shelters like we were suddenly in the Arctic."

"I always thought they were preparing us for some secret mission at the North Pole," Austin said sarcastically. "Little did we know, we'd end up in this post-apocalyptic winter wonderland instead." They both laughed at their shared memories, finding humour in the absurdity of their past experiences compared to the situation they faced in the present. The cold in the air had provided a stark contrast to the warmth in their laughter, creating a moment of brotherhood amid the snow-covered wilderness. They stood for a moment, appreciating the solitude of their surroundings. The soft crunch of snow underfoot punctuated the silence as they both stopped laughing, listening to the quiet morning.

"I'll head back to the RV today," Ben suggested. "See if I can find a spare tyre in town and get it changed over so we can get the hell out of here. We might be able to make it further south before we get snowed in." Austin nodded, scratching his stubble absentmindedly.

"You'll take Reece with you."

"Sure," Ben said before looking back towards the ranch house. "What about them?" Austin's eyes darted back and forth between the building and the surrounding snow-covered landscape.

"It would help to have some extra muscle around."

"I'll get going to town." Ben paused, looking back at the barn. Reece had already stepped out to move the remnants of the previous nights' fire inside the cover of the barn doorway, shielding it from the light snowfall.

"But first," Austin clapped his friend on the shoulder. "Coffee."

Chapter Twenty-Six

The snowfall thickened with each passing week, so gradual that no one even noticed when Christmas and New Year slipped by. A spare tyre for the RV proved impossible to find, and Ben and Reece had driven it back to the ranch with painstaking care, every jolt a reminder that the single wheel now bore the heaviest part of the vehicle, a spot meant for a tandem set. As the groups grew closer and the nights bit harder with winter's chill, Chase and Tyler finally relented, allowing everyone to stay in the house. Alex had given up his upstairs bedroom to Su, MJ, and Sam, while Val and Chantelle claimed one of the downstairs bedrooms for themselves. Alex had moved into the remaining downstairs room, leaving the last bedroom a topic of heated discussion.

"You guys need more sleep than I do. If you're gonna be running around town in the snow to find scraps for the next few months, you'll need rest." Beth protested relentlessly, her objections falling on deaf ears.

"We're happy in the lounge by the fire." As he smiled, Austin's hand reached out and rested on Beth's shoulder, offering a comforting and reassuring touch. Ben's demands were less warm.

"You're taking the bedroom, Beth." His tone was stern, his voice tinged with anger. She eventually accepted the decision, though her resentment lingered quietly beneath the surface. She nodded submissively, unsure of why he seemed resentful towards her. Their plan to head south had been quietly abandoned. Even the most determined among them recognised the truth - a journey through the snow, no matter how prepared, would exact losses they weren't willing to sacrifice. Luis' words cut into Austin like hot needles, reminders of how often he had warned that the dead weight would drag them down. He knew he could make it south on his own, the survivalist in him had toyed with the thought during particularly low moments, but the idea of leaving anyone behind was unthinkable. Not Ben or Reece, who could handle the trek alongside him, but Ben wouldn't leave Beth, and Beth would never abandon the others. Every time the intrusive thought surfaced, he shoved it back into the recesses of his mind. Morale withered as the days blurred together, each one spent inside, prisoners to the beautiful, indifferent snowfall outside. The fire in the old hearth remained alight constantly, flickering across makeshift beds strewn across the floor where Austin, Ben, Reece, Chase, and Tyler slept. Card games became infrequent, and conversation even rarer. The creaking floorboards echoed in the quiet house, each sound amplified by the oppressive stillness. Meals were cooked, supplies tidied, tasks performed, but the motions felt automatic, almost ritualistic. Austin sat before the fire, staring into the flames with a faraway look, lost in thought. Ben, perched on the couch pushed against the back wall, flipped a quarter over his knuckles absentmindedly, his expression taut and contemplative. Reece leaned against the wall, silent, observing the group like a sentinel, his gaze sharp even in stillness. On the adjacent beds, Chase and Tyler exchanged brief, loaded glances, words unnecessary to convey the shared unease. Outside, the cold seemed to gnaw at the very bones of the house, seeping in with every gust of wind and dusting of snow. Beth, normally the fire in the group, was the last to admit defeat. She sat by a frosted window, eyes tracing the delicate dance of snowflakes, the distant mountains blurred beneath their weight. Her expression held a quiet yearning for the world beyond the ranch, a longing for movement, for freedom, for anything other than this suspended purgatory. Val tried to lift the mood for Chantelle's sake, her faint smile never quite reaching her eyes. Alex sat in a corner, drumming his fingers on his knees, restless yet restrained. Su hid behind the pages of a book, seeking escape in ink and paper from the monotony that pressed against every wall. Sam and Chantelle busied themselves with MJ, finding small pockets of amusement, though even their energy waned as the weeks passed. The days rolled seamlessly into nights and back again, indistinguishable from one another. Conversations dwindled to silence, the deck of cards on the table gathering dust, the fire's crackle echoing the unspoken tension that wrapped itself around the group. Tyler, unable to endure the stagnation any longer, rose from his bed and drifted to the kitchen window. He traced patterns in the frost with a fingertip, lost in the endless white expanse outside. Chase joined him, and for a moment they stood side by side, silent witnesses to the frozen panorama, the world outside as cold and untouchable as the weight pressing down inside.

"We'll get through it." Chase whispered gently.

"I know," Tyler sighed and cocked his head. "Just worried about dad."

"I know," Chase looked back towards the silent group in the lounge room, frozen in their places. "It's nice you reconnected with him before this, otherwise you'd've been a wreck worrying about him at home." Tyler's hand gently caressed Chase's face, following the line of his beard down to his chin. Their attention snapped to the doorway, and they instinctively released each other. Beth stood there, framed by the dim light, a stack of grimy bowls and utensils clutched in her hands. The edges of her fingers were smeared with dried food, and a small streak of ash dusted her sleeves. For a moment, the quiet weight of the moment hung between them, punctuated only by the clatter of the bowls as she shifted her grip. She offered them an exhausted half smile, walking into the kitchen and gently placing the items in the sink.

"Don't mind me—"

"We were just—"

"I'm not stupid," Beth's face flushed. "It didn't take much to figure it out."

"How long have you known?" Chase looked between Beth and Tyler, relaxing his body.

"After we moved into the house, it didn't take long to catch on," she laughed. "I've seen the way you two huddle in the corner. The way you press yourselves against each other when you have a quiet conversation." Tyler shuffled awkwardly on his feet.

"We thought we were being subtle." He said, before sharing a smile with Chase that conveyed a silent sense of relief. Tyler gently placed his hand back on Chase's face, the warmth of the moment reflected in their affectionate expressions. Beth observed the tender moment between them, witnessing the beauty of their intimacy. She shifted her gaze back to the lounge room, yearning for some semblance of human interaction herself. Chase placed a quick kiss on the side of Tyler's lips where they met his cheek.

"Why'd you keep it a secret?" She asked.

"It's hard, the... *industry* we're in," Chase sat down at the opposite end of the table in the kitchen. "National Guard, Army... we weren't sure how they'd react."

"It's never come up in conversation but I don't think any of them are homophobic." Leaning against the counter, Beth braced her posture with her arms on either side, stretching her neck up and looking towards the ceiling.

"My dad," Tyler began, taking a seat next to Chase. "He

didn't really get it. We only started to reconnect just before this —" He paused, gesturing outside. Chase took his hand, intertwining their fingers.

"I get it. When my mum found out I was dating a girl in high school, she flipped," Beth paused, thinking about her parents back home. "But that was a long time ago." She shook her head to clear her mind of the thoughts that threatened to overwhelm her, then she returned to the sink to finish washing the dishes.

"It must be hard," Chase stood, walking over to her. "Not knowing what's going on back home, or if they're—"

"Chase," Tyler interrupted him. "Don't." Tears welled in her eyes as she pressed her hands to the edge of the sink, willing herself not to break. Chase reached out, resting a gentle hand on her shoulder. When the tears fell, he pulled her into a hug, letting her cry silently against his chest.

"I'm sorry," she murmured. "I'm just really tired." Ben entered the kitchen, brow furrowed as he took in the scene. Chase nodded toward him, silently inviting him to take over. Ben's arms were steady as he wrapped around her, and for the first time since the world ended, Beth let herself truly cry. The kitchen, simple and dimly lit, became a sanctuary for raw emotion. Sobs echoed softly, each one a release of months of fear, grief, and exhaustion. Chase stepped back, giving them space, while Tyler retreated to the living room with a quiet gesture for Chase to follow. Beth clung to Ben, feeling the warmth and steadiness of his embrace weaving a small but profound sense of safety around her. His strong, steady arms provided a sanctuary, allowing her to release the pent-up emotions that had been weighing on her heart. Slowly, the crying subsided, leaving a quiet calm in its wake. Ben didn't rush her. He stayed close, letting her collect herself, and when she finally pulled back, puffy-eyed but calmer, she managed a small, grateful smile. The weight on her chest felt lighter, even if only by a fraction, and for a moment, in that cold winter house, she felt she wasn't alone.

Beth jumped at the knock on her bedroom door. Ben's cautious gaze met hers as he peeked into the dimly lit room, pausing as if weighing whether to step inside. She sat up against the pillows, the oversized shirt hanging loose around her shoulders, her bare legs stretched out before her. Her skin prickled with awareness of his eyes on her, every inch of exposed flesh a reminder of how vulnerable she felt. She tugged the shirt down over her thighs, trying to reclaim a shred of modesty, but it only made her more conscious of how much he could see. The slight movement drew a quiet tension between them, the space charged with the unspoken. Every breath, every flutter of her heartbeat seemed louder in the small room. Ben remained at the doorway, careful and deliberate, his presence both steady and electrifying. The dim shadows flickered across her legs and torso, highlighting the tension in her posture. For a moment, time stretched. The quiet of the room pressed in around them, the sound of her breath mingling with the faint rustle of fabric. Vulnerable, exposed, and fully aware of him, Beth felt the weight of anticipation coil tight in her stomach, a pulse of need and nervousness that neither of them spoke aloud.

"I wasn't sure if you were sleeping." He whispered, unwilling to wake the rest of the house.

"I don't sleep," she closed her book, placing it gently on the side table. "Not really."

"I just—" he paused, biting the inside of his cheek. "I wanted to make sure you were okay. But I'll let you rest." He took a step back, slowly closing the door behind him and turning into the hallway.

"Ben," she hesitated, her voice louder than she intended. "You can come in." Entering the room without a moment's hesitation, he swiftly closed the door behind him. She observed him from head to toe, examining how ordinary he appeared without his uniform. As the door clicked shut, the room seemed to contract, leaving an air of anticipation in its wake. The soft glow of ambient candlelight cast a warm hue over Ben, who now stood in the quiet space with Beth's gaze fixed upon him. Her eyes lingered on the subtle details of his appearance, noting the absence of the structured uniform that often defined him. In the subdued lighting, his features softened, and the vulnerability that occasionally peeked through the facade of normalcy became more apparent. For a moment, neither of them spoke, the room filled with the tension of shared moments and hidden feelings. Beth, still sitting up against the pillow, her knees up against her chest, found herself caught in the quiet intensity of the exchange. Ben, sensing the weight of the unspoken, took a tentative step closer. Their eyes met, and in that shared gaze the room had shifted, once a mere backdrop was now transformed into a canvas for the intricacies of human connection. Beth felt a mixture of curiosity and vulnerability, a sense that the ordinary had been replaced by a moment charged with unexplored possibilities. Ben, breaking the silence, spoke softly as his words carried a sincerity that echoed in the confined space.

"Beth," he said softly. "I'm sorry I've been so cold."

"We're all cold." She quipped, gesturing to the window where the snow lay quiet and unmoving outside.

"Always with the jokes." He took another step closer and sat at the end of the bed, facing the wall. The room held a delicate balance, a tableau frozen in time. Beth, the openness in her eyes reflecting both resilience and a hint of sadness, watched as Ben grappled with his own vulnerabilities.

"What's wrong?" She asked quietly. With his gaze fixed on an indistinct point on the wall, he took in a deep breath.

"I've been keeping a lot inside, and it's time I let someone in." He let out a slow exhale as Beth listened, her eyes tracing the lines of his profile. The admission hung in the air, and for a moment, the outside world disappeared, leaving only the hushed exchange within the confines of the room.

"You know you can talk to me, Ben," she began. "Whatever you—"

"Back in Redding, when I had separated from Reece and Val, I ran into Luis."

"What?—"

"He held me at gunpoint, and he said something that—" He paused, and the words played over again in his mind, fresh as the day he heard it. She scooted herself closer to him, as she gingerly crossed her bare legs in front of her. Ben looked down at her smooth skin, watching the goosebumps form over her legs as she got closer. As the snowflakes outside clung to the window, the shared vulnerability in that space became a bridge connecting two souls weathering the storm together.

"What did he say?"

"He said," Ben swallowed hard. "There will come a day when that girl dies, and I want you to be there to watch."

"Why?" She whispered softly.

"I thought he was gonna shoot me, and instead he left with those words which've lingered in my mind *every second* since he spoke them and I just can't get the thought of you—"

"Hey," she whispered softly, taking her hand and placing it on the side of his face, turning him to look at her. "I'm not going anywhere." He looked at her warm gaze, one which bore into his soul as the candlelight created a soft glow around her.

"Beth—"

"Is that why you raced to find me in the clearing at the campsite?"

"What?" Ben asked, confusion etched into expression.

"You stormed through the trees and hugged me, and—" Beth's eyebrows furrowed in concentration, her lips slightly parted as she searched for the right words to say. She leaned in closer to Ben, her eyes flickering with uncertainty in the dim candlelight.

"I don't really remember," he took her hand from his face and held it on his lap. Scanning his eyes, she hoped that his memory would be restored of the events of that evening. He noticed the sadness in her eyes, cautiously stroking the back of her hand with his thumb. "What happened?"

"You kissed me." She whispered softly.

"I kissed you?" Ben exclaimed, his shock and amusement unconfined as she nodded solemnly. "I don't remember."

"I know," she said. "You were exhausted."

"I was determined to get back to the campsite," nodding gently, he continued stroking the back of her hand. "The way he said it, I thought he'd done something to hurt you. I thought I was going to return to you dying and that's what he meant—"

"He didn't do anything to me."

"But, your split lip—"

"It wasn't him," she smiled. "Sparring accident. It was nothing." Her smile faded as quickly as it had formed, leaving a hollow ache in its place. Guilt rose unbidden, a sharp, unwelcome reminder of the kiss she had shared with Austin - a memory she shoved away as quickly as it surfaced. The warmth of it lingered at the edges of her mind, and with it, a confusing pull she wasn't ready to confront. Ben noticed the shift immediately. He hesitated for a fraction of a second, then slowly reached out, his hand hovering before resting gently against the side of her face. His touch was cautious, questioning, as if seeking permission to bridge the invisible distance that had suddenly appeared between them. Her eyes flicked toward his, and for a moment, the room seemed to shrink around them, the space between them charged with unspoken words. She wanted to tell him it meant nothing, that it wasn't real, but the truth tangled itself in her throat, leaving only tension and uncertainty. Ben's gaze softened, patient yet insistent, waiting for her to decide whether to close the gap, or lean back. And in that suspended moment, she realised how fragile the line between desire, guilt, and loyalty could be. The first brush of lips was soft, questioning, then deeper and hungrier. His hands cradled her face, thumbs tracing the curve of her jaw before sliding down, fingertips grazing the hollow of her throat. A shiver chased down her spine as his mouth moved against hers, slow and deliberate, each kiss pulling her further under. He tugged his shirt free and discarded in a careless heap on the floor. Her hands mapped the hard planes of his stomach, the flex of muscle beneath warm skin. A push, gentle but insistent, and the mattress dipped beneath her. The weight of him pressed her into the sheets, his hips settling between her thighs, the heat between them undeniable. Snow whispered against the window, but inside, the air was thick and charged. His mouth left hers, trailing fire down her neck, teeth scraping just enough to make her gasp. Her fingers tangled in his hair, tugging, and his hands slid lower, tracing the dip of her waist, the flare of her hips, then lower still, peeling away the last barrier between them. She arched her back as cool air met her bare skin, and then heat when his palm slid up her thigh slowly. Her own hands found the waistband of his jeans, the button giving way with a quick snap. The zipper hissed open, her fingers brushing against the hard line of him beneath the fabric. He bit his lip with a sharp inhale, his body tensing under her touch. Then he was standing, stripping away his jeans, and she was lost in the sight of him - all lean strength and coiled tension, shadows playing over his skin in the dim light. She sat up, reaching for the hem of her shirt, lifting it over her head in one fluid motion. His gaze burned over her, dark with want, tracing the curve of her body like a starving man presented with a feast. Her breasts rose and fell with each breath, soft and flawless, begging for his hands and his mouth. Her lips, plush and parted, trembled as she bit down on the lower one, stifling the moan that threatened to escape. Her hips swayed, the dip between them deepening as she clenched her thighs together, every muscle taut with anticipation. He leaned into her, the mattress dipping under his weight, and his mouth found her skin. First her calves, the tender flesh yielding under his lips, then her knees, where he lingered, savouring the way she shuddered. Her thighs were next, and she gasped as his kisses trailed higher, each press of his lips igniting a fire that burned hotter with every inch he claimed. His tongue flicked against her hips, and she arched into him, her stomach quivering as he worked his way up her body. When his mouth finally met hers, it was with a hunger that bordered on desperation. Her arms wrapped around his neck, pulling him closer, her nails digging into his shoulders as she surrendered to the kiss. Her body opened to him like a flower under the sun, and he slid into her with a smoothness that drew a stifled moan from her lips. Her fingers twisted in the sheets, the fabric crumpling beneath her as she adjusted to him, her legs wrapping around his hips to pull him deeper. The heat between them was electric, a current that crackled and snapped as he began to move, his thrusts deliberate and unhurried. Her breath hitched, her chest rising rapidly against his, the sensation of her skin against his driving him wild.

"Are you okay?" His forehead pressed against hers, their breath mingling as he whispered.

"Yes." Her lips found his again, this time with a ferocity that matched the pounding of his heart. Her tongue danced with his, each movement coaxing more from her, pushing them both closer to the edge. His hands roamed her body, tracing the curve of her waist, the dip of her spine, before gripping her hips firmly. The sound of her moans, low and throaty, filled the room, each one spurring him on. Her nails raked his back, leaving trails of fire in their wake, and he groaned, the pleasure and pain driving him deeper and faster. The rhythm between them became erratic, frantic, as they chased the peak together. Her cries grew louder, mingling with his, a symphony of desire that echoed off the walls. The sheets rustled beneath them, the sound blending with the sharp intake of their breaths, and she bit into his shoulder to stifle another loud moan. The world outside ceased to exist, the snow falling silently beyond the window nothing more than a backdrop to their passion. There was only the heat of their bodies, the slickness of their sweat, the way they fit together as if they were made for each other. Her head tossed back, her hair a wild tangle against the pillows, and she cried out, her body clenching around him as he placed his hand over her mouth. She bit into his fingers, and he followed, his own release crashing over him like a wave, pulling them both under until they were gasping, trembling, clinging to each other as if letting go would shatter the fragile reality they'd created. In that moment, savouring the aftershocks that rippled through them, as they surrendered to the intimacy, the boundaries that separated them from the outside world dissolved, leaving only the shared warmth and the silent echo of their entwined bodies in the room.

Chapter Twenty-Seven

Beth sat by the ranch window in the lounge room, watching the world outside awaken from its winter slumber. The once snow-covered landscape was thawing, revealing patches of green beneath the melting frost. Winter's cold, harsh grip had slowly loosened, giving way to the first whispers of spring. Small buds peeked from the trees, tentative yet resilient, while the fields, once blanketed in white, began to shimmer with hints of life. The air carried a subtle freshness, tinged with the scent of rain and the faint fragrance of emerging flowers. The symphony of winter was silent, punctuated only by the occasional crunch of snow underfoot or the distant trickle of melting streams, was giving way to the lively chorus of birdsong and rustling leaves. The warmth of the sun brushed against her skin, a gentle reprieve from months of biting cold. Winter's rigid, monochrome world was giving way to a riot of colour - greens, yellows, soft pinks and purples, each bloom a testament to resilience and rebirth. Beth marvelled at the way nature recovered, its quiet persistence mirroring her own journey. The ranch, long cloaked in stillness, was now a canvas of renewal. And yet, even as life returned to the world outside, her thoughts lingered on the fragile and complicated connections within the walls of the house. She couldn't shake the memory of that night with Ben - his presence, the comfort of his touch, the intimacy of their shared vulnerability. A warmth had sparked between them, fleeting yet undeniable. In the days since, however, Ben had grown both protective and distant, a silent guardian whose attention was divided between the group's safety and the unspoken barrier that now separated them. He ensured she ate, he watched over her rest, yet he maintained a careful detachment. The distance frustrated her. She wondered if that night had meant more to her than it had to him, or if their connection had been simply a moment of shared need, a temporary escape from the cold reality surrounding them. His routine of venturing into town and scouring abandoned houses for supplies offered a convenient justification for his absence, a pretext for solitude that left her longing for the closeness they had shared. Eventually, she had offered her bedroom to Chase and Tyler, a pragmatic decision in the fleeting sanctuary of the ranch. Ben had bristled at the gesture, his protective instinct clear, but she had ignored it, knowing the need for privacy outweighed any minor protest. Beth traced the budding trees with her gaze, the subtle breeze brushing against her cheeks through a cracked window. Spring's arrival mirrored the delicate ebb and flow of human connection - fragile, tentative, yet persistent. She allowed herself a brief exhale, a moment of reflection on the tension, the longing, and the small sparks of warmth that still existed in the midst of survival. Meanwhile, Austin, Ben, and Chase prepared for a day-long expedition across town, seeking supplies in houses long thought picked clean. Each step into the abandoned neighbourhoods was a reminder of how precarious their world remained, even as the landscape outside hinted at hope and renewal. Reece watched the sudden stir of life in the room, a stark contrast to the months of frozen inactivity and quiet despair. The space, once heavy with idleness and the oppressive weight of waiting, now hummed with purpose. Plans were forming, movements were deliberate, and a subtle energy pulsed through the group. He stepped forward slowly, careful not to startle Beth, and his voice carried a soft steadiness that seemed almost foreign in the house after so long.

"Beth? Are you alright?" He asked. She looked up at him warily, still tracing circles in the window. His lips curved slightly into a concerned frown, his eyes fixed on her face. She smiled, weariness flickering across her face.

"Just... thinking—"

"You look sick." Reece's arm extended towards Beth's face, his fingers lightly brushing her forehead as he examined her. Beth's face was pale and her eyes were tired and glossy. Her shoulders shook ever so slightly in the cool air of the ranch, her teeth chattering as she tried to suppress her shivers.

"I'm fine." She whispered. Val's concern sharpened as Reece updated her on Beth's worsening condition, and a ripple of unease moved through the house. The air felt heavier, each glance exchanged carrying silent acknowledgment of the situation's gravity. Tyler, recognising the seriousness, once again offered the bedroom, now transformed into a makeshift hospital space for Beth's recovery. Val adopted a professional stance immediately, slipping into the precision and calm of her nursing training. Her hands moved with purpose as she assessed vitals, adjusted blankets, and ensured Beth's comfort. Yet beneath the clinical efficiency, there was a subtle undertone of personal worry. Beth watched Val move, the sharp contrast between her own weakness and Val's competence striking her. Each time Val entered the room, the N95 mask framed her face, a reminder of the fragility of Beth's condition and the precautions necessary to protect the rest of the group. The mask didn't hide the intensity in Val's eyes, though - the same vigilance she had shown on the road now focused entirely on Beth. The room, once filled with the faint hum of conversation and routine, now held the tense quiet of watchfulness. Every measured breath and deliberate action reminded Beth of how precarious her state had become, and how dependent she was on the careful hands and unwavering attention of those around her. Val left the room as soon as Austin, Ben, and Chase had returned from their supply run.

"Beth's sick." She said dryly, her tone clinical. The three of them exchanged glances, a faint edge of worry crossing Ben's face, though he said nothing and it disappeared just as quickly.

"What is it?" Austin asked.

"Honestly," Val snapped a glove from her hand and tossed it into a plastic bag. "No idea. Could be a viral respiratory infection. A mild flu, maybe RSV. Could be a gastrointestinal bug. Could even be malnourishment or exhaustion, but out here even something mild can get serious fast. She was barely back on her feet before we got stuck in this paradise, and now she's down again—"

"Is she okay?" Ben's voice was monotone, clipped, and Austin noticed the tight set of his jaw, the lack of emotion lurking beneath the calm.

"She will be," Val said, removing her mask. "Fluid, rest. That's all she needs... for now."

"For now?" Chase pressed.

"Until she gets better and needs nothing else," she glanced back briefly at the door, a shadow of concern flickering in her eyes before she turned away. "Or she gets worse and there's nothing we can do for her." Austin scanned the room, studying each person, before settling on Val.

"Anyone else sick?"

"Well," Val sighed, rubbing the bridge of her nose. "Chantelle's been feeling sick the last few days, but no fever, so she's probably just tired like the rest of us. Su's got a headache, but she barely drinks any water and she doesn't eat much, so it's probably related to her heart condition. And Alex, he's been up and down all winter, so who the fuck knows." She pulled another pair of gloves from her bag and headed for the stairs, her steps brisk and deliberate.

"Where are you going?" Austin called after her.

"Doing my rounds."

"Do you need anything?—"

"Yeah, a fucking doctor would be great." Her voice carried a note of sharpness as she stomped up the stairs. Austin's brow furrowed as he looked around the room once more.

"If anyone goes into any of those rooms, make sure you have a mask on," Austin added, his tone stern. "We don't want anything spreading."

The grip of fever held Beth in its relentless embrace, weaving a haze of delirious dreams. Reality and imagination blurred, and the faces of those she cared about flickered through her mind like fleeting shadows. In the swirl of her fever, Ben and Austin appeared, their voices whispering incoherent words, their forms shifting and merging in the surreal landscape of her subconscious. One moment, she was in Ben's comforting presence, his reassuring smile a tether to calm. They wandered through fragments of familiar landscapes, sharing moments frozen in time. The next, Austin emerged, his stoic figure a pillar of strength amid the fevered chaos. The dreams twisted and intertwined, a kaleidoscope of memories, laughter, and hardship. Days drifted by in a feverish haze where time lost its shape, and the lines between past and present dissolved. The phantom images of Ben and Austin lingered, their voices echoing in her delirium. Then, in a sunlit clearing, a voice called her name. The brilliance of the afternoon sun blurred her vision, and she reached toward it, sensing the rhythmic pulse of a heart beneath her hand as she rested it on a shoulder. When the figure turned, it was Luis, his gaze piercing, a hunting knife raised, and suddenly plunged into her shoulder. A jolt of pain tore her from the dream, and she screamed. Beth's eyes snapped open, sweat clinging to her forehead, the dim light of the room searing into focus.

"Jesus Christ, Beth! You scared the shit out of me." Val's breaths were ragged, her hand pressed to her racing heart. Beth opened her mouth to speak, but her voice refused to come. Her body felt locked, every muscle heavy and unresponsive, as if the nightmare still held her in its grip. Austin entered the room abruptly, his face tight with concern and alertness, scanning as if expecting an attacker to appear at any moment.

"What happened?" He asked, eyes darting around, muscles tense and ready for a fight.

"Nothing," Val said, shaking her head. "She must've been dreaming." Austin's shoulders eased slightly as he nodded, his gaze lingering on Beth for a moment before he turned and left. Beth sat up suddenly, the sterile scent of disinfectant filling her senses. She clutched at her shoulder and then pulled her hand back, expecting blood, but there was none. The haunting visions melted away, replaced by the stark reality of weakness and fever. Val remained close, her concern clear, watching every flicker of movement as Beth began the slow climb back to awareness.

"How long?" Her words were like dried leaves rustling in the wind, faint and fragile on her lips. The hoarseness in her voice hinted at the depths of exhaustion and pain that radiated through her body.

"Five days," Val offered a reassuring smile. "Welcome back." In the gradual clarity of waking from her fevered dreams, Beth wrestled with the lingering images of Ben, Austin, and Luis. The edges between dream and reality blurred, leaving her with a gnawing sense of yearning and disorientation. Reece appeared in the doorway, calling for Val's attention. Austin needed to discuss Beth's condition, and estimate when she might be well enough to travel south. As Val passed him in the doorway, his gaze flicked back to Beth, heavy with concern. He gave her a slight grin, moving closer to her.

"How're you feeling?"

"You speak Korean," her unexpected and misplaced comment caught him by surprise. "How do you speak Korean? It's been on my mind forever." Taking a seat in the chair by the bed, he raised his eyebrows in amusement.

"And you're only asking now?"

"Sorry, I've been busy." She quipped hoarsely. In response to his unexpected laughter - a genuine sound she had never heard from him before - Beth stirred on the bed. As she pushed herself upright, a fit of wild coughing seized her, each convulsion drawing in sharp, ragged breaths. Her chest heaved with the effort, the sudden intake of air leaving her dizzy and flushed.

"Here." Reece took the glass of water from the side of the bed and helped her take a small sip before she sat back and closed her eyes.

"Just like old times, hey." She smiled at him, and he laughed again.

"I never actually took care of you last time," he mused. "That was all Val and Chantelle's doing." They sat in silence for a while as she tried to control her breathing, the sudden amusement and exertion of energy seemingly draining her very quickly. "My wife was Korean." Reece offered suddenly with a bittersweet mixture of sadness and fondness, jolting Beth from her meditative state. She turned her head to him a little, her tone laced with surprise and intrigue.

"Really?"

"Really," his face contorted with emotion. "We met in Busan."

"When?"

"My father was in the navy, and we were stationed there for a while when I was sixteen. Docked at the Jinhae Naval Base for joint training exercises. Her father was the *Daeryeong*, the captain."

"Childhood sweethearts," Beth smiled, her words like a whisper carried on a rough sea breeze. Reece's broad shoulders tensed, his expression shifting to one of sadness and longing. "Can you translate something for me?" She sat up a bit more, wincing at the struggle.

"Sure."

"Su's mother, she asked me to call her *e-o-mma*," Beth sounded out carefully. "And called me *sonn-ye-o*. What do they mean?" Beth felt a small jolt of energy from Reece's touch as he placed a gentle hand on her arm.

"*Eomma* is an informal and affectionate term for mother in Korean," he looked over at her with a smile. "And *sonnyeo* is an expression of affection towards someone who's not part of their family."

"Why?"

"You must've made some impression on her—"

"I didn't do anything." Beth's voice cracked as she thought about their final moments together, and her final moments alone.

"You helped save her family," Reece offered her a reassuring glance. "That's probably more than anyone'd done for them in a long time." Beth's eyes flashed with tears as they glistened, betraying the pain and longing she felt in that moment. Her lips quivered and her hand shook as she brushed away a stray tear that rolled down her cheek. Beth's gaze flicked to Reece's face, his expression filled with warmth and understanding. His eyes crinkled at the corners as he gave her a reassuring smile. A dark and heavy weight settled in the pit of her stomach, like a stone sinking in an endless sea of sorrow. Tears threatened to spill from her eyes as she held back a sob, the pain and longing for what could have been radiating from her like a tangible aura. In that moment, she felt the depth of her grief and sadness, overwhelming and all-consuming. In their shared silence, Reece's gentle touch and comforting smile reminded her that she was not alone in her pain, that there was still warmth and understanding in this world. And for a brief moment, the weight lifted and she found solace in that small glimmer of hope.

"What happened?" Austin pressed Ben as they walked around the perimeter of the ranch.

"What d'you mean?" Ben's voice was devoid of emotion, the words coming out flat and clipped, like the snap of a branch underfoot. Austin stopped in his tracks.

"That. That *tone*. You're cold and distant, and don't blame the winter because you were fine through December and most of January." He said. Ben faced his friend, grappling with the realisation that Austin had always been a confidant for everything he needed to share. The profound value of their friendship complicated the distinction between seeking comfort as a friend and maintaining the necessary respect for him as their commander.

"I did something you asked me not to do." Ben responded after a long silence.

"What did you do?"

"I—" he paused, seeking the right words to say. "I complicated things." The quick realisation dawned on Austin's face and he rubbed the bridge of his nose.

"When?"

"Weeks ago." Ben continued walking as Austin paused for a moment, pushing aside the strange pang of envy which had washed over his body, and jogged up to Ben, falling in line beside him. The rhythm of their footsteps echoed the unspoken tension between them as they walked in silence. The vastness of the ranch sprawled around them, a silent witness to the complexities of their shared predicament.

"I thought you understood how important it was to keep things simple." Austin finally spoke, his voice carrying a mix of disappointment, jealousy and concern.

"I do," Ben replied, his gaze fixed on the snow-covered mountains. "But emotions, relationships, they're not exactly things you can control or simplify, Austin—"

"I get it, emotions can be messy," Austin sighed, realising the depth of Ben's struggle which was just as deep and confusing as his own. "But we can't afford distractions, especially now—"

"I know," Ben nodded in reluctant agreement. "And I messed up, but it's not just about the mission. I miss genuine human connection. I can't just turn off how I feel—"

"I'm not here to reprimand you. We're all dealing with our demons, but we need to find a way to navigate this without jeopardising everything we've worked for," Austin shook his head, his voice rising in frustration. "I don't care if you're with her, I don't care if you're *in love* with her," Austin found himself lying on both counts as his expression stiffened. "Just don't let it sacrifice your morals, don't let it make you irrational, don't let it make you forget what's really out there—"

"That's the point!" Ben exclaimed loudly, defeated. "What's out there? Surviving day to day? That's not a life. I just needed something... *something* to make me feel like there could be anything on the other side of this." Austin swallowed hard, his body tensing as he thought about a life beyond the apocalypse. A life he never got to have with his girlfriend, a life beyond surviving. His wall was crumbling, letting through feelings he had long kept locked in a world that demanded only survival, and he realised more than anything he wanted that for himself too. Austin placed a gentle hand on Ben's shoulder.

"Just don't let it change you." He said softly. As they continued their patrol around the ranch, the weight of their conversation lingered, overshadowed by the impending challenges they faced in a world reshaped by chaos and uncertainty.

Chapter Twenty-Eight

Ben had avoided checking on Beth during her illness, a pattern that had not gone unnoticed by the rest of the group. His explanations - early trips to town, exhaustion on return - were thin veils that failed to fool anyone. As days passed, with Beth swinging between fever and fleeting calm, the others rotated through care. Val and Chantelle ensured she had food, fluids, and comfort. Even Austin and Su had spent a few nights at her side, passing the time with a deck of cards. Ben's absence during these moments became increasingly conspicuous, leaving a subtle, unspoken tension hanging over the household. One evening, Beth found the strength to join the group for dinner. The fading winter sun spilled across the dining room, casting a golden glow on the faces around the table. The chill of the season lingered, but the faint promise of spring hinted at renewal. Conversation turned to plans for moving further south, and Ben, who had been distant until now, finally spoke up, breaking the silence that had grown as heavy as the winter air.

"I've been thinking about San Diego," he leaned against the wall, folding his arms as his body stiffened. "Instead of Los Angeles."

"Los Angeles is closer." Su protested, unsure of the already lengthy walk with her daughter in tow.

"San Diego is probably safer," Austin interjected, observing the concerned look on her face. "We'll make sure MJ gets there." Su offered him a half smile, one filled with a mixture of appreciation and concern. Austin nodded in solicitude, and his eyes briefly met Beth's, recognising the unspoken concern mirrored in her gaze. The absence of Ben's usual assertiveness in their decision-making process didn't escape anyone.

"I agree," Val added, her gaze flickering between the faces around the table. "We need to avoid LA, bypass it through San Bernardino, and down to San Diego." She traced the open map on the table with her finger. Beth, though still recovering, offered her support with a nod. A subtle tension persisted, however, leaving an unspoken understanding that the dynamics within the group were shifting.

"We don't know what's going on in San Diego," she started, glancing around the room and settling her eyes on Ben. "But we saw what was happening further up the coast, and I'd rather not be a part of that—"

"That was *months* ago," Ben interjected, a cold expression matching his unwavering tone. "We don't know where they've moved on to or who they even were—"

"*If* they moved on." Beth said under her breath, and Ben shot her an angry glance.

"What're our options, then?" Austin pressed, a hint of frustration seeping through at the growing disdain between the two. Tyler's eyebrows were furrowed in concentration, his lips pursed as he thought about their options.

"Do we stay here?" His fingers drummed anxiously on the edge of the map, his eyes flickering between the faces around the table.

"Spring is almost here," Chase added. "We can hunt and

stockpile provisions for next winter. The house is big enough for all of us—"

"Barely," Val scoffed. "Do you guys wanna continue sharing the living room? And I'm not confining myself in this tiny space with these two shooting daggers at each other." She gestured between Ben and Beth, who both looked away in opposite directions.

"We could convert the barn." Chantelle chimed in, a light tone in her voice which contrasted the tension in the room, seemingly oblivious to the animosity between Ben and Beth. With a solemn expression, Sam looked down at his feet as he thought about the past few months of endless boredom.

"It would give us something to do." He whispered.

"It's not safe on the mainland, so close to the coast as we are," Austin protested. "We need to stick to the original plan. Head south, find a boat, get to Catalina Island." Ben sneered through gritted teeth.

"It might not be safe there—"

"It might not be safe anywhere!" Austin's voice rose, nearly shouting. "What the fuck d'you wanna do then? Because you've been quiet for days and *now* you suddenly have an opinion. So shoot, tell me what your plan is." Ben, who had been leaning against the wall by the window throughout their conversation with his arms crossed, suddenly stood up straight and balled his hands into fists.

"Austin—"

"No," Austin raised his hand dismissively at Ben. "We're heading south once Beth is well enough for the trek. She needs her strength and we need to wait for the last of winter to pass. It'll be roughly two weeks, allowing an extra day or two for rest. This conversation is over—" Ben burst towards the door, swinging it open with a forceful motion, and stormed off outside into the fading dusk light. Austin shook his head, gazing down at the table, his arms braced on either side of the map. The tension in the air grew thin, reflecting his dwindling patience. "Excuse me." He said finally, walking calmly outside to follow Ben into the field.

"Here," Val handed Beth a second tin of food. "Get your strength up. I have a feeling Austin'll wanna head off sooner rather than later."

"Let's get you to bed." Su ushered MJ and Sam upstairs, Chantelle in tow to help keep the little girl entertained before it was time to turn in for the night. Alex pushed himself to his feet and excused himself, saving what little strength he had left for the journey south, which he figured could start any day by the sound of it.

"Make sure she eats a fucking bran bar." Reece smiled, and Val shot him a playful smirk. He dropped into a chair across the room, propping his feet up on the dining table.

"Reece—"

"What?" He leaned back, folding his hands behind his head. "We're all done with dinner." He quipped, earning a light laugh from her as she gathered the plates, tins, and cutlery, carrying them to the sink. Beth ate in silence, savouring each bite of her second tin, quietly recognising her strength returning with every mouthful. Val, Chase, and Tyler took their seats at the table. Val laced her fingers together, her movements careful, and leaned forward slightly.

"Something's going on with those two." Val said, looking back to the door where Austin and Ben had disappeared. Chase looked towards Beth, who chewed silently, staring at him, unsure of what to say.

"Any ideas?" He asked. She swallowed slowly, trying to postpone her response as long as she could, hoping someone would say something to fill her silence. After a moment, no one had offered any insight.

"I'm not sure." She said softly, taking another mouthful of food, hoping no one would ask her about either of them. She could only imagine how much any of them knew.

"You and Ben aren't exactly subtle." Val said, her expression stoic. Beth swallowed her food and tensed her body.

"What's that supposed to mean?—"

"Is that what this is about?" Tyler furrowed his brow. "Ben and Beth? What's Austin gotta do with it?"

"Austin doesn't like complication," Reece sighed, removing his feet from the table and leaning forward on his elbows. "He's very straight forward and likes to stick to a plan."

"And?" Chase looked between Reece and Beth. "What's changed?"

"We found Beth," Val shrugged. "Before it was just me and Chantelle, and she's sixteen so that's an obvious *no*. And they're like brothers to me—" She paused, glancing up at Beth. Tyler looked around the room, settling his eyes on Val.

"So she's the first thing that's come along—"

"I'm not a *thing* that came along!" Beth slammed her fist onto the table, her heart skipping a few beats before she uncurled her hand and pressed her palm into the wood. "Can you all stop talking about me like I'm not here? I'm sitting *right here*, so ask me." The four of them shot glances at one another, some concerned, some laced with confusion, but ultimately Val met Beth's gaze with curiosity.

"Alright," she said. "Which one did you sleep with?" Beth clenched her jaw, her fingernails digging into the wood of the table.

"Ben."

"And Austin's pissed about it?"

"Obviously." She said through gritted teeth.

"Because it made Ben shitty about... *something*?"

"Apparently." She took in a low, deep breath before releasing the tension in her body. "I don't know why Ben is mad at me. I don't know why Austin is mad at him. You'll have to ask them about it—"

"You just told us to ask you." Val raised an eyebrow before

sighing. She rolled her eyes before looking over at Reece, who had a playful smile on his lips.

"Well, that cleared up absolutely nothing," he smirked, before looking around the room. "So, what do we think?" Chase raised his eyebrows at him.

"About Ben and Beth?"

"About San Diego." Reece pursed his lips together with an amused expression.

"I think San Diego is the best idea." Tyler voiced, placing his hands on the table.

"San Diego," Val agreed, Chase nodding in quiet agreement. "Then how do we convince Ben?"

"He won't like it," Beth offered quickly, the room turning to her in unison while she looked at each of them. "But he won't leave us. He won't—" She paused, feeling the need to speak out loud that he would never abandon her, despite the current animosity. It was almost as if she was trying to reassure herself more than anyone else.

"Despite appearances," Val continued slowly, focusing her gaze back onto Chase and Tyler. "Ben and Austin are close. Ben will follow his orders."

"Austin's kept us alive so far," Reece said slowly. "I'll follow him anywhere."

"Then we will too," Chase stood, walking towards the living room. "We recognise loyalty when we see it, and as far as I'm concerned I'd rather not be the one in charge."

"Ben!" Austin's face was contorted in a fierce determination as he yelled out to his friend. His muscles were tense as he charged forward, his feet swiftly pounding against the ground. "What the fuck is wrong with you?" With a sharp intake of breath, Ben spun around to face Austin, the sound of heavy footsteps growing closer and closer behind him.

"Me? What the fuck is wrong with *you*? You're gonna get us all killed!"

"You're the one acting like a lunatic!" With a forceful push, Austin shoved Ben's chest, causing him to stumble backward.

"Don't touch me!" Ben instinctively lunged forward in response, but then quickly refrained from further confrontation.

"Look," Austin raised his hands to his chest before Ben could protest further. "I get it, it's dangerous, but we can't stay here and we can't go north. We won't survive a winter there. We barely survived one here—"

"What if we run into whoever those guys were? What if they're in San Diego?"

"They could be anywhere!" Anger brimming, Austin tossed his arms up and brought them down hard against his legs, the smack echoing his frustration. Ben's face contorted with frustration, his brows furrowed and his jaw tense as he argued.

"What if they looted LA through the winter and they're already headed south to San Diego?"

"What if they headed to San Francisco? What if they came across another group and they all killed each other?—"

"What if, what if, *what if*!" Ben yelled in frustration, grunting heavily as his breath escaped his lips and danced on the cool spring evening air. They both paused, locking eyes with each other. Austin scrutinised Ben, examining the frustrated and irrational state that seemed to have consumed his friend from head to toe. Taking a deep breath, Austin decided to address the underlying tension, his expression changing to one of deep concern.

"You've been avoiding her, Ben. Why?"

"I don't know what you're talking about." Ben's jaw tensed

as he looked away, his eyes fixed on the mountains in the distance.

"Cut the bullshit," Austin raised an incredulous eyebrow. "You've barely been in the same room with her, let alone checked on her when she was sick. The others've noticed, and so have I." Ben remained silent, his frustration evident in the clenching of his fists as Austin pressed on. "We've had this discussion, and I'm not dealing with it anymore. You're either with me, or against me." Austin pursed his lips with anger. Ben's gaze hardened, and he finally met Austin's eyes.

"Austin—"

"No," Austin took a tentative step towards him, raising a cautious hand. "I'm done with you side-stepping the question. Give me something."

"You don't understand." Ben said softly.

"Then *help me* understand," Austin implored. "You're letting this affect the entire group, and it's not fair to anyone. It's not fair to me. You're my brother, I'd die for you." Ben maintained his silence, clenching and unclenching his fists as he stared at the ground. Austin sighed, and spun around on his heel to head back towards the house.

"I'm afraid." Ben called out sombrely as Austin stopped in his tracks, standing in the middle of the open field, looking up into the evening sky. His breath danced in the air before it disappeared into the night. The weight of Ben's words hung in the air, and Austin sighed, his shoulders slumping. He turned back to his friend and took a few steps towards him. Pausing, he looked at Ben's face, neither wanting to say a word.

"Afraid of what?" Austin pressed, finally breaking the silence that hung in the air.

"Everything," Ben shrugged and shook his head. "I have never been more afraid of anything in my entire life."

"Losing her?"

"Losing anyone!" Ben yelled in frustration. "You, her, any

of them, and it lies on us. All of their lives, every decision we make and everything we do lies on us and I'm just—"

"It's okay," Austin shook his head, his expression softening. "I'm afraid too."

"This... *stigma*," Ben sneered, as if the words were bitter in his mouth. "Being the tough, protective ones. It's unfair."

"Nothing about this is fair," Austin offered him a half smile. "But we can be tough and protective and still have feelings." He swallowed the lump forming in his throat.

"*Feelings*," Ben scoffed. "Like hate? Anger? Fear?—"

"Fear is natural, Ben. It doesn't make you weak. It makes you human," Austin sighed. "We're all scared, but we can't let it control us. We have each other, and that's what matters—"

"And love?" Ben asked, looking over the mountain peaks.

"Love?" Austin raised an eyebrow. He thought for a moment, his eyes darting between the mountains and the ranch house, and then back to Ben. "That makes you human too." They both stopped and looked around, soaking in the peaceful quietness of their surroundings.

"I'm sorry." Ben whispered slowly, taking in a deep breath.

"I need my friend back," Austin said. "I need my *brother* back." The words hung heavy in the air and pierced through Ben like hot needles. He took another deep breath and exhaled sharply, the weight on his shoulders feeling a little lighter.

"I'm sorry I've been such a dick."

"Yeah you've been a huge pain in my ass," Austin replied, giving him a reassuring smile. "But I wouldn't be a very good friend if I just gave up on you."

"I feel like I've let you down."

"You could never," Austin's head tilted to the side, his smile warm and genuine as his comforting eyes crinkled at the corners. "We're family. We're in this together. There's no room for blame or guilt. We adapt, we support each other, and we keep moving forward. We've all got our struggles, and you're not alone in yours." Ben nodded, a sense of gratitude washing over him.

"Thanks."

"Anytime, brother." Austin's voice was low and soothing, like a calm river running through a peaceful forest. Each word seemed to wash away the tension and fear in Ben's mind. Ben looked back towards the house, a sense of vulnerability washing over him.

"I should probably talk to her—"

"Fuck, *please* talk to her," Austin laughed. "For everyone's sake." As they made their way back, the night sky above them twinkled with stars, and their sense of kinship slowly reignited.

Ben found Beth in her room the next morning, rifling through her backpack and belongings as she prepared for their imminent departure. He knocked gently on the door, asking to come in - a request she granted with obvious reluctance. He could feel her hesitation, the unspoken question of whether he should just leave her alone. But Ben had promised Austin the night before that he would settle the tension between them, and he needed to do it before they left. Silence hung thick in the room, heavy as the winter fog they both longed to forget. The curtains barely moved, and the air seemed still, as if even the inanimate surroundings recognised the hostility between them. No rustling sheets, no shifting footsteps - just Beth and Ben, suspended, each waiting for the other to speak. Their unspoken words filled the space, crowded and stifling, pressing down with every shallow breath and the occasional shuffle of belongings. Ben finally gave in, a solemn expression flashing across his face.

"I wanted to say I'm sorry—"

"For what?" Her mouth barely moved as she spoke, the corners turned downwards in a slight frown.

"For everything," he took a step into the room, leaving the door open behind him. "For treating you the way I've treated you." Her eyes flicked up towards him for a heartbeat, then darted away, refusing to meet his gaze.

"It's nothing—"

"It's *not* nothing," he stepped forward, grabbing her arm lightly. "Will you look at me please?" She let her book fall onto the bed, eyes fixed on his hand gripping her arm. He eased his hold, taking a small step back. Slowly, she turned to face him, looking up with a sharp glare that burned with barely contained anger.

"You have my attention."

"I've been treating you like shit. Between the campsite and here, and then after that night—"

"We really don't need to do this." Her lips pressed tightly together.

"We really do—"

"I think we have bigger things to worry about than a one night stand, Ben." She fired at him despondently as he sat down on the end of the bed.

"That's what you're mad about? That's what you thought this was?" Ben shifted uncomfortably.

"What else would it be?—"

"I'm not used to being vulnerable, Beth."

"And that's my problem?" She asked angrily as he looked down at his feet. He paused, unsure of what to say to negate her rising temper. Thinking for a long moment, she sat down on the chair across the room, facing him.

"I'm gonna tell you what I told Austin last night," he said slowly as she sat silent, staring at him with a blank glower. "I'm afraid. I'm genuinely afraid of moving forward. We can't go north, I don't wanna go south. I'm afraid—"

"Of what?"

"Everything," he looked her up and down, taking in her expression which had smoothed over from anger to mild concern. "I'm afraid of making the wrong decision. I'm afraid of losing you, or Austin, or any number of those people out there counting on us to make sure we're all okay."

"Austin's in charge, so those aren't your decisions to make," she shook her head. "We're not going to lose anyone—"

"But we could," he met her gaze with a solemn expression. "We could lose anyone at any given moment and the thought of losing you makes me—" He paused, swallowing the lump in his throat. She leaned forward slightly as he closed his eyes, trying to hold back his emotions from her.

"Ben—"

"Every time I convince myself that everything could be okay, I let myself get close to you, and then my mind is filled with the thought of losing you and I can't bare it."

"So you keep your distance." She smiled softly at him. He nodded and looked down at his feet again.

"Yeah, and I treat you like shit to keep you away. I don't know how to keep you safe and—" he paused, staring at the floorboards. "And *care* about you the way that I do." He avoided the word, the one word that felt like a vice around his chest, squeezing the life from him. To say it aloud, or even to himself, was to risk unraveling completely.

"Guess we're both learning the hard way," she murmured, a faint smile tugging at her lips. "I'd kill for some internet right now, so I could Google how to survive feelings during the apocalypse—"

"Thank you." Ben stood and took her into his arms to hug her tightly. She hesitated before hugging him back, her tense body language relinquishing as she melted into his arms.

"What for?" Her question was muffled by his chest pressing against her face.

"Because," he smiled. "When you make jokes at me I know we're okay."

"Yeah," she whispered, hugging him tighter. "We're okay."

Chapter Twenty-Nine

They had done their best to leave the ranch as they had found it, with Su and Chantelle insisting on preserving every last piece of its history. Parting from the place proved far more difficult than anyone had anticipated, the fleeting sense of security it provided leaving a tangible ache in their chests. Yet, everyone understood the necessity of moving forward. The RV had been abandoned early on. Ben had recognised that winter's neglect had rendered it useless, and so they had set off on foot. The days blurred together, the hours measured in the rhythm of their footsteps, punctuated by the occasional shallow rest or a hurried meal. Their first challenge had been MJ. Su, Sam, and Chantelle took turns shouldering her when fatigue struck, each step seeming heavier than the last, until they could no longer shoulder the weight after only a few days. They raided an abandoned Walmart for food and supplies, dragging out a sturdy, large pram that could accommodate her. The spring air carried a slight warmth, but it offered little comfort when muscles ached and lungs burned from long hours of walking. Beth, despite having recently recovered from her fever, pushed herself harder than anyone expected. She refused to let her weakness slow the group, forcing herself to keep pace even when dizziness and nausea threatened to overtake her. Each morning, she rose determinedly, tying her boots tight and adjusting her pack, hiding the exhaustion behind clenched teeth and a stiff back. Alex fared worse, and his strength waned unpredictably. Some days he managed a steady march, other days a cough wracked his body and he could barely lift his pack. By the end of the seventh day, the group improvised. They scavenged a small hand cart from one of the empty stores along the way. It became a lifeline - Su, Alex, and even Beth took turns riding when the strain of walking grew too great, while others took shifts pushing and pulling it down the highway. Even Austin, usually unyielding, allowed himself brief pauses to ensure no one was overexerting themselves, despite the planned journey taking longer than he had hoped. The cart was crude, heavy when loaded, and prone to snagging on stones, but it offered a reprieve from the relentless march, a small victory that kept spirits from breaking entirely, and to Austin's delight, they began to speed up. Even with these accommodations, the trek remained arduous. Every day tested their patience and endurance. The monotony weighed on their morale, and small arguments or frustrations flared as fatigue mounted. Yet, they pressed onward, driven by necessity and a stubborn desire to reach the safety of the southern coast. After two weeks on foot, the spring days stretched longer, the sun lingering over the horizon with a tentative warmth. The air, scented faintly with new growth, offered a fragile comfort, but exhaustion gnawed at them all the same. Each evening, when the group finally halted, muscles stiff and spirits frayed, they allowed themselves only a brief reprieve before setting up camp and preparing for the next day. Two weeks of constant movement had transformed the journey into a rhythm of endurance - walk, rest, carry the weak, push the cart, repeat. Through it all, their shared burdens - physical, mental, and emotional - bound them tighter, forging the kind of cama-raderie born only of hardship and survival.

"I never thought I'd miss the days of freezing to death at the ranch, bored out of my mind." Beth quipped to Ben as they passed through the Angeles National Forest on the Mojave Freeway, just north of San Bernardino. Before Ben could reply, Austin halted them to gather.

"We're approaching more residential areas," he said. "And I want to make sure everyone has their guard up. I know you're tired, but we can't afford to lose focus." They nodded in silent compliance.

"Standard formation?" Reece asked, receiving a nod of confirmation from Austin. Reece then adjusted his assault rifle, readying his sniper equipment for long-range scouting at the rear.

"It's gonna get dark soon," Austin continued. "We'll stop at the next hotel along the freeway." They pressed on through the day, leaving the mountainous terrain behind. Gradually, houses started to emerge on the horizon, signifying the outskirts of town. They continued along, looking beyond the highway for a hotel to spend the evening. Night began to set in slowly as Ben approached Austin from behind.

"We need to find a place to settle for the night." Ben whispered.

"I know," Austin said, glancing back at the group, several of whom were starting to lag. "I don't wanna stay in town—"

"I don't think we have a choice," Ben followed Austin's gaze behind them. "They won't survive another few hours on foot."

"There," he nodded towards a sign in the distance, reading it aloud. "Budget Lodge." Austin veered slightly to the right, heading for the exit. Without hesitation, they swept methodi-cally through the motel, clearing each room one by one until they were satisfied it was empty. MJ, once laid down on the bed, drifted off almost instantly, the exhaustion from the day evident in her small frame. Su and Chantelle stayed close, tending to her quietly, whispering and adjusting blankets with gentle care. The rest of the group gathered in a room next door, spreading out backpacks and taking stock of their supplies. The walls were thin, but the enclosed space offered a sense of safety that the roadside could never provide. Every rustle or creak drew their attention, the tension of constant vigilance hanging heavy in the air as they waited for the night to pass.

"Pick a room. Get some rest," Austin commanded. "We're leaving at first light." Val took a long swig from her canteen, wiping away the water dribbling down her chin as she spoke.

"We're exhausted—"

"Before you say it, no," Austin gave her a sharp look. "We're not staying here for two nights in the middle of the town."

"Big cities are dangerous," Tyler added. "We can push on to the south side of town and stay somewhere for a few nights once we're out of the area."

"Agreed," pulling out his map, Austin traced the paper with his finger. "We'll continue along highway 15 until we find something." Ben glanced cautiously at Beth before looking back at the map.

"And if we don't? It's a big county, we might not make it out of here in a day's walk, not the way we're going—"

"Then we rest for another night somewhere and keep going until we're out of town," Austin gave his friend a reassuring look. "Besides, we don't have a choice."

"We'll be fine," Reece added dryly. "But we should get some sleep if we're gonna make an early start tomorrow."

As she sat up in bed, her eyes settled on the broken clock hanging on the wall. Beth surveyed the emptiness of the room, feeling the weight of solitude pressing in. Her gaze drifted to her worn-out boots, her aching feet a quiet testament to the ground they had covered. Outside, the desolate city offered no comforting hum of life, only the stark contrast to the weariness settling within her. Her mind, exhausted from the relentless journey, toyed with the idea of seeking solace in the quiet night. And then there was Ben, the familiar face that lingered in her thoughts, a tether in the unsettling stillness. The need for connection eventually triumphed over the fatigue in her body. With a determined exhale, Beth stood, the bed springs creaking beneath her as if echoing her inner debate. She slipped into her jacket, the cool night air brushing her skin as she stepped into the external corridor. The muted glow of the moon guided her to Ben's door. Her hand hovered for a moment before knocking softly. The rhythmic thrum of her heartbeat filled the silence, anticipation coiling in her chest. After a pause that felt endless, she knocked again. The door creaked open slowly, revealing Ben. Their eyes met, holding a quiet understanding that needed no words. Time seemed to suspend itself in that space between them, the tension heavy with unspoken need. Finally, with a subtle nod, he stepped aside, letting her enter. The door closed behind them, sealing out the emptiness of the city. She moved to his bed, slipping off her jacket and boots, grateful she hadn't laced them tightly for the short walk. Ben, shirtless, approached from behind, lifting her shirt slowly over her head, pressing a gentle kiss to her shoulder. Beth stayed facing away from him, her gaze fixed on the tousled bedcovers, absorbing the quiet intimacy of the moment.

"Were you asleep?" Beth murmured softly, feeling his head shake in response. She turned to face him and smiled, cupping his face in her hands.

"Couldn't sleep." Ben's hands gently gripped her lower

back as he leaned in to kiss her, his touch soft and tender, as if afraid to hurt her. Beth could feel the warmth and strength radiating from his embrace, bringing a sense of security and trust that she had craved since that night. The air between them thickened with need, electric and unspoken, as Ben pulled her close, his body flush against hers. Every inch of him radiated a heat that made her shiver. She could feel the urgency in the way his hands trembled against her waist, the way his breath hitched when their hips brushed. His lips crashed into hers with a hunger that was raw, desperate, as if he'd been starved for her touch and now couldn't get enough. The kiss was deep, consuming, tongues tangling in a rhythm that was both frantic and tender, each movement drawing a soft moan from her throat. Their bodies moved together, instinct guiding them, as the world outside faded into a distant hum. His fingers trailed down her spine, leaving a trail of fire in their wake, slipping under the hem of her shirt to push it upward, revealing the soft curve of her stomach. She arched into him, her hands gripping his shoulders, nails digging into his skin as he peeled the fabric away, letting it fall forgotten to the floor. His mouth left hers, trailing kisses down her neck, his teeth grazing the sensitive skin of her collarbone, making her gasp. He knelt before her, hands sliding down her thighs, fingertips tracing the delicate skin behind her knees, sending shivers up her legs. His breath was hot against her stomach as he hooked his fingers into the waistband of her pants, pulling them down slowly, inch by excruciating inch, his eyes never leaving hers. The fabric pooled at her ankles, and he tossed them aside, his gaze raking over her with a hunger that made her pulse quicken. Her hands moved to the knot at his waistband, trembling slightly as she untied it, the sound of fabric pulling against fabric filled the silence. She pushed his pants down, her palms skimming his thighs, feeling the heat radiating from him. He stepped closer, his body pressing into hers, the roughness of his chest against her soft skin making her breath catch.

His hands slid up her sides, fingers brushing the swell of her breasts, unhooking her bralette with practiced ease and letting it fall away. His mouth found hers again, his kiss slower now, deeper, as if savouring every taste of her. His hands roamed her body, exploring every curve, every dip, every inch of her skin. She moaned softly into his mouth, her hips pressing against his, feeling the hard heat of him against her. His fingers traced the curve of her hipbone, sliding lower, teasing her, leaving her gasping and writhing beneath him. He nudged her legs apart gently, his hand sliding between her thighs, fingertips brushing against her, making her whimper. His touch was deliberate, slow, each stroke sending sparks of pleasure through her, building a fire deep within her belly. She clung to him, her nails digging into his back, her breath coming in short, shallow gasps as he explored her, his touch growing firmer, more insistent. Her body arched into his hand, her hips rising to meet his strokes, her moans growing louder, filling the room.

"Shh, someone will hear." He silenced her with his mouth, his kiss swallowing her sounds, his tongue tangling with hers.

"I don't care." She broke the kiss, her head falling back, her breaths coming in ragged gasps as he continued to stroke her, his touch driving her wild. Her hand found his chest, feeling the rapid beat of his heart beneath her palm, matching the rhythm of her own. Her thighs fell open, and Ben didn't hesitate. He let his weight fall on top of her, and Beth's breath caught in her throat, her fingers tangled in the sheets, her body trembling. Ben leaned down, his lips brushing hers in a tender kiss before he pushed forward, sliding into her with a slow, deliberate thrust that made her cry out. Beth's legs wrapped around his waist, her heels digging into the small of his back as she matched his rhythm, her body rising to meet his with every thrust. The room was filled with the sound of their ragged breaths and the occasional whimper that escaped Beth's lips. Ben's forehead pressed against hers, his eyes closed as he drove into her. She could feel the tension building inside her, coiled tight like a spring ready to snap, and she clutched at him, her body trembling as the pleasure threatened to overwhelm her. Ben's thrusts became faster, harder, his hips slamming into hers with a force that made her cry out, her nails raking down his back. Her body convulsed, her cries muffled against his shoulder. Ben groaned, his own release crashing over him, his hips stuttering and his body trembling with the intensity of it. He collapsed against her, his weight pressing her into the mattress, his breath hot against her neck as they both struggled to come down from the high. Beth's hands smoothed over his back, her fingertips tracing the faint marks her nails had left, and Ben kissed her temple, his lips brushing against her skin in a tender caress. They lay there, tangled together, their bodies still joined, the heat between them slowly fading but the intimacy lingering, wrapping them in a cocoon of contentment. The world outside ceased to exist, leaving only the two of them, lost in each other, their hearts beating as one. In the quiet of the room, they found solace in each other's arms, a sanctuary from the chaos of the world, a fleeting moment of peace in the storm of their lives.

Reece awoke to the sound of muffled footprints outside the rooms. In the early dawn light he failed to see outside his window, the awning of the rooms above casting a shadow on the corridor outside.

"Always the early riser." He cursed Austin's ability to wake up on queue, doubting he probably ever went to sleep.

"This room." A hushed voice from outside made his heart skip. Instinctively, he reached for his handgun. Before he could react, the door burst open, and a searing pain exploded down the back of his neck. He crumpled to the floor, groaning, and looked up to see the cold barrel of a gun aimed at him. Rough hands grabbed him, hauling him to his feet. Reece scrambled for footing as he was dragged along the exterior corridor. Ahead, he caught sight of another person, seized by the arm and forced down the motel's external stairs. Kneeling in the car park below, Austin craned his neck, eyes wide, as he watched Reece being brought down by two men.

"What the fuck did you do to him?" Austin's question fell on deaf ears. A man stood behind him with his arms folded. Austin glanced over his shoulder, staring at the handgun nestled safely in its holster at the man's side. Before he could even flinch, a knife appeared at his chin.

"Don't even think about it." The man holding the knife brought Austin's head around slowly to face the motel once more. He looked up at the man, then past him to the motel, where his friends were being dragged out room by room. Su clutched MJ tightly, the child wailing in her arms, while Sam followed slowly behind. Val knelt beside Austin, her gaze fixed on the ground, frozen in place.

"Val," he whispered. "Are you okay?" But she said nothing, her mind filled with memories of Spokane that rendered her paralysed with fear. On the other side of her, Chantelle cried in short, desperate bursts. Each sob was cut off by a man's harsh command until a sharp slap sent her sprawling to the floor. She stayed still, stifling every sound, while Val didn't dare flinch. Austin squeezed his eyes shut, every fibre screaming to move, but he stayed frozen - one wrong twitch, and they'd all be dead. Chase, Tyler, and Alex were brought down the stairs next, moving towards Austin and kneeling at his side. He shot them concerned glances, gesturing subtly toward the gun holstered on the man behind him. Tyler scanned the parking lot before shaking his head and looking back at Austin. Austin's eyes returned to the motel, flinching as he saw Beth and Ben being escorted from the same room.

The man with the knife looked down at him with a blank stare.

"I said, *don't even think about it.*"

"I wasn't—"

"Better not be," he interrupted, then slowly walked over to the stairs. "Put her with the others." Beth glanced at Austin, fear tightening her chest, before she was pulled toward the other side, the separation of men and women strikingly clear. Ben looked at Austin, a growing expression of concern adorning his face as he knelt beside him, raising his hands behind his head as everyone else had done. A man appeared from a 6x6 military truck, walking over to them slowly. Another pulled Chantelle back to her knees as he assessed Beth, Val, Chantelle and Su one by one. Beth stared at him, watching him as he walked, noting the way he had a sense of authority about him. Val continued to stare straight ahead of her, frozen in time, removing herself emotionally from the situation as Chantelle sobbed silently, looking down at the ground. Su clutched onto MJ and rocked back and forth slowly, trying to sooth her daughter.

"He'll like these ones." Another said, circling the women slowly.

"What about this one?" Standing behind Su and MJ, another pointed carelessly at the small child crying in her mothers arms.

"You know how he feels," he paused, looking back at them. "Take care of it." A piercing, guttural cry ripped through the air as Su's arms were torn from around MJ. The child screamed, thrashing violently, but it was futile - one of the men swept her away with terrifying ease, carrying her to the far side of the motel. Su lunged, desperate, her hands clawing for her daughter, but a cruel blow smashed into the back of her head. She crumpled onto the concrete with a sickening thud, blood mixing with dust, leaving her motionless. Austin surged forward, every instinct screaming to protect, to reach MJ, but a rifle's stock collided with his abdomen. Pain exploded through him, doubling him over, and he collapsed mere feet from Beth. Their eyes locked in a fleeting, frozen moment, and they knew there was nothing they could do. Beth's chest tightened, a raw, choking panic swelling inside her as she closed her eyes. The world had contracted to the ragged screams of MJ and the lifeless slump of her mother. And then a gunshot. The sound cracked like the sky itself had shattered. MJ's scream ended abruptly, replaced by a horrific silence that pressed against Beth's eardrums, leaving her gasping for air as if the sound had been ripped from her chest. Her stomach dropped, bile rising, the sharp tang of fear and helplessness flooding her senses. The child's small body, a fragile weight she had never imagined could be taken so violently, lay somewhere beyond her sight, and Beth felt herself sway, powerless, sickened to her core. The parking lot seemed to collapse around her. Dust hung in the air, mingling with the metallic scent of blood. The sight of the man, the brutal efficiency, MJ kicking and screaming, the utter hopelessness of it all made Beth's mind seize. Austin, shaken, turned his head towards the side of the building before pressing his forehead into the ground. The world had become a cruel, endless night, and they had nowhere to run, nothing to hold onto except the fractured remnants of people they loved.

Chapter Thirty

The ten-minute drive to the airport stretched endlessly, each second a cruel echo in the back of the military truck. Su lay unconscious on the floor, bound and gagged, her small form unnervingly still against the tense quiet that filled the vehicle. Austin sat across from Beth, his eyes fixed on Su, watching over her helplessness with a mix of grief and anger. Beth stole a glance at Ben, who sat wedged between Val and Tyler, his gaze stubbornly avoiding hers, yet betraying a turmoil he could no longer hide. The restraints dug into their skin and added a sharp edge of discomfort to an already suffocating ride. The silence was oppressive, heavy with the gravity of their situation, broken only by the dull hum of the truck and the occasional shuffle of shifting limbs. At the front, a man gripped the cab with one hand, rifle in the other, his movements precise and unrelenting. Reece's eyes flicked to the second truck trailing behind, noting the disciplined yet unorthodox formation. These weren't soldiers - they were something else entirely. A militia with ruthlessness baked into every movement, organised but chaotic, leaving Reece unsettled, aware that conventional rules did not apply here. He tried to catch the attention of Austin and Ben, but their focus was immovable. Austin's gaze never wavered from Su, grief and helplessness etched deep into his face. Ben's gaze had finally settled on Beth, his eyes silently pleading, asking for forgiveness in a way no words could convey. The open-air truck rattled forward, the wind biting through the silence, carrying with it the metallic tang of fear. In that weighty quiet, every heart beat a little faster, every breath a little shorter, and the prisoners felt the sharp edge of hopelessness pressing down from all sides. A man's voice broke through the quiet as they stopped in the middle of the runway at the airport.

"We have no room for them here. You'll have to drive them up."

"That's a long drive." Another man complained as Beth looked up at the sky, the morning light slowly filtering through the city as it rose.

"We could just kill 'em." Another laughed, looking back at the truck. Concerned glances rippled through the group as Austin's gaze never left Su, her small, bound form on the floor consuming his focus. Beside him, Ben strained against his restraints, the tight cords cutting into his wrists, his frustration and helplessness plain on his face.

"*Don't. Move.*" The man standing with them in the back of the truck raised his rifle at Ben, and he reluctantly complied. The man smirked, looking around at the group while Beth looked up at him. She focused her gaze, unwavering. Her eyes met his as he looked her up and down, smirking with a lascivious expression that made Ben sick as he watched.

"We have to drive the trucks back anyway. Besides, you know our orders," another man called out to the group on the ground, looking at Val, Chantelle, Su, and finally back at Beth. "He'll want all of them." The seven-hour drive stretched like a cruel eternity, each mile a reminder of their helplessness. Cramped in the back of the truck, the group's predicament felt almost unreal, a nightmare played out in slow, jarring motion. The air was thick with unspoken dread - every glance between captives carried the weight of shared fear. The truck's rumble sent bodies jostling against each other, the confined space amplifying every shallow breath, every nervous shuffle. Beth's back ached, and her hands were numb from the restraints. Outside, the world seemed impossibly distant, while inside, the casual laughter of the men in the front cab cut through the tension, twisting it into something sharper, colder, and utterly disorienting.

"We could pull over for the night," one of them had suggested. "Have our own fun before we get to the—"

"I'm not in the mood," another turned to look at the women lined up on the benches, arms bound behind them and gags pulling their cheeks tight. "I wanna get back, been out here too long. Besides, that one looks like she bites. I'm too tired to deal with that." Beth glared at him before he turned to face forward once more. Their conversation of violence seemed phenomenally casual, almost as if they were discussing dinner plans. Ben shot Austin a look of dejection as he listened to the men discussing the vile things they would do, if they had been bothered to pull over for the night. The rhythmic hum of the engine droned on, an unsettling metronome to their silent thoughts. Each mind churned with fears of escape, of MJ, and the uncertain fate that awaited them. Occasionally, they stole furtive glances at one another, searching for reassurance, or perhaps a shared understanding of the dread pressing down on them. Then, abruptly, the truck shuddered to a stop. Su was hauled out first, carried across the harsh concrete parking lot. Beth followed, her steps tense as the man holding her arm forced her down the steps. She yanked free with sharp indignation, her anger sparking against his frigid grip. Each movement felt amplified in the silence, every detail of the surroundings pressing in as if the world itself had narrowed to the concrete underfoot and the looming threat of their captors.

"Oh, he'll like you." He smirked at her, the voice lingering with an air of malice and amusement.

"Fuck you." She muffled through her gag. A sharp crack split the air as he slapped her across the cheek, sending her stumbling into the back of the truck. Ben, still seated, lunged for her, but two men grabbed him from either side, yanking him down face-first onto the unforgiving concrete. A rifle pressed into the back of his neck, and pain shot through his body as a knee slammed into his spine, pinning him, while his cheek was crushed against the rough ground. Beth took a tentative step toward him, only to be yanked back by the man who had struck her, his grip harsh and unyielding. The metallic tang of fear and sweat filled the air, mingling with the muffled cries and the dull thuds of bodies hitting the concrete. Each movement, each desperate struggle, felt simultaneously futile and unbearably immediate.

"If you move again, we'll shoot her." The man's gaze flicked between them, sharp and unrelenting. Ben froze immediately, the muffled groans of protest stifled by his gag.

"And if *you* move again," another man snarled, fixing Beth with a predatory stare. "We'll shoot him." Beth's muscles tensed, her chest heaving as she fought the instinct to lunge, to resist, but the cold evening air filled her lungs instead. Slowly, painfully, she ceased struggling, the weight of helplessness settling over them both like a thick, suffocating fog.

"Have we calmed down?" The first man asked Beth, his rifle still pressed against Ben's neck. Her heart raced as she slowed her breathing and looked down at Ben who met her gaze with concern. She nodded and relaxed her tense posture, trying to feign compliance. They lifted Ben from the ground, escorting him across the parking lot. Beth paused and looked around at the seemingly familiar place, her eyes catching the faded signs around her - Alcatraz Cruises. Austin's steps were measured and careful, each one guided by the rifle-wielding man beside him as they moved toward the ferry. Beth remained on the pier, her eyes darting over every shadowed corner, every possible escape route, every object that might serve as a weapon. Her pulse raced as her mind raced faster, calculating and desperate. Reece was her next sight, his movements restrained by a guard just behind him. Their eyes met for a fleeting moment, and she felt the weight of his silent warning. He shook his head slowly, a quiet, almost sorrowful gesture that spoke volumes - whatever plan she had, it wasn't going to work.

"Come on." Another man grabbed her arm. He yanked her toward the ferry and shoved her onto the deck. The boat rocked violently as the waves slammed against its side, and she lost her footing. She hit hard, sprawling onto her side, pain lancing through her hip and slamming against her skull. Groaning, she tumbled next to Su's still form, her body rolling slightly with the motion of the waves. The cold air stung her face, and for a moment, the world tilted violently, leaving her gasping for breath through her gag while her heart hammered in her chest.

"We took care of the kid," a man walked over to Alex. "But what about this one?"

"Let him decide." Another said.

"You know how he feels about old people." The man replied, waving his knife around casually. Tyler flinched in his chair, but refrained from moving.

"He looks fit enough. Might be of some use." Another spoke up, bringing the ramp inside the ferry and walking towards the front. They all jolted back as the ferry lurched sideways, a few of the men cursing as they steadied themselves.

"*Sorry,*" a crackled voice came over a handheld radio. "*I'm still getting used to it.*" Austin was still in a trance as Ben leaned into him, his voice muffled by the gag.

"What do we do?"

"I told her I would protect MJ." Austin muffled back as

Ben looked at him with a concerned expression, his brow furrowing.

"No talking!" A man approached Ben, rifle raised and ready to strike. The ferry lurched violently with a wave, and Ben instinctively recoiled as the man stumbled but quickly regained his balance. Cursing under his breath, the man scanned the deck, glancing toward the front of the ferry before glaring back at Ben. He planted himself against a post, seeking a steadier position. Beth rolled onto her back, staring at the ceiling of the ferry, trying to calm the queasy churn in her stomach as the open water tossed the vessel like a toy. Her gag loosened, and she spat it from her mouth, drawing in a deep, shuddering breath. The air filled her lungs like a lifeline. The engine's roar and the slap of waves against the hull seemed louder than ever. Then a muffled cry cut through the chaos.

"Min-ji!" Su screamed, the piercing noise cutting through the gag. She sat up and looked around the ferry, her wide eyes reflecting both confusion and fear. "*Nae ttal eodi isseo*? Where is my daughter?"

"He doesn't like children." A man walked over to her, tightening the gag as she screamed for her child. The muffled cries blended with the rhythmic crashing of the waves as the man at the helm steered the vessel swiftly across the water.

"Can we shut her up?" Another walked over to Su as she wailed on the floor.

"Let her cry," one said. "Maybe she'll get it out of her system before we get there."

"You killed her daughter," Beth looked up at him, recognising him as the man who ripped MJ from Su's arms. "It'll take more than fifteen fucking minutes to get over that." He looked down at her, walking slowly, then crouching over her. He placed a gentle hand on her face, but Beth refused to recoil. She swallowed hard, her heart hammering in her chest.

"Shame," he said, his voice soft, almost intimate, yet laced with menace. "Guess we'll have to get rid of the problem." His left hand gripped the side of Beth's face, forcing her gaze onto Su. In one fluid motion, his right hand snapped up, pistol aimed at Su's temple, and the trigger clicked. The boat lurched violently with a wave, and the bullet zipped past Su's hair, scorching air and splintering the ceiling above. Time froze, and Su's sobs caught in her throat, her small body rigid with fear. Beth's own breath left her in a harsh, trembling gasp she hadn't realised she'd been holding. Relief and shock collided violently in her chest. Bile rose, burning her throat, but she swallowed it back, refusing to give him the satisfaction. He pressed closer, whispering into her ear. "Lucky for her, she gets a second chance. Don't pretend to be tough. It won't do you any good. So sit still, and be quiet like a good girl." He pressed a mocking, gentle kiss to her forehead, tightened her gag, and strode to the other side of the ferry. Beth's eyes darted to Ben, wide and frantic, and in that moment she saw everything - fear, helplessness, exhaustion - mirrored in his gaze. They were all prisoners in the same hopeless nightmare. She was lifted to her feet as the ferry docked at Alcatraz, her unsteady legs struggling to find purchase as the boat rocked against the pier. The cold wind cut at her face, but there was no time to register it - they were immediately marched up the winding hill toward the prison. Beth stole a glance back at Austin, whose blank gaze seemed drained of all emotion, leaving her stomach heavy with unease. While the men were escorted around the side of the building, the women were halted at the main cellhouse entrance. The spot where the gift shop had once stood was now stripped bare, chairs lining the walls like grim placeholders. She watched the men disappear around the corner, none daring to look back. A shove from behind pushed her through the doorway. The sudden change from the bright, open air to the dim, enclosed space made her head spin, forcing her to blink repeatedly as her eyes adjusted. The door slammed shut behind them with a solid thud, the echo reverberating through the empty room. Silence followed, oppressive and complete, pressing down on the four of them like a physical weight. In the quiet, Beth's chest tightened, each breath shallow, each heartbeat magnified in the stillness.

"Where are we?" Val's muffled question trembled through her gag.

"The gift shop." Beth replied, her voice muffled as she scanned the room, though there were no souvenirs left on the shelves. The dim light caught on the glossy white tiles, reflecting cold and sterile against the group. She tried the door with her forearm, but it wouldn't budge.

"It's locked from the outside," a hushed voice called from the adjacent room. "Please, this way." Beth pushed past the others, every step echoing on the concrete floor. A short, plump woman stood before her. Her kind eyes, sharp and unnerving, seemed to peer straight into Beth's thoughts. She gestured toward a bench, calm, but the room's stillness made Beth hesitate, her chest tightening.

"What's going on?"

"Please, sit—"

"Not until you tell us what's happening." Beth's stance was firm, wary. The woman's dirty apron hung tattered at the hem, her fingers long and thin, her grey hair neat at the shoulders.

"You need to wash." She said softly, raising an eyebrow.

"Who are you?" Beth demanded through her gag.

"I'm Maureen," the woman smiled, but it didn't reach her eyes. "I'll take care of you while you're here."

"Take care of us?" Val muttered, moving closer to stand beside Beth.

"Yes," Maureen said, gesturing to the bench. "Sit. If you don't, your friends will get hurt." Val and Beth exchanged wary glances before lowering themselves cautiously. Chantelle obeyed silently, and Su remained frozen, catatonic in the corner. "Come on, it's okay." Maureen motioned for Su to join them.

"Your friends murdered her daughter." Val spat through her gag.

"Not *my* friends," Maureen corrected bluntly. "But they don't like children here."

"So they kill them?" Chantelle cried, pain and fear sharpening her words.

"Yes," Maureen said. Silence fell, thick and heavy. Su was ushered forward by a young woman with dark brown hair, her skin glinting in the dim light. "This is Jennifer. We're going to take your gags off now. Do not scream." Beth's throat tightened.

"If you scream, they'll hurt your friends." Jennifer added softly. Finally, the gags were removed. Beth swallowed hard, tasting freedom and bile at the same time.

"What the fuck does that mean—"

"We're taking off your binds now," Jennifer said hesitantly. "Please... don't hurt me."

"Hurting us won't help," Maureen interjected. "But if you do, he will—"

"Yeah, we fucking get it." Val's glare cut through the room. Maureen pursed her lips together before stooping behind Beth. The restraints were stripped away, one by one, wrists raw and tender.

"You need to remove your clothes." Maureen stood, walking to the other side of the room to fetch a basket. Returning to them, she placed the basket gingerly at their feet. In the dimly lit room, the air was thick with tension, heavy enough to press against their skin. Vulnerable and exposed, the group moved cautiously under Maureen and Jennifer's watchful eyes. Su sat motionless, her catatonia amplifying the oppressive stillness, a living void in the centre of the room. Then something shifted. Her vacant eyes snapped to Jennifer, pupils flaring with a raw, almost feral intensity. In an instant, Su lunged, a storm of rage and grief, her body colliding with Jennifer's. The two women toppled to the cold floor, limbs flailing in desperate, chaotic struggle. Slaps echoed sharply, muffled screams ricocheted off the walls, and the faint scent of sweat and fear filled the air. Beth's heart lurched as she took in the scene - Su, on top of Jennifer, slapping wildly, screaming for her daughter. Maureen ran toward the chaos, but Val's firm grip on her upper arm froze her in place.

"Don't." Val commanded, her voice low and dangerous. Beth surged forward, tackling Su from behind, pressing her down, arms wrapping tightly around her flailing wrists.

"Su, stop! *Please*!" She cried, voice ragged, trembling with panic and fury. Su's screams for MJ turned into strangled sobs, her body quaking against Beth's hold, every second stretching like an eternity. The two women collapsed into a tangle on the floor, Beth holding on with all her strength, fighting against both Su's grief-fueled desperation and the biting reality of their helplessness. A door burst open. A man appeared, and Su's sobs hitched, but Maureen raised a hand toward him.

"It's okay, Kevin." She said. The man nodded, eyes briefly scanning Val and Chantelle, taking in their naked forms before smirking and leaving as abruptly as he had entered. Beth's muscles burned as she continued to restrain Su, straddling her on the cold floor, wrists locked against her frantic thrashing. Slowly, the heart-wrenching cries began to fade, giving way to ragged, silent sobs that shook Su's frame. The room seemed to exhale with the cessation of her screaming, leaving only the oppressive hum of fear and uncertainty. Beth finally helped Su to her feet, supporting her trembling frame. Maureen gestured toward Jennifer, who picked up a sponge from the bucket, preparing to begin the forced washing. Beth, Val, and Chantelle washed themselves slowly, eyes constantly flicking toward Su, ready to respond to any sudden flare of panic or grief. From outside, a gunshot cracked through the air, sharp and unnerving. Maureen and Jennifer ignored it, but Beth's gaze snapped to the door, a spike of panic lancing through her chest. The world outside the room was merciless, the walls around them barely a shield against the cruelty waiting beyond.

"Just target practice." Jennifer said quietly, almost indistinctly. Once they were done, Maureen and Jennifer disappeared from the room, closing the door behind them.

"D'you think they're gonna hurt 'em?" Chantelle whispered.

"Of course they are." Beth said flatly, her voice numb. Val's eyes darted between the grimy windows.

"Who are they?"

"Not Mountain Gate. Too organised." Beth stood, pacing around the room.

"Ex-military?" Chantelle wrapped her arms around her knees.

"Too disorganised." Val countered with a scoff.

"Somewhere in the middle." Beth muttered. She checked the door, but it was unsurprisingly locked. Maureen returned with four grey dresses.

"Please, put these on. He wants to see you," she said. Beth snatched the dress, throwing it to the ground. Maureen hissed, picking it up and thrusting it back into her hands. "I don't think I need to repeat myself again, so you'll just have to wait and see for yourself. Now, you can either put this on, or Kevin will walk you outside naked. It's your choice." Beth's jaw tightened, and she nodded, swallowing as she donned the dress. As they emerged from the building, Beth's arm was yanked suddenly, stumbling across the gravel. Their bare feet ached from the relentless march. The four of them were brought into the recreation yard. Their eyes fell on the posts where Austin, Ben, Reece, Sam, Tyler, and Chase were tied. Tyler sobbed silently. And there, on the cold ground, lay Alex, his lifeless eyes staring into nothing, a gunshot wound to his head.

Chapter Thirty-One

Tears streaked down Chantelle's cheeks as she was roughly shoved into line between Beth and Val, her body trembling from shock and fear. Each step felt like dragging her soul across broken glass, and she struggled to steady herself as the sight of Alex's lifeless body on the ground ingrained into her memory like a vice. Su followed slowly behind her, her movements obedient and mechanical, but the sorrow radiating from her every step only deepened the sense of helplessness that hung over the group. Beth and Val exchanged haunted glances, and Chantelle's sobs threatened to escape again, though she fought them back, swallowed by despair and the unbearable weight of what they had just witnessed.

"What did you do?" She cried. A man emerged from the shadows across the yard, his hands clasped behind his back like a predator sizing up prey. His blonde hair whipped in the wind, but it did nothing to soften the cold, calculating tilt of his head. Every step he took was deliberate and measured, carrying an almost theatrical patience as if savouring the fear he inspired before even speaking. His eyes, sharp and unblinking, scanned the group with a predator's precision, and the faintest curl of a smile hinted at a cruelty that promised nothing but pain.

"He was deemed unnecessary."

"*Unnecessary?*" Val's hand clenched into a tight fist, her nails digging deep into her palms as she struggled to contain the surge of anger and helplessness coursing through her. Her jaw tightened, teeth grinding together, and a low, restrained hiss of frustration escaped her throat. Every instinct screamed to fight, to lash out at the cruel reality before them, but the sight of Alex's lifeless body and the unrelenting control of their captors kept her frozen. The tight coil of rage and fear twisted in her chest, making each shallow breath feel like a battle against despair itself.

"Yes." The man's lips were set in a thin, straight line, his eyes piercing and cold as he spoke.

"People aren't unnecessary." Beth fired at him.

"They are here," he leaned in close and examined her, smirking. "You have a fire in you. He'll like you." Beth squared her shoulders, planting her feet firmly as she faced the stranger, who towered over her by a full foot, every inch of his presence radiating cold, deliberate menace.

"So I've been told—"

"What's your name?" He smiled at her, dragging a finger down the side of her face softly as she recoiled.

"Don't touch me." She spat, the words dripping with contempt as she recoiled.

"It might not be me you have to worry about," he laughed, gesturing around him as he walked over to where the men were tied up, eyeing them off one by one. "But we can talk about that later. You've been brought out here because of your little outburst." He looked at Su, a smirk playing on his lips while she continued to stare blankly into the distance. He motioned to one of his men, who strode confidently toward Chase. A brutal punch to the gut sent him collapsing to his knees, his arms sliding helplessly down the pole behind him. Beth surged forward instinctively, running to the middle of the yard, but the man raised a single hand, stopping her in an invisible chokehold of authority. The air around him seemed to thicken, each breath she took scraping against the icy weight of his presence. Even without touching her, he radiated a bone-deep cold, a suffocating darkness that made her muscles seize and her heart hammer as if trying to escape her chest. Her gaze darted to Ben, and a sharp, searing pang shot from her throat straight down to her toes, leaving her trembling and teetering on the edge of hysteria. The man smirked, a slow, cruel curl of his lips that made Beth's stomach knot. With a casual wave of his hand, another of his men stepped forward, striking Ben squarely in the jaw. His head snapped violently to the side, a sickening crack echoing through the yard, and a spatter of blood hit the gravel at their feet. The impact reverberated through the air, and for a heartbeat, everything seemed to stop. -Beth's chest tightened, her hands trembled, and the world narrowed to the sight of Ben, stunned and bleeding, at the mercy of these monsters. She froze between the two groups of her friends, eyes flicking to the men stationed around the yard. Their rifles were trained on the groups, poised and ready, each trigger finger an extension of the commanding man's will. One wrong move, one flinch, and someone else would die. Slowly, deliberately, he walked toward Val, Chantelle, and Su, inspecting them with a gaze that seemed to peel away every layer of their defences, and the air around him grew heavier with menace. "Are you unnecessary?" He looked down at Val, who shot Beth an ambivalent glance. Beth nodded at her desperately, furrowing her brows and looking over to Su who was still catatonic.

"I—" she stammered. "I'm a nurse."

"Good, you can go to the infirmary," he continued on to Chantelle and raised an eyebrow at her. "And you?"

"She was a student," Val said before Chantelle could

respond. "I was training her. She belongs with me in the infirmary—"

"Liar!" The man smirked, giving a small, almost lazy nod. One of his men stepped forward without hesitation, driving a vicious blow straight into Austin's eye. The impact landed with a sickening crack, snapping his head sideways as blood sprayed from the split skin beneath his brow. He staggered, barely staying upright against the post as his eye began to swell almost instantly. Beth recoiled where she stood, her breath catching as she fought every instinct to move, to run to him. But she didn't dare. Alone in the open space of the yard, she felt completely exposed - every inch of her vulnerable under the watch of rifles and that man's unrelenting gaze.

"I'm in high school," Chantelle said quickly. "I was in high school. Please, I'm only sixteen—"

"Sixteen!" the man laughed, looking around the yard. "Still such a *child*." They froze, bracing for it, for the words that would condemn her. Waiting for him to say that children were unnecessary. Waiting for Chantelle to be killed where she stood. He looked her up and down slowly, deliberately, before leaning in close, his face near hers as if he were breathing her in, savouring the moment. Chantelle's body went rigid, her breath caught somewhere between her lungs and her throat. Then he spoke. "But you *look* old enough." The shift was instant, like a vice loosening. The air rushed back into their lungs.

"Thank God." Val whispered, her voice breaking, breath hitching as she fought to steady herself. Beth willed every fibre of her being not to move, unsure of what any of them would do while she slowly looked around the yard again. It seemed that the other men had almost been trained into responding to one word commands. Words that displeased this authoritative figure triggered a response that forced them to be violent towards someone else as punishment, but they didn't look as if they enjoyed it as much as he did. Her stomach turned as she tried to imagine what it had taken to break them down into this - what kind of hell had carved that kind of compliance into a person. The man let out a quiet grunt as he finished inspecting Chantelle, then shifted his attention to Su.

"You?" He looked down his aquiline nose at her. She remained silent, staring into the distance, completely suspended in animation. Her distant gaze stared straight through him as he cocked his head from side to side, moving around her as if trying to silently grab her attention, but she was barely present.

"Su—" Beth's voice was barely audible as she pleaded for the woman to break her silence, praying that he wouldn't hurt someone else for her disobedience.

"I'm talking to you." The man's hand was large and rough, with calloused skin and dirt under his fingernails. As he waved it in front of Su's face, she flinched slightly, her eyes staying fixed on the distance.

"She was a housewife," Beth said, the lie coming quicker than she expected, even as she realised she had no idea what Su had been before everything fell apart. "She's just exhausted." She held his gaze, forcing every part of herself into stillness, willing her expression into something steady, something believable. Not too defensive, not too soft. Just enough truth wrapped around the lie to make it hold.

"She lost her husband, her sister, her mother, and one of your men just murdered her daughter." Val's voice cracked through the air like a gunshot, sharp and piercing as she hurled her words at him.

"Oh, no. What a shame," he said sarcastically. "She seems obedient enough. She'll be fine in the kitchen." Snorting, he finally moved back towards Beth. "He'll want to see *you*." Beth fought the urge to flinch at her wonder of who this other man was. He scanned her from head to toe, sizing her up and silently judging her worth.

"Don't you want to find out if I'm necessary?" Sarcasm dripped from her mouth like venom.

"No need," he laughed. "You're definitely necessary." Beth glanced back at Ben. He was already watching them, his glare hollowed out by something deeper - desperation and defeat. His body slumped against the post that held him upright as their eyes met for a fleeting second, and it was enough. No words, just a shared understanding of what necessary really meant for women with no specific assignment. Her gaze shifted to Austin. He didn't look up. His eyes were fixed on the ground, empty, as if whatever fight he had in him had been beaten out as soon as they were tied up. She looked between them all. Bound, bloodied and barely holding themselves upright. Dirt streaked their faces, dried blood clung to their skin, and their bodies trembled under the strain of the ropes cutting into them. And then it hit her. This hadn't just happened, they'd already been beaten. Not for information, not for resistance, just because they could be. The punches, the blows in front of them, that wasn't punishment. That was theatre, a message. A cold, sickening realisation settled deep in her chest. It didn't matter what they did. They were going to get hurt anyway.

"And what about them?" Beth whipped around to glare back at the man who was still circling the courtyard. "Are they necessary?"

"All muscle is necessary," the man waved his hand at another who grabbed the women one by one to usher them back inside. "You're dismissed. Hopefully you've learned your lesson."

In the hushed confines of the prison walls, Val was led down a corridor by her silent escort. As she walked, she observed a few women clad in grey dresses, their downcast eyes avoiding any form of interaction as she passed. The cells displayed a stark contrast, with some bearing personal touches and cosy blankets, while others remained barren and unoccupied. Upon entering the infirmary, Val was greeted by a man donned in a doctor's coat. His acknowledgment was accompanied by a nod towards the escort who had brought her there. The air in the infirmary carried an unmistakable atmosphere of tension and restraint, leaving Val to wonder about the intricate dynamics at play within the confines of the institution.

"She's a nurse." The man who had escorted said.

"Perfect." The doctor smiled, and then paused, waiting for the man to go. The man stood firm, staring at nothing in particular towards the back wall. Val cautiously darted her eyes between the two, trying to discern who had the power in the room before settling her eyes back on the doctor who raised an eyebrow at her escort.

"He asked me to—"

"Thank you," the doctor's voice dripped with sarcasm and superiority, a sharp contrast to the robotic tone of the escort's response. "You can leave now." The escort barely moved his gaze from the back wall before turning and marching himself out the door and back down the corridor, his boots heavy and footsteps echoing as he left. Val stood straight, her body stiff with fear as she turned to face him, her voice laced with disdain.

"Who are you?"

"I'm Doctor Horn," he said. "But you can call me Bryce when they aren't around." Val looked around the room, seemingly kitted out with an array of medical supplies and equipment. She spotted her medical kit from her backpack on a table in the back room. Her mind flickered between her distant memories of scouring Redding for supplies, finally settling on the unnerving memory of the men hoarding medical provisions into the back of a truck.

"You didn't waste any time going through our shit." Val could almost taste the bitterness in the air as her words dripped with frustration and loathing.

"All of your items will be catalogued and distributed accordingly," he looked down at a clipboard, running a pen down the page. "And it seems you all had a lot on you to sort and categorise." She maintained her silence, looking around the room, taking a step towards her things. "Please don't. I would hate to have to call someone in here. Do I need to call someone in here?" He asked calmly. She shook her head, still looking around the room at all of the items, noticing a scalpel on the bench. "I know what you're thinking." The doctor's voice had a sharp, biting quality to it.

"What's that?"

"That you want to hold me hostage with that scalpel over there," his fingers drummed impatiently against his clipboard, the sound of his nails clicking against the metal echoing in the room. "Or you want to strangle me to death with my stethoscope—"

"Among other things." Her eyes darted around the room, still refusing to make eye contact with him.

"I can assure you, the only thing that is going to do is anger Victor and he will torture your friends until you're completely catatonic," he looked up from his clipboard over his glasses. "And they will have no use for a catatonic nurse."

"Victor?"

"Blonde hair, hook nose, carries himself like authority is something he owns rather than earns," he placed his clipboard on the bench and folded his arms. "I assume you've met him, otherwise you wouldn't be in here."

"I think so," Val walked over to the bench and leaned against it, folding her arms to mirror his stance. "Are you allowed to talk about him like that?"

"Who's going to tell them? You?" His laughter burst out unexpectedly, almost like a reflex. The sudden sound caused Val to jump in surprise, and she regarded the man with a wary eye, scrutinising his actions that seemed to lack any concern for his own safety. "I am their only doctor and there is no one left here who I love. They can't hurt me anymore." His casual, almost careless manner in an environment that should have been tense set her every nerve on edge. The contrast between his indifference and the danger around them sharpened Val's instincts, leaving her on high alert, every movement scrutinised.

"What did they do to you?"

"They murdered my daughter." He said, his face impassive.

"Why?"

"Because they don't like children here," the words fell from his mouth without any weight or emotion behind them. "So she became unnecessary."

"Became?"

"She was necessary, until she wasn't," his voice was a void, a black hole sucking in all feeling and leaving nothing but emptiness in its wake. "And I don't have the correct equipment here for a... termination." Val paused, weighing each word with full awareness of its meaning and consequence. The room's tension pressed down on her, sharpening the stakes of the conversation. She braced herself for his response to the question she was about to ask, fully aware of the fragile power dynamics at play within the prison.

"If someone isn't assigned a job, what do they do?"

"Someone?"

"A female."

"Ahh," tilting his head to the side, he narrowed his eyes at her. "Do you really want me to answer a question you already know the answer to?"

Staring through Chantelle as if she weren't there, Beth could barely find the stomach to eat the food in front of her. Chantelle mirrored her, reeling from the conversation they had both had with Maureen earlier. Chantelle's hands were folded gingerly in her lap, while Beth had braced herself on the table, elbows locked and fingers tight on the metal top. Chantelle's expression and body language was soft, almost as if she were trying to mitigate the pain within her as she replayed the conversation over in her head. Beth's body was stiff and her face was contorted in pain as she tried hard to force the lump in her throat back down into her stomach before she gagged on her own anxiety. Still barefoot and led along the gravel path, Beth and Chantelle had approached a small garden where Maureen diligently tended to various flowers. The vibrant hues of the blooms contrasted with the bleak surroundings of the prison, creating an unexpected oasis in the midst of hardship. The scent of the flowers wafted through the air, momentarily alleviating the oppressive atmosphere within the confines of the prison walls.

"I had a feeling you two would be brought to me at some point." Maureen was working diligently, tending to the flowers without breaking her focus, not looking up at either of them. Her gentle words had drifted through the air, a stark contrast to the fragility of the blossoms she had lovingly tended to in the garden.

"Brought to you for what?" Beth's words had been sharp, her tone indignant.

"A chat," Maureen had stood up slowly, bracing her hands on her knees to straighten herself up. She cursed her ailing knees before dusting herself off. "Let's go for a walk—"

"Fuck." Beth mouthed silently to herself as she closed her

eyes and thought about the garden, the walk around the grounds that Maureen tended to, and the evident dissimilarity of the beauty that surrounded them, followed by the harrowing conversation. Bile rose in her throat, and she forced it back down. Beth watched Su move slowly around the kitchen, though her efforts seemed minimal. She moved about, eyes distant, performing her duties with a detached air. Her thoughts lingered on the daughter she had been forcibly separated from, and the oppressive weight of her captivity pressed down on her. Beth watched cautiously as Maureen, overseeing the operations, noticed Su's lack of enthusiasm. Approaching her, she spoke with a measured tone.

"Su, every role here is essential. We all contribute, and we all reap the benefits. Embrace your place in this community, and you'll find solace." Maureen smiled delicately at her. Su glanced at Maureen, visibly distressed, her expression a mix of resentment and resignation. The kitchen felt like a cage where she was forced to play a part in an unsettling drama. Beth slammed her fists into the table and stood up. She walked through the kitchen doors and braced herself on the bench inside.

"Leave her alone." She commanded, her voice stern and authoritative. A man walked over to her as Maureen held up her hand dismissively, before gesturing around the room.

"Su needs to learn her place here—"

"Her *place*?" Beth fired at her. "Like mine and Chantelle's *place*?"

"Exactly." Maureen nodded. In a defiant and spontaneous act, Beth impulsively seized a kitchen knife from the counter. Before she could fully process her actions, the man swiftly clasped both of her arms at the elbows, forcibly escorting her out of the kitchen.

"Let go of me!" She protested, her pleas met with the man's unwavering grip. Beth's protests echoed through the air as the man firmly restrained her, his grip unyielding. He pulled her away from the kitchen, the cold knife still in her grasp, her fingers tensely wrapped around the handle, the unfamiliar surroundings added to her disorientation. "Let go of me!" She repeated, her voice rang out with a mixture of frustration and fear. She squirmed in his grasp, attempting to free herself from the imposing hold that restricted her movements. The man, seemingly indifferent to her protests, continued guiding her away, the knife a potential threat in her hand. He swung her violently to the right, causing her hand to collide with a support post in the dining hall. Beth winced as her hand made contact with the concrete, the force making her fingers release the knife. It clattered to the floor, the sound echoing in the tense atmosphere of the dining hall. "Let me go!" Beth demanded, attempting to pull away from his grasp. The man, indifferent to her protests, continued to escort her towards the doors. She struggled against his hold, staring at Chantelle, hoping she would pick up the knife and aid in her rescue. Chantelle, however, remained seated, staring blankly into the distance.

"Ben!" Austin called, straining against his own restraints. "Ben, wake up!" His words trembled with urgency, carrying across the small distance, but he could do nothing else to reach him.

"Oh," Ben's voice came out as a low, distorted grunt as he lifted his head, scanning the recreation yard. "We're still here." Every one of them had slumped against their posts, bodies sagging with exhaustion. The unforgiving ropes bit into their wrists and shoulders, keeping them tethered in place, their weariness etched into every strained line of their faces. Even in the dim light, their hopelessness was palpable, a weight pressing down on the yard as if the very air mourned with them.

"Where's Sam?" Austin's gaze shifted to the unoccupied post as Ben roused. Slowly regaining consciousness, a sense of panic washed over him. With each passing second, his mind became clearer, and he became more aware of the dire situation they were in.

"Where's Beth?"

"I don't know." Austin responded, taking note of the haphazard positioning of armed men aimlessly roaming the vicinity, out of earshot.

"They were—" Ben looked up at where the women had been standing in the yard earlier. "Were they wearing grey dresses? Was that *real*?"

"Really strange," Reece said groggily, looking over at them. "You're in shock, Ben. Try to calm down." Ben lowered his head and nodded thoughtfully, studying the intricate patterns in the dirt and mud beneath his feet. Turning his attention to Tyler, Reece glanced at Alex's body on the ground.

"I'm okay." Tyler lied as he gazed at the sky and shut his eyes. Chase's face was grimy with sweat and dirt, his eyes narrowed as his head rolled to the side, revealing a jagged scar that ran from his ear to his jawline.

"It's okay not to be." He said. They all sat exhausted in the dirt, gazing out into the distance. They stole glances at each other every now and then, but no one had the energy to speak anymore. The weight of the day was crushing them, with the dirty ground offering no relief, their lips dry and mouths parched from lack of food and water. As dusk settled, casting long shadows across the desolate recreation area, the tight bindings around their hands began to loosen. The mysterious figures behind their release worked quickly and efficiently, allowing the captives to rub their wrists and regain some mobility, before their hands were bound behind them once again. The air was thick with tension as they cautiously looked around, uncertainty etched on their faces.

"Where are we going?" Austin's voice cracked as he protested, his words swallowed by the heavy silence around them. No one answered. The quiet stretched, thick and suffocating, amplifying the tension in the yard. Every member of the group grappled with their own spiralling thoughts - fear, anger, and helplessness colliding as uncertainty gnawed at their nerves. Each step, each bite of the ropes holding their wrists together seemed magnified, a constant reminder of their powerlessness.

Chapter Thirty-Two

Beth was yanked into a well-lit parlour by two men, their grips firm and unrelenting. They planted her roughly into a chair in the centre of the room, its cold legs scraping slightly against the floor. Her eyes fluttered as they adjusted to the brightness, taking in the sight of Val, Chantelle, and Su standing rigidly in a line along the wall to her left. Each of them seemed tense, their bodies taut as if anticipating the next command. The room felt oppressive despite the light. The wide space magnified every movement, every shuffle of feet, and the unspoken weight of what was about to happen pressed down on her chest. She shifted her feet uncomfortably, and attempted to stand.

"Don't. Even. Think. About it." A man raised a finger sharply, forcing Beth to freeze mid-breath. His gesture toward her right made her shift her gaze, revealing Ben, Reece, Chase, and Tyler pressed against the wall, kneeling with their hands bound tightly behind their backs. Their heads hung low, bodies slumped with exhaustion, yet the rigid tension in their shoulders betrayed a readiness for punishment at any moment. The dim lighting made it hard to take in all the details at once, and Beth's eyes flicked nervously around the room before

landing on Austin, slumped but tied to a chair beside her. The sight of him, restrained and vulnerable, twisted her stomach into knots. Her chest tightened, each shallow breath a struggle, as the reality of their captivity pressed down like a physical weight. Every subtle movement of the men around them carried a threat, a reminder that one wrong glance, one wrong breath could trigger a sudden, brutal act. She sank slowly back into the chair, digging her nails into the wooden arms.

"What the fuck?" She let out a sudden, sharp laugh - half disbelief, half nervous energy. The sound ricocheted off the walls, startling even her own ears. Out of the corner of her eye, she caught Austin flinch, the movement almost imperceptible but enough to make her heart skip. The echo of her laughter felt intrusive in the oppressive silence of the room, as if it had no right to exist here, and she froze instantly, chastising herself for breaking the careful quiet.

"Is this funny to you?" The man's voice snapped sharply through the room, tinged with surprise and barely contained frustration, each word vibrating with a dangerous edge that made the air itself seem to tighten around them.

"No, this is insane," she laughed again, then her nerves settle before clearing her throat. "Who are you?"

"My name is Marcus," he approached Beth with a lightness to his step, his lips upturned in a smug smirk. "And this is a *lesson*." She glanced to her right. The dim light was just enough to see Austin's disheveled appearance. Sweat glistened on his forehead, and his clothes were wrinkled and torn.

"A lesson?" She asked quietly, looking back at Marcus.

"Yes," Marcus' smirk was like a rogue wave, just visible enough to be perceived but hiding a sense of danger beneath its surface. "Everyone learns a lesson when they come here." His sadistic, self-absorbed behaviour was oddly playful. "I thought you'd learn it in the yard, but apparently not."

"Apparently not." Beth echoed. She couldn't tell if he was completely insane or simply enjoying himself with their torment. A small fire crackled in the back corner of the room. He strutted over to where the women were waiting, each one avoiding his eyes as he walked by.

"I learned my very first lesson after I arrived here and started helping people," Marcus turned on his heel to face Beth and Austin. The air around her seemed to grow colder and her skin tingled with goosebumps as he approached. "I learned that sometimes people don't really care when we threaten them, when they think that out there is better than in here." There was a quiet tension in the room, heightened by the occasional creak of the chair as Austin shifted in his bindings.

"Where's Sam?" He asked, looking up at Marcus.

"Having a drink with his new friends. He was *oh so happy* to tell me what you did to his mother," Marcus replied joyfully, looking between Austin and Beth. "He decided he'd rather be on my side than yours. Though, he did plead with me to be nice to his sister." He looked over to Su, whose gaze hadn't left her feet. "But that will depend on *his* behaviour. Now, come on, don't you want to know what the lesson is?" He teased menacingly, a hint of frustration in his voice as he looked back towards Beth.

"Okay," Beth's mouth was suddenly dry with fear, a metallic tang filling her senses. "What's the lesson?"

"I'm so glad you asked!" Marcus rushed towards her, placing his hands on either side of the chair and leaning in close. "The lesson is that if any of you step out of line, then someone *else* gets punished. Quite simple, isn't it?"

"Fuck you." Beth recoiled, gagging slightly on the over-powering stench of sweat and grime that clung to Marcus. He strode toward Su with a terrifying deliberation and slapped her across the face, the dull thud of her body hitting the floor echoing in the room. Beth sprang upright, shoving the chair back with a sudden force.

"*Sit.*" Marcus pointed a gleaming knife at her, his tone sharp and deliberate, the single word slicing through the air like a threat made flesh. Her fists clenched at her sides, but she obeyed, lowering herself slowly into the chair, spine rigid. Her nails bit into the wooden arms, her eyes darting across the room. His men didn't flinch at her defiance - they were puppets trained with ruthless precision, moving only when their master willed it. "Now, we've had some defiant people in here but I feel like you are going to be extra difficult." She gulped, inhaling deeply and exhaling slowly as her body trembled with fear and adrenaline.

"Something tells me you'd like that—"

"Oh, yes, I do love fucking with people. Please give me a reason to do so," he walked over to one of his men, looking over at Beth as his tone changed from a light playful menace to dark and vitriolic. "Like Tim here, who tried to escape with his wife and sister, so I let him watch while my men took turns with poor Maya and Tamara. Unfortunately, they didn't survive the ordeal, but Tim listens now." Ben flinched and shifted on his knees. Austin looked over at him and shook his head quickly. Marcus scuffled Tim's hair as the broken man stood unwavering, looking straight ahead, holding his rifle firmly at his chest despite the rough mocking gesture.

"Tim *listens* now?" Chase asked cautiously. Marcus closed the distance in two long, deliberate strides and slammed a blunt fist into Tyler's jaw. The sickening crack echoed in the room as Tyler's head snapped sideways, and he slumped slightly against the wall.

"I am talking to these two!" Marcus barked, jabbing the tip of his knife toward Austin and Beth. The blade caught the light, glinting sharply, a silent promise of what could come if they dared to move. Every muscle in Beth's body stiffened as the cold gleam of the weapon pressed against her awareness, and she froze in place, heart hammering. "So as long as you behave, everything is good!" Beth let out a low, sharp gasp as two men materialised behind her, forcing her arms down onto the chair's wooden rests. The pressure was crushing, pinning her so tightly that even the tiniest movement felt impossible. Still, she thrashed violently, trying to wrench free, her legs kicking against the floor in a futile attempt to slide the chair backward. Her bare feet skidded uselessly against the concrete, the friction too little to give her leverage. Marcus's gaze swept the room with clinical precision, flicking from Chase to Tyler, lingering on Reece, and finally resting on Ben and Austin. Their faces - etched with fear, pain, and barely contained defiance - drew a faint, cruel curl of a smile to his lips. He relished the control, the way every twitch and flinch responded to his presence. Another man approached the fire with a slow, deliberate gait, retrieving a glowing branding iron. The molten tip shimmered ominously in the flickering light, casting warped shadows across the captives' faces. Beth's chest heaved, her breath coming in short, ragged gasps, heart hammering as icy dread slithered up her spine. The metallic scent of iron and smoke filled the air, pressing down on her like a weight, and Marcus's eyes lingered on her with calculated patience, waiting for the fear to take root fully. Ben struggled to raise from his kneeled position, placing a foot in front of him.

"Beth!—"

"*Don't. Move.*" Marcus's voice cut through the room like a whip, low and deliberate. His hand moved with unnerving speed, pulling a handgun from his jacket. He leveled it at Chantelle across the room, the barrel unwavering, unflinching. Chantelle whimpered, eyes snapping shut, trying to shrink inside herself. Beth's gaze snapped between her and Ben.

"Ben, don't!" she gasped. "Shut your eyes—"

"Keep your eyes open, *Ben*," Marcus interrupted, almost teasing, his tone eerily casual. The gun stayed trained on Chantelle, unwavering. Ben's stare locked on Beth, helpless as the men forced her down, their grips ironclad, preventing even the smallest escape. Every futile struggle, every strained breath, Marcus seemed to drink it in, savouring the helplessness like a fine indulgence.

"We get it," Austin's jaw tightened, anger and frustration coiling in his chest as he looked up. "You don't have to do this —" Marcus's eyes slid to him, sharp and calculating, as if reading the defiance like a book. He tilted his head slightly, a slow, deliberate motion. He gestured silently towards Beth, and Austin's gaze shifted reluctantly, the weight of Marcus's control pressing down on him like a physical force. Every nerve in the room seemed to hum with tension, each heartbeat a reminder that one wrong blink, one wrong move, and Marcus's playfulness could turn lethal in an instant. They watched in unbearable, stomach-churning agony as the man with the branding iron advanced toward Beth. Each deliberate step seemed to echo in the room, each one heavier than the last. The air around him felt thick and hot, like the metal he held was radiating pain even before contact. Beth's eyes widened as the iron hovered over her forearm, the anticipation alone twisting her stomach into knots. When it finally pressed down, a searing scream tore from her throat, jagged and raw, scraping against the walls. The sound was sharp, unrelenting, echoing in the parlour until it felt like it would shatter something inside her. Ben's gaze darted between Beth, Chantelle, Austin, and Marcus, his body taut, every muscle straining with tension. Rage and helplessness wrestled inside him, his fists clenched so tightly his knuckles were white. He could feel his heartbeat thrumming in his temples, a chaotic drum that mirrored the panic rising in his chest. One wrong move, one flinch, and Marcus's cruelty would rain down again. He forced himself to stay still, even as his mind screamed to intervene, to tear the men off her, to stop the pain. Austin's body trembled violently, feet pushing into the floor as though grounding himself could somehow give him leverage to act. The raw, metallic scent of burning flesh made bile rise in his throat. Beth's cries cut through him, a knife twisting in his chest with every high-pitched wail, every desperate gasp. His stomach heaved, yet he could do nothing. Marcus stood back, arms loose at his sides, his expression deceptively calm, like a conductor watching a symphony of agony unfold. There was a method to his cruelty, an artistry in the way he savoured the suffering without lifting a hand. Each flinch, each flaring eye, each tremble of Beth's body was a silent affirmation of his power. The other captives could only watch, their own fear thick in their lungs, their hearts hammering as their helplessness stretched taut like a wire. Time dragged on, minutes melting into one another, every second a drawn-out eternity of torment. When the branding iron was finally removed, Beth sagged forward in the chair, gasping, sweat and tears mixing on her face, her arm a screaming monument to the pain she had endured. She trembled violently, gripping the sides of the chair as though her fingers could anchor her to something solid in the chaos of her body. And finally, just as her body had been threatening all day, the bile clawed its way up her throat. She barely had time to brace herself before it spilled into her lap, staining the fabric of the chair, thick and cloying. A sharp, acidic tang filled her mouth, and some dripped down in viscous rivulets onto the floor, hissing slightly where it hit the concrete. She hadn't eaten in over a day, so there wasn't much, but what little there was turned into a sickly yellow mess, a brutal reminder of her body's betrayal and her own utter exhaustion. Every ragged breath she drew tasted of acid and fear, and the putrid tang of panic lingered in the air, mixing with the faint, lingering stench of burnt flesh.

"Ahh shit," Marcus sighed, scratching his stubble absentmindedly. "Now you've ruined my chair." Austin's jaw was tight to the point of pain - his whole body shook, fury and impotence burning like acid in his veins. Ben's gaze never left her, raw grief and impotent rage blazing behind his eyes, each inhale tasting of fear and frustration. Marcus's steps echoed across the room as he moved toward Ben, slow and deliberate, eyes sharp and predatory. Each movement was a reminder that nothing, no scream or flinch or protest would be ignored. The silence that followed Beth's torment was suffocating, heavier than the screams themselves, a cruel reminder that the next moment could erupt in pain again. Everyone felt it, a silent, shared dread that pulsed like a heartbeat through the room - the inescapable, lingering truth that Marcus thrived on control, that their suffering was a tool, and that mercy was a stranger here. Even in the brief stillness, the smell of burned skin lingered like a ghost, a mark on their senses that would not be forgotten. Beth's breaths came in ragged bursts, each one a reminder of the cruelty just inflicted.

"Fuck." Tyler gagged violently, his body jerking as bile forced its way up. It spilled over his lips, running down his beard in thick, hot rivulets, splattering onto the floor below. Each heaving breath rattled in his chest, the taste acrid and bitter.

"Jesus Christ, you're not all gonna vomit, are you?" Marcus spun around the room, turning abruptly towards Austin. "Because if *you* do I'd really prefer that you lean forward a bit. I like these chairs—"

"No." Austin said softly. His hands shook, a silent promise of retribution forming in his rigid frame. Ben's body remained coiled, taut with restrained fury, eyes burning with the knowledge that action was impossible yet inevitable when the moment came. And Marcus, calm, deliberate, unstoppable, loomed over them all - an unyielding shadow of menace that made the room feel smaller, the air heavier, and hope a fragile, flickering thing. His eyes darted between Austin and Ben before he let out a light laugh and sighed.

"This one cares about you," Marcus leaned over to look at Ben before standing and redirecting his eyes towards Austin. "This one too—"

"Go fuck yourself!" Beth screamed, her fingers digging into her arm as she rocked forward, the sweat on her neck matting her hair to her skin. Every nerve in her body screamed in pain and fear. Marcus circled behind Ben with predatory ease, and then, with brutal precision, slammed the butt of his handgun into the back of Ben's skull. Ben's body crumpled to the floor with a hollow thud, a muffled groan escaping his lips. His restraints held him fast, and even as the pain radiated through him, he could do nothing but struggle against the unforgiving bonds. The room seemed to shrink around them, the scent of sweat and fear thick in the air, each second stretching unbearably.

"Excuse me?" Marcus leaned down, pressing the cold barrel of his gun hard against Austin's temple. His voice was low, deliberate, every word dripping with menace. "Did you say something?" Austin's took in a sharp breath. Beth's gaze shot to him, her eyelids quivering as she shook her head.

"No." She whispered, her voice barely audible as she swallowed the lump rising in her throat. Marcus moved with unnerving grace, snatching the glowing branding iron from the man who held it and stepping over to return it to the fire. The faint sizzle as it touched the coals echoed in the quiet room, making her flinch. Then, almost too casually, he strode back toward her. Crouching low, he reached up and tilted her chin with a deliberate gentleness that made her stomach twist. Her eyes met his, and for a heartbeat, the soft motion felt like a trap - a predator's intimacy that promised pain, not comfort.

"Now, if any of my men try to touch you, show them that brand," he whispered softly, nodding toward her scorched arm with a smirk. "And it'll remind them not to." Marcus seemed to glow with satisfaction at the suffering he had orchestrated, his grin widening as Beth blinked up at him, her gaze unfocused and hazy from pain and exhaustion. A thin thread of anger lingered beneath the daze, but it was tangled with nausea, shock, and the raw fatigue of having been broken. Her eyes, glassy and half-lidded, flickered toward him with a quiet resistance rather than full fury. "You really want to hit me right now, don't you? Go on, *do it*." Marcus whispered, leaning closer, reveling in her limbo between defiance and disorientation. Beth's lips pressed into a tight line as she shook her head slowly, her body trembling from the effort of staying upright and aware, her mind barely able to process the threat as the oppressive tension wrapped around them both.

"No—"

"Do it, and I'll slap your friend here," he said, nodding toward Austin, who looked up at her with wide, uncomprehending eyes. "Don't, and I'll shoot him in the head." He tilted his head, resting the barrel of his gun against his own temple like it was nothing. Beth's body trembled, sweat trickling down her face, her chest rising and falling in ragged gasps. For a heartbeat, uncertainty froze her, but Austin's gaze was steady, pleading and unwavering. It ignited a spark of resolve. Without hesitation, she swung her hand and struck Marcus across the face. The slap echoed sharply through the room, a brief, jagged crack of defiance cutting through the oppressive air. Red welts bloomed instantly on his cheek, a small, raw proof of her anger and exhaustion interwoven. Austin's jaw clenched as pain shot through his head from the immediate retaliation - the butt of Marcus' handgun smashed into the side of his skull, snapping his neck to the side. His groan was guttural, ragged, and Beth's stomach churned.

"I'm sorry." She whispered, closing her eyes and bowing her head, teeth digging into her lower lip as she fought back a sob, the weight of helplessness pressing down on her chest.

"Have we all learned our lesson?" Marcus raised his arms mockingly, a cruel grin stretching across his face. A few of them nodded in silence, their movements slow, tentative, as if afraid to draw his attention. Beth lifted her gaze, trembling.

"Yes." She whispered, her voice raw, barely audible.

"Good." Marcus dropped his arms and walked over to her. Without warning, he pressed his lips to her forehead. Beth flinched violently, and Ben recoiled beside her. Her skin crawled at the intimacy, the violation, as Marcus' eyes lingered for a heartbeat too long.

"You should get that looked at," he said casually, nodding toward her arm. "We don't want it getting infected. And for God's sake, clean yourself up. You stink." Beth's gaze dropped. Her arm throbbed, the skin bubbling and blistering where the branding iron had seared the flesh. The letter M, encircled and raw, glared back at her like a permanent scar, a mark of ownership that left her stomach twisting in helpless rage. He had branded her link cattle. "Now you may all go. I'm bored." Ben was hauled to his feet, his eyes catching hers one last time, apology written across every line of his face. Reece, Chase, and Tyler followed silently. Val, Chantelle, and Su were next. Beth's gaze sought theirs, but they all avoided her eyes, leaving a silent, suffocating tension between them. Finally, Austin's restraints were removed.

"I'm sorry." Beth mouthed a quiet, heavy apology. He only nodded in response, his face pale and tight, before being led from the room.

"Take her to the infirmary," Marcus instructed one of his men, his voice chillingly calm. "And bring her something nice to eat. She should be rewarded for her... *good behaviour*."

Chapter Thirty-Three

Val's hands moved carefully over the raw, branded flesh of Beth's arm, swabbing it gently with antiseptic. Each pass brought a sharp sting that made Beth flinch, but she held herself upright, eyes fixed on some distant, unmoving point as though staring could keep the pain contained. The antiseptic scent hung heavy in the air, clinical and sharp, mingling with the faint tang of blood and sweat still clinging to her skin. Neither spoke. Their silence was dense, almost oppressive. Every tiny sound made Beth's muscles twitch with instinctive tension. Val's hands were steady, but her fingers trembled slightly, the residue of fear from Marcus's presence still lingering. Beth's chest rose and fell in shallow, uneven breaths. Her mind wanted to drift, to find a space far from the room and the memory of what had happened, but the echo of Marcus's smirk, the weight of his control, pressed like a shadow against her back. Even here, even with Val tending to her, the two of them alone in the solitude of the infirmary, she couldn't fully escape it.

"The guards told me what happened in the kitchen," Val finally broke the silence, not daring to look Beth in the eyes. "You know, before we were all dragged into that room—"

"And?"

"*And,*" Val pressed. "If you'd kept your cool then maybe he wouldn't've been so—" She trailed off, her fingers slowing as she dabbed at Beth's arm.

"So this is my fault?" Beth scoffed, looking at Val for the first time since entering the infirmary. "He would've branded me either way—"

"But we might not've been dragged in there to see it," Val stopped dabbing and looked up at Beth. "Maybe think of others before you do something stupid again and put the rest of us in that situation." Beth stared at her, wide-eyed and unblinking.

"With all due respect, fuck you, Val—" Beth winced as Val pressed the antiseptic harder into her skin, pain searing through the fresh brand. "You have no idea what happened in that kitchen, why I grabbed that knife—"

"Chantelle was there," Val hissed, turning to put the gauze on the tray. "You could've gotten her killed—"

"You have *no fucking idea* what I did for that girl." Beth snatched her arm from Val and stood, walking across the room to the bench and slamming her fists into the metal counter. Metal clashed with metal, and a clipboard fell to the floor with a resounding clang. "Maureen took us for a walk and told us that Victor loved my spirit, but Marcus might prefer Chantelle. All fresh and pure and young. She said Marcus would most likely choose her, but Maureen had the final recommendation. His last girl died less than a week ago, and he was itching for another... but he didn't want any of the others here. That's why we were brought here. He wanted someone new, exciting, and unbroken. I *begged* Maureen to tell him to choose me to save Chantelle, and for a moment, I saw some humanity in her eyes... right before she slapped me and told me to be grateful for whatever we had. Then we left, and I thought Chantelle was fucked. But then—" Beth's eyes drifted to her arm, blistered and raw, pain searing from shoulder to wrist. Her back ached from being held down, her mouth tasted like poison, and she felt sticky and unclean from the sweat that still clung to her dress.

"Beth, I—"

"No," Beth snapped and turned to face her, hands digging into the counter to stop herself from throwing something. "I don't want to hear it, Val. You don't like me. Never have. But don't act like I'm the worst person you've ever met. You're angry, fine. But don't take it out on me. I don't want to be here any more than you do. I grabbed that knife because Maureen was going after Su. Because I was *furious*. Because I knew she'd pick Chantelle for Marcus. Because we were told what we were gonna become, and then shoved into the dining hall to sit there while the men looked us over like we were... fuck, I don't know... inventory? Fresh meat? It made me sick. I'm sorry my temper got you thrown in that room with me, but—" Doctor Horn cleared his throat. Both of them jumped, and Beth spun toward him, heart still hammering, and he raised a single eyebrow, calm and unshaken.

"You're lucky no one else was standing in the hallway," he said lightly. "You must be Beth, I'm Doctor Horn."

"How long've you been standing there?" Val asked, swallowing the lump in her throat.

"Long enough," he said. "Come on, back on the cot. Let Val finish dressing your wound." Beth hesitated, then walked slowly back to the cot where Val continued to dress her arm. The air hung heavy with tension, and Beth navigated the space cautiously.

"Don't worry, this happens to everyone. You'll stop blaming each other... in time." He said casually. Beth rolled her head toward the doctor, face scornful.

"Excuse me?—"

"People come here and blame their friends and their loved ones because blaming Marcus and Victor only causes pain for others. They yell and scream until they're defeated and have nothing left," he explained, raising his eyebrows. "Though you seem to be handling that better than the others." He gestured to the brand on her arm.

"How much of our... conversation did you overhear?" Val asked, not looking up from the wound.

"All of it."

"So you know Beth threw Chantelle to the rest of the wolves while she only has to deal with Marcus—"

"Ahh," he cocked his head. "You think the wolves are worse than the hawk?" Beth and Val exchanged an awkward glance, then looked back to the doctor. He sighed, and pushed his glasses up his nose.

"The wolves will eat you quickly. If you're nice enough, they can be tamed with a kind word or a light touch. A treat, every now and then. But the hawk? He dismembers his prey slowly. He holds it in his talons, precise and cold. He is an intelligent, *patient* killer. He'll hunt other prey for a quick meal, but when he's bored of the hunt, he returns to his nest to feast on his prized catch." Beth glanced down at her arm, bile threatening to rise again, but she had nothing left to give. Val stopped wrapping her arm, fingers shaking as she slowly looked up at Beth.

"So the wolves—"

"Are the better choice," the doctor said, tapping his clipboard. "Well, the illusion of choice. Beth seems to have picked for Chantelle, and your daughter got the better end of the deal. The den is easier to hide than the nest—"

"Can I be excused?" Val asked.

"Of course," he said, taking the half-wrapped bandage from Val. She hurried from the room, clutching at her stomach and covering her mouth. "Anyway, do you have any questions?" He continued wrapping Beth's arm, winding the bandage slowly in a dizzying motion.

"Yeah," she said blankly. "How the fuck do we get out of
here?"

"I meant about your wound. Aftercare, etcetera." He
replied, ignoring her indifference. Beth's gaze flicked to the
doorway.

"No—" She paused as a woman suddenly appeared,
balancing a tray of food. Her steady glare seemed to convey a
steady mix of distaste and obedience.

"I was told to bring this to the infirmary," she said, placing
the tray down quickly. She glanced at Beth's bandaged arm
and scoffed. "Lucky." Then she walked off, soft red hair flow-
ing, figure gliding instead of stepping. Beth raised an eyebrow
at the doctor.

"Lucky?"

"Sabrina tried very hard for a promotion," he said,
watching her disappear. "Alas, she isn't exactly Marcus' type.
Already broken by this place. But then again, neither are
you—"

"And this makes me lucky?" Beth asked, gesturing toward
her bandaged arm.

"Some girls prefer the devil you know," he said, walking
over to set down his clipboard. "Sabrina likes to be in charge.
The men pick her first, and they treat her well... for the most
part. She wanted an extra level of... protection, I suppose."

"Lucky me." Beth scoffed, sitting up to take some food
from her tray. She glanced at her bandage, then noticed the
concern etched on the doctor's face.

"Can I get you anything else?" He asked.

"No thank you, Doctor Horn." She said softly.

"Call me Bryce. We might as well get acquainted a bit
better. We'll be seeing a lot more of each other," he shrugged.
"Oh, and you can stay in one of the recovery rooms tonight.
You've had a rough day. Saves you walking all the way back to
your cold cell. The room will be locked—"

"Is that for my safety, or theirs?" Beth asked sarcastically, eyes blank. He smiled and left her alone to eat her late dinner.

A solid week had passed since that night in the parlour, though Austin couldn't quite figure out how many days exactly. The repetitive labour made time stretch thin, each motion blurring into the next. Dawn had already spilled pale light across the yard, the early spring sun cutting through the lingering chill. He wiped the sweat from his brow, grimacing as the ache in his arms reminded him just how much work he'd endured, and how much of himself he'd left behind in the days since.

"Keep working!" a sharp voice cut from the courtyard's edge. One of the guards was staring him down. Austin shifted his attention to Reece, who was sawing through a log with methodical precision. They'd been assigned the tedious task of reconstructing one of the collapsed outer structures - a job that felt meaningless, especially after seeing the rows and rows of empty cells. There was already enough room for the bodies they had. He bent to clear rocks and debris from the wrecked building near the pier where they had arrived. Thoughts of escape flitted through his mind, teasing him, before he pushed them aside. One wrong move here could mean death, or worse - the death of someone else. Glancing at Ben, he noticed the robotic way he moved through the yard. His eyes tracked the rocks he shifted, but his mind seemed elsewhere, distant and unreachable. Austin approached the pile of stones Ben had been working on. The sharp tang of the ocean carried on the wind, brushing past them both, a fleeting reminder of the world outside this prison of stone and labour. He lowered himself to the ground next to a large stone as if he were about to assist in lifting it.

"Ben," he spoke softly. "We can take them—"

"What?" Ben's mind was foggy. The smell of salty sweat and exertion hung heavy in the air around him, mixed with the metallic scent of blood from the cuts on his hands.

"We can take them," Austin repeated. "We get a plan together with the others, and we—"

"No." Ben's face twisted with anger, jaw locked tight as he forced the word out through gritted teeth, his eyes narrowed with barely contained frustration.

"What?"

"I said *no*." The rock hit the ground with a dull thud as they released it. On impact, it split slightly, fragments breaking away as a fine cloud of dust lifted between them, hanging in the tense, unmoving air.

"Ben—"

"Look around, Austin," Ben whispered angrily. "We aren't going anywhere, and anything we do will likely get the girls killed—"

"But—"

"No buts." Ben pushed past his friend, returning to his pile of debris.

"Hey, I said keep working!" The same guard who had berated Austin earlier strode toward them, his expression set with purpose, a faint, unsettling smirk tugging at his lips. Feigning obedience, Austin gave a short nod and turned back to the pile, bending to pick up a rock. He held it there for a moment, turning it in his hand, feeling the rough edge scrape against his thumb. Solid and real, something he could actually use. His mind flickered, quick and dangerous. His eyes met Reece's, who gave him a sharp shake of his head. Austin ignored it. With a small, decisive nod to himself, he turned on his heel and hurled the rock. It struck the guard high in the back. He lurched forward with a grunt, his rifle slipping from his grasp and clattering to the ground. Austin moved before the sound even settled. He sprinted forward, closing the distance in seconds, and slammed into him, driving him to the ground. The impact knocked the air from the guard's lungs as they hit hard. For a split second, everything stilled, then the courtyard shifted. What had been forced labour twisted into something else. Something volatile. The guard recovered fast, swinging blindly. Austin took the hit, then drove a punch into his ribs, then another. Fists collided with bone and muscle, each impact sharp and brutal. Around them, men began to gather. Some laughed, some jeered, but no one stepped in. Austin barely registered them. His movements were rough, unpolished - fuelled by exhaustion, anger, something desperate clawing its way out. Every strike was less about winning and more about feeling something that wasn't help-lessness. The guard retaliated with equal force, slamming a fist into Austin's jaw, snapping his head sideways. Still, Austin didn't stop, he didn't think, he just hit back. The fight spiralled into chaos, messy and violent and breathless.

"What do you think you're all doing?" Victor's voice boomed through the courtyard, a commanding roar that momentarily silenced the sounds of the brawl. "Get back to work, *now*!" The crowd's murmurs turned into whispers of fear and submission as the group dispersed rapidly, leaving Austin and the guard on the floor. Looking up at Victor, Austin spat blood at his feet.

"Fuck you, *sir*." He smirked. Victor's oily face shone in the morning sun as he stood over Austin. Relishing in his perceived authority, he raised his foot quickly off the ground and kicked Austin square in the jaw.

"Take him." He spoke casually, flicking a dismissive hand through the air as he turned and walked away from the scene, as though it were nothing more than a minor inconvenience. Two guards stepped in immediately, each grabbing one of Austin's arms and hauling him back from the confrontation.

The crowd, a restless mix of prisoners and guards, began to disperse, their murmurs fading as the moment passed, though the tension it left behind lingered heavily in the air. Austin twisted slightly in their grip, just enough to cast one last defiant glare toward the guard he had fought. There was no apology in it, no regret - only a quiet, unspoken promise that this wouldn't be the end of it. As he was dragged away, Ben's gaze shifted toward the main structure of the prison, a cold dread settling deep in his chest. He forced himself not to follow the thought too far, not to picture what might be waiting inside, but the fear lingered all the same - thick, suffocating, and impossible to ignore.

Confined to her cell for a week, no one came for Beth. She endured long, monotonous stretches of silence, staring at the walls and tending to her injured arm. The only human interaction she had was when Val arrived to change the bandages, her visits brief and wordless. The rest of the time, Beth sat in stillness, her mind circling back to that night with Marcus. The memory lingered, sharp and inescapable, replaying in fragments she couldn't shut out. At times, the urge to move overwhelmed her - to run through the halls, screaming, searching for Ben, and Austin, and the others. She imagined grabbing a knife from the kitchen, forcing her way through anyone who stood between her and them. But the thought never made it past her body. Fear held her in place, rooting her to the bed, to the floor, to the walls that closed in around her. Each time she considered stepping beyond the threshold, her mind caught up, dragging her back with quiet, suffocating reminders of what one wrong move could cost. Not just her, but them. The door was left unlocked during the day. She knew that. The corridor beyond was there, waiting. Still, she didn't move. Days blurred together, marked only by the slow shift of light through the dirty windows outside. Morning bled into evening, then into night, until time itself lost its shape. So she stayed where she was, staring, thinking and imagining. She imagined finding them, one by one. Slipping through the halls unnoticed, reaching the pier, taking the ferry, or anything that would float, and leaving this place behind. She imagined Ben first. The way he would pull her in, bury his face in her hair, like he needed to know she was real. Then Austin, steady and certain, and back in control. Leading them away from the island, back to the mainland, further west. As far from this place as they could possibly go. Sabrina appeared in her cell doorway, like an unwelcome poltergeist stuck in the foundations and sucking the life from it's occupants. She folded her arms and leaned against the side, waking Beth from her trance.

"He'll leave you alone for a while." She smirked. Beth looked up at her, a half faded, half questioning look across her face.

"Who?"

"Marcus," Sabrina offered. "It's what he does. He'll leave you alone after whatever he did to you that turned you into... *this*." Beth returned her gaze to the blank wall in front of her.

"He hasn't done anything to me."

"Wow, so all he's done is brand you and you're already a mess?" Sabrina scoffed and entered the cell, leaning against the wall where Beth's gaze was fixed. "Just wait until he actually puts his hands on you. I can't wait to see what you're like then." Beth didn't lift her eyes at first, studying the woman's figure instead. Her slender frame strained against the plain grey dress, the tight material clinging to her hips, the sharp line of bone visible beneath it. There was a gauntness to her, but she held herself with a rigid kind of control, as though sheer will alone kept her standing. When Beth finally looked up, she

met a stern, unyielding gaze. Dark green eyes, cold and authoritative, stared back at her. Red hair fell in loose waves over her
shoulders, striking against the dullness of the room. A bruise
bloomed across her cheekbone, a quiet testament to the
violence that lingered on the island.

"This?" Sabrina smirked, raising her hand to her
discoloured cheek. She took a seat next to Beth, relaxing her
body a little and placing her hands on the edge of the bed,
bracing her posture. "Victor's the worst, but he's quick."

"Quick?" Beth turned her head to face Sabrina, her eyes
heavy and weary from exhaustion.

"Violence excites him, so once he's done with beating the
shit out of you he's quick at the end," she gestured down to
Beth's bandaged arm. "But you don't have to worry about
him—"

"Then why are you telling me this?" Beth could taste the
bitterness in her mouth as she spoke, a combination of fear
and disgust.

"I'm telling you for the sake of your friend."

"Chantelle?" Beth's energy lifted slightly. "Where is she?"

"Infirmary," Sabrina's face was expressionless. Her eyes
narrowed, and her lips pressed together. "She's new and exciting, but the novelty will wear off soon."

"The guys we came here with," Beth snapped her head
towards her quickly. "Do you know where they are?"

"I haven't seen them," Sabrina said. "But I assume they've
been taken to the worksites."

"Worksites?"

"Rebuilding some of the collapsed structures around the
island," Sabrina rose abruptly, already moving toward the
corridor. "I have to go." Before Beth could protest, she slipped
out of the cell, her pace quick but controlled. Beth stood and
followed to the metal frame, watching as she disappeared
down the corridor, her footsteps echoing faintly against the
concrete.

"Marcus wants you." A strong male voice from behind startled her, and she whipped around to see a man standing at the far end of the corridor. This was it, the moment Marcus would have her alone. The hawk hunting his prey, but she had to walk right into the nest.

Chapter Thirty-Four

Fear gripped her instantly, sharp and suffocating. Before she could react, the man closed the distance and seized her arm, his grip tight enough to make her wince. He dragged her down the dim corridor, her feet stumbling to keep up. The air was stale, thick with the scent of rusted metal and old sweat, pressing in around her with every step. She was hauled into Marcus's room, stark and cold, the space she thought was a parlour. She hadn't noticed the bed in the background last time. And he brought her right back to the place where she had been tortured. She couldn't escape the memory - she would be reminded of it every single time. He stood near the window, nothing more than a dark silhouette against the fading light. The man released her and stepped back toward the door, turning to face them. He fell still, almost statuesque, as if waiting for instruction.

"Ah, Beth," Marcus drawled, his voice oily with malice. "How are you feeling?" She shivered, but not from the cold in the room. Memories clawed back unbidden - the searing pain, the smell of burning flesh, the fear etched into her friends' faces, the sickening crack as Ben's head met the floor, the way

Austin had looked at her when he had been hauled away. It all came rushing back, suffocating and relentless. She wondered how many more memories she would collect in this room before the nightmare was over. "Tell me, how did it feel?" He moved closer, his breath warm against her cheek as his gaze drifted to her bandaged arm. Every instinct in her body screamed to pull away, to run, to do anything, but she stayed rigid, limbs frozen, heart hammering so violently she was sure he could hear it. Beth fought to smother the panic rising in her chest, clenching her fists at her sides. She bit down on her lip until it throbbed, tasting iron.

"It was nothing." She said, her voice tight and brittle, far too controlled. Her words were a shield, fragile and trembling, masking the storm of fear she wouldn't let him see.

"Lies," Marcus said with a smirk. "But let's talk about more recent betrayals." She squared her shoulders, fists clenched so tightly her knuckles ached, and took a careful step toward Marcus. Her eyes locked onto his, blazing with forced intensity. The light from the window carved sharp shadows across her face, lending her an air of defiance, but beneath the surface her heart thudded erratically, and a cold tremor ran through her limbs she struggled to contain. Every step felt like walking on a wire strung high above a chasm, and she willed herself not to falter.

"I haven't done anything—"

"Not you," he interrupted dismissively, raising a hand to silence her. His voice, cold and deliberate, cut through the chill of the room. "Your leader, Austin, has been struggling to keep up with his workload. You didn't pick a very strong person to lead you." Each word slammed into Beth's gut, twisting and burning as she recoiled slightly, tasting the metallic tang of blood on her lip from where she had bitten down hard. That taste only fueled her determination not to show weakness. "Poor Ben couldn't keep up," Marcus continued casually, indifferent. "He collapsed into a heap the day after you last saw him here, so I've had my men beat him every day since. Oh, and Tyler's dead," he lied, watching her face crumple. "An outburst over his father's death was his undoing." Beth's eyes widened, her face paling, her hands clenching into fists as shock and grief churned through her. Her mind whirled, thoughts tumbling uncontrollably, her heart pounding in heavy, desperate beats. "Reece is dead too," Marcus added, twisting the knife further. "He tried to steal a weapon, so we put him down on the spot." The room seemed to shrink around her, thick with the scent of fear, and the cacophony of her own racing thoughts drowned out everything else. "Chase saw reason," Marcus continued, a cruel smirk on his lips. "He's one of my men now, no longer forced to pay for your defiance—"

"Now I know you're lying," Beth shot back, her voice trembling but fierce. Her eyes blazed, her body tense, fists tight at her sides. "If you'd really killed Tyler, he'd never do that. For someone who makes a blanket rule of punishing people for lies and bullshit, you sure don't mind bending your own rules when it suits you—"

"And lastly, Sam," Marcus said, voice sharp as he cut her off. "He's adapted well to his new role among my ranks. But then again, he joined quite early on." Beth's thoughts flitted to young Sam, barely more than a child in this broken world, now a pawn in Marcus's cruel game. That part she believed - she remembered his absence from the parlour room, and his anger with her over his mother's death. Anger surged, overwhelming fear for a moment. She slapped Marcus across the face, and the sharp sound echoed in the room.

"Fuck," she whispered, covering her mouth with trembling hands. "I—" His eyes flashed with anger, then something darker, a smile creeping across his smug face. In one swift, unstoppable motion, he dragged her toward his bed, her resistance futile against the strength he wielded. Marcus's thick fingers dug into Beth's jaw, forcing her face up to meet his cruel, hungry gaze. His breath reeked of stale whiskey and rotting meat, hot and wet against her trembling face.

"Your spirit has *intrigued* me, Beth," he growled, his free hand sliding down her throat, squeezing just enough to make her gasp. "Now I want to see if your actions speak louder than words." The sting of the slap still lingered on Marcus's cheek as he pinned Beth to the bed. Her pulse hammered under his grip, her chest rising and falling in frantic little hitches as he squeezed harder, before releasing her throat. She coughed, and gasped for air rapidly. The mattress groaned beneath her, springs squealing, his massive thighs caging her in.

"Get off me!" Beth could feel the pressure of Marcus's body on top of her, his weight pressing down on her like a heavy stone, trapping her against the soft mattress. The sharp crack of flesh on flesh sent a shockwave of pain through her skull, her vision swimming as her head snapped to the side. A thin trickle of blood seeped from her split lip, and Marcus licked it away with a slow, filthy drag of his tongue.

"You taste like fear." Marcus sneered, his grip tightening on her arms. Beth clenched her jaw, refusing to give him the satisfaction of a reaction. But as his hands roamed over her body, an involuntary shudder ran through her. She choked back a sob, her fingers clawing at the sheets as Marcus's rough hands tore at her dress.

"Please." She whispered, hoping against hope that some shred of humanity remained within him, but Marcus was beyond reason.

"*Please*?" He laughed cruelly at her plea and continued to strip away her clothes, his touch rough and violating. The fabric ripped like wet paper, baring her pale, trembling flesh inch by inch, and she realised why the dresses were so tight and stretchy - the fabric was so easy to tear. She wondered how many dresses they had hidden away, how many they had stored for every time one got ruined. Then she snapped herself back into reality. This wasn't the time to disassociate, to leave her body and pretend she wasn't there, not like the last time. A surge of primal rage overtook Beth, her small frame trembling as she fought back against his grip. She clawed at his face with her nails, her feet flailing and kicking out in a desperate attempt to break free. Marcus was strong, his grip unyielding as he tightened his hold on her. A loud crack echoed through the room as he struck her across the face again. A searing pain exploded from her jaw, radiating through every nerve in her body.

"Fuck—" She clutched at her face in agony as she tried to regain her bearings. She wanted to scream and lash out again but she knew it would only make things worse. He paused and looked over her as she lay still on her side, breathing heavily and swallowing hard, trying not to move. Slowly, he pulled Beth onto her back, holding her wrists down as she stared up into the ceiling, thinking about nothing but the pain radiating through her body. The lump in her throat grew as he held her thin wrists together with one hand and lifted her dress with the other, fumbling at her hips as he struggled to remove her underwear. Cursing, he let go of her hands and fumbled with his belt, the buckle clinking like a death knell. She looked up at him as his attention wavered, wondering if she could seize the opportunity she had with his distracted attention. She swallowed hard, daring not to breathe as she mustered what little strength she had to potentially fight him off. Looking up slowly above her head, she noticed the long torch on the side of the bed, wondering if it was close enough for her to reach. With one swift movement, before even thinking about her actions, she braced her feet on the bed and lunged at the side table, grabbing for the torch as it knocked to the floor.

"Fucking bitch!" Marcus cursed as he lunged at her, causing them both to topple over the edge of the bed and land on the ground with a heavy thud. She let out a loud scream as she desperately reached for the torch, fumbling to grab it as it rolled across the floor just beyond her reach.

"Get off me!" She howled, but with his knees firmly planted on either side of her body, Marcus held her down as she fought against his grip. He leaned over her, reaching for the torch and picking it up in one smooth movement. He kept himself on top of her, pinning her to the floor with his torso as he pressed his face against her cheeks. His breath was hot against her face, and she gagged from the smell. The weight was crushing, and she could feel the pressure from the torch he held across her wrists. The torch she thought might save her was now used to easily pin her down with his one hand. Pressing his heavy body against her small frame, she was completely powerless to him now.

"I knew there was a fight in you I would enjoy." He said, stopping for a brief moment, catching his breath. He slowly moved his hands and pulled his pants down. She shifted slightly, trying to move out from underneath him, but there was no room for her to do so. She let her body go limp as she disassociated from the moment. Her eyes drifted from his face to the ceiling as she closed them. She could get through this, she told herself. She had done it before, when her husband sold her for food when they were starving. But this was different. Last time, he fumbled and grunted his way through it, barely leaving a mark on her. Marcus was different. She tried to pay no attention to his hands roaming her body, his tight grip leaving marks on her skin. Marcus didn't give her time to beg. He grabbed one leg, forcing them apart with a brutal yank, his fingers digging into the soft flesh of her inner thigh. And then she could no longer ignore it. The first thrust was agony as Beth's back arched off the hard floor. A ragged scream tore from her throat as Marcus buried himself to the hilt in one brutal stroke. The second thrust was a punishment, and her body jolted hard against the worn carpet, folding it beneath her. It dug into her back, her choked sobs mingling with Marcus's filthy growls. The third thrust was like ice coursing up her spine, and she felt something snap as Marcus leaned down, his teeth sinking into the tender flesh of her shoulder. Beth squeezed her eyes shut, tears streaming down her cheeks as his pace turned erratic. With each forceful movement, Marcus let out a victorious grunt while she lay there, unable to fight back. Her skin was marred and torn by his rough hands, and the rug protested as it crumpled beneath her, creasing and moving, acknowledging her suffering as he indulged in his twisted desires.

"I am not here." She whispered to herself, and then she was gone, her mind slipping from her body, untethered, as if she were watching herself from far away. The ache in her muscles, the pounding of her heart, even the echo of Marcus's words - all of it felt distant, unreal, like a scene playing out through a fogged window. Time stretched and thinned. The room, the bed, the walls, the floor - they all blurred together, and for a moment, she wasn't Beth at all. She was nothing. When he had finally satisfied himself, he walked away, leaving her behind - a broken form crumpled on the stained rug, laying in a pool of her own blood, mixed with their sweat and his semen dripping down her thighs and onto the carpet. Beth remained frozen, every muscle taut and aching, her thoughts a chaotic mix of terror and rage. The memory of his smirk, the weight of his presence, lingered like a shadow pressing against her chest. She could hear the measured, laboured rhythm of Marcus's footsteps as he dressed and left the room, each step echoing in the quiet, and his final words hung in the air, curling around her mind like smoke she couldn't shake.

"You'll learn to obey soon enough, Beth." He said her name with a venom that crawled into her bones, making her shiver uncontrollably. Tears traced hot paths down her temples as she lay flat on the floor, barely able to breathe through the trembling. She tried to shift, to roll over, but pain flared through every muscle. A sudden spasm of nausea hit, and she curled in on herself, rolling to her side. Bile and remnants of her meal spilled onto the carpet, her body betraying her in the only way it could, leaving her gasping and hollow, suspended between fear and helplessness.

"Do you need help getting up?" The man stood at the door, his back turned to her, waiting for her to collect herself so he could escort her back to her cell.

"Have you been here the whole time?" She coughed, forcing herself onto her knees, and finally leaning against the bed.

"I have to watch—" the man swallowed, his face etched with a hint of fear. "It's the rules." His voice cracked, a fissure of fragility that belied the control he tried to hold. Beth felt it deep in her chest. He was broken too. Not in the same way, not the same shape of fracture, but broken all the same. "Do you need help—"

"No." She said. With a deep, shuddering breath, she willed herself upright, each movement sending jagged jolts of pain through her body. Her teeth were clenched as she forced one foot in front of the other. Tugging her torn sleeve over her shoulder, she caught sight of herself in a crooked, cracked mirror hanging askew on the wall. Her once vibrant green eyes stared back, dull and hollow, swallowed by shadows she barely recognised. Bruises bloomed across her face like a cruel tapestry, each mark telling a story she wished she could forget. Her lip was split, one eye swollen shut, and a purple ring bruised her neck. She traced the damage with her gaze, detached, as if observing someone else entirely. The pain radiating through her limbs was sharp and insistent, a tether to the grim reality she could not escape. Unable to meet her reflection any longer, she turned away, each step echoing on the concrete floor like a hammer on her nerves. The man waiting at the door seemed vaguely familiar now, and then she recognised him - Tim, the man Marcus made an example of the night she was branded. He gestured, and she followed, her body heavy with exhaustion and dread. The hallway stretched on, dim and oppressive, shadows crawling along the cracked walls. Her bare feet felt numb against the cold concrete, and every step seemed longer than the last, each one dragging her deeper into the prison's claustrophobic grip. When Tim finally halted at a door, she realised they hadn't been heading back to her cell. A chill ran through her as she stepped inside, into another cellblock. It was even more desolate than her own, the gloom pressing in from every corner, the silence punctuated only by distant, hollow echoes. She paused, heart hammering, and let herself be swallowed by the shadows, her mind drifting somewhere far away, untethered, as if she might float out of herself and disappear entirely.

"Last cell." Tim's voice was cold as he shut the door behind her, the click echoing through the corridor. Beth's swollen eyes flickered, struggling to adjust to the dim light. She peered into the cells lining the corridor, each and every one empty, waiting for the next unfortunate soul. Her steps were cautious, measured, senses stretched taut. The air was thick with the musty, stagnant smell of neglect. Each cell she passed seemed to pulse with its own quiet despair, a capsule of isolation that hinted at countless untold horrors. Her unease coiled tighter with every step, her heartbeat echoing in her ears. When she finally reached the last cell, she dropped to her knees without hesitation, ignoring the searing pain through her body and pressing her hands against the metal bars. Her fingers trembled slightly as they gripped the cold steel, the faint taste of fear and hope mingling in her mouth.

"Austin." Her voice was barely more than a whisper, soft and tentative, trembling with the weight of everything she'd endured. It drifted across the cold space between them, nudging him from the edges of sleep. His eyes cracked open, heavy and sluggish, and he turned his head toward the bars, the dim light catching the weariness etched into his features.

"Beth," he said gently. "You're alive."

"So are you." Beth pressed her head against the cold bars, bracing her aching body as best she could. Austin shifted against the wall inside the cell, crawling over to sit as close to her as the bars allowed. She reached through and grabbed his hand tightly, tears streaking her dirt-smudged cheeks.

"Beth," Austin murmured, voice low and rough, trying to orient himself in the dim, oppressive space. "How are you here?" Her grip on his hand tightened.

"What did they do to you? Marcus told me that they killed Reece and Tyler, and Ben was—, and Chase had joined him, and Sam—," she paused, the bile rising in her throat again. "I'm so happy to see you—" She swallowed it down, studying his battered face, the way his eyes seemed empty yet restless, half-lost in exhaustion, struggling to stay semi-conscious. When he turned fully towards her, his fatigue seemed to ebb for a moment as he took in the full picture - her bruised, bloodied face, her torn clothing, the silent toll of her ordeal.

"Fuck," he breathed, reaching through the bars to brush her hair from her face, revealing the dark bruises and split lip. The sight set fire through him, a mix of rage and helplessness. "What happ—"

"Don't ask," she begged, tears spilling down her cheeks. "Please, don't ask."

"Marcus..." Austin growled. "Did he—"

"*Don't ask.*" Beth's voice trembled. Her pelvis ached, and a knot formed deep in her stomach. She forced a shallow breath. Austin sneered, holding the side of her face with his hand, his bruised knuckles red with dried blood. Looking up at him, she shook her head, a wave of defeat adorning her face.

"I'll kill him—"

"How? Marcus and Victor, they're so sadistic and cold, and everyone else seems too scared to do anything." Her words were fragile, a delicate spiderweb, shimmering with the weight of her pain and fear, threatening to collapse at any moment. "How long have you been in here?"

"Since about midday," he removed his hand from her face, straightening his back on the concrete. "I got into a fight this morning, they had me on the post in the yard for a bit, and now I'm here." He winced, arching his neck.

"Are the others okay?"

"Since I last saw them this morning, they're all still alive if that's what you mean," Austin's jaw clenched and his muscles tensed as he spoke. His body still felt the effects of the fight he had been in, and his punishment afterwards. "Okay is a stretch."

"He told me that Reece and Tyler were dead, and you had a mental breakdown, and Chase was with them now, and Ben —" A tear rolled down her cheek as she willed her body not to cry, banging her head against the metal bars, the sound echoing and bouncing off the concrete walls.

"Hey," he leaned in, angling his body closer, pressing his forehead gently against hers through the bars. The warmth of him was a startling contrast to the chill of the metal between them. "Nothing he said is true. He's just trying to break you." Austin murmured, his voice low and steady. Her hands tightly clenched the metal bars, her knuckles turning white from the force.

"I know—"

"You have to remember that," he pleaded. "Anything he tells you is a lie and he's just trying to break you."

"He's already broken me." Her voice trembled despite her best effort to keep it low and controlled. She fought the urge to bang her head against the bars, to dull the ache of the emotional torment that consumed her.

"No, he hasn't," Austin swallowed hard, wincing at the pain in his ribs, but his eyes stayed locked on hers. "You're stronger than you think."

"That might've been true," she whispered, voice barely audible. "Before today."

"What do you mean?" He asked. She recoiled, pulling her head back from the bars, meeting him with wide, haunted eyes, a mix of fear and disgust.

"I gave up. I just lay there... and I let him—"

"Time's up," Tim barked, storming down the corridor. "You have to leave."

"No, please," Beth's eyes grew wide, pleading. "I need more time—"

"Now." He grabbed her arm, yanking her to her feet and hauling her down the corridor. She wrenched free, sprinting back to the cell, collapsing against the bars and sinking to the cold floor.

"Don't tell Ben about this," she begged, voice cracking. "*Please*, Austin... he'll get himself killed." Austin nodded, helpless, as Tim seized her again, dragging her along the corridor. "Promise me!" She screamed after him as the outer cell door slammed shut behind her.

"You need to keep quiet," Tim hissed as they moved, the twisting passageways echoing with each step. "Or you'll get us both in trouble—"

"Look around you, Tim," she spat, yanking her arm free again. "I'm already in trouble." He froze in the corridor, his domineering presence filling the space, and she recoiled, stepping back instinctively.

"I'm not unfamiliar with your situation, Beth," he said, his tone cold and measured as he advanced. "And I do feel sorry for you. I really do. But we need to get you back to your cell."

"Why did you take me to see Austin?" Her voice was flat, her body planted like a stubborn anchor. She refused to move.

"There's no one left here for them to hurt if I make a mistake," he said, taking another measured step, his gaze fixed on her. "But if you don't move now, one of your friends're gonna get hurt."

"Why did you take me to see Austin?" She persisted, standing firm and inhaling deeply. Taking her arm once more, Tim pulled her down the corridor, continuing to her cell. He hurried them both through the concrete maze with determination.

"You hadn't seen your friends for a week. I thought it would help you—"

"Why're you trying to help me?" She asked cautiously, confused by his defiance.

"After Marcus does this he likes to be alone for a while."

"That doesn't answer my question." She pressed angrily as they approached her cell, a guard at the opposite end startling as they entered the corridor. Throwing her in, he stepped in after her.

"Stay here for the rest of the day!" His voice boomed, sharp and commanding, echoing off the walls of the cellblock. She looked up at him, noting the dissonance between his rigid, cold face and the force behind his yell - it wasn't meant for her, it was for the guard stationed down the corridor.

"I am in charge of you when he isn't around," he whispered softly, almost silently. The words seemed louder in the quiet space and he made sure the other guard couldn't hear him. "And Austin or Ben will be in charge of the next girl he likes once you're gone." Her eyes filled with desperation and fear as she looked up at him. "My wife was his favourite." Beth swallowed hard, her hands shaking.

"Where is she now?"

"Shut up!" Tim punched the leather mattress, and it crackled beneath his fist. Beth let out a scream, and then a low gasp as she stepped back and slammed herself against the wall. "He lied to you," he whispered. "Marcus never let any of the men rape Maya, but he wanted you all to think it—"

"Why?"

"That's the kind of person he is—"

"Maureen said the last girl only died days before we

arrived," Beth whispered, looking down to the floor. "Oh God, Tim, I—"

"Her body is still fresh, floating somewhere out there in the bay," his voice was low, steady, almost unnervingly calm. "After we tried to escape, he did his worst, or so I was told. He left her after he was done and she broke the mirror in his room and slit her wrists. It happened so fast—"

"The broken mirror," her voice was strained and hoarse, like sandpaper scraping against rough wood. She sat down on the bed slowly. "I'm so sorry—"

"Beth," he knelt down and brought his face close to hers, almost too close for comfort. "One of your friends will watch the next girl get raped and beaten endlessly so they know what he did to you before her. That is the kind of person he is. So when I beg for you to follow what I am asking, it's for your own good, because I know what he is capable of doing to people."

"And now you know what he did to your wife." Beth whispered remorsefully, a tear rolling down her cheek.

"And now I know what he did to my wife," Tim's face twisted with disgust and anger as he echoed Beth's words, his eyes narrowed and his jaw clenched tightly. "And up until today I was pissed, and sad, but now I get it. I understand why she broke that mirror and—" he paused, cracking his knuckles absentmindedly. "The best thing I can do now is help people here, until he's put down, or until I am."

"Can you take me to see Ben?" She pleaded softly.

"No. You need to swear at me now, loudly," he whispered. "So I can slap you and storm off. I have appearances to keep up, and I've spent far too long in here already." Closing her eyes and nodding reluctantly, she tilted her face up towards him and took in a deep breath.

"Fuck you!" She yelled, as his hand swung down past her face and into the mattress again, the crack echoing off the walls. She startled, a sharp, ragged sound escaping her throat -

neither scream nor grunt, but something caught somewhere in between, raw and instinctive. Nodding with a small gesture of gratitude, he offered her a half smile as he marched defiantly from her cell, sliding the door closed with a thud and walking down the corridor. Alone now, as the adrenaline drained and the weight of it settled, she pulled her knees tight to her chest and buried her face in the torn fabric of her dress, her sobs quiet and unrelenting in the quiet cellblock.

Chapter Thirty-Five

Chantelle's body was a canvas of purples and reds, an abstract map of the cruelty she had endured. She lay curled on the infirmary bed, shivering despite the room's warmth. Shadows flickered across her bruised face, and every so often a subtle tremor ran through her cut legs, as if her flesh remembered each blow even while her mind tried to forget. Val moved with practised care, hands soft and steady as she tended to Chantelle's wounds. The cool ointment slid over the cuts, a rare comfort in their harsh reality. Leaning closer to adjust a bandage, Val's brow furrowed, her touch gentle yet precise. The faint hum of a lantern nearby was the only sound, broken only by the occasional shuffle of Val's movements and the soft scrape of gauze against tender skin. The air smelled faintly of antiseptic and sweat, mingling in a way that made the room feel both clinical and intimate. Chantelle's breaths came shallow and uneven, her chest rising and falling as though even that small motion demanded effort. Her eyes, when they flickered open, were distant, unfocused, like a candle struggling against the wind. Val paused for a moment, glancing down at the battered form before her. Every bruise, every cut, every small mark told a story of endurance she could only imagine. She traced a line along Chantelle's arm with her thumb, careful not to press too hard, feeling the subtle twitch of muscle beneath tender skin.

"You don't have to move more than you can bear," she whispered, almost to herself, steadying the smaller, trembling body before her. "I'll talk to Doctor Horn tonight, and maybe he'll let you sleep in one of the treatment rooms—" A bead of sweat slipped down Chantelle's temple, catching the harsh light and dripping onto the sheets. Val dabbed it gently away, her fingers lingering briefly against the warmth of Chantelle's skin. For a moment, the girl seemed almost weightless, suspended somewhere between pain and numbness, the room around her blurred and distant. She made no sound, her lips pressed together, her fists loose but rigid in their restraint. The silence was oppressive, yet strangely protective, as if the walls themselves had absorbed the echoes of the torment outside. And somewhere in the back of Val's mind, she realised that despite what lay before her, it was nothing compared to the bruises and cuts she had dressed on Beth's body earlier that day. The brutality of one man had outweighed what three had done to Chantelle, but the thought brought no comfort at all. Chantelle's eyes fluttered, dark pools reflecting fear, pain, and defiance all at once. Her lips parted, but no sound emerged, as if her voice had been stolen along with everything else. She turned her head slightly, a motion small but deliberate, a silent refusal that carried as much weight as any words. Val exhaled slowly, a breath filled with empathy and frustration. She knew the signs of trauma - how it could lock someone inside themselves, leaving them mute and catatonic, a prisoner of memory. She continued her work, wiping away a stray tear with the pad of her thumb, feeling the slight shiver of muscle beneath her touch. Val rested a light hand on Chantelle's shoulder, grounding her without pressing, offering presence without demand. For a long, unbroken moment, the two of them existed in that quiet space. Val tended the wounds, and

Chantelle endured them, the room holding the unspoken truth of suffering and the fragile strength it took to survive. Every blink, every tremor, every exhale became part of the silent rhythm they shared - healer and wounded, connected through quiet persistence, through a language beyond words, through a strength that only pain could forge.

Moonlight seeped through the barred window, casting long, skeletal shadows across Reece's cell. He lay on his back, staring at the ceiling where the light formed an eerie lattice over the concrete. Silence hung over the row of cells, broken only by the occasional shift or muted cough from one of the other men. Ben was a quiet presence in the cell to his left. To his right, Austin's painful groans with every laboured breath filtered through the dark, the slow rhythm a reminder of the exhaustion that weighed on them all. Reece shifted, trying to ease the ache in his body against the unforgiving cot, but comfort was a luxury long since stripped away. His thoughts drifted to Val, Chantelle, Beth, and Su. His gaze hollowed, and a surge of helpless anger coiled in his chest. He clenched his fists, the rough blanket biting into his palms, grounding him in something real. Then, footsteps, abrupt and measured, drawing closer. The sound echoed through the corridor, a steady rhythm that signalled the changing of the guard. The current sentinels - a seasoned guard with his trainee in tow - moved off without a word, their departure as quiet as their watch had been. Sam had stood over them for the past twelve hours, and the shock on their faces when he first appeared had said enough. That hadn't stopped them from trying. Every attempt to speak to him had been met with a sharp blow through the bars from his trainer, followed by nothing more than a cold, silent scowl from Sam himself. He was one of them now, and there was nothing they could do. Another figure emerged to take their place - solo, seasoned, a new silent sentinel against the dark. Reece stilled, every muscle tightening, coiled with instinctive tension. The man paused, scanning the cells with a slow, deliberate sweep before stepping fully into the row, the heavy door swinging shut behind him with a dull, final thud. He moved with purpose, boots soft against the stone, until he stopped just outside Reece's cell.

"Name's Kevin," he said in a low voice, his eyes scanning the corridor. "You can talk freely now." Reece's heart pounded in response to the unexpected declaration, a mix of wariness and cautious hope flaring within him. He remained silent though, wary of traps and tricks as he sensed Austin and Ben stirring in their respective cells, the tension in the air thick enough to choke on. Kevin waited, patient as if time were no concern to him. There was something about his stance, a lack of rigid authority that suggested sincerity, or perhaps it was just another layer of deception in this place where trust had become an endangered sentiment. Reece's gaze moved from Kevin's face to the shadows on the walls, invisible threads connecting him to his friends in the shared uncertainty of the night. They were all caught in the same storm, battered by waves of fear and defiance. For now, words remained unspoken, a silent pact among them as potent as any spoken promise. They were together in this, even in the stifling quiet of captivity. The silence stretched thin, as if the men held their breath in unison, reluctant to give voice to their thoughts within walls that had heard too much. Kevin's eyes remained steady, a quiet challenge posed to their collective mistrust. "Look—"

"Is Sam really one of you?" Reece pushed himself up and took two quick steps toward the bars, staring Kevin down through the dim light. "Or is that some kind of trick?" Kevin raised an eyebrow, slow and unimpressed.

"A trick?"

"Yeah," Reece shot back, voice low and edged. "Like he's playing guard to get in our heads. I'm thinking Su got threatened, and we're all supposed to just sit here and swallow it—"

"Sam was pretty eager to be done with you," Kevin cut in, tone flat. "Didn't take much. Kept going on about his mother—"

"Bullshit!" Austin forced himself upright, pain flaring through his ribs as he crossed the small space of his cell. His hands closed around the bars, grip tightening. "He wouldn't do that to Su." From somewhere down the row came a sharp rustle. Ben shifted hard against the wall, fabric scraping concrete. A quieter movement followed, Chase adjusting on his cot, breath slipping tight through his teeth. Tyler coughed once, dry and rough, then went still again.

"That's what Su said too," Kevin replied, drifting a step closer to Austin's cell, careful to stay out of reach. "They had a fight in the dining hall. A loud one. Something about their mother, and a girl. Min-ji, I think. Sam blamed her for everything. Said he hated her for forgiving you. Something like that—"

"Something like that?" Austin's voice sharpened and Kevin scratched at his stubble absentmindedly.

"My Korean's not perfect—"

"*Dangsin-i geu mal da al-a-deureotdaneun geo... dareun nomdeuldo ara?*" Reece cut in, slower now, deliberate. Kevin's head snapped toward him, a flicker of surprise before it flattened into something sharper. He turned fully towards him.

"*Nal sog-ilyeogo handamyeon... geugeon an tonghanda,*" he said, a faint smirk tugging at his mouth. "But no, no one else knows. They got no idea I understood a damn thing." He rolled one shoulder. "Like I said, I'm rusty, and they talked fast. But whatever else he said, it was enough. Su went at him—"

"Bullshit," Austin snapped again, his voice low this time,

grip tightening on the bars. "If that were true, one of us would've been—"

"You think someone wasn't?" Kevin cut in, voice turning harder. A heavier shift sounded from Ben's cell - his weight hitting the wall, a breath forced out slow through clenched teeth, but he stayed silent.

"Who?" Austin demanded. Kevin let it hang for a moment.

"Chantelle. Three guards took it out on her. Made Su watch," he said at last, his words slower now, and the air around them tightened. "Made *everyone* watch, right there in the dining hall. Sam was one of them. Didn't hesitate, didn't stop. So no, he's not pretending. If he can do that and walk away like it's nothing—" The words settled, thick and suffocating.

"Where is she?" Reece's voice cut through, low and lethal.

"In the infirmary. Look, I know you got no reason to trust me. But not everyone here is with Marcus and Victor. Not really. You showing up," he gave a small shrug, searching for the right words. "It... *changed* things. Some of us've been talking. You five, you're different. Strong, loyal. The first real tight group of muscle that's been brought here in a while—"

"Yeah? And that's supposed to make us feel better? Or more worried?" Reece let out a slow breath through his nose. Kevin's mouth twitched faintly.

"Depends how smart you are." He said. From down the row, Ben shifted quickly. The scrape of movement echoed off the concrete, tension coiling tight in the sound of it. When he spoke, his voice was low, controlled, but there was something raw underneath it.

"Kevin," he used the name carefully. Not friendly, but not hostile, like he was testing it. "How's Beth? Is she safe?" Austin's head turned sharply toward the sound of his voice, jaw tightening. Kevin noticed, and there was the faintest flicker in his expression before it flattened again.

"She's with Tim," he said. "He's... a good friend. She's not alone—"

"That's not what I asked," Ben pressed, the restraint in his voice thinning. "How *is she*?" Austin stepped in before Kevin could answer.

"Ben—"

"Don't," Ben snapped, sharper now. "Don't do that. Not here." A heavy silence settled between them, stretched tight across the corridor. Kevin tilted his head slightly, watching the exchange play out.

"I'm little surprised," he said slowly, almost casually. "You didn't ask Austin—" Austin's eyes snapped toward him, a mix of irritation and disbelief. He wanted desperately to step forward, to explain in person, but the bars held him back.

"What the hell is that supposed to mean?"

"He's seen her." Kevin met Austin's gaze without flinching. The words landed like a blow, and Ben went still.

"What?" Ben wasn't loud, which made it worse. His voice came again, tighter, cracking at the edges. "You've seen her?" Austin's grip tightened on the bars, knuckles whitening.

"Ben—"

"*When*?" Ben fired back.

"Yesterday, after the fight I got into—" Austin paused, his glare at Kevin softening. "*You* dragged me into solitary—"

"Yeah," Kevin said slowly, leaning in just enough so only Austin could hear. His voice dropped to a rough whisper. "By starting that fight, you gave yourself the chance without even knowing it. I figured I'd—" Ben slammed his fists against the bars, the echo ricocheting through the corridor.

"I can't believe you didn't tell me!"

"She asked me not to!"

"Enough!" Reece barked, sharp, cutting through the chaos, though the tension behind his command still trembled. Ben pressed his face against the cool metal, his eyes burning, muscles coiled, jaw tight. His hands lingered on the bars, trembling just slightly. Kevin let them sit for a heartbeat, watching, then finally broke the pause.

"Like I said," he muttered, almost to himself. "I'm on your side."

"Then tell me how she is," Ben's voice was lower now, controlled, but it still held an edge of intensity that cut through the air like ice. "Either of you—"

"She's alive," Kevin's gaze drifted somewhere between the cells, unfocused but deliberate. His voice was low and rough. "You don't wanna know any more than that." Silence followed, and Ben didn't argue this time. The fight drained out of him all at once, leaving something heavier behind. He turned away from the bars, pressing the back of his head against the cold metal, eyes closing as if that might shut out the images forming. Nothing Kevin had said was enough, and somehow it was already too much.

The tepid water cascaded over Beth's head, running down her back as she dragged her fingers through her hair, tearing at the tangles left by sweat and neglect. Each strand she freed felt like a small, bitter victory. Her thighs stung where his residue clung stubbornly to the hair, and she pressed the sponge harder, scrubbing until her knuckles burned. The blood would wash away, the rest would not. The bite on her shoulder, stitched crudely by Val, itched beneath the healing skin. Bruises bloomed dark across her arms, thighs, and stomach. Every movement sent pain through her body, sharp and grinding, like glass caught in her joints. When she shifted her weight, the dull throb in her hips flared, a reminder that her body was still a battlefield. She cursed under her breath, frustrated by how easily the surface filth lifted while the deeper damage stayed buried, permanent. Water ran over her face, rinsing away tears she hadn't realised had fallen. Beneath it, something colder settled in. Less than a day had passed, and already the edge of it had carved into her, sharpening her, hollowing something out and replacing it with control. The shower house smelled faintly of rust and soap, its cracked tiles and broken nozzles offering a fragile kind of privacy. For a moment, she let herself take it. Not comfort, just control, just the outer layer, and it was enough. She scrubbed her legs once more, forcing herself to endure the sting, to turn the pain into something she could manage. Then the sound of boots against wet concrete cut through it. Beth stilled, her body tightening as she straightened, every ache still there, but contained now, locked down and sharpened into something usable.

"Mind if I join you?" Jennifer asked, her voice echoing slightly in the damp room. Her silhouette was slim against the light filtering in from a grimy window. Beth inclined her head once. Jennifer took a seat beside her. For a few moments, they sat in silence as Jennifer slowly undressed and washed herself. Then her voice cut through the quietude, tentative as water trickled down her shoulders.

"Stephanie, my sister, she's here too," Jennifer confided, reaching her arm over her shoulder to wash her back, turning away from Beth. "She's, you know, one of them. The girls they —" Jennifer paused. Beth's chest tightened slightly at the words, but she said nothing. Jennifer struggled to reach her arm around her neck, wincing in pain and clutching her elbow.

"I'm sorry," Beth said, leaning towards her and reaching for the sponge. "Here, let me—" Jennifer flinched, and Beth recoiled.

"I'm sorry," Jennifer shuddered. "I just... you get kinda conditioned to flinching when someone comes up behind you."

"I know." Beth replied flatly, dropping her hands into her lap.

"Can you?" Jennifer held the sponge over her shoulder. "My arm... I just can't quite reach."

"Sure." Beth took the sponge, her movements measured and deliberate, almost clinical as she wiped dirt from Jennifer's back. She noticed the bruising, acknowledged it, and moved on. No blood, no nail marks, no teeth marks, just bruises.

"I get a few rough hands every now and then," Jennifer murmured, as if reading Beth's thoughts. "But they never hurt me too bad. They know I take care of the girls, and you."

"So you're close to Sabrina?" Beth's tone carried a quiet edge, sharper than intended, and Jennifer let out a low scoff. Beth finished wiping the last of the dirt away before handing the sponge back to her.

"Close is a stretch," Jennifer said, turning around and gazing into Beth's cold eyes before she continued washing her arms and legs. "I'm supposed to make sure you're all eating and bathing, you know, watching out to make sure you're not losing it? Nip that in the bud before you go too far and can't come back. But she needs less care than the rest. Don't let her get to you. She's mostly bark, very little bite. The worst she'll do is *try* to make you get yourself killed, or kill yourself, so she can have another crack at Marcus, but that's it."

"Noted," Beth stood, wrapping a towel around herself, shivering not from the chill but from the rawness of what they shared. "And me?" Jennifer paused, letting the sponge drop back into the bucket. She studied Beth's face first, not just looking but watching, tracking the stillness there, the absence of anything that might give her away. Her gaze dropped slowly, deliberate in its path, to the way Beth held the towel. Too tight, knuckles pale, fingers rigid rather than relaxed. Then lower, to her stance. Knees locked, not from ease but from control, like if she let them bend she might fold entirely. Even her toes curled faintly against the concrete, gripping for balance, betraying the tension the rest of her body tried to conceal. Jennifer lingered there a moment longer, piecing it together, reading the quiet contradictions between what Beth showed and what her body refused to hide.

"I haven't had time to really assess you yet—"

"*Assess* me?"

"It's why I take care of you and the girls," Jennifer smiled. "I was studying behavioural psychology and applied behaviour analysis at UCLA. So I guess that made me... necessary." Beth shuddered at the word.

"I thought you were young," Beth mused, the first hint of something other than coldness breaking through. "Maybe only a little older than Chantelle—"

"I'm only seventeen," Jennifer said with a quiet laugh. "Child prodigy, or whatever. Taking care of you keeps me safe. You're important to Marcus, and I'm important to you, so the others know if I'm hurt too bad, Marcus will throw a tantrum. Where were you headed when you got taken?" She asked, quickly changing the subject.

"Are you curious?" Beth narrowed her eyes. "Or assessing me?"

"Both." Jennifer's answer landed like a stone in still water. "South."

"Huh, smart. We were headed north, trying to find our dad when it all went down. He was in San Francisco for work, then the pandemic hit," Jennifer went on, eyes distant, scanning beyond the grimy wall. "We waited for a few weeks and he never came back so we left home. Got snatched up as soon as we hit the San Jose—"

"Think he's still alive?" Beth's voice was soft, almost cold, betraying none of the fear she felt.

"Maybe," Jennifer's eyes filled with tears, mirroring Beth's own fears. "But I'll probably never find out." She put her sponge in the bucket and reached for a towel, her movements slow and numb. They shared a solemn look, trapped in this merciless limbo, clinging to memories of a different time. The steam from the buckets diminished, a misty veil that clung to Beth's skin as she and Jennifer exchanged a look of silent solidarity. It was a fleeting moment of connection before the creak of the door heralded an abrupt intrusion upon their fragile tranquillity.

"Move along now." Maureen's voice cut through the haze, sharp and unyielding. Beth opened her mouth, words perched on her tongue, but they died there. Her attention snagged on the new arrival - a woman fresh from the mainland, eyes wide, the raw terror of the unknown painted across her face. Silence spoke louder than any cry, and Beth felt the air thicken with it, heavy and suffocating. The stranger's gaze fixed on Beth's shoulder, the fresh stitches tracing the unmistakable shape of a bite. Her eyes lifted slowly to Beth's face, widening as they took in the bruising along her cheekbones and around her eyes. Beth arched a brow, then flicked her gaze briefly towards Maureen.

"Make sure she's more prepared than we were." Beth said through gritted teeth.

"No need," Maureen's hand pressed firmly to her shoulder, before handing over a new grey dress to Beth. "Jennifer here is so preoccupied with the others that Marcus thought you could use a friend of your own." No further words, no hesitation, just an insistence that left no room for argument. Beth took the dress without a word, letting her eyes flick once more to Jennifer, who lingered in the middle of the room, watching the newcomer with a quiet, grim understanding of what it could mean for her.

Chapter Thirty-Six

Chantelle's gaze lingered on the gleaming edge of a kitchen knife, its blade catching the dim light that filtered through the barred windows of the dining hall. The cacophony of clinking dishes and muted conversations blurred into a distant hum as her thoughts narrowed into something darker, more focused. For weeks, the image of the knife had flickered at the edges of her mind like a morbid beacon, each time her resolve faltering before it could take shape. Her fingers tightened against the coarse edge of the metal table, knuckles whitening with the strain of holding herself in place. She could almost feel the cold handle in her palm, the weight of it, the finality. Every muscle in her body coiled, ready to move, but something deeper held her there, a stubborn, instinctive refusal to let go.

"That one." A familiar voice cut across the dining hall, but Chantelle barely registered it. Before the thought could form, a hand closed tight around her arm and yanked her from the bench. The world lurched, and light fractured through streaked glass as she stumbled barefoot down the corridor, her body dragged faster than she could keep pace. The concrete bit into her feet, her balance slipping with each forced step as she was hauled through the yard and thrown into a storeroom. She landed hard against a stack of concrete mix, the impact knocking the breath from her lungs. She pushed herself up slowly, turning to face him, her eyes narrowing against the dim light.

"Sam?" Chantelle let out a shaky breath, her body folding in on itself despite the effort to hold steady. "What're we doin' in here?"

"Initiation." He said simply, his hand hovering at his belt. Nausea twisted through her gut, sharp and sudden, but her face remained blank, her voice quiet when she spoke.

"You already had yours—" A sound from the corner snapped her attention sideways. A boy stepped out from the shadows, hesitant and uncertain.

"This is Jorge," Sam said, nodding towards him. Chantelle's eyes widened. He couldn't have been more than fourteen. Something in her chest twisted at the sight, the realisation settling in with a dull, sinking weight. She supposed some children were necessary, if Victor wanted them broken in young. She looked back at Sam, searching his face for something familiar, something human. The boy who had sat with her through the cold winter and played with MJ. The boy who had promised he's take her bowling one day.

"Sam—"

"He's here to see how it's done." He stepped closer, closing the distance between them, then startled as the door burst open. Both Sam and Jorge turned, their bodies tensing as a large figure stormed into the room, filling the space with his presence. Chantelle instinctively drew her knees in tighter as he moved toward her.

"Victor wants this one tonight," the man said, grabbing her arm and hauling her to her feet. "Find someone else." Sam stepped forward, his hand catching the man's arm, his voice sharper than it had any right to be.

"You can't—"

"I fucking can." The man moved fast, slamming Sam back into the stone wall. The crack of his head against it echoed through the room, and his body crumpled, folding in on itself as he hit the ground. A smear of blood followed the motion, dark against the stone. For a moment, everything stilled. Chantelle stared. The world seemed to tilt, her breath catching somewhere in her throat. The boy on the floor didn't look like the one she remembered. The warmth was gone, replaced with something hollow, something unrecognisable. Whatever he had become, whatever he had done, it didn't stop the sharp, disorienting jolt that ran through her chest. "Fuck—"

"I—" Jorge stammered, panic flooding his voice. "I didn't wanna be here. I swear, I—"

"If you say *anything* about this," the man cut in, grabbing Jorge by the front of his shirt and lifting him off the ground. His feet barely touched the floor as he struggled, hands clawing at the grip on him. "I'll tell them I found you in here fighting over her, and *you* killed him."

"But—"

"She'll back me up," he said, nodding towards Chantelle. "And that's not an argument you're gonna win." Jorge's gaze snapped to her, desperate and searching. Chantelle held it for a moment before giving a slow, deliberate nod.

"Okay—" he gasped. "I won't say anything—" The man dropped him. Jorge hit the ground hard, scrambling before bolting for the door, disappearing into the shadows without looking back.

"Sam." Chantelle whispered, the name barely leaving her lips as she leaned forward. The man crouched beside the body, pressing his fingers to Sam's neck.

"Fuck," he muttered, more certain this time, before standing and turning back to her. "Are you okay?"

"You're Tim, right?" Chantelle said slowly, her voice steadier than she felt, as though something inside her had already shut down what needed to be felt. "The one who follows Beth around?"

"Yeah," Tim replied, running a hand over his face. "Are you okay?" Her eyes drifted back to Sam. His stare was fixed, empty, unseeing. Whatever had been left was gone.

"Yes." She said after a moment, her eyes closing briefly.

"Good." Tim exhaled through his nose, rubbing at the bridge of it. "This isn't how I wanted this to go—"

"What're you doin' here?" She asked, pulling her knees in tighter, grounding herself in the pressure.

"You need to leave," he said, pulling her up and brushing the dust from her dress, his movements quick and efficient. "A lot of people saw Sam take you from the dining hall, most of them are still there. You go back to your cell, get under your blankets, and don't move. Make sure no one sees you. Stay there all night. Can you do that?" She glanced once more at Sam, something flickering across her face before it flattened again. He caught her chin, forcing her to look at him. "Hey. Stay with me. Can you do that?"

"Yes," she said, straightening, forcing her body into something functional. "What about... him?"

"I'll deal with it," Tim said, his voice lower now. "We'll move him later. Dump him in the bay—" He gave a small, humourless breath. "Not how I planned my night." Chantelle swallowed, nodding once before turning toward the door. She hesitated at the threshold, something catching in her chest, then stepped back and wrapped her arms around him. He froze, caught off guard, his hands hovering uncertainly at his sides.

"Thank you." She said, her voice quiet, tight with something she couldn't fully name.

"Yeah," he muttered, shifting slightly. "Don't mention it. Literally, *don't fucking mention it.*" She nodded, then slipped out into the night, the door closing softly behind her.

Beth sat on the cold, hard floor of her cell, knees drawn to her chest, arms wrapped tightly around them. The dim morning light filtering through the high window in the corridor cast long shadows that stretched across the room like fingers grasping for something just out of reach. She closed her eyes, trying to shut out the world and the constant dread gnawing at her insides. Across from her, perched on the edge of Beth's cot, her new friend sat in still silence, hands folded neatly in her lap. They had barely spoken, yet she had become a constant presence, lingering like a shadow Beth hadn't asked for. Beth watched her, taking in the impassive face, the hollow, unfocused eyes. She knew she should say something, offer some kind of comfort, but the thought felt distant and unreachable. Holding herself together took everything she had. There was nothing left to give to anyone else. The creak of the hallway door snapped her back. Footsteps followed, deliberate and confident. Beth's gaze flicked toward the entrance to her cell as Sabrina sauntered in, a smirk resting on her lips as though she carried some private joke with her. Without asking, she lowered herself to the floor beside Beth, her presence immediate and unwelcome, pressing into the small space like it belonged there.

"Who's your new friend?" Sabrina's voice was syrupy sweet, tingling with malice. Beth remained silent, glancing up and shaking her head. "Oh, come on. Why don't you introduce me—"

"Leave her alone." Beth said, her voice calm.

"Why don't you go get some dinner so I can have a chat with my dear friend Beth?" Sabrina smiled, but there was no kindness in it.

"I'm supposed to stay here with her—"

"It's okay, Estelle," Beth said. "Go eat. Just because I don't want to doesn't mean you shouldn't—"

"I don't think I should—"

"Estelle?" Sabrina raised an eyebrow, her voice low. "Fuck off." Her tone was light and commanding. Estelle rose to her feet, quickly disappearing down the corridor towards the dining hall. Sabrina turned to Beth, her eyes filled with mischief, and something playful. "Guess what? One of your precious friends has decided to join the ranks. Can you believe it?"

"No," Beth whispered quietly. "Please, do enlighten me."

"He's a guard now." Sabrina almost sang as the words escaped her lips, seemingly with triumph. Beth's heart hammered in her chest, but she refused to let the fear show, because she knew what this was. She turned to face Sabrina, her gaze steely.

"I know what you're doing," she said, her words clipped. "Don't even bother—"

"Oh, but it's true," Sabrina's smile widened as she leaned in closer, her breath hot against Beth's ear. "Desperation changes people, makes them do things they never thought possible. You should see Austin, all dressed up in his little uniform, strutting around like he owns the place. Or is it Ben? I always get those two confused." Beth felt a surge of anger rise within her, but she fought to keep her composure.

"I knew you were delusional, but if you get those two confused, then you're a fucking idiot," her voice was low and filled with contempt. "So which is it, Sabrina. Are you an idiot, or are you a liar?" Sabrina's face faltered, but only for a fraction of a second.

"Oh, Beth—"

"Don't bother. I don't care," Beth sighed. "This place, whatever it's done to you, it's turned you into a monster." Sabrina recoiled slightly, as though struck, but then her expression hardened, and the cruel glint returned to her eyes.

"We're all monsters here, Beth," she rose to her feet, dusting off her hands as if ridding herself of something unpleasant. "Some of us just hide it better than others."

"You think you hide it well?" Beth raised her eyes to meet Sabrina's dark gaze.

"In this new world, it's adapt or die," Sabrina said as she made her way to the metal door frame. "It looks like your friend chose to adapt." With a final cold laugh, she exited the cell, leaving Beth alone once again, surrounded by silence and the weight of uncertainty. She slowly raised herself and walked over to the metal doorframe, peeking around the corner and down the corridor. Sabrina's silhouette shrank against the dimming light as she paused at the threshold, casting a backward glance over her shoulder. "I've bet you've had both, right? Whichever one it is, I wonder if I'll give them something you never could—" With a sudden burst of fury, Beth lunged forward from the shadows of her cell, her fingers clawing into a fist that found its mark on Sabrina's cheek. She stumbled, a hand flying to her face where a red imprint began to bloom. Her eyes, wide with shock, quickly narrowed into slits of malice. Before Beth could ready another strike, the air was split by the shrill clack of boots on concrete. A guard rounded the corner, his presence like a damper on the fire that had leapt from Beth's spirit.

"What's going on here?"

"She attacked me," Sabrina spat out, her eyes filled with fake tears as she regained her poisonous composure. "I was walking to the dining hall for breakfast and she just... she *attacked* me!" The act was good, too good. It was the kind of voice spoilt rich girls used on their fathers to smooth over another maxed-out credit card, and Beth knew she wasn't going to win this one. The guard didn't hesitate. His hands were steel traps closing around Beth's arms, wrenching them behind her back as if she were nothing more than a rag doll. Beth writhed, trying to twist away, but her strength was no match for his iron grip. She felt her body being dragged back-ward, her bare feet scraping helplessly against the floor. The pain coursed through her body, her injuries barely having a chance to heal. She relented, letting her form fall limp against him. The guard grunted, his breath hot and foul against her neck. As they disappeared around the corner, leaving the scene of the brief tumult behind, Beth's defiance was replaced by a sinking dread. Her mind raced with thoughts of Ben and Austin, of the twisted words Sabrina had left her with, and the chilling possibility of truth tangled within the lies.

Muscles trembling as he hefted another stone into place, the weight of Ben's work was a relentless force against his dwin-dling strength. He wiped a grimy forearm across his brow, leaving a streak of dirt in its wake. The spring sun was a harsh overseer, but even it couldn't compare to the steely eyes of the guards who patrolled ceaselessly. A rough hand clamped down on Ben's shoulder, squeezing with an authority that brooked no argument. Startled, he stumbled, the rhythm of labour abruptly severed. Before he could utter a word in protest, a second guard grabbed his other arm, yanking him away from his task without a word. Ben protested then, his voice hoarse as he tried to plant his feet firmly into the ground. Resistance sparked within him, a desperate kindle of defiance against their silent treatment. His body swayed from the sudden pull, and he could feel every ounce of weariness dragging at his limbs, betraying him. The guards were implacable, faces hidden behind mirrored sunglasses that reflected Ben's own haggard image back at him, a ghost of the man he used to be. They tightened their grip, propelling him forward with brute effi-ciency. The fight drained out of Ben like water through a sieve, his attempts to resist growing more feeble with each step as hunger clawed at his insides and fatigue clouded his vision.

"Where are you taking me?" His question dissipated into the stifling air, unanswered. Austin dropped a stone on the ground and marched over, abruptly stopped by a guard in his path. The guard's hand rested heavily on his weapon as he glared at Austin with cold, unyielding eyes.

"What're you doing?—"

"You know better than to interfere." He growled, stepping forward to block Austin's path again.

"But he did nothing wrong!" Austin insisted, gesturing towards Ben's retreating figure. "We've just been working silently like you asked—"

"It's not your concern." The guard's expression remained unchanged as he spoke through gritted teeth.

"It *is* my concern!" Austin snapped back, frustration boiling within him. The guard's grip tightened on his weapon and for a moment, Austin feared he would use it, but the guard simply sighed and shook his head.

"Just stay out of it," he muttered before turning away and calling over his shoulder. "I'm not in the mood for a fight." Austin watched them go, jaw tightening as Ben was dragged from the yard. There was nothing he could do, and that was the worst part of it. The uselessness of it sat heavy in his chest, grinding against his ribs. With a slow breath, he forced himself to turn back to the work in front of him, shoving his hands into the pile of debris as if the effort alone might quiet his mind, but it didn't. Every movement felt mechanical and detached. His thoughts circled back, again and again - to Ben, and to Beth. Something had happened. He could feel it in the way Ben had been taken. Too fast, much too sudden. It didn't sit right. Whatever Beth had done to trigger it, whatever had set this in motion, it wasn't good.

Consciousness returned to Beth in fragments, a slow and reluctant tide dragging her back under. Her head throbbed in time with her pulse, a dull, relentless rhythm that filled the cramped storeroom. She blinked against the dim light seeping through the gaps in the wooden slats, her vision struggling to settle as shadows shifted just out of focus. The pain came next. Her wrists burned with a deep, grinding ache that made her flinch as awareness snapped fully into place. She tried to move, instinctive and immediate, but the sharp pull of restraints stopped her short. Rough bindings cut into her skin, holding her arms tight against the chair. Panic stirred low in her chest, not explosive, but tight and suffocating, like it had nowhere left to go. She forced herself to breathe through it, slow and controlled, even as her pulse refused to follow. Across from her, something shifted. Beth's gaze snapped up, focus sharpening as another figure came into view. He was slumped forward in the chair opposite her, his chin resting heavily against his chest, his body slack in a way that didn't look like rest. It looked wrong - too still, too quiet. For a second, her chest tightened, something dangerously close to panic clawing its way up her throat. He looked worse than she remembered. Worn down and beaten into something quieter, smaller. The sight of him hit harder than the restraints, harder than the pain still threading through her body.

"Ben," she called softly, her voice strained. No response came, and she forced more strength into her voice. "*Ben!*" His eyelids flickered, then opened, glazed with confusion. Awareness returned, and with it the brutal reality. Their eyes met, silent questions hanging heavy between them. The lines of struggle, exhaustion, and defeat marked his face, mirrored on her own bruised skin. A shiver passed through her as she tested her bonds, the rope biting into wrists already sore and raw. Ben shifted slightly, grimacing at the effort, his eyes following a rat scuttling across the floor as if its intrusion were nothing unusual. Time had warped here, and hours bled into one another. Beth stared at him, thinking of all the words she wanted to say but could not summon. Her tears mixed with grime on her face, bitter and gritty. The pale light of dusk traced the contours of his hollowed eyes and the deep impressions the ropes had left on his wrists. He finally groaned after hours of silence, his voice barely above a whisper. His throat was parched, the dehydration making the slightest word a struggle.

"Beth—"

"You're awake." She tilted her head, trying to catch his line of sight. He rolled his head slowly until his eyes met hers, and she could see that he finally focused on her instead of staring idly at nothing.

"What did you do this time?" He asked, attempting a smile.

"Nothing that justified being tied up and locked in a dark room all day," she whispered, shaking her head angrily. "I'm sorry—"

"What did you do?"

"I slapped another girl," she confessed. "You know Sabrina?"

"Not really," he winced against his restraints. "But you're right, they wouldn't give a shit about a catfight. Why'd you slap her?"

"She told me you or Austin were one of them now—"

"Never." His face crinkled into a warm smile, softening the hard lines of exhaustion etched across his face. His eyes sparkled with affection as he gazed at her. She looked at his blood stained shirt and scuffed knees, noting the healed scrapes and bruises on his skin.

"Are you okay?"

"These fucking ropes are destroying my wrists." He winced again.

"Stop moving then." She said, more a scold to herself than to him, frustration with her own pain bleeding through. He froze, finally looking at her properly, taking her in for the first time. Ben closed his eyes after he had taken in all he could before he couldn't bear to look at her any longer.

"What happened to you?" He asked softly. Taking in a deep breath, she swallowed hard as she looked down at her bruised legs and arms.

"Use your imagination—"

"I don't want to," his voice sliced through the air with a sharp tone, like a hot knife through butter. "If I think for one second—"

"Hey," she snapped, her voice raw. "Look at me." Ben slowly lifted his gaze to her, taking in the soft expression, the faint gleam in her eyes that stood out against the bruises and cuts on her face. For the first time in a long while, he saw something he hadn't thought he'd ever see again - tiny sparks of hope flickering through her battered exterior. He couldn't decide if it was real, or simply a mask for his benefit. Her lips curved into a hesitant smile as she inhaled sharply, her voice trembling as she spoke. "I don't wanna lie to you, so don't ask me what he's done. But for what it's worth, I'm okay Ben." A smile spread across his face at the sound of her saying his name, savouring the way it rolled off her tongue. He had missed her voice during their time apart, and now he drank in each word. As twilight deepened, the door creaked open. A guard entered, carrying a tray with scant rations, but his eyes lingered on Beth with a chilling intensity. She met his gaze evenly, hiding the fear clawing at her insides. Ben's breaths grew shallow as the guard approached, body tensing. Despite his fatigue, a quiet resilience held him upright - a silent declaration that he would protect Beth if he could. Beth drew on that inner strength to steady herself as her own resolve wavered.

The guard knelt by Ben with a bottle of water, holding him while keeping his gaze fixed on Beth. She tensed under the leer. When he held the bottle to her lips, she parted them slightly. He spilled some down her chin, watching it trail to her collarbone. Closing her mouth, she clenched her jaw as he ran his thumb over her chin, wiping away the water, then tracing down her neck and along her collarbone. Ben watched uneasily. The guard huffed, glancing at the brand on her arm with visible frustration.

"Shame." He cocked his head to the side, contemplating silently as his eyes darted from Beth's face to her brand and back again. Before Ben could fully react, the guard was gone. And so they remained, two figures bound, confused and exhausted, left alone in their dark tomb.

Chapter Thirty-Seven

Chantelle's tears dried almost as quickly as they'd fallen, the warmth of the sun pulling them from her skin. She sat on the stone bench, the courtyard offering colour without comfort, its blooms wasted on a grief that refused to soften. Her fingers traced the worn edges of the book in her lap, a fragile tether to a home that barely felt real anymore. Her gaze drifted to the sliver of water beyond the walls, her thoughts turning, unbidden, to Sam. She wondered where his body had ended up. Caught on the rocks maybe, or dragged under, hopefully gone without a trace. She wondered how long it would be before someone noticed he was missing. How long Jorge could keep his mouth shut. Footsteps approached, light but deliberate, breaking through the quiet. Chantelle didn't look up, she didn't need to. Maureen carried herself in a way that always made itself known, something measured and watchful beneath the softness she tried to wear. Chantelle swallowed, forcing the tightness from her throat, steadying herself before lifting her gaze.

"Chantelle, dear," Maureen began, her voice coated in practised warmth. "This is Estelle." Sunlight caught the girl fully as she stepped forward, Jennifer lingering a few paces behind her. Estelle stood rigid, her hands trembling where they clutched at the fabric of her grey dress. Her eyes moved too quickly, scanning the courtyard like she was searching for an exit that didn't exist. Fear hadn't dulled her - if anything, it sharpened her, made her look too aware, too present for where she was.

"Hello." Chantelle said softly, the word careful and measured. Maureen's hand pressed lightly at her back, urging her to stand. It felt heavier than it should have.

"You know how Jennifer takes care of my girls so diligently?" Maureen continued. "Estelle here is to be Beth's own personal... *friend*. Help her understand our ways." *Our* - the word snagged in Chantelle's chest like barbed wire. These wasn't her ways, they never would be.

"Of course." Chantelle replied, smooth and agreeable, the lie easy now. She gestured for Estelle to follow and started walking, her pace steady and controlled. Jennifer and Estelle both fell in beside her, quiet but watchful, taking everything in - the flowers, the walls, the sky above them. Chantelle glanced towards Jennifer. "So what exactly're we teachin' her?" Jennifer's gaze flicked between them.

"Beth's been a little... dark lately—"

"No shit," Chantelle muttered. "Wouldn't you be?" Jennifer huffed under her breath, stepping up beside the low wall overlooking the water.

"Maureen thinks Estelle isn't doing her job—"

"My job?" Estelle's composure cracked for a second, something sharper breaking through before she caught it. "I don't even know what that is. What am I doing here?" Her voice wavered despite her effort to steady it, her eyes drifting toward the horizon like she could reason her way out of it. "She told me to shadow Beth, to look out for her. That's all." Chantelle's jaw tightened.

"Guess she thought Beth'd just open up to you and it'd all fall into place."

"Beth isn't much of a talker." Estelle said, brow lifting slightly.

"No, she's not," Jennifer said, folding her arms as she leaned back against the wall. "My job is to keep all the girls in check. Well, was my job. Guess I've been demoted. Guess they figured Beth needed something more... *specialised*." Her eyes flicked over Estelle. "You've got a background, right? Psychology? Psychiatry?"

"I—" Estelle faltered, swallowing hard. "Clinical psychology." Jennifer let out a slow breath.

"Yeah. That tracks." She turned back towards the ocean, bracing her hands on the stone. "You watch her. Everything. Make sure she eats, make sure she bathes, make sure she doesn't disappear into herself. And when she starts to go insane—"

"Talk to her," Chantelle cut in, her eyes settling on Estelle. "Keep her grounded. Don't let her drift."

"I still don't understand—" Estelle's voice tightened, her gaze flicking between them.

"She's in shock." Chantelle said quietly, not unkindly, just matter-of-fact.

"Yeah, no shit," Jennifer muttered, dragging a hand down her face before pushing off the wall. "Listen to me. You don't have time to sit in that. You need to get your head straight, *fast*, or this place will eat you alive." Estelle went still. "Beth is Marcus' personal entertainment," Jennifer continued, her tone flattening into something colder, more precise. "That means everything he feels gets taken out on her. Your job is to make sure she doesn't break. Not physically, that's not up to you. Mentally. You keep her from going under. Think you can do that?"

"I—, but—"

"Jesus," Jennifer exhaled, rubbing her temple. "Counsel her, console her, that's it. Get it? Pretend you're in a constant therapy session with one single patient and all you have to do is keep her from going insane. Like I'm supposed to be doing with Chantelle right now." She glanced sideways, raising her brows. "So when Maureen asks, we had a *great* session."

"Sure." Chantelle said, the word easy and hollow.

"One more thing," Jennifer went on, turning back to Estelle. "You've got a rare position here. Beth's his favourite. That makes you valuable by association. No one's going to touch the thing keeping her functional. So you do your job, and you remain necessary—"

"Enjoying the tour?" Sabrina's voice cut through them, her shadow falling long across the stone. She leaned lazily against the wall, that same crooked smile pulling at her mouth, her eyes already locked onto Estelle.

"Sabrina." Chantelle said, her voice flat.

"Take a good look girls," Sabrina said, tilting her head slightly, her gaze dragging over Estelle. "This one won't last long at this rate." Estelle's lips parted, the breath catching in her throat.

"Appreciate the concern," Jennifer replied dryly. "We'll make sure she knows how things are done." Sabrina's smile sharpened, but she said nothing more, just watched them a moment longer. They kept walking, far from Sabrina's scrutinising gaze and her mocking laughter that filled their ears.

"Where does that leave you?" Chantelle asked after a beat, glancing toward Jennifer. "Now that you ain't watchin' Beth." Jennifer didn't hesitate.

"Same as the rest of you," she paused, just long enough for it to land. "Nothing's protecting me anymore."

In the cellblock, Austin sat on the edge of his cot, rolling a small pebble between his fingers, a quiet act of defiance against the monotony. Sleep had been a choice he'd refused. Every time he closed his eyes, he saw Beth - her hair tangled with dried blood at her brow, the split in her lip, the bruising that swallowed her skin in blues and blacks. But it was her eyes that stayed with him. Steady, unyielding, like she was telling him she'd make it through, no matter what they did to her. Whatever he was dealing with in here didn't come close, so he didn't complain.

"Kevin, why wasn't Sam here at his post today?" Reece's voice cut through the silence, dragging Austin out of it. He blinked, the pebble stilling between his fingers. The question sat there for a second before it landed, and with it came the realisation - he hadn't thought about anyone else, not properly. His jaw tightened, and he dropped his gaze to the concrete wall ahead.

"Kevin," Austin called as the guard came into view, the faint jangle of keys marking his shift. "Where's Ben?" Kevin leaned against the bars, casual, like none of it mattered. His eyes dragged over Austin, taking him in, measuring what was left of him.

"Taken for questioning." Kevin said, shifting his weight.

"Why?"

"Look, you didn't hear this from me," he said, his words slow. "But Sam's missing." The pebble slipped from Austin's fingers, hitting the ground without a sound that mattered.

"Missing?" Austin furrowed his brow, confusion setting in. "What does that have to do with Ben?"

"Nothing," Kevin shrugged. "But Beth's with him too, so I imagine he's just there for motivation. If they get nothing out of them, then one of you'll be next."

"So neither of them did anything wrong?" Chase called from further down the row, his voice tight.

"Well, no," Kevin said with a faint smirk, stepping back

and angling his gaze down the corridor towards Chase. "Official story is, Beth attacked Sabrina. Everyone thinks this is just punishment. But they won't get anything out of them. Neither of them know a damn thing—"

"And how do *you* know?" Austin asked, keeping his eyes fixed on Kevin. His face changed, a slight expression of guilt hiding behind a mask of indifference, but he remained silent. Austin looked up slowly, something colder settling behind his eyes. The draft through the broken window didn't touch him. It didn't register. Instead, a crooked grin pulled at his mouth, and then he laughed. It was quiet at first, but wrong in a place like this. It echoed anyway, and the others shifted.

"What's so funny?" Tyler asked, his voice rough, unused. Austin shook his head, that grin still sitting there, something sharper behind it now.

"Beth," he said, like the name meant something more than just a person. "She attacked Sabrina."

"And?" Chase frowned, not following. Austin leaned back slightly, the tension in his shoulders easing for the first time.

"She's still fighting," he said, the relief threading through his voice despite himself. "Just like I told her to." He let the words sit there, holding onto them like proof. Like something they hadn't managed to take yet.

The sound of heavy boots thudded closer, each step slow and deliberate, the rhythm of it settling deep into the bones of the room. It wasn't hurried, it didn't need to be. The kind of power that announced itself like that never did. Marcus filled the doorway when he appeared, his frame swallowing what little light filtered in from the corridor behind him. For a moment, he didn't move. He didn't need to. The space seemed to contract around him, the air thickening, pressing in on Beth's chest until breathing felt like work. Her body reacted before her mind could catch up. Every muscle locked. Her spine went rigid against the chair, shoulders drawing tight as if bracing for an impact that hadn't come yet. A sharp, sour heat rose in her throat without warning, bile clawing its way up, sudden and violent. She swallowed hard, forcing it back down, her stomach twisting in protest as the taste burned at the back of her tongue. Her lips parted on instinct, but she shut them again just as quickly, jaw clenching as she fought to keep control. It was automatic, conditioned, and Ben saw it all. The way the colour drained from her face, the way her fingers curled slightly against the restraints - not pulling, not fighting, just reacting. The way her breathing hitched once, shallow, before she forced it steady again. It wasn't just fear, it was deeper than that. It was something learned, carved in through repetition, until his presence alone was enough to make her body turn against itself. Marcus stepped inside, and the door groaned shut behind him with a dull finality, sealing the room. He moved slowly, unbothered, his boots dragging faintly against the floor as he began to circle them. Not pacing nor restless, just observing like he had all the time in the world. His gaze settled on Beth first, lingering there, taking in every detail with a quiet, deliberate interest that made her stomach lurch again. She swallowed once more, harder this time, forcing it down, forcing herself still. Her eyes stayed forward, unfocused, like if she didn't meet his gaze then she might disappear from it. Ben's jaw tightened as he tracked Marcus' movement, every instinct in him screaming to move, to do something, anything, but there was nothing. All he could do was watch the way Beth's body betrayed her, the way she shrank inward without actually moving, like she was trying to take up less space under his attention. Marcus moved past her, slow and deliberate, his presence dragging through the room like something heavy and suffocating. The silence stretched with him, thick and oppressive, broken only by the faint, uneven rhythm of Beth forcing herself to breathe through the nausea clawing at her throat.

"Where's Sam?" Marcus asked, almost too casually. The question hung heavy between them as Beth and Ben exchanged a confused glance. "And don't lie to me, because I'll know."

"I have no idea what you're talking about." Beth whispered, her voice hoarse.

"Lies!" Marcus snapped, the word cracking through the room as his hand lashed out. The backhand landed hard against Ben's cheek, snapping his head to the side with a sharp jolt. Ben didn't cry out. He barely reacted beyond the movement itself, his jaw tightening as he slowly brought his head back to centre. No blood, no split skin, nothing lasting. Marcus was holding back. That was worse. He stood over him, unmoving for a beat, watching. There was nothing impulsive in it, nothing uncontrolled. Every movement was deliberate, restrained, like he was pacing himself for something far worse to come. "Where is Sam?"

"I promise you," Beth said, louder now. "I have no loyalty to him. If he's escaped, and I knew, then I'd tell you—" Another hit cracked through the air, this one driving into Ben's jaw with a dull, sickening force. His head jerked with it, the sound of impact echoing off the walls before the silence swallowed it again. Beth's lips pressed tight, her jaw locking as the reaction hit her before she could stop it. Heat surged up her throat, sharp and acidic, bile rising fast. She swallowed hard, forcing it back down, her throat working against it as she fought to keep it there. She didn't look away.

"Escape is impossible from this place," Marcus said, his voice low and controlled, a stark contrast to the crack of violence that had come moments before. "It's why we chose it. You should understand that by now." He moved again, slow and deliberate, circling them like a hawk. Not pacing, stalking. His gaze dragged over them as he passed, heavy, assessing, like he was already deciding where to apply pressure next. A predator with patience, not hunger. "He's here somewhere, hiding and waiting." He stopped just behind Beth, close enough that she felt it before she saw it - the shift in the air, the weight of him at her back. Her shoulders tensed instinctively, her breath catching for half a second before she forced it steady again. "Waiting for all of you to try something, waiting for his moment. There aren't a lot of places to hide on this island. When we find him, and we will—"

"Why would he ever help us? You made such a show of him joining your ranks," Ben's stomach turned as he lifted his gaze to Marcus, voice tight with revulsion. "He wouldn't even think of helping us—" Marcus's slow, deliberate movement to Beth's shoulder made Ben's blood run cold. He trailed a finger along her collarbone, and then lowered the fabric ever so slightly. When the bite mark was revealed, Ben's breath caught, his fingers clenching at his sides. Then Marcus ripped the stitched flesh free with one quick movement. Beth's scream shattered the air, jagged and raw. Ben's fists tightened, every instinct screaming to strike, to protect, but he was powerless. His stomach twisted again as he watched the fire consume her shoulder. Flames licked at her neck, tears threatening to spill, but she clenched her jaw, hiding every ounce of it from them. Blood trailed down her skin, catching at the neckline of her dress, staining the grey fabric dark.

"I can see this is going to be harder than I thought," he began, voice low and threatening as his gaze lingered on Beth, then shifted to Ben. "You know, I love her spark. She's feisty, isn't she? Out of all the ones I've had, she's my *favourite*." Beth remained silent, defiant even in her vulnerability, her chin lifted in a challenge that spoke louder than words but her pounding heart and uncontrollable shaking gave her away. Ben's jaw clenched, muscles working as he slowly fought against the ropes binding him to the chair. The implication in Marcus' tone was clear, but no argument would come from his lips. He would do nothing to endanger her. "Have you ever had her, Ben?" Marcus' question hung in the stale air between them, a baited hook awaiting its catch. Silence and stillness was Ben's only reply, a resolute fortress against the onslaught of Marcus' perverse interrogation. "Answer me!" Marcus snapped suddenly, backhanding Beth across the cheek. The sound of the strike echoed through the room. Ben's determination wavered, and his suppression broke with a single, weighted nod.

"Yes." He whispered, a mixture of shame and rage filled his eyes, but he held Marcus' gaze, refusing to be cowed.

"Ah," Marcus murmured, a cruel smile twisting his lips as he traced Beth's arm with a finger, eyes flicking to Ben. "It must sting, Ben. To watch her here, with me, and know there's nothing you can do. That she's *mine*, while you can't even reach her." The air seemed to convulse with tension, thick and suffocating, charged with hatred and the faint pulse of defiance. Marcus leaned in close, the acrid stench of tobacco and sweat filling Ben's nostrils, his presence a suffocating weight, a predator's claim on both mind and body.

"Ben, no—" Beth's breath caught in her throat, her words completely inaudible, bile rising hot and bitter, but she forced it down, choking back the nausea, unwilling to give Marcus the satisfaction. Ben's eyes burned, dark with raw with uncontrolled rage. Time slowed as he surged forward, forehead crashing into Marcus' nose with a sickening, wet crack. Blood erupted like a twisted fountain, hot and coppery, streaking down Marcus' face and splattering across the floor. His lips parted in a strangled gasp, eyes wide with shock and fury, crimson dripping onto his collar. For a suspended moment, silence held. -the predator staggered, the prey now towering with uncontained wrath. Then Marcus' head snapped back, fury igniting like wildfire, eyes alight with a terrifying, predatory gleam. His hands lashed out, grabbing at Beth with lethal precision, but even in that instant of chaos, the room seemed drenched in the smell of iron and fear. Every beat of their hearts echoed like a drum of impending violence, and Beth's stomach twisted again, bile threatening to rise as she swallowed hard, holding herself together while the storm of blood and rage collided before her.

"You'll pay for that," he snarled through bloodied teeth. "*She'll* pay for that." His hands moved quickly, releasing Beth from her binds, not out of mercy but as a means to an end. She fell to the floor, disoriented for just a heartbeat before instinct kicked in. As Beth scrambled to gain her footing, Marcus gripped her arm with the force of a vice. She lashed out, her legs flailing, trying to find purchase against the slick concrete floor.

"Let go of me!" Her screams echoed off the walls, a chilling symphony of terror and defiance. Ben lurched forward, raw fury burning in his chest, but the ropes bit into his wrists, biting through muscle and skin. Every pull sent sparks of pain up his arms, his knuckles whitening as he strained against the unyielding bonds. The frustration coiled inside him like a living thing, writhing with each futile tug, his body trembling from both rage and the searing ache that flared with every movement.

"Beth!—"

"None of you seem to learn your lesson!" Marcus howled, driving a fist deep into Beth's ribs. She curled instinctively, arms shielding her stomach, but the blow slammed through her like a hammer, organs rattling under the impact. Ben writhed against his ropes, skin tearing, each futile pull sending sparks of pain. Beth coughed violently, ribs screaming as if each breath carried fire, and Marcus didn't relent - his boot smashed into her back, and she arched with a cry as the thunderous crack of shoe against spine reverberated through the room.

"Stop!" Ben roared, every muscle quivering with rage, fists straining against the unyielding binds. He couldn't move, couldn't stop it, and the helplessness coiled around his chest like a living thing. Marcus dragged Beth toward the door, her screams trailing behind, and slammed it shut with a final, echoing thud, leaving Ben trembling, bloodied, and furious.

Chapter Thirty-Eight

Austin scanned the decrepit yard, his gaze drifting over the others as they worked. The sun bore down on them, heat soaking through fabric, sweat clinging to skin, but he barely registered it. His focus had narrowed to a single point -a plan. He bent slowly, picking up a heavy rock, testing the weight of it in his hand. His jaw tightened, breath steadying as he measured the angle. Not too much, not enough to cripple him, just enough. He dropped it. The rock slammed into his ankle with a dull, crunching impact, pain flaring sharp and immediate. His leg buckled on instinct, and he let himself go with it, collapsing to his knees in the dirt. A low, strangled sound tore from his throat as he grabbed at his ankle, fingers digging in hard. The pain was real, hot and pulsing, but controlled, contained. Exactly what he needed.

"Get up, you idiot!" One of the guards snapped, hauling Austin roughly to his feet by the arm.

"I think it's broken." Austin ground out, his face tightening as he clutched at his ankle, letting the tremor in his hands sell it just enough. The guard swore under his breath, clearly annoyed.

"Fine. Infirmary. *Move.*" Two of them took him, one on either side, dragging him forward with little patience. Austin let his weight sag between them, limping hard, jaw clenched as if every step cost him. As they turned the corner, out of sight of the yard, the tension in his expression eased just slightly. Not enough to give him away, but enough. A flicker of something sharper replaced the pain. A small, controlled victory. He leaned heavier into them, letting himself be half-dragged, half-carried toward the infirmary, where Val worked. Her compassion was worn thin, dulled by the things she was forced to see, but not gone.

"Val." He breathed as he was pushed into the sterile white room, the smell of antiseptic temporarily overpowering the stench of despair that hung in the air outside.

"Let me see." Val said, her voice low and efficient as she knelt to examine his foot. Her fingers were gentle, a stark contrast to the harshness that surrounded them. One of the men stood at the door, eyeballing them as she worked. Austin glanced at Val, a silent plea for privacy that took her a moment to understand. She cautiously examined his ankle, turning it in her hand as she held it tight. Austin's face contorted in agony, his features twisted and strained as he struggled to keep up his act.

"It might be broken," Val turned to the guard at the door. "This could take a while."

"I'll wait—"

"He's not going anywhere," Val's tone was sharp. She gestured towards the ankle. "Are you gonna stand there all day?" He let out a sigh of defeat and made his way to the door. As he exited, he cast one last glance over his shoulder and looked Austin up and down before disappearing through the doorway and closing the door behind him. They waited for a moment, listening for the footsteps to fade down the corridor. "So what happened?"

"I dropped a rock onto my foot so I could see you—"

"Fucking stupid," she snapped. "As if you don't get hurt enough around here without doing shit like this to yourself. You could've done some real damage—"

"I wanted to know how Chantelle is," Austin whispered quickly. "I haven't seen her around. Is she—"

"No." Val's eyes darkened as she flicked a glance toward the door, then leaned in closer. "She's not okay. I can't keep doing this. Treating her, treating Beth. I can't keep seeing them like that." Her voice cracked, the strain slipping through despite her effort to hold it together. "They rape my daughter, Austin, and I can't do a fucking thing about it." The words landed heavy between them, thick with sorrow and rage. Val's hands faltered against his foot, a brief tremor breaking through her composure before she forced them steady again. Austin exhaled slowly, the sound low and hollow, carrying the weight of something close to defeat.

"I'm sorry."

"You're lucky this isn't broken." Wiping away a tear and composing herself, Val patted Austin's ankle lightly.

"Hey, watch it." He winced in pain and recoiled. "It still hurts."

"Keep your head down, Austin," she murmured, finishing her inspection and standing up. "And don't do anything stupid like this again."

"I needed to see you." He lifted his eyes to meet her steady gaze. She rose without a word, drawing in a slow breath as she moved to the bench. Leaning back against the counter, she folded her arms across her chest.

"Well, you've seen me—"

"Val," urgency laced Austin's tone. "We can't stay here. We need to leave." She raised her gaze to meet his, her expression neutral.

"No shit," she scoffed quietly, disbelief etched in her features. "But in case you hadn't noticed, we're on an island,

Austin. There's no boat, no way off this rock without them noticing—"

"But there're boats, Val. Motorboats. I've seen them," he leaned forward, eyes intense and voice barely above a whisper, his gaze never leaving hers. "Every time we go down the hill to unload supplies from the ferry, they're there, tied up at the pier." Val's expression flickered, the seed of hope taking root despite the despair that had long since claimed the soil of her resolve. She glanced towards the door once more, then back at him, a silent question hanging between them. Her hands paused, hovering over the bandages on the tray as Austin's words echoed in her cluttered mind. The echoes of distant conversation from down the corridor was the only thing that punctuated the silence between them. She looked at him, searching for fire in his eyes to convince her that an escape plan could work. His jaw was set with determination, his eyes alight with something fierce and unyielding.

"Alright," she whispered, conviction building in her voice. "We escape, or we die trying." Austin's eyes softened for a moment, gratitude mingling with the fire that kept him from breaking under the weight of their grim reality. They had no plan, no allies, nothing but their will to survive.

"We won't die trying." He offered her a half smile, tilting his head and furrowing his brow as he thought of his friends rallying to follow him into the abyss of escape.

"We might," she placed her hands on the bench gingerly as she gazed down at the floor. "But I'd rather be dead than stay here." The sound of sudden footsteps on the concrete came from the next room, and both Val and Austin tensed as their conversation was abruptly interrupted. Doctor Horn, the island's unwilling physician, stepped into view, leaning heavily against the wall, his glasses askew and his lab coat stained with the evidence of his daily torment.

"Your spirit is admirable," he said, his voice low and strained. "But you're dreaming if you think escape is possible."

He shuffled into the infirmary, his eyes darting nervously towards the door.

"Perhaps it is a dream," Val said, her voice flat, stripped of anything soft. "But I'm not interested in accepting this as reality—"

"You think I haven't dreamed?" Doctor Horn let out a hollow laugh. "That I didn't want to take my daughters hand and run away as far away as possible? I know your pain, Val. I watched my daughter die in this place. Dreams don't change the fact that Marcus controls everything here."

"Then help us." Austin's face was set in a stern expression, his jaw clenched and his eyes blazing with determination. The old doctor hesitated, his eyes flickering to the ground before meeting Austin's steady gaze.

"I've done too much watching, too little acting," he confessed, a tremor in his voice betraying regret. He looked towards Val, his expression hardening. "I watched them murder my daughter. I won't have you watch them murder yours. If you're set on this mad course, I have a condition—"

"Name it." Val challenged, her pulse quickening.

"Kill Marcus," he stated, completely devoid of any emotion. "He is the demon that haunts this place. Free us all from his tyranny." A heavy silence filled the room as the gravity of the request settled upon them. To kill was no small thing, even a monster like Marcus. Yet, in the face of their own hellish circumstances, morality seemed a luxury they could ill afford.

"Without Marcus, we might stand a chance." Austin murmured, more to himself than to the others.

"Less likely for him to seek retaliation," Val said. "I don't think anyone else would come after us—"

"Victor might." Austin winced as he shifted his foot on the bed.

"Victor could swing one of two ways," Doctor Horn raised a pensive eyebrow. "He could be thankful you rid him of his obstruction to authority, or he would take your escape as a blow to his pride and follow you to the ends of the earth to seek revenge."

"Two extremely possible scenarios." Lost in thought, Val ran her tongue across her teeth slowly.

"Two equally possible scenarios," Austin added dryly, looking around the floor at nothing in particular as he too lost himself in his thoughts. "Guess we'll have to take him out too —" They remained silent for a long moment, each thinking of other scenarios and escape plans they could implement as their time to strategise wore thin.

"Will you do it?" Doctor Horn pressed, his eyes searching theirs for the resolve he lacked, breaking both of them from their thoughts. "You'll have to, if you want to take Beth with you and not be followed." Val exchanged a glance with Austin, a silent communication passing between them. To kill a man was to cross a line from which there was no return. But then again, they had crossed countless lines already, and Marcus and Victor were malevolent. Austin stared at the doctor stoically, the agreement sealed with a nod.

"Why don't you come with us?" Val asked, taking a small step forward as she dropped her hands to her side.

"I have nothing left," Doctor Horn said, his voice barely above a whisper. "With Marcus dead, I can rest easy knowing I did something right before my time is up. Besides, you can't take everyone with you. Someone needs to stay behind and pick up the pieces of what I imagine won't be a peaceful escape." With that, he turned away, leaving them with the weight of their newfound conspiracy. As Doctor Horn's footsteps receded, Val felt the inevitability of their path settle around her. They would escape, or die trying. And if fate proclaimed it, they would be executioners too.

Beth's body trembled with each suppressed sob, her tears soaking into the coarse fabric of the pillow that smothered the sound. The room lay still in the aftermath, the air thick with something unspoken that clung to her skin like a second layer she couldn't wash away. A thin line of blood slipped from the cut on her forehead, stark against her pale skin. The metallic scent hit her hard, sharp and overwhelming, mixing with the stale heat of sweat and fear. She tasted it on her tongue, iron and salt, her tears dragging it down her face - hers, Ben's, Marcus' - all of it blurred together into something she couldn't separate anymore. The click of the door handle cut through the haze like a live wire, snapping her back into Marcus' room.

"Come on, we've gotta go," Tim's voice cut through the stillness, low and urgent. "You've been laying there for almost an hour. He'll be back soon." He stood silhouetted against the light from the hallway, a figure made of both fear and resolve. Beth scarcely moved, her limbs heavy and disobedient, her spirit shattered into countless shards of broken determination.

"Are you taking me back to the storeroom?"

"Yes."

"Then you need to give me a moment." She hesitated, using the bedsheet to wipe the blood from her face, not wanting Ben to see her broken and bleeding though she knew there was nothing she could do to make herself look any less dishevelled. She forced herself to put on her clothes, every movement sending a jolt of pain through her battered form. She tried to ignore the throbbing ache, the physical manifestation of the barbarousness she had suffered at Marcus' hands. Tim watched her with a pained expression, his heart heavy with guilt and sorrow. He wanted to comfort her, but he knew

that they didn't have time for that now, and it wasn't his place.
They needed to get out of there before Marcus returned. As
Beth struggled to get her dress back on with one hand, Tim
moved forward and helped her, ignoring her nakedness, his
touch gentle and careful. She gave him a small smile of gratitude before steadying herself on his arm. In Tim's eyes, a
mirror of her own terror, she found a flicker of strength that
wasn't her own. It was enough to straighten herself up properly, just enough to turn her head towards him, her gaze
hollow.

"I know my post is designed for me to see what he did to
my wife," Tim started, his voice shaky with forethought. "But
she wouldn't've fought back the way you do."

"Tim—"

"And I didn't do enough to protect her, or my sister, so he
wouldn't've taken anything out on her the way he has with
you." He paused, questioning whether the conversation was a
help or a hindrance.

"Is that supposed to make me feel better?" Her voice was
barely audible as she closed her eyes and placed her fingers on
the gash on her forehead. She watched the blood drip onto her
fingertips, bringing them down to eye level to inspect it, and
wiped her bloodied fingers on her dress.

"It seems he's more entertained by you than anyone I've
seen." Tim studied her carefully, visually taking in every inch
of her. He admired her resilience and strength as she stood tall
in the midst of chaos that would have broken most people.

"Seems so," she took a small step towards the broken
mirror, lifting her dress to wipe the blood from her face. "This
won't stop bleeding." Tim's hand extended with a white cloth
in his palm, his face a mixture of concern and guilt as he met
her gaze.

"Come on, if he finds you here when he gets back—"
Tim's words trailed off, but the implication hung in the air, a
silent scream louder than any cry Beth could muster.

"I know." She whispered, exhaustion threading through her voice as she pressed the rag harder against her forehead. She forced herself forward, each movement slow and mechanical, detached from the pain flaring through her body. Tim stayed close at her side, his hand steady at the small of her back, guiding without pushing. They moved toward the doorway together, slipping out into the corridor. Beth didn't look back. She didn't need to. Every step away from that room felt like distance carved out of something suffocating, even if it was only temporary. The corridor stretched ahead, dim and endless. Her steps faltered, uneven, but she kept moving. Tim guided her through it in silence, his grip careful and deliberate. When they reached the storeroom, the cold hit her immediately, biting through what little warmth she had left. He led her to the chair and eased her down. The ropes followed, tight and practiced, securing her in place once more. Nothing about it was unfamiliar.

"Easy." He whispered, as if his voice could somehow alleviate the sting of the ropes against her raw wrists. Beth remained stoic through it all, her gaze fixed on a point somewhere far beyond the concrete walls that caged them. Across from her, Ben was still bound in his chair, his wrists raw from his attempts to free himself and his eyes never leaving her face, tracing every line of anguish etched into her features. His expression grew darker the more he studied every new cut and scrape. His eyes trailed from her broken face, down to her torn dress which had ripped at the seams of her shoulders, further to her limp arms where new bruises had formed at her forearms, and finally at her legs where soft trickles of blood had streaked down from her pelvis. Tim and Beth both remained silent, as Tim crouched down beside her and raised the rag to her forehead, trying to stop the bleeding. His efforts were futile, as no amount of pressure seemed to lessen the oozing that formed every time he relinquished the pressure.

"It's okay," Beth whispered. "Just leave it. I'm not gonna bleed to death."

"I'll try to convince Marcus to let Val take a look at you." Tim continued wiping blood from her arms, looking down at her legs as he maintained his gentle pressure with the rag. He hesitated, then swiftly dabbed at her legs and wiped the blood from her thighs.

"Don't touch her." Ben hissed, shifting uncomfortably in his chair.

"Your anger is misdirected." Tim said quietly, before standing and walking to the table in the room. He slowly unscrewed the lid from the canteen and offered Ben some water, which he gladly gulped down before moving back to Beth as she took light sips before shaking her head. The liquid felt harsh against her throat and although she was thankful for the hydration, she could barely swallow enough for it to make any difference.

"Thank you." Closing her eyes, she whispered softly as Tim placed the canteen back onto the table. He walked out silently, closing the door behind them, leaving them in the dark store room alone.

"Beth," Ben started, his voice choking with regret. "I'm so sorry. I should've spoken up, we should've stayed at the ranch just a bit longer." His words hung heavy between them, a testament to their shared guilt and the weight of decisions made and unmade. The air was thick with unsaid confessions and apologies, each one a reminder of their reality, a sharp contrast to the dreams they used to harbour. But here, in the dim light of the storeroom, only the raw truth of their situation remained, as undeniable as the bindings that held them. Beth's chin lifted slightly, a subtle defiance against the despair that threatened to consume her.

"Don't," she said softly, her voice a quivering thread in the stifling silence of the storeroom. "None of us could've predicted this. We all went along with it." Her eyes, though clouded with pain, held an unwavering resolve as they met his. In the dimness, Ben's face contorted with anguish. He leaned forward as much as the ropes would allow, aching to bridge the space between them.

"How are you so—" he faltered, searching for something that didn't sound wrong. Nothing would come, no comforting way to ease the question he wanted to ask. "How are you—"

"Not falling apart?" Beth cut in, a faint edge of disdain in her voice. "I don't know, Ben. Adrenaline, maybe. I sit in that cell all day and stare at the ceiling, pretend I'm not here. I don't even know how much time passes—" She shifted slightly, jaw tightening. "But when I'm out of it... I can't afford to break down." Ben huffed a quiet breath, a small, almost disbelieving smile pulling at his lips. He could see it there, that spark. Faint, buried deep, but still there. Something sharp beneath the exhaustion.

"I'm sorry," he said, the words rough, dragging themselves out of him. "I keep replaying it. Thinking I could've done something different—"

"Stop," Beth's voice was softer now, but no less firm. "We're not doing that. Not anymore. None of this is on us." She held his gaze, steady, grounding. "And I can't afford to have you fall apart either—"

"Beth—" His voice caught, thick with something he couldn't quite get out, his chest tightening as the words pressed up, ready to spill. The metallic groan of the door cut straight through it. The moment snapped. Victor's shadow stretched across the floor before he stepped inside, long and dark, swallowing what little space they had carved out for themselves. The door swung open behind him, careless, and he sauntered in like he owned every breath in the room, a smirk carved deep into his face. His eyes gleaming with malicious pleasure as they flicked between Beth and Ben.

"Aren't we cosy in our little nest of despair?" Victor

drawled. Ben's jaw clenched, every muscle in his body tightening with a mix of anger and exhaustion. His hands, bound to the chair, balled into fists as Victor circled them like a predator taunting its prey. "I hope we're comfortable." Victor's voice dripped with feigned concern as he leaned down, bringing his face close to Beth's, examining her bruises with mock sympathy. Beth turned her head away, her breath hitching in her chest, but Victor reached out, tilting her chin back towards him with a single finger.

"Don't touch me—"

"Now, now," the coldness in his eyes belied his warm tone. "No need to be shy—"

"Leave her alone." Ben growled, the words laced with a venom that surprised even himself, echoing off the walls with a desperate intensity. Victor straightened up and laughed, a sound devoid of any real humour.

"Oh, the *gallantry*. But let's not pretend, we both know you're not in any position to make demands. Where's Sam?" He asked, his tone light.

"Marcus already questioned us," Ben said, measured and careful this time. "We don't know anything."

"You've had him since day one," Beth added, her tone flatter and colder than his. "He wouldn't be on our side even if we begged." Victor let out a quiet breath, something almost amused, but it didn't reach his eyes. No movement, no sudden violence, no raised voice. Just that look, patient and unblinking. The kind of stare that didn't need force to pull something out of you - it just waited until you gave it up yourself.

"Alright then. You leave me no choice," Victor announced, his voice casual as he pulled a gun from the holster at his side and began toying with it idly. He allowed the silence to swell uncomfortably. "There's a way out of this room for one of you. A simple choice, really." Ben felt his heart stutter in his chest, an icy dread seeping into his veins as Victor laid the gun down on a table within their sight but far out of reach. "You've wasted our time, so now only one of you gets to walk out of here. Whomever gives Sam up will walk, and the other will be rendered... *unnecessary*." The air hung heavy with the implication, a silent edict of violence that promised freedom at the cost of their souls. Ben's breath hitched as his gaze shifted to Beth, whose eyes were wide with horror, reflecting the monstrous game that Victor had laid out before them. Victor took a small step towards the door before turning back to face them. "Either one of you will walk away, or you will both starve to death in the dark."

Chapter Thirty-Nine

al's hands remained steady, but it was a discipline, not a comfort. Beneath the surface, something twisted tight and restless, threatening to slip through if she let her focus waver for even a second. She dabbed at the fresh wound on Chantelle's arm with precise, measured movements, her touch careful, almost clinical - like if she stayed exact enough, she wouldn't have to feel it. The sterile scent of the infirmary clung to the air, sharp and artificial, but it did nothing to mask the copper tang of blood that seemed permanently soaked into the walls. It followed her everywhere now. No matter how much she cleaned, how much she scrubbed, it never left. Chantelle wouldn't look at her. Her eyes fixed on a chipped section of wall, unblinking, as if there was something there worth studying, something safer than meeting Val's gaze. Val noticed it immediately. She always did. The avoidance, the distance, the quiet retreat into somewhere unreachable. Her grip tightened slightly around the cloth before she forced it to ease, smoothing the motion into something gentler. She could catalogue every injury. Every bruise and every split in the skin. But this, this quiet and hollow withdrawal, there was nothing she could stitch back together. And that was the part she couldn't stand.

"Chantelle," Val began, her voice a soft entreaty amidst the hushed murmurs of the infirmary. "Why can't you talk to me?" She paused, ensuring the bandage was secure before locking eyes with her charge. Chantelle grunted, and the sound was like a small, wounded animal, a single note of acknowledgement amidst the cacophony of thoughts inside her mind. "Can you tell me what's been happening?" The question lingered between them like the delicate thread of a spider's web, fraught with the potential to unravel or hold fast. Val waited, not just for an answer, but for a sign that the bond they shared hadn't been irreparably damaged. Chantelle's gaze finally met Val's, and it was like a window shuttering closed.

"The fuck d'you think's been happenin'," her voice was filled with a white-hot anger, devoid of the warmth Val had once coaxed from her. "And why bother? Not much you can do beyond patchin' me up." She glanced at the entrance to the infirmary as if expecting someone.

"Chantelle," Val's voice trembled. "Please don't be so unkind—"

"Unkind? I'm past carin', "Chantelle spat. "You think your kindness means somethin' here? It's a weakness. I used to know how to handle myself, *remember*?"

"Of course, I do," Val said, her temper rising against her will. "But that doesn't mean—"

"Before you took me in, before your picture-perfect idea of bein' a mother," Chantelle cut her off, her voice rising with each word. "That old life, it would've served me better here. But you... you made me soft!" Chantelle's voice was sharp and harsh, like a knife slicing through the air. Each word seemed to pierce the silence of the infirmary with a forceful, angry tone.

"Soft," Val's mouth tightened, her heart pounding in protest. "Is that what you call being cared for? Being loved?—"

"*Love*?" Chantelle spat out the word as if it were venom. "The kinda love that left me unprepared for this hell. My real mother would've made me tough enough to survive—"

"Your real mother is right here," Val hissed, her voice sharp. "That *woman* who gave you up was a coked-out alcoholic who left you alone at home every night so she could score behind a run-down pharmacy. All I ever wanted was for you to live. Not just survive, but truly live." Val felt the sting of tears but fought them back.

"Look around, Val!" Chantelle's laughter had a hollowness to it, like a shell of its former self. "This ain't livin', and because of you I'm not even good at survivin' anymore—" Val's fist slammed into the metal tray, the sharp crack splitting the room as bandages and instruments scattered, clattering across the concrete in a harsh, uneven chorus. The sound hung there. Chantelle flinched, her body recoiling instinctively. Val stood frozen for a beat, her hand braced against the cot, chest rising too quickly. Then it hit her - the tremor. Her fingers curled in on themselves as if she could contain it, her shoulders drawing inward, her body folding slightly as she fought to pull herself back under control. When Val finally forced herself to look at her again, the sight hit harder than anything she'd seen in that room. Chantelle was afraid of her. It was there in the way she held herself, in the way her shoulders had drawn in, in the way her eyes flicked up only for a second before dropping again like she'd been burned. Not fear of the men, not fear of what they did to her, but fear of her. Val's throat tightened. She had stitched torn skin, set broken bones, cleaned wounds that should have killed them. She knew how to fix damage. She knew how to put things back together. But this, this was something she had done. Her hand dropped slowly from the cot, her fingers still trembling, and for a moment she didn't move, didn't speak, like if she stayed still enough she could undo it.

"Chantelle—" Her voice came out quieter than she expected, rough around the edges. Chantelle didn't answer, didn't move. And that hurt more. Val took a step towards the head of the cot, slower this time. Measured, like approaching something fragile that might shatter if she got it wrong again. "I didn't mean—" she stopped, jaw tightening. "I'm sorry." The words felt useless, empty. There was no version of them that fixed this. Chantelle's lip trembled, just barely, and then it broke. A sharp breath hitched out of her, like something inside her had snapped loose, and suddenly she was moving. Stumbling forward more than stepping, collapsing into Val like her body had given up holding itself together. Val caught her instantly. Her arms came around her without hesitation, pulling her in, holding her tight as Chantelle folded against her, sobs tearing out of her chest in broken, uneven bursts. She clutched at Val's shirt like she was drowning, fingers twisting into the fabric as if it was the only thing keeping her above water.

"I'm sorry—" Chantelle choked, her voice cracking apart. "I'm so sorry, I— I didn't— I didn't mean—"

"Chantelle, no," Val's grip tightened, one hand pressing firmly against the back of her head, anchoring her there. "No. You don't apologise. Not for this."

"I'm sorry, mama," Chantelle sobbed, the word slipping out of her like something pulled from deep inside, raw and unguarded. "I'm so sorry—" Val's breath caught. For a second, everything else fell away - the room, the blood, the noise, all of it - and there was just that word, fragile and familiar and devastating all at once. Her hold on Chantelle tightened, pulling her closer, pressing her cheek against the top of her head.

"You've got nothing to be sorry for," she said, her voice low, steady, even as something inside her threatened to fracture. "*Nothing*. Do you hear me?" Chantelle shook against her, sobbing harder, her body wracked with it now, all of the fear and pain pouring out all at once. Val held her through it.

Didn't let go, didn't loosen her grip. One hand moved slowly over her back, grounding, steady, the same motion she'd used a hundred times before, back when the worst thing she'd had to fix was a scraped knee or a bad dream. "This isn't your fault," she murmured, quieter now, but firmer. "None of it is." Chantelle's fingers tightened in her shirt, clinging.

"Mama." She whispered, her sobs quietening to a whimper. Val closed her eyes for a brief moment, pressing her lips to the crown of her head.

"I'm getting you out of here," she said, the words low, certain, not a comfort but a promise. "I don't care what it takes. I don't care who I have to go through." Her hand stilled against Chantelle's back, her grip unyielding. "I will get you out."

Ben's hands strained against the bindings, his eyes wild as they locked onto Beth. The whites showed, frantic, flicking between her and the gun on the table like he was trying to will her to understand without saying a word. The air in the storeroom sat thick and sour, sweat and fear clinging to every surface. Beth tasted it, sharp and metallic at the back of her throat, adrenaline turning her mouth dry as she tried to swallow past it. The distant clang of metal doors and muffled cries blurred into nothing, all of it swallowed by the look on his face. He was shaking, every muscle in his body pulled tight, cords standing out as he fought the restraints, the rope biting deeper into his skin with every failed attempt. His gaze didn't leave hers. It wasn't just fear - it was a plea, urgent and desperate. Cutting straight through the noise and landing exactly where it hurt.

"Beth, please," he implored, every muscle in his body

tensed, braced for an end he seemed to have accepted. "Make something up. Tell him Sam tried to swim to the mainland and find help." Beth, her own wrists chafing against the coarse rope that held her, shook her head vehemently, her jaw set hard. A single tear betrayed her stoic facade, trailing down her dirt-streaked cheek.

"No," she responded, her voice unwavering despite the crack of emotion threatening to break through. "They'd see right through it. They know this area, Ben. They have men everywhere scavenging for supplies, and they know that we know it. They aren't gonna believe that Sam swam off alone to find help." The gun lay at the table beside them, a cold piece of steel that offered a grim solution, yet neither would even look at it, its presence a stark reminder of their predicament. In this twisted game of survival, love had become the unexpected variable, altering calculations and defying the oppressors' rules. They sat there, two souls united in defiance, refusing to play their captor's cruel game. "You tell them that you got into a fight, pushed him over a cliff. Tell them it was an accident—"

"*You* tell them that," he snapped, his voice raw. "You do it—"

"And when would I have had the time?" Beth scoffed, her eyes darting towards the gun. "Someone has their eyes on me all day, every day. No one's buying that. It has to be you."

"I won't kill you," Ben's voice was strained, his words a desperate plea that reverberated in the heavy silence. "So you're gonna have to kill me. Shoot me, and then tell them I confessed to you—"

"Shut up, Ben," she glanced down at the ropes binding her to the chair, then at her arm where her bandages had come loose, exposing the branded M encased in a circle. "Or what if... what if he attacked me?"

"What?"

"What if he was so enraged about his mother's death, that he wanted revenge, and he attacked me?" Beth narrowed her eyes before lifting them to reach Ben's gaze. "He attacked me and I told him that he wasn't supposed to touch me, but he didn't care. One of the guards, no idea who, he saw it and pushed him off the cliff. I didn't recognise him—" her voice was soft, cold and calculating. "It was dark, and he told me to go back to my cell, so I did."

"It's a tough sell," Ben looked down at the brand. "Like you said, you're watched all the time—"

"And it still leaves the problem of you being killed for the lie—"

"Do it—"

"No," she snapped. "I'd rather starve to death with you in the dark." Beth studied the deep lines of strain etched across Ben's face, the silent resolve in his eyes. She leaned forward, close enough for him to feel her breath, her voice a whisper meant only for him. "You're stronger than me, Ben. If one of us is going to make it out of this prison, it's you. And I can't —" her breath hitched, and she swallowed a lump forming in her throat. "I won't survive without you." Ben's expression softened, the edges of his desperation blurring into something else, something tender yet heavy with unspoken truths. He shifted, the chair creaking in a melancholic rhythm.

"Beth," he began, his voice thick with an emotion he dared not name. "I won't survive without you either—" Ben paused, his eyes glistening with unshed tears, his jaw clenched tightly as he fought to regain his composure. His hand trembled as he winced against the tight ropes that had eaten through the skin on his wrists.

"You have to, Ben," she urged, her heart hammering against her ribs. He shook his head, a wry, painful smile touching his lips. "The others need you more than they need me—"

"You don't understand," his eyes locked onto hers, a storm of feelings swirling within their depths. "I have no interest in surviving this if you don't walk out the other side with me."

They remained still, the space between them thick with everything left unsaid. It settled there, heavy and unspoken, until it became something solid. A quiet understanding neither of them needed to voice. Whatever came next, they would face it together. The storeroom door creaked open. Victor's shadow stretched across the floor before him, swallowing what little light the room had. The temperature seemed to drop as he stepped inside, his presence carrying something darker than anger, something colder.

"Time's up," Victor's voice cut through the silence. "Have you lovebirds decided who's more necessary?" His smile was all teeth, devoid of emotion. Beth's gaze didn't waver, the fire in her eyes belying the vulnerability of her bound form.

"Get fucked." She spat with venomous clarity. Victor's hand moved with a viper's swiftness, striking not Beth but Ben, the sharp sound reverberating off the walls. Ben's head jerked to the side, a red mark blooming across his cheek, but his expression remained resolute, his jaw set in silent defiance.

"Wrong answer." Victor sneered, amusement flickering in his cold eyes. He sauntered forward, fingers dancing along the knife at his belt as if contemplating its use. Instead, he reached down and untied their bonds with deliberate slowness, the ropes falling away to reveal their raw, chafed skin. He gestured towards the gun that lay on the table, an offering soaked in malice.

"What *exactly* are you expecting us to do?" Ben rubbed his wrists, the sting from the slap still lingering, but he made no move towards the weapon. Beth, too, remained motionless, her spine straight as steel, her chin lifted in challenge. Their united front was unspoken - neither would entertain Victor's twisted game. They both remained seated, neither moving for the gun nor the door. Victor's smile faltered, his brow creasing in irritation. "Reach for the gun? Threaten the other for information in order to save ourself? We're not playing your game." Ben stared at Beth, who offered him a silent nod in solidarity.

"Well then," he said, his tone deceptively calm. "I suppose we'll just have to wait and see how long this little act of bravery lasts." Victor's patience was thinning, a dangerous glint in his eye as he circled them like a shark scenting blood.

"Well then," Beth glared up at him coldly. "Better take a seat. You're gonna be here a while." The silence was tense as Victor considered his next move against her mocking jest.

"I'm getting bored," he drawled, the threat in his voice unmistakable. "And unnecessary pieces get discarded." Beth's breath hitched, her eyes darting to Ben, whose own gaze was locked on Victor with an intensity that spoke volumes.

"Please Beth," Ben's voice cracked, barely above a whisper as he turned to her. "Tell him." The unspoken weight of their predicament hung heavy between them as Victor's lip curled into a semblance of a smile.

"Ben!—"

"Tell me what?"

"She knows," Ben said quickly, darting a panicked glance towards the gun. "She confessed. I'll tell you what she said if you keep her alive—"

"You fucking idiot!" Beth screamed, her fingers digging into the arms of the chair. Victor smirked, extending the gun towards Beth with a flourish. It was a grotesque offering, the metal cold and impersonal. Her hand trembled as she took it, the weapon foreign and unwelcome in her grasp.

"Tell me what you know, Beth. And then claim your freedom from this room," Victor cooed, pressing the barrel of his own gun against Ben's temple, his finger teasing the trigger. "If you don't do it, I will, and then your precious Austin pays the price for your disobedience." The air seemed to crystallise around them, time stretching taut as Beth lifted the gun to look at it, her arm shaking with the gravity of the choice forced upon her. Kill Ben, or don't, and he would die anyway, but Austin would pay for it. Ben's eyes implored her to act, his life offered up in sacrifice for hers, and for

Austin's. Beth's fingers tightened around the grip of the gun, a tremor running through her as she quickly pressed the cold muzzle to her own temple. Her heart hammered against her chest, a defiant drumbeat in the silence of the room. Ben's voice was a distant echo, filled with raw desperation.

"Beth!"

"I'll tell you what you want to know, but you're not gonna like the answer," she whispered softly as she smiled at Ben. "But you keep him alive. He's necessary, you need the muscle. Marcus can find another prize to brand—"

"Don't!" He pleaded as she met his gaze, reading the unspoken love and terror that swirled within its depths. Then, with a sudden flicker of resolve, she whipped her arm around, pointing the gun directly at Victor's smug face. She gasped loudly, the noise breaking through the tension like a thunderclap. Her finger squeezed the trigger, but instead of the anticipated blast, there was only a hollow click. The gun was empty - a cruel joke, a tormentor's ruse. She stared at Victor, the realisation dawning in her wide, frantic eyes. Victor's expression twisted into one of mock disappointment.

"Oh dear, Beth. That was the wrong move." He tutted, shaking his head in feigned pity and waving a finger at her. The standoff hung heavy in the air, the threat of violence lingering like a cloud about to burst. Beth's hand dropped to her side, the useless weapon now just a weight dragging her down. It was then that the heavy door crashed open, and Marcus stormed into the room, his presence commanding immediate attention. His brows knitted in anger, his eyes shooting daggers at Victor.

"What the hell do you think you're doing?" Marcus barked, stepping forward with authority that challenged the balance of power in the room. Victor, his smirk fading under Marcus's glare, shrugged nonchalantly, brushing off the gravity of the moment.

"Just a little fun, *Marcus*. You asked me to question them—"

"Fun?" Marcus's voice was a low growl, and he stepped forward until he was inches away from Victor's face.

"Yes Marcus, fun." Victor's expression was stoic, a look of fear flashing over his eyes before he returned to his usual smugness.

"I asked you to question them, not have them kill each other. In case you're forgetting, we still have structures to rebuild and Beth is *mine*!" Marcus' hard stare locked with Victor's for a charged second before he turned on his heel. "I'm in charge here, not you. Remember your place before I determine *you're* unnecessary. Do as I ordered, return them to their cells." The reluctant obedience in Victor's movements betrayed his annoyance as he gestured for Ben to rise from his chair. Beth's legs felt like lead, but the defiance that sparked within her gave strength to her weary limbs. As she stood upright, she caught Ben's eye, confusion and terror set deep within his gaze.

"Move," Victor grunted, ushering them out with a nudge of his boot. As Beth stumbled into the corridor, she glanced at Tim standing defiantly as Marcus stormed off at the other end. "Take her to her cell." Victor commanded, his tone filled with anger as he pulled Ben down the hallway. Ben turned to look at Beth, nodding at her as he wearily marched off without her.

"Come on." Tim said, pulling Beth down the corridor.

"Why did Marcus let us go?" She hissed.

"You're his to play with," he replied coldly. "Not Victor's—"

"Did you fetch him to save us?" Her tone was thankful, but littered with anger and resentment that her saviour was also her biggest tormentor.

"I knew it was the only way to get you out of there," he turned a corner quickly, dragging her along as her broken body struggled to keep up. "Once Marcus cools off about Victor, he'll take it out on you."

"As long as he doesn't touch Ben for—"

"For what?" Tim snapped, stopping so suddenly that she crashed into him. "For literally nothing?" He observed her, cowering in the dim light, bruised and broken and fearful of his sudden, unexpected anger. Beth's eyes widened with fear and confusion as she opened her mouth, struggling to form words, her lips trembling and her face pale. "I'm sorry," he whispered, placing a gentle hand on her arm. "I didn't mean to scare you—"

"You didn't." Swallowing hard, her dry throat scraped as she winced. They marched in silence for a while, before it was broken with a stark realisation.

"Marcus won't take it out on Ben, but Victor will." He said, and she thought about why they were in there in the first place.

"Do you know what happened to Sam?" She pressed, her legs struggling to keep up.

"Yes."

"And?"

"And nothing," he said, turning another corner before they entered the corridor where her cell sat at the other end. "You know what you need to know."

"I need to see Austin." Beth whispered urgently. His eyes flicked to her, then away, a muscle twitching in his jaw as he pushed her into her cell.

"Beth, I can't. There's no way of getting to him right now." He spoke in hushed tones, aware of potential listening ears nearby.

"Then you have to get a message to him," she insisted, desperation edging her voice. "Tell him we need to find a way to be alone. It's important." Tim hesitated, his gaze meeting hers. The conflict in his eyes spoke volumes, but so did the determination that slowly took its place.

"I'll see what I can do." He murmured, gesturing at the water he had hidden under her pillow and closing the door with a resounding clang that echoed the turmoil churning inside her. Alone in the cold embrace of concrete walls, she clung to the hope that Tim would succeed, and that Austin would understand the urgency of her request.

Chapter Forty

Jennifer sat at the far end of the dining hall, her back angled toward the wall, a position chosen out of habit rather than comfort. The room carried its usual low hum, cutlery scraping against plates, muted conversations weaving together into something dull and indistinct. It was the kind of noise that became background quickly, something the body learned to ignore if it wanted to survive. Estelle sat across from her, untouched food cooling on her plate. Her fingers toyed with the edge of a fork, turning it slowly between her thumb and forefinger, her attention elsewhere entirely. Jennifer watched her for a moment before leaning back slightly in her chair, folding one arm across her stomach.

"How are you going with her?" Jennifer asked, her tone even, like she was asking about the weather. Estelle blinked, pulled back into the moment.

"Beth?" She asked, as if there were any doubt. Jennifer's gaze didn't shift.

"Who else would I be talking about?—"

"Her walls are so hard to break through." Estelle let out a quiet breath, dropping her eyes to the table. Jennifer nodded once, like that confirmed something she already knew.

"That's not unusual."

"I know," Estelle said quickly, though the way her fingers tightened around the fork betrayed her. "I just thought there would be something. Some kind of entry point."

"There is," Jennifer replied. "You just don't get to choose what it is, or when she lets her walls down." Estelle huffed out something that might have been a laugh if it had any humour in it. Her gaze drifted across the room, watching the other girls eat, talk quietly, exist in that strange, subdued way they all had. Then it shifted back to Jennifer.

"She's been missing from her cell," Estelle said after a moment, her voice lowering slightly. "Gone for over a day now." Jennifer's expression didn't change, but her eyes sharpened just enough for Estelle to notice the concern.

"Gone where?" She asked.

"I assume Marcus' room," Estelle shrugged, though there was tension in the movement. "But I don't really know. You know this place better than I do." Jennifer leaned back a little further, her chair creaking softly against the concrete floor.

"He doesn't keep them there for that long."

"What do you mean?" Estelle's brow furrowed.

"A few hours," Jennifer said. "Sometimes less. He gets bored." The words sat there, blunt and unpolished. Estelle's grip on the fork loosened slightly, the metal clinking softly against the plate as she set it down.

"Then where is she?" She said quietly, her mind already moving ahead of her. Jennifer didn't answer immediately. She reached for her cup instead, taking a slow sip like she had all the time in the world. It wasn't avoidance, exactly. It was calculation.

"Infirmary maybe," she said eventually, setting the cup back down. "If something'd happened that mattered, you'd know about it—"

"Would I?" Estelle frowned.

"Yes." Jennifer said. There was no hesitation in it. No softness either - just certainty. Estelle shifted in her seat, her posture tightening.

"She doesn't want me there," she said, the words coming out before she could filter them properly. "I can feel it. Every time I'm near her, she shuts down further."

"That's not about you—"

"It feels like it is," Estelle said, glancing up. "I'm supposed to help her, and she won't even look at me half the time. If she doesn't engage, if I can't get through to her—" She trailed off, but the implication lingered anyway. Jennifer watched her carefully now, reading the edges of the panic creeping in.

"You think they'll reassign you."

"Wouldn't they?" Estelle swallowed. Jennifer leaned forward slightly, resting her forearms on the table.

"They don't move people because something is difficult," she said. "They move people when they're useless. You know, *unnecessary*." Estelle's jaw tightened at that, the word landing harder than she expected.

"I'm not useless." She said, a quiet edge slipping into her voice.

"I didn't say you were," Jennifer replied. "I'm just telling you how they think." Estelle exhaled slowly, dragging a hand through her hair before letting it fall back to her side.

"I've had patients who've resisted," she said, more to herself than to Jennifer. "People who didn't want help, who fought it. But this... this isn't resistance. It's like she's already decided I don't matter." Jennifer's gaze softened just slightly, though it didn't reach her expression fully.

"You're not there to matter," she said. "You're there to keep her functional." Estelle let out a hollow laugh.

"That's a bleak job description."

"It's an accurate one." Jennifer said. Silence settled between them again, heavier this time. Around them, the dining hall continued as if nothing had shifted, as if this conversation wasn't slowly tightening something beneath the surface.

Estelle glanced toward the entrance, her eyes lingering there for a second longer than necessary. Jennifer followed her gaze briefly before returning her attention to Estelle.

"That doesn't bother you?" Estelle asked, searching her face. Jennifer held her gaze evenly.

"It doesn't help me to be bothered."

"That's not what I asked—"

"Of course it bothers me," Jennifer tilted her head slightly, considering her. "I just don't waste energy on it." Estelle pressed her lips together, absorbing that.

"You're very good at compartmentalising." Estelle let out a breath through her nose, her shoulders dropping a fraction.

"You'll need to be too." Jennifer said. Estelle looked down at her hands, flexing her fingers slightly as if testing them.

"I don't know if I can—"

"You will, or you won't last." Jennifer shrugged lightly. There was no cruelty in it, just fact. Estelle nodded slowly, though uncertainty still clung to her. Their quiet conversation snapped clean in half. Both women startled slightly at the sudden presence of a man neither of them had heard approach.

"Estelle."

"Kevin." Jennifer gave a small, acknowledging nod, her tone even.

"Beth is back in her cell." There was nothing in the delivery. No concern, no urgency. Just information, dropped and left where it fell. Estelle shot a quick look toward Jennifer, something like relief flickering across her face before she pushed back from the table. Her movements were quick and light, almost too eager as she made her way out of the dining hall without another word. Jennifer watched her go for a beat, then leaned back in her chair, her attention settling fully on Kevin.

"You know," she said lightly, tilting her head, a faint, humourless smile touching her mouth. "We were *just* discussing her whereabouts for the last day and a half." Her eyes held his. "You wouldn't happen to know anything about that, would you?" A pause stretched between them. Not awkward, not hesitant, just weighted. Kevin didn't answer straight away. His gaze drifted instead, slow and deliberate, sweeping the room, the doorways, the scattered groups of people who weren't paying attention, and the ones who might have been. When he looked back at her, there was something tighter in his expression.

"You don't get to know everything here," he said finally, his voice low. "And you can't keep digging like you used to. Not now." Jennifer's brow lifted slightly.

"Not now that I'm not protected?" She finished for him. Kevin didn't deny it. Silence settled again, thinner this time, stretched over something sharper. "I'll be fine." Jennifer said, her voice steady, though her eyes flicked once around the room, quick and instinctive. Kevin's jaw shifted, like he didn't quite believe her but wasn't going to argue it.

"Watch your back," he said, his tone colder now, more deliberate. "That's not a threat. It's a warning." He stepped away before she could respond, disappearing back into the movement and noise of the hall like he'd never been there at all. The scrape of cutlery, the low murmur of voices, all of it carried on unchanged. But his words didn't leave with him. They lingered, and something about them sat wrong in her chest. Quiet and insistent, like a shift she couldn't see yet, but knew was coming.

Days passed, and still Tim couldn't shake Beth's request. It sat in his chest like something lodged too deep to pull out, grinding against every thought he tried to replace it with. His knuckles blanched around the grip of his rifle, the metal biting into his palm as his gaze fixed on Austin across the yard. He hadn't been a man who courted conflict. Not like this. Not when the cost was written so clearly in blood and consequence. But something had shifted, something that refused to quiet, no matter how many times he told himself to leave it alone. Desperation crept in slow, then all at once, clawing at his insides until it was impossible to ignore. It wasn't just Beth's voice anymore, it was the look she'd given him, the weight of it, the expectation that he might actually do something. His jaw tightened. With a slow, controlled breath, he pushed the hesitation down where it couldn't reach him. His shoulders squared, tension settling into every line of his body as he rose to his feet. Every movement felt deliberate now, measured, like stepping onto a path he already knew he wouldn't be able to walk back from.

"Hey, you!" Tim called out, loud enough to turn heads. He marched towards Austin. "Keep working!" Austin looked up, confusion lining his brow. The clatter of rocks and murmur of conversation faded into a suspenseful hush as Tim marched over with deliberate, heavy steps.

"Me?"

"I said *keep working*!" Tim growled, shoving Austin's shoulder with rough force. The yard tensed, sensing the brewing storm. Austin, caught off guard, stumbled back but quickly regained his footing. His eyes narrowed, searching Tim's face for the reason behind the aggression. Austin raised his fist angrily, his reaction fuelled by exhaustion and frustration. He swung once, but missed. Tim raised the butt of his rifle and smacked Austin on the side of his head, causing him to collapse to the ground. Tim leaned over him firmly, leaning in close under the pretence of anger. His voice dropped to a whisper for Austin alone. "Beth needs to talk to you. Fight me." Confusion flickered in Austin's eyes, replaced swiftly by his comprehension. Standing, he gritted his teeth and pushed

Tim back with a force that spoke more of urgency than malice.

"Fuck you!" Austin shouted, throwing a punch that grazed Tim's jaw, sending a clear message to the onlookers. Tim reeled from the blow, more from the necessity of the act than from pain, and lunged forward, tackling Austin to the ground. The scuffle escalated quickly, fists flying with more show than intent, each man playing his part in the desperate charade.

"Break it up!" Bellowed a guard, barreling through the crowd. He seized Austin by the collar, pulling him away from Tim.

"He started it!" Tim feigned his protest, picking himself off the ground.

"He attacked me for no reason!" Austin tried to lunge forward, a futile attempt against the guards' grip.

"Enough of this," the guard snarled. "Maybe a night in solitary'll cool your head." With a rough yank, Austin was dragged forward, defiance lighting his gaze. As he was hauled away, there was a fleeting moment where his eyes met Tim's, a silent thanks passing between them before he disappeared from view. The yard slowly returned to its cacophony of noise and movement, but the seed of conspiracy had been planted, germinating in the shadows of the confrontation. Austin was locked up again, but this time it was a step towards something greater.

The stale crust of bread crumbled between Ben's fingers, each bite a gritty reminder of the scarcity they endured. A narrow shaft of light from the high window sliced through the dimness of his cell, casting long shadows across the concrete floor. He chewed slowly, conserving energy, his thoughts circling the last few days like a wound he couldn't stop prodding.

"Quite the performance the other day." The voice slid through the silence, smooth and edged with something sharp. Ben looked up to find Victor leaning against the bars, arms folded, that same crooked grin pulling at his mouth.

"Didn't realise you were such a fan." Ben said, brushing crumbs from his hands. Victor pushed off the bars, stepping closer.

"Oh, I am. Just not of you." His gaze flicked, deliberate. Ben didn't rise to it.

"Where am I?" He asked. Victor's smile lingered, amused by the question.

"A quieter part of the island. Not many people pass through here," he glanced down the corridor like he owned it. "Less noise. Fewer interruptions."

"What do you want?" Ben's jaw tightened. Victor studied him for a moment, like he was deciding how much to give.

"You stay here until it's done."

"Until *what's* done?" Ben stilled. There was a pause, then Victor exhaled through his nose, almost a laugh.

"There's going to be an execution," he said. The word landed heavily. Ben's stomach dropped before he could stop it. His mind went straight to Beth, fast and brutal, the image already forming. Victor caught it, and a low laugh slipped from him. "Relax. If it was her, you'd know by now. So you could sit here and stew in it."

"Then who?" Ben's gaze hardened. Victor stepped closer to the bars, lowering his voice like it was something valuable.

"Marcus," he said slowly. Ben didn't move, didn't react. But something shifted behind his eyes. Victor watched it, pleased. "Things are about to change. I'm taking over—"

"And you came to tell *me* that?" Ben asked.

"I came to offer you a place in it," Victor said simply. "You join me, you don't end up on the wrong side of what comes next." His gaze sharpened. "And Beth stays protected." Ben let out a quiet breath, something bitter curling at the edges of it.

"You expect me to believe that?"

"You should," Victor said, unfazed. "She's valuable. I'm not stupid enough to waste something like that—"

"That's not protection," Ben said, his voice low. "That's ownership with better marketing." Victor's smile flickered, thinner now, tilting his head slightly and studying him again.

"You're thinking emotionally. That's your problem."

"And you're not thinking at all," Ben shot back. "You just want power." Victor didn't deny it.

"Call it what you want," he said after a beat. "But when this place tears itself apart, and it will, you'll want to be standing with the man holding the gun, not the one kneeling in front of it." Ben leaned back against the wall, arms folding loosely, like he had all the time in the world.

"Then I guess I'll take my chances." He said. Victor held his gaze a second longer, something colder settling in behind his expression.

"A war's coming," he said quietly. "Make sure you're on the right side of it." Then he stepped back, the moment snapping as quickly as it had formed, and disappeared into the corridor. Ben didn't move, but the word execution sat heavy in his chest, tangled with everything Victor had just set in motion. And for the first time, the walls of the place felt like they were holding something bigger than control. They were holding something waiting to break.

The sound of hurried footsteps echoed down the dimly lit corridor, sharp and out of place against the usual dead quiet in her cellblock. Beth's head lifted slowly from where she sat hunched on the cold concrete floor, her body stiff from hours spent in the same position. Across from her, Estelle straightened where she sat on the edge of the cot. She'd been there for days now, trying - soft questions, careful words, anything that might reach her. It had gotten her nowhere. One-word answers, if that. More often just silence, or a sideways glance that shut the attempt down before it could even start. Still, she hadn't stopped trying. Beth barely spared her a look now. Her attention fixed instead on the corridor as Tim came into view, his face flushed, his movements quick and urgent. There was none of his usual restraint, none of the careful distance he kept around the others. He motioned to her, sharp and insistent. Beth pushed herself up too fast, her body protesting as the world tilted for half a second beneath her feet. She steadied, breath catching, eyes locked on him.

"Come on, quickly," Tim whispered harshly, glancing over his shoulder as if expecting pursuit at any moment. "I suggest you take a quick lunch." He motioned towards Estelle, who sighed heavily before walking down the corridor. Beth followed him, her heart pounding in her ears. They navigated through the labyrinth of cells and corridors until they reached the outer cells, still more isolated and forlorn than the rest.

"How long do I have?" Beth's breaths came in short gasps, the gruelling treatment she had undergone for days finally taking its toll on her stamina.

"I don't know, but make it quick. I'll come get you when time's up," Tim said, his voice a mix of bravado and regret as he handed her a key. "Here." She turned it in her hands, rubbing the metal with her thumb.

"What's this?"

"The key to his cell door." He smiled, turning on his heel and closing the outer door behind him. She offered him a look of gratitude as he left, before slipping into the cell where Austin sat against the far wall, his presence immediately grounding her.

"You cost me a day of food and water to be in here." Austin quipped, a weak attempt at humour that didn't even come close to loosening the knot in her stomach. It just sat there, tight and unrelenting, as if her body already knew this moment mattered too much. When he lifted his gaze, it hit her full force. There was nothing casual in it. No distance, just something raw and searching that caught her off guard and held her there. The lock clicked beneath her fingers before he fully registered the action. The sound rang out in the quiet. Austin stilled, the shift in him immediate. The sharpness dropped from his posture as he pushed to his feet, something lighter taking its place. He didn't speak. He just watched her. She didn't give him time to think. Crossing the space between them in a few quick steps, she collided into him, arms wrapping around him with a desperation she couldn't quite contain. For a second, there was hesitation in his confusion, just a flicker, before his arms flung around her, strong and certain, pulling her in like he wasn't letting go. The contact knocked the breath from her lungs. It was warm and solid and real. Her grip tightened, fingers bunching into the fabric of his shirt as if he might disappear if she loosened it. She buried her face against him, the tension in her body finally cracking, something fragile and long-held slipping loose under his hands. For the first time in what felt like an eternity, she didn't feel like she was bracing for something. She just held on, and he did too. Her heart stilled, anxiety removing itself from the tension in her body.

"Hi." She whispered. Her breath came uneven against his chest, each inhale catching as his arms tightened around her waist, pulling her closer like he needed to make sure she was real.

"Hey," he pressed his face into her hair, eyes closing, the tension in his body finally giving way as something steadier settled in its place. For a moment, he let himself have it - the quiet, the warmth, the simple relief of her being able to touch her - and felt it undo him far more than he expected. "We're getting out of here."

"How?" She murmured, his warm neck pressed against her face.

"Leave that to me," Austin said, letting her go and they both lowered to sit on the cot softly. "I'm not taking no for an answer."

"Neither am I," she countered. "I want in on the plan. I can fight too." He looked into her grey eyes, once green with life and hope were now flat and distant. Except for the tears he observed welling up, there was no fight he saw inside of her.

"I told you to stay strong." He placed a gentle hand to the side of her face.

"I *am* strong," she began, her eyes filling with more tears than she wanted to allow. "Let me help."

"Is Ben okay?" Austin pressed, with the sudden realisation that he hadn't already asked about his friend.

"Ben's fine," she hesitated, considering her next words. "At least... he was the last I saw him. Victor tried to get us to turn on each other, but then Marcus intervened and I haven't seen him since."

"Neither have I," Austin wiped a small tear from her cheek. "So you've been returned to the public eye but he's still missing? Probably not a good sign—"

"No," she said softly. "Probably not. I'll see what Tim can find out." A silence settled between them, close and suffocating, filled with the thoughts they couldn't risk speaking aloud. It stretched out, pressing into the small space, making the air feel heavier than it should have. Beth sat beside him on the edge of the cot, her hands clasped tightly in her lap, her gaze fixed somewhere on the floor. She didn't trust herself to look at him for too long, not when everything she was holding back sat so close to the surface. Austin shifted slightly beside her, the faint creak of the cot loud in the quiet.

"Do you remember, at the campsite? When you told me it

felt like a prison?" Austin's expression softened, the lines of worry etching deeper into his features. Beth sighed, breathing heavily as a surge of emotions - the campsite, the ranch, the safety they hadn't registered at the time - it took hold of her, causing tears to cascade down her cheeks.

"Yes. Why?"

"How do you feel about it now?" He gazed at her as her eyes glistened. She let out a low, disbelieving laugh between sobs.

"The campsite wasn't so bad." She sniffed, turning away from him to wipe her face with her sleeves. A click from the other end of the corridor stilled her heart, and she turned back to Austin, her face filled with panic.

"Shit," he whispered, pulling Beth into a quick hug. "It'll be okay. We'll—"

"We need to leave," Tim marched into the open cell, his face worried. "Marcus is looking for you." Beth pulled herself from Austin's embrace and snapped her head towards the door.

"What are we gonna tell him?"

"We'll think of something," Tim leaned in to grab her arm. "But we have to leave, *now*." He pulled her from the cell, locking the door behind them. Austin stepped forward urgently, reaching through the bars and grabbing onto Beth's dress.

"Wait—"

"We have to go, Austin." Tim hissed.

"Listen to me," he said, his tone low and intense. "I'm going to come for you. When the time comes, be ready. Trust me." Her hand covered his, warmth spreading through the chill of the metal that separated them.

"I trust you," she whispered. "With my life." Austin held her gaze, something steady passing between them, unspoken but understood. It wasn't hope, not really. Not something fragile. It was quieter than that. It was harder. Something that refused to bend, no matter what this place tried to take from them. His hand tightened around hers, like he could anchor her there just by holding on. Then she was gone. Tim's grip closed around her arm, sharp and unyielding, tearing her from him before either of them could react. Austin's hand fell empty as she was pulled down the corridor, her steps stumbling to keep pace. He didn't move, he couldn't. He just watched as she was dragged further away, her figure swallowed slowly by the dim light, until there was nothing left of her but the echo of her words still sitting heavy in his chest.

Chapter Forty-One

The noise tore through the prison like a hurricane, a violent rush of sound funnelling through tight corridors, dragging everything in its wake. Shouting, metal slamming, gunfire cracking somewhere too close. There was no time for plans. No time for whispered conversations in shadowed corners. No time to think, only to react. Kevin burst into the cellblock, his footsteps heavy and fast as he moved straight for Reece's door. The lock clanged open, and he shoved a rifle into his hands. Reece's rifle. He looked down at it, feeling the familiar weight settle into his grip, something steady cutting through the chaos. A small, disbelieving smile pulled at his mouth before he glanced back up Kevin was already moving, unlocking Chase and Tyler's cells. He dropped a bag of weapons between them, barely slowing. Before either of them reached for it, they closed the distance. Arms wrapping around each other, quick and tight, like they didn't trust the moment would last. Chase's hand came up to Tyler's face, grounding, and he kissed him. Kevin nudged Tyler's arm with the butt of his rifle.

"Plenty of time for that later." He said, kicking the bag closer.

"What's happening?" Reece asked, stepping forward, the confusion finally breaking through.

"An uprising." Kevin crouched, dragging their weapons from the bag and handing them out. "Not the one I planned on. But if you wanted a distraction, this is it."

"An *uprising*?" Chase echoed, checking the rifle, slotting the magazine in with a sharp click before shaking out the tension in his shoulders.

"Victor wants this place for himself," Kevin said. "He's got people here, more on his side than Marcus—"

"And that helps us how?" Tyler stepped up beside Chase, their hands brushing for half a second before pulling apart.

"They'll be too busy killing each other to notice you escaping," Kevin's gaze snapped between them, sharp and urgent. "It's now, or maybe never." Reece hesitated, the weight of it settling in, then forced it down.

"We don't even know where Austin or Ben are—"

"Tim's already on his way to Austin," Kevin cut in. "And I've got a pretty good idea where to find Ben—"

"And the girls?" Chase pressed. Kevin dragged a hand over his face, tension flashing through him.

"Beth's with Marcus. Tim and Austin'll go after her."

"I'll find Val." Reece said, jaw tightening.

"Then we'll hit the kitchen," Tyler said, glancing towards Chase, who gave a short nod. "Chantelle and Su should be in the dining hall for dinner—"

"A lot of the fighting'll be there," Reece said. "You'll need backup. I'll take a gun for Val, we'll meet you there." He paused for a beat, looking down at the floor. "Do we bother looking for Sam?—"

"Sam's dead," Kevin said flatly. The words landed hard. Confusion, disbelief, and a flicker of anger passed between them. Kevin saw it, and swore under his breath.

"What happened?—"

"It was an accident. I'll explain later. You wanna stand here talking about it, or do you want out?" His voice sharpened. Silence stretched for half a second too long, then Reece nodded.

"We get out," he looked between them, something firm settling into place. "Do what you have to do, then meet at the docks. Don't wait. Get the fuck out—"

"There are three motorboats," Kevin cut in. "But the second one of 'em starts, they'll hear it. They'll know exactly where you're headed." Reece exhaled through his nose, adjusting fast.

"Alright. If you make it there first, you wait. As long as you can," his eyes flicked between them, making sure it landed. "But if they show, don't hesitate. You take a boat and you go." His grip tightened around the rifle, knuckles whitening. "And don't look back."

Moving with a predator's silence through the maze of corridors, Reece kept low and measured, each step deliberate. The chaos echoed around him - shouts, gunfire, metal slamming - but he filtered it out, narrowing his focus. Doors lined the hallway, each one a potential threat. None of them mattered. Only one did, the infirmary. He reached it and stilled, pressing his ear to the cold metal. No movement, no voices, just the distant violence bleeding through the walls. His heart pounded anyway as he gripped the handle and pushed inside. The sharp sting of antiseptic hit him first, cutting through the blood that clung to his clothes. His boots struck the sterile floor, and then something moved. An arm locked around his throat from behind, steel flashing as a scalpel pressed tight against his neck, right over his pulse.

"Val!" Reece barked, going still. She didn't hesitate - the

blade pressed harder. He reacted fast, twisting and grabbing her arm, hauling her over his shoulder in one sharp motion. She hit the ground hard, the breath knocked from her as he followed, pinning her wrists down. "Val, it's me!" He hissed. She froze, and for a split second, her eyes stayed hard, then softened as recognition hit.

"Reece," her grip slackened, the scalpel slipping from her fingers and clattering against the floor. "I thought—" A voice cut in from the doorway, soft and casual.

"Is it time?" Doctor Horn stood a few feet away, something hollow in his expression. Not fear nor panic, just acceptance. Reece's head snapped up and he pushed off Val, hauling her to her feet as his fingers tensed around his rifle.

"Time?" He echoed.

"Reece," Val said quickly, stepping between them, her eyes flicking back and forth. "He's not the enemy." Reece's jaw tightened.

"Explain—"

"He heard Austin and me talking," she said. "About getting out. He didn't say anything. He kept it quiet." Reece's grip on the rifle didn't loosen. Doctor Horn shuffled uncomfortably on his feet.

"Though I didn't realise it would be so soon—"

"This wasn't the plan. Something else's happening," his gaze locked onto the doctor. "Why didn't you say anything?" Silence stretched, and gunshots cracked somewhere in the distance. Doctor Horn's face shifted, something breaking loose beneath the surface.

"In return for a favour." He said flatly. Reece's eyes narrowed.

"What favour?"

"I need you to kill me." He took a tentative step towards Reece, and Val recoiled.

"That wasn't the deal!—" She grabbed his arm, and the doctor moved instinctively, shoving her back. She slammed into the counter with a sharp crack. Reece lunged forward, grabbing him by the collar and slamming him against the wall. The rifle came up, finger tightening on the trigger. For a second, he thought about it. Then he exhaled hard, and instead drove his fist into the doctor's jaw. The crack echoed through the room as he collapsed, unconscious before he hit the floor. Val steadied herself against the counter before rushing forward, dropping beside him. Two fingers pressed to his neck.

"He's out cold." She said, breath uneven. Reece stood over them, the adrenaline still buzzing through his body, something darker settling underneath. "The fuck was that?" She glared at him.

"I'm not killing anyone I don't have to," he said, voice low and controlled, but tight. The weight of what he had nearly done sat heavy in his chest. He glanced toward the door, toward the chaos waiting outside. "Come on," he added, sharper now. "We're running out of time."

The smell of blood and gunfire thickened with every step Chase and Tyler took toward the dining hall, settling heavy in the back of their throats as they moved past bodies sprawled across the corridor - some twisted where they had fallen, others facedown in spreading red pools that caught the dim light. Chase checked the magazine of his rifle out of habit rather than need, his thumb brushing the metal as if expecting it to come up empty. Tyler's eyes tracked the layout ahead, mapping angles, exits, lines of fire - the compound burned into his memory like something he could navigate blind.

"Chantelle and Su," he muttered, not looking back. "In

and out." Tyler stayed close behind him, jaw tight, eyes flicking over every doorway they passed.

"There'll be too many guards for just us, especially if they've got the girls locked down in there—"

"They won't," Chase cut in, voice low and controlled. "They'll be too busy tearing each other apart." Tyler didn't answer, but the silence between them wasn't agreement, it was restraint. They edged forward, slower now, the distant noise swelling into something louder and less controlled. Gunfire cracked in uneven bursts ahead, echoing through the concrete like it had nowhere to go, layered with shouting and screaming, the kind of sound that came when structure broke and no one was in charge anymore. Chase lifted a hand slightly as they neared the opening to the dining hall, signalling Tyler to hold, and then leaned just enough to look. The space beyond was wide, open, and completely blown apart. Tables had been overturned into makeshift barricades along one wall, bodies piled between them. Some were moving, most were not, while gunfire tore back and forth across the room in sharp, disjointed bursts that made it impossible to tell who was shooting at who. Near the far end, two men were locked in a brutal, clumsy fistfight, swinging wildly as if the rest of the chaos didn't exist, until a shot cracked from somewhere off to the side and one of them dropped mid-swing, the other staggering back a step before a second round hit him too, both of them crumpling without either side claiming it. No one even looked.

"Fuck," Tyler swore under his breath. "This is... chaos."

"Keep it together," Chase said, pulling back slightly. "I count eleven along the wall, barricaded. Can't see into the kitchen." Tyler leaned in just enough to get his own angle, eyes narrowing as he tried to cut through the movement.

"You see Chantelle or Su?"

"Negative—" A sudden blur of movement broke from the corner of the room. A girl they didn't recognise sprinting, panicked, her breath tearing out of her as she ran for open space, and the gunshot that followed came from somewhere neither of them could place. It punched straight through her back, dropping her hard onto the concrete with a force that echoed louder than the shot itself. Tyler flinched despite himself, his gaze locking on her, then snapping back to Chase.

"These girls don't deserve this," he hissed, anger bleeding through now. "We have to get in there—"

"We have to get Chantelle and Su," Chase snapped back, sharper this time, the control slipping just enough to show the strain underneath. "We can't save everyone." Tyler held his stare for a second longer than he should have, something raw sitting behind it, something that hadn't been there before all of this, before the prison, before the lines got blurred and then erased entirely. When he looked away, it wasn't because he agreed. Gunfire erupted again, louder this time, a concentrated burst from somewhere deeper in the kitchen, answering shots ripping back through the dining hall in a chaotic exchange that sent people ducking, shouting, scattering without any clear direction. Plates shattered under stray rounds, metal tore, someone screamed for help and was immediately drowned out by another volley. "There's no way in without getting pinned," Chase muttered, eyes tracking movement, calculating, already shifting the problem into something solvable. "We're not getting a clean look at anyone in there." Tyler didn't respond right away, his attention snagging on something further in - a body sprawled across one of the tables, half-lit by the flicker of overhead lights that were struggling to stay on. Dark curls were matted with blood, the side of her head obscured where something had torn through, and even from this distance, the contrast of her skin made her stand out against everything else around her.

"There," Tyler said quietly, nodding toward the table. "Is that—" Chase followed his line of sight, squinting slightly as he tried to make it out through the movement, through the bodies, through the chaos that refused to settle long enough for certainty.

"I don't know," he admitted, his jaw tightening. "It could be. Could be one of the others too. Those sisters?—"

"Jennifer and Stephanie," Tyler said, the names catching in his throat as he tried to place the face with what little he could see. "I can't tell." For a second, neither of them spoke, the noise of the room filling the space between them.

"This is fucked," Chase said finally, quieter now, more to himself than anything. "We're not getting in there to check. We head to the docks, link up there—"

"No," Tyler shook his head immediately, eyes still fixed on the room. "We said we'd wait for Reece and Val. We wait."

"And how long do you want to crouch here?" Chase turned on him, frustration cutting through the control he'd been holding onto. "Until someone spots us? Until we get dragged into that?" Tyler met his gaze this time, not backing off.

"You go then," he shot back, voice low but edged. "Fucking leave. I'm waiting as long as I can."

Kevin's boots echoed through the abandoned wing at the other side of the island as he descended deeper into the forgotten cellblock. The air was damp, heavy with neglect. He paused at Ben's cell, where moonlight sliced through the barred window. Ben's head snapped up, fingers clenched around the bars.

"Kevin? What the hell's going on?—"

"Victor's men are taking over," Kevin said, keys jangling as he unlocked the cell. "Everyone's scattered. Fighting's taking place mostly in the main cellblocks." He thrust a handgun towards Ben. "Take it." Ben hesitated before accepting the weapon, its weight foreign after months without one. He turned it over in his hands, looking at it curiously.

"How'd you find me?"

"Had an idea where you'd be." Kevin started walking, and Ben followed slowly. The door creaked open under Kevin's hand, revealing the night beyond. He jerked his chin toward the courtyard. Ben lingered at the threshold, then moved forward onto the silver-washed concrete. His eyes swept the perimeter, the distant popping of gunfire muffled like firecrackers heard underwater.

"I haven't been to this side of the prison before."

"I have," Kevin said casually before following Ben out. "Once."

"So what's the plan?" Ben felt the weight of the handgun again, turning it over slowly.

"Everyone's headed for the docks." Kevin began walking towards the main cellblock, his gait even and calm.

"I need to find Beth—"

"Tim should have her by now," Kevin paused, turning to face him. "The plan is to get to the docks—"

"*My* plan is for me to find Beth," Ben said, voice low. "That's all that matters—"

"Fuck," Kevin muttered. "Victor said you'd be stubborn." Ben glanced down at the handgun again, and something about it tugged at him. It was too light, it felt wrong. The balance sat strangely in his palm, the weight not pulling where it should. His grip tightened slightly, thumb brushing the slide as if the answer might be there. And then a flicker of recognition crossed his face - Kevin had handed him an empty gun.

"What's your plan, then?" Ben asked.

"Tim'll take Beth to Victor," Kevin said casually. "And your friends, the ones who don't get killed in the fighting, they'll go back to their cells—"

"Why let them out to begin with?" Ben hissed, taking a small step towards him.

"Gotta let them think they have some hope, right? It was Victor's idea—"

"And what makes you think I won't tell them?—"

"Beth," Kevin said, the one word falling flat between them. His eyes were vacant and cold. Ben's jaw tightened, his fists balling at his sides. Anger and rage coursed through him like he hadn't felt, the finality of everything hitting him all at once. Kevin gestured with his rifle for Ben to walk in front of him, raising it. "Come on. Victor wants you too." Ben walked slowly in front of him, raising his hands to his chest. The chaos grew louder as they approached the main cellblocks, his heart racing.

"Why tell me now?" Ben pressed. "Why not wait until we were inside and in the thick of it—"

"You're not going inside," Kevin snapped. "Like I said, Victor wants you alive. Can't have you getting shot now can we?"

"Victor wants me alive?"

"Yes."

"Good." Ben's breath came in ragged gulps, his heart pounding a relentless rhythm against his ribs. He felt the bruising thrill of defiance surge through him as he spun around, seizing Kevin's rifle with a reckless, desperate grip. The clatter of the weapon filled the night air, punctuated by a dry crack that echoed as Ben swung it fiercely, his makeshift strike landing soundly on Kevin's jaw. Kevin staggered backward, dazed, blood splattering across Ben's cheek like a warm rain. Ben wiped at it with the back of his hand, adrenaline masking the sting of the burn left by the heated metal. The drizzle turned the rifle slick in his hands, and for a terrifying second, it slipped. Kevin lunged, eyes burning with a wild fury as he swung the rifle toward Ben's head. Ben twisted to the side just in time, feeling rather than seeing the weapon whistle past him. He lashed out with his boot, connecting solidly with Kevin's ribs. The impact sent Kevin staggering backward, gasping for air. But he was quick, too quick, recovering to launch into a flurry of punches that slammed into Ben's gut. Each blow pushed him back until he managed to catch himself. He raised an arm to block another jab and retaliated by grabbing Kevin's arm, twisting it sharply behind his back. Kevin let out a pained grunt but fought through it, yanking free and pivoting to face Ben once more. Without giving Kevin a moment to regain his composure, Ben charged forward. They hit the ground hard, rolling over rough concrete as each struggled for dominance. The fight was brutal and clumsy - neither gave an inch as they grappled with one another. A burst of rage propelled Ben onto his feet long enough to grab hold of Kevin's rifle again. A primal yell ripped itself from Ben's chest as he squeezed the trigger. The bullet caught Kevin just off the centreline of his face, a ragged and ugly wound that punched through the soft tissue of his cheek and sent a cloud of shattered teeth and blood in a pink mist across the air. For a heartbeat, Kevin's head snapped backward, his arms pinwheeling as if trying to catch the violence that had just passed through him. The wound was catastrophic, tearing away a wet crescent of skin and muscle, leaving a crater where the flesh had been. Kevin's eyes, wide with shock, fixed on Ben's face for one eternal second before rolling upward. His body crumpled, a marionette with severed strings. The wet gurgle of his final breath bubbled through the wound, then silence. Ben wiped Kevin's blood from his face with a trembling hand, then steadied himself. He checked the rifle and slung it over his shoulder. Gunfire still popped in the distance as he turned toward the main cellblock, his mind narrowed to a single thought.

Austin's pulse hammered in his ears as he followed Tim through the corridors, each step heavier than the last. The rifle sat awkward in his grip, his body still catching up to the demand being forced on it. Hunger, exhaustion, weeks of being worn down - it all dragged at him. But not enough to stop him, not now. They reached Marcus' door. Austin didn't hesitate. He raised the rifle, and Tim gave a single nod, and the door burst open. Candlelight flickered wildly, shadows snapping across the walls. Austin didn't need to see clearly, he didn't need to adjust his eyes to the light. He heard it. The scuffle, the low, animal growl from Marcus, Beth's breaths sharp and strained and wrong. Then he saw it - Marcus on top of her, ripping at her dress, a sudden crack across her cheek. Something inside Austin snapped. He didn't think, didn't aim, and he didn't hesitate - he launched. They hit the ground hard, the impact rattling through the room. Austin was on him instantly, fists flying wild, brutal and unrelenting. Each punch landed with a sickening crack, bone and flesh giving under the force. Marcus fought back, snarling, trying to shove him off, but Austin didn't stop. Every scream he'd heard, every bruise, every broken piece of them - it all came out at once. Beth pushed herself upright on the bed, her chest rising sharply as she watched. She snapped her head towards Tim, watching as he stepped lightly, slowly, across the floor.

"Shoot him!" She shouted. There was no shock in her eyes, no horror - only a distant sort of indifference as if she had seen too much to be moved by violence anymore. Tim stepped forward, steady and controlled, rifle raised, but he didn't fire.

"I don't have a clear shot." He said. Austin didn't hear any of it. It wasn't until Marcus fell limp, his struggles ceasing, that Austin's frenzied assault came to an end. Panting, he rose to his feet, his chest heaving. His hands were slick with blood that was not his own, and for a moment, he swayed, caught in the aftermath of adrenaline and wrath. Beth pushed herself up from the bed, her movements measured and deliberate. She closed the gap between them, reaching out with her own blood-stained hands to touch Austin's arm. Her fingers felt warm against his skin, the contact bringing him back to the present, pulling him from the edge of the dark abyss into which he had plunged.

"Austin?" Beth said softly, her voice cutting through the haze that clouded his mind. "It's over." He looked at her then, and really saw her, taking in the blood that splattered her clothes and the calmness that settled over her features. It was as if the chaos around them couldn't touch her, couldn't penetrate the wall she had built around herself.

"We have to go," Tim lowered his rifle, eyes darting towards the door. "Marcus' guards'll be—"

"You go," Beth urged. "We'll be right behind you." Her tone was insistent but gentle, as though coaxing Austin from a dream. Tim paused for a moment, looking between Beth and Austin. Something shifted, and he nodded at her.

"I need to take care of something. See you at the docks." Tim said before disappearing through the door. Beth turned back to face Austin, leaning in closer. She gazed into his eyes, hoping she would still find the man she knew inside.

"Austin?—"

"Beth." He pulled her into him without hesitation, one hand gripping her waist as he crashed his mouth against hers. The kiss was rough, desperate - messy with blood and sweat and everything they hadn't said. She felt it immediately. The heat of him, the tremor beneath his strength, the way he held her like if he let go, she'd be taken again. Her body ached, every bruise and split screaming in protest, but she didn't pull away. Her fingers caught in his shirt, grounding herself as his grip tightened, pulling her closer, like he was trying to erase the space this place had forced between them. The air still stank of violence. Marcus' blood streaked across both of them, smeared between them where they pressed together. She broke from the kiss with a sharp breath, her heart racing, her body caught between pain and something far more dangerous.

"What are you doing—"

"I love you," his forehead dropped to hers, breath uneven, voice low and wrecked. "I shouldn't. I know I shouldn't... but I do." Her gaze drifted past him, landing on Marcus' body sprawled across the floor, lifeless and still. Then back to Austin - his face, his hands, all of him marked in blood.

"Austin," she whispered, her voice low. "I—" A pause, hollow and desperate.

"You love Ben," he said before she could say anything more. "We need to leave." Beth nodded, taking one last look at the room that had defined her for weeks. She frantically searched the pile of clothes Marcus had left on his couch, finally producing a handgun from the abandoned holster. Austin looked at Marcus, the weight of his actions settling heavily on his shoulders. Without a word, he allowed her to lead him away from the corpse, away from the room where death lingered like a spectre. The corridor was a tunnel of uncertainty, each shadow a potential threat as Austin and Beth moved with haste. His hand gripped hers, the warmth between them an unspoken promise - a lifeline in the suffocating dark. Their breaths came fast and shallow, synched in a rhythm born of desperation, every line of his body tensed as he peered around every corner before leading her safely through the labyrinth. They edged forward, but the burst of gunfire that had erupted earlier tore through their plans. Guards swarmed the passage, a barrier of bodies and bullets between them and freedom as the two of them retreated to find another way, their escape delayed but not deterred.

Chapter Forty-Two

The corridor smelled of smoke, blood, and gunfire, thick and clinging like a second skin as Reece and Val came around the corner, boots heavy against the concrete, every sense screaming alert. The clatter and chaos inside the dining hall and kitchen spilled out into the hallway - shouts, gunshots, the crash of overturned tables and metal. Reece's hand gripped his rifle a little tighter, the knuckles whitening as he fell into step beside Val. She was silent, sharp-eyed, reading the space as if she could absorb it all at once, her posture tight with contained tension. Tyler turned his head as he heard their footsteps approaching, relief washing over him as Reece and Val crouched down beside them.

"Have you found them?" Reece asked, voice low but insistent, cutting through the noise. His eyes flicked to Chase first, then Tyler, noting the way both exuded control, even in the middle of all this madness. Chase shook his head, keeping his expression blank.

"Negative." He said, voice measured, clipped, a touch of that hard edge Tyler had come to recognise as the warning not to press too far. Tyler's hand rested lightly against Chase's back for a fraction of a second before falling to his side again, eyes sweeping the corridor ahead.

"No sign of Chantelle?" Val's gaze was sharp, darting between them, and she caught Chase's eye first. Her voice was quiet, but there was a fierce insistence beneath the calm. She grabbed Reece's arm with sudden decisiveness, enough to make him catch her intent without words. "I have to find her." She said, the single sentence carrying the weight of fear and restraint. Reece nodded once, a sharp, compact motion that somehow held reassurance. He adjusted the strap of his rifle across his shoulder, fingers brushing the scope with practiced ease. He lifted it, peering through the chaos, past overturned tables and the noise echoing in the room beyond. The dining hall opened into a wide, broken space, littered with the detritus of sudden violence. Bodies sprawled across the floor, some limp, some twitching, caught mid-motion in the delirium of the fight. Gunfire erupted in uneven staccato from the far end, closer to the kitchen, punctuated by metallic crashes as chairs toppled and plates shattered. He adjusted the scope, narrowing in along the wall closest to the kitchen doorway, scanning the bodies scattered among the debris. His pulse hammered in his ears as he caught sight of something, someone, half-hidden just inside the kitchen's threshold, lying prone, the angle only partially visible but enough to catch his attention. The figure was still. The body seemed smaller, the dark hair pulled partially across the face, and Reece's breath caught slightly.

"I think I see Su," he hissed, leaning slightly back from the wall, eyes still locked on the scope. "There, just inside the kitchen." They all followed his gaze without hesitation, jaws tightening, and Val's fingers gripped Reece's arm more firmly.

"I *need* to find my daughter." She whispered, determination ringing through every syllable, the faint tremor in her voice belied by the steel in her eyes. Before Reece could make a move, a flash of movement caught the corner of his eye, a shadow shifting too fast in the chaos, too purposeful. The report came next, sharp and immediate, a crack of gunfire aimed precisely in their direction. Concrete splintered at the edges where the bullets struck, and Reece barely had time to shove Val down, hurling them both behind a protruding corner. The gunfire followed in uneven bursts, ripping through the corridor in short, unpredictable staccato that made their ears ring.

"Move!" Chase barked, breaking the frozen calculation for them. Tyler's hand landed briefly on Reece's shoulder, a grounding push before he followed Chase, both moving fast but calculated, each step a blend of urgency and tactical sense. Val scrambled to her feet, the grip on Reece's arm firm, the unspoken coordination between them a bond forged in chaos. Reece adjusted the rifle for mobility as they ran down the corridor, their footsteps heavy. The gunfire followed, sporadic and chaotic, bullets whizzing past in a deafening chorus, but the corridor offered cover just enough to stay ahead, enough to keep the chance of survival alive. Every step carried the weight of possibility, the risk of being too slow, of a single misstep that would cost them everything. Reece's eyes stayed forward, scanning, mapping, calculating while his heart pounded in time with Val's, her presence a stabilising anchor in the storm of violence around them. Chaos swirled behind, ahead, and all around, but they moved forward. Even as the corridor seemed endless, even as gunfire and screaming filled the distance behind them, Reece's focus remained on the doorway, the figure just beyond, and the fragile, desperate hope that they could find Chantelle before the violence swallowed everything whole.

The courtyard lay under a thin smear of moonlight, the ground cracked and littered with detritus from the chaos that had swept through the island. Tim's boots struck the concrete in a measured rhythm, each step cautious, each glance flicking toward shadows that might conceal unseen threats. His chest tightened with a low, simmering dread as he rounded the corner of a collapsed wall and froze. Kevin was there, sprawled awkwardly, dark hair matted, the stillness of his body claiming the night like a stubborn truth. Blood had pooled beneath him, the slick red catching the pale light and glinting with a finality that twisted in Tim's stomach. Something in Tim coiled, a bitter, aching spike of frustration. Ben had done this, and the understanding sank into him, heavy and unyielding, and for a moment he couldn't move past it. Then he saw Victor. The man stood tall, impossibly calm in the chaos, a shadowed silhouette against the faint light spilling from the upper courtyard. His gaze swept over Kevin's body, detached, and when he finally looked at Tim, the expression was a mix of amusement and faint irritation. Tim's pulse jumped, rage flaring before he could even think.

"Why aren't you fighting for the prison you're trying to take over?" He demanded, voice low but sharp. Victor's smile was slow, deliberate, the kind that suggested danger wrapped in ice.

"Why would I?" Victor said, his voice smooth, almost conversational as if discussing the weather. "When I have all of you to do the work for me." His gaze flicked down at Kevin's still form, and a faint shrug accompanied the offhand comment. "Although with this display of ineptitude, I wonder how everything's going in there. Kevin was supposed to bring Ben to me, but I suppose he was unnecessary. Couldn't get the job done. Couldn't even finish the simplest task." The words were knives sliding through Tim's veins, each one cutting sharper than the last. Fury rose like a tide. Without thinking, he lunged forward, fists swinging toward Victor with a mix of desperation and calculated rage. Two figures materialised at his sides in an instant, hands locking around his arms, yanking him back with brutal efficiency. He struggled, kicking and twisting, but their grip was unrelenting, muscles coiled and steady. He could see the amusement in Victor's eyes, hear the faint click of something metallic in the distance, but he didn't care. He had to get to him. Victor's voice was soft, teasing, almost bored as he stepped closer. "Where is she? You were supposed to bring her to me—"

"I finally saw what you and Marcus are," Tim's chest heaved, anger and disgust pressing against his ribs. His voice cut through the night, raw and deliberate. "I changed my mind." Victor's expression didn't shift, but his eyes glittered with something darker, sharper, and deadly.

"Oh," he said, voice low and dangerous. "Can you see *this*?" Tim barely had time to register the motion before a blade flicked upward, clean and precise, slamming into the side of his face. Pain erupted instantly, hot and white, metal slicing through bone and sinew. His vision erupted in fire and shadow, blood spilling into his eye, burning, blinding him entirely. He fell back onto the concrete, screaming into the night, hands clawing at his face, the world dissolving into a red haze, then black. The courtyard, the blood, Kevin's broken form, all faded into indistinct shapes and sounds. He was trapped in the darkness of his own body, the last thing he felt the cold press of Victor's control, the inevitability of being overpowered, the finality of failing too late. Victor crouched slightly, surveying him with detached calculation, like a predator examining prey that had failed to escape. Around them, the distant bursts of gunfire and chaos carried on, indifferent to the small, merciless confrontation that had just occurred. Tim's limbs thrashed weakly, rage giving way to panic and the sickening clarity that he was utterly vulnerable, utterly at Victor's mercy, and utterly alone. The courtyard's silence pressed down, heavy and complete, broken only by the soft drip of blood onto cracked concrete. Kevin's body remained where it had fallen, a testament to failed plans, while Tim's consciousness teetered on the edge, swallowed by pain and blinding darkness, leaving only Victor standing unchallenged, calm, and inexorably in control.

The outer door slammed behind them with a resonant crack that echoed through the compound, the noise swallowed almost instantly by the chaos outside. Reece, Val, Chase, and Tyler burst into the open air, the night cold against their skin, hearts still hammering from the adrenaline of the dining hall and the gunfire that had marked every step of their way. For a moment, relief flickered - a brief, fleeting thought that maybe they had made it through, at least for now. Then Ben appeared. He was staggering up the incline toward them, his movements uneven, each step heavy with pain, the subtle hitch of his body betraying something far worse than fatigue. Tyler's eyes caught him first, sharp and instinctive, and he broke into a run, cutting across the debris-strewn courtyard with long, urgent strides. Reece followed immediately, adjusting his rifle for speed. Ben's hand lifted instinctively to his side as he moved, and when he looked down, the sight made his stomach lurch. Blood coated his fingers, dark and slick, seeping through the fabric of his shirt. He faltered, stumbling against a chunk of rubble, teeth gritted, breathing ragged. Tyler reached him first, closing the distance in seconds, grabbing him under one arm, steadying him against the slope. Reece was there a heartbeat later, hands on his other arm, as they lowered him to the ground.

"You've been hit." Tyler said sharply, voice cutting through the night air. Ben's eyes flicked between them, a mix of pain and frustration twisting his features. He tried to speak, but his words were hoarse. Val came running, taking in the scene in an instant, crouching beside him, her hands reaching for his wound with practiced speed. Her fingers pressed against the fabric, probing carefully.

"It's gone clean through," she said, voice tight, low, urgent. "He's losing blood, fast." Ben groaned, struggling against the weight of exhaustion and panic, voice strained.

"Where's Beth?" No one answered him. He tried again, eyes searching theirs, fear and anger mingling in a sharp, frantic edge.

"I can't treat this here." Val said finally, voice steadier now though lined with tension.

"We can't go back to the infirmary. It's too dangerous." Chase said, his eyes scanning the courtyard. Val's eyes flicked to her backpack.

"I might have something that could help him, but I'm not leaving without finding Chantelle." She said. Reece's gaze hardened, and he leaned down slightly, eyes locking with hers.

"Ben needs you more right now." He searched her eyes, knowing she wouldn't leave him to bleed out on the ground. Val's jaw tightened, a flicker of frustration crossing her features. Then, with a short, decisive breath, she nodded.

"Chase, Tyler. Help me get him down to the dock," she glanced up at Reece, voice sharp and almost desperate. "You bring my daughter back to me. Do you understand?" Reece nodded firmly, a silent promise burning in his eyes, and without another word, he set off across the courtyard, slipping between broken walls and overturned debris, scanning every shadow as he moved. Chase and Tyler hoisted Ben between them, each adjusting his weight carefully as he slumped, limp from blood loss and exhaustion. Tyler's hand pressed instinctively against the side wound through the thin fabric of his shirt, trying to slow the flow while keeping pace. Val moved slightly ahead, eyes forward, calculating angles, watching for threats, scanning the courtyard as they navigated toward the hill. The ground sloped downward, littered with shattered fragments of concrete and debris from the chaos that had erupted earlier, but they moved quickly, urgently, carrying Ben with precision born of survival instinct. Each step was measured, every movement careful yet swift, the three of them forming a shield around him, keeping him steady against the pull of gravity and the creeping, relentless exhaustion threatening to drag him down. Above them, the echoes of distant gunfire and shouts punctuated the night, a reminder that danger had not stopped, that the prison remained alive with violence and death. But they moved as one, a single, purposeful unit, pushing Ben toward the docks where the small chance of extraction awaited. When they reached the dock, they laid his body on a bench, Val kneeling beside him.

"What do you need?" Tyler pressed, kneeling beside her.

"Get my kit from my bag," she said, her voice cutting quietly through the night, sharp and commanding. "Follow everything I say, and he might just make it. And you," she turned towards Chase, motioning up the hill. "Don't take your eyes off that hill, and if anyone comes down that's not one of our own, you shoot to kill."

Beth and Austin rounded the corner, the outer door just beyond their reach, their boots scuffing lightly over broken concrete, breaths ragged from exertion and adrenaline. The corridor ahead opened into a small side hallway, a space cluttered with debris, overturned chairs, and the remnants of hastily abandoned belongings. The metallic tang of blood hit them first, subtle but unmistakable, and then the shapes came into view. Three figures were slumped against the far wall, partially hidden in the shadows. Estelle lay sprawled across the floor, one arm bent at an unnatural angle, her face pale and streaked with blood, chest rising and falling shallowly. Beside her, Maureen's body had gone still, twisted grotesquely on the cold concrete, blood seeping into the floor beneath her. And between them, Jennifer sat with her back against the wall, legs splayed, head tilted slightly, the blood on her clothes streaked with grime and dust. She was hurt badly, but conscious, eyes widening as they took in Beth and Austin. Austin moved first, grabbing Beth's arm, urging her to keep moving.

"We can't—" He started, but Beth jerked her hand free, snapping it out of his grasp.

"No," she said sharply, voice low but fierce. She darted forward, kneeling beside Jennifer, crouching close. Her fingers brushed a streak of blood from Jennifer's cheek, wiping away the tear that had escaped down the pale skin. "I've got you." Beth murmured. Jennifer's lips parted in a weak, painful smile.

"We... we were trying to find Stephanie," she said, her voice hoarse, trembling. "We thought... maybe we could get her and make a run for the docks. The fighting... maybe it would give us cover." Beth glanced toward Austin, whose grip tightened on his rifle, ready to pull her away, but she shook her head slightly, focusing on Jennifer.

"Great minds think alike." Beth said quietly, voice soft but carrying a hint of determination. She pressed a hand against Jennifer's shoulder, steadying her, grounding them both in a moment that felt impossibly fragile. Jennifer coughed, lips moving as if forcing words through pain.

"Maureen, she caught us," she said. "We begged her... begged her to come with us. But she wouldn't. She—" her voice broke, and she shook her head. "She stabbed Estelle first, and then me. Before I got the knife... before I—" Her eyes met Beth's, a flicker of shame, of horror, and sorrow burning in their depths. "I killed her." Beth's hand tightened slightly, brushing over Jennifer's hair as she held her close.

"We'll figure it out," she whispered, her voice steady though her chest felt tight. She looked up at Austin. "We can't just leave them." Austin's jaw clenched, frustration radiating off him in sharp, tense movements. He reached out, grabbing Beth's arm again, trying to pull her back.

"Beth, we can't. We don't have time!—"

"No!" Beth yanked her hand from his grip again, sliding to her knees beside Jennifer, meeting her gaze. "I'm *not* leaving her!" She said firmly, her voice carrying a note of steel that cut through Austin's frustration. Jennifer's gaze softened, pain etched deep into every line of her face.

"It's okay. Leave me." She whispered. Beth shook her head vehemently, brushing her fingers over Jennifer's cheek again. A sudden eruption of gunfire ripped through the courtyard outside, the staccato reports echoing down the corridor and bouncing off the walls like thunder, and Beth's heart jumped. She glanced at Austin, who tensed, fists clenched around the rifle.

"Stay here for a second," he ordered sharply, voice low but urgent. "I'll be right back." He opened the outer door a crack before sliding out, keeping his body low. Jennifer reached out weakly, fingers brushing Beth's arm.

"Go," she said quietly, though her eyes betrayed her longing. "I won't leave without my sister." Beth pressed a hand over Jennifer's and nodded, swallowing hard against the lump in her throat.

"I hope we meet again someday." She whispered, voice breaking slightly but holding on to resolve. Beth lingered for a moment longer, glancing down at Jennifer and then at the two others. Estelle's shallow, uneven breaths rattled her, a stark reminder of how fragile life remained in the midst of this chaos. Maureen's lifeless body reminded her of the stakes, of the cost, of what had already been lost. Then Beth pushed herself up, pressing against the wall, moving toward the door. The night air hit her face, carrying the acrid stench of gunfire and smoke. Her eyes swept the courtyard, already alive with movement and violence. Bodies ducked, men firing indiscriminately, bullets whizzing past, ricocheting off metal and concrete. Austin was crouched behind a low wall, rifle raised, taking heavy fire from somewhere deeper in the compound. His frame shuddered with each shot, but he remained focused, calculating, eyes sharp beneath the brim of his hood. Beth pressed herself against the building's corner, her back flat, every sense alert. She watched him, noting every movement, every twitch, every adjustment he made to stay alive. The chaos stretched around her, a violent storm, but she held herself still, a silent observer and guardian, heart thumping in sync with the distant gunfire. She could feel the pull of urgency, the need to act, the desperate tension of survival twisting her chest. But she waited, allowing herself a fraction of a second to take it in - to mark the sight of Austin's calculated movements, the spray of bullets, the chaos of the courtyard that mirrored everything the prison had become. Austin's eyes flicked across the courtyard, catching a glimpse of movement further down. There, pressed low against a crumbling wall, was Reece, slouched and still, every muscle coiled as if willing himself invisible. The gunfire roared around them, but neither side had noticed their presence. Austin's hand shot up - a quick, sharp motion to signal Beth to stay put. Without hesitation, he vaulted forward, sprinting across the open stretch, diving for the partial cover of the wall, and pressed himself tight against Reece's side, feeling the solid weight of his companion beneath the storm of bullets.

"Val, Ben, Chase and Tyler are at the dock," he said through ragged breaths. "I came back for Chantelle. We can't find her—"

"Su?" Austin asked, but Reece shook his head. He glanced back at Beth, crouched behind cover, and motioned sharply for her to stay put. "Beth's with me." Reece took one look towards her before glancing back at Austin, his expression tight.

"Ben's hurt bad." He said. Guilt and anxiety tightened in Austin's chest. Beth's eyes tracked them, silent and pleading, as the chaos of the courtyard pressed in from every side. She scanned the ground ahead, weighing the route to the opening that led down to the docks, knowing bullets and shouting wouldn't wait, and neither would time. They were so indescribably close to freedom, and then a sight caught her eye. Chantelle was being dragged through the outside passageway, towards the storerooms she and Ben had been kept in.

"Austin!" She called out, but the gunfire and yelling drowned out her hoarse voice. Her mind turned with frustration, battling the thought of leaving Chantelle behind. She cursed as she ran towards the storeroom, leaving Austin and Reece's fading silhouettes behind. Beth barrelled through the ajar door, her eyes wide as she watched the guard pin Chantelle to the ground.

"Stop!" Her friend's protests were muffled, her struggles weakening against the brute force of the man atop her. Anger coiled tight in Beth's stomach, a visceral, searing heat that demanded action. The guard was too focused on his vile intent to notice the shadow that loomed behind him, Chantelle's screaming in his ear muffled the blast of the door as she had barged through. Beth's fingers trembled, but her aim was steady as she levelled the handgun she'd taken from Marcus. Everything else faded away, leaving only the guard, Chantelle, and the cold weight of the firearm in her hands.

"You heard her. *Stop*." Beth commanded, her voice quiet but laced with deadly resolve. The guard turned, a sneer twisting his features as he saw the petite figure challenging him. It was the last expression he'd ever make as Beth pulled the trigger without hesitation. The gunshot echoed through the storeroom, a stark and final punctuation. The guard's body went limp, collapsing beside the trembling form of

Chantelle. Beth didn't flinch at the sight of blood pooling beneath the man's head. There was no room for shock or grief in her heart, only the fierce satisfaction of having protected one of their own.

"Where the fuck did she go?" Austin hissed, scanning the courtyard with frantic eyes.

"It's no use," Reece said. "We have to go. They're pressing towards the dock. It's now or never—"

"I can't leave her—"

"You think I wanna go back down there and tell Val we can't get to Chantelle?" Reece grabbed Austin's arm. "We stay, we die."

"Fuck, Beth—" Austin whispered, before pushing himself from the ground and racing down the hill. Reece followed close behind, their heavy footsteps drowned out by the gunfire above them. They reached the dock in time to see Chase and Tyler lowering Ben into a motorboat.

"Where is she?" Val yelled, her voice tight.

"We couldn't get to her." Reece replied, the words heavy with unspoken dread. Val's eyes widened with alarm, a tempest of fear and anger brewing in their depths.

"Then we can't leave." Val stated, the determination in her voice leaving no room for argument. But even as she spoke, the reality of their situation settled upon them like a shroud. The harsh truth was unrelenting - they couldn't save everyone, and their window of escape was closing rapidly.

"Val, we have to go." Austin urged, his gaze locked on Ben's limp form. They had come so far, lost so much, and yet the thought of abandoning any of their own was unthinkable. But as the seconds ticked by, stolen by the inevitability of their circumstance, they knew there was only one choice left to make.

"I'm not leaving her!" Val screamed, as Reece lifted the butt of his rifle, knocking her out with one swift motion and catching her in his arms as she fell.

"Let's move." Reece said finally, a command laced with sorrow, as he threw Val over his shoulder.

"Beth?" Chase's voice was tight, searching. Austin shook his head, lips pressed hard, the weight of the choice written across his face. With heavy hearts, they climbed into the boat, leaving behind the ghosts of those they could not carry with them. Austin fired a few rounds into the motorboats alongside them. Each hiss of air and water signalled slow destruction, a small measure of sabotage against what might pursue them. Pain gripped Austin's chest, a vice squeezing tight as the compound's chaos rumbled above - shouts, gunfire, the pounding of boots down the hill. Men sprinted toward the docks, some still trading fire, others racing for their own escape. Every second felt like a countdown. The engine roared, ripping them from the dock, cutting through the water with brutal urgency, leaving the compound and its horrors behind. But the memory of those left behind clung like smoke, heavy and bitter.

Chantelle's sobs tore through the storeroom, her body convulsing as if trying to reject the horrors of the night. Beth's chest thudded with every beat, a grim reminder that they were far from safe. She crouched beside her friend, the air thick with the residue of violence and fear.

"Chantelle!" Beth grabbed her shoulders, shaking her. "We need to move!" Chantelle's eyes were glazed, lost in panic, trapped inside her own terror. Every second they lingered was a risk they could not afford. With a surge of desperation, Beth drew back her hand and snapped it across Chantelle's cheek. The sharp crack echoed off the walls, forcing her friend's attention back.

"What the fuck, Beth!" Chantelle hissed, pressing her hand to her cheek.

"Get off the fucking ground!" Beth snapped, fierce and relentless. She yanked Chantelle upright, and the sting of reality ignited her adrenaline. Together they bolted through the storeroom door, feet hammering against cold concrete. Darkness stretched before them, shadows flickering like restless ghosts. Breath came sharp and shallow, lungs burning, legs screaming, but escape propelled them forward. Beth led, hauling Chantelle up the hill toward the pier. At the top, they froze for a heartbeat, surveying the chaos below. Guards swarmed the docks, flashlights slicing silver arcs across the ground, shouts piercing the night. Spotlights from generators swept the pier, hunting for any fleeing figure. But the boats were gone. Her eyes darted across the dimming horizon, desperate. Every instinct screamed urgency. She grasped Chantelle's arm, tightening her hold, and raced to the edge of the compound. Hands clutched the rough stone fence, scars of battles past biting into her palms. She hoisted herself just enough to peer over. There, against the dark water, the faint silhouette of Austin cradling Ben on the back of a disappearing boat. His posture spoke of raw tension - every muscle coiled in readiness to flee, yet anchored by loyalty. Across the distance, she knew he could see her in the scanning lights. In that instant, all chaos fell away. She read him in a glance - torn, determined, burdened. Beth's heart ached in the silence between them. No words could cross the space, but the understanding was absolute. Survival demanded distance, yet connection held stronger than fear. She drew a ragged breath, letting purpose settle into her bones. Slowly, deliberately, she nodded. Austin's response was almost imperceptible, a subtle shift in stance, a language only they could speak. Then he turned fully toward the vessel that would carry them to a fragile dawn. The boat cut through the water, shoving the night and all its horrors behind them.

"Is that them?" Chantelle's frantic cries disappeared into the void. "Did they leave us?—"

"Yes," Beth whispered. "We're on our own." Chantelle sank beside her, sobs muffled into her hands, knees pulled tight. Beth watched until the last shadow of them faded into the black. Around her, the dim torchlight of patrolling guards flickered, indifferent to her vigil as they approached. The ocean breeze whispered promises of freedom that might never be hers. Beth pressed her hands into the stone wall, eyes locked on the dark horizon where her friends had vanished, and in that moment, as the waves swallowed their silhouettes, she understood the weight of the night. The chaos, the loss, the narrow threads of survival - they all belonged to the same story. She drew a deep, shuddering breath, letting it fill her chest. The world had shifted. The night had claimed its measure. And as she watched, silent and unbroken, Beth accepted the truth. The night had claimed its dominion.

Afterword

Dear Reader,

Thank you for taking the time to step into this story. Whether you devoured it in one sitting or lingered over the pages, I'm genuinely grateful you chose to spend your time here.

If you enjoyed this book, a quick review makes an enormous difference to independent authors and helps other readers discover my work and allows stories like this to keep finding a home.

You can leave a review by visiting my website and finding the various links to Amazon, GoodReads, and other platforms.

www.ceshorland.com/dystopia-series/deadweight

Thank you again for reading, and for supporting independent authors. It truly means more than you know.

With all my love and appreciation,
CE Shorland

Content Notes &
Trigger Warnings

The following section provides a chapter-by-chapter breakdown of content that may be distressing to some readers.

This guide is intended to help you make informed decisions about how you engage with the story, whether that means preparing for certain themes, reading with awareness, or choosing to skip particular sections.

If you continue through this guide, please keep your mental and emotional wellbeing in mind. Some of the content may be challenging, and it's important to pause, take breaks, or step away if needed. This guide is here to support your reading experience, not to pressure you - how you engage with the story is entirely up to you.

While much of the story is dark, there are also moments of compassion, resilience, and fleeting hope. Acts of kindness, tenderness, and small sparks of joy appear amidst the difficult circumstances, reminding readers that even in the harshest situations, humanity endures.

Due to the nature of this format, some entries may contain contextual spoilers, though no names are mentioned. Reader discretion is advised.

While care has been taken in the portrayal of sensitive material involving minors, this story contains scenes that some readers may find distressing. Violence involving minors is not described in explicit detail, however, references to harm, including injury, death, and the aftermath of traumatic events are present. This includes the off-page death of a young child, the death of a teenage character, and references to sexual violence involving a minor, with focus placed on the aftermath rather than the act itself.

The novel also contains frequent interpersonal conflict, including heated arguments between friends and loved ones, which some readers may find emotionally confronting.

Themes of complex relationships are explored throughout, including emotional intimacy involving multiple characters. While no explicit commitments are established, some readers may interpret these dynamics as infidelity or find them distressing.

As a broader note, scenes throughout the novel include varying degrees of violence, injury, and death, with descriptions of blood, physical harm, and their aftermath.

Real-world locations are referenced throughout the story, often depicted in a state of abandonment and decay. Readers familiar with these places may find these portrayals unsettling. A full list of locations can be found below:

- Eatonville, Washington State
- Spokane, Washington State
- Redding, California (and surrounding areas)
- San Bernardino, California
- Los Angeles, California
- San Diego, California

- Catalina Island, California
- San Francisco, California
- Alcatraz Island, California
- Australia (in general)
  - *The main female character is Australian and, having become stranded in the United States during the events of the story, occasionally references her home.*

Chapter 1

- Starvation and physical deterioration
  - A female character is found severely malnourished (prior to the start of the novel) and is cared for by others.
  - The novel opens with her disoriented and regaining her bearings.

Chapter 2

- Suggestive sexual threat / coercive attitudes
  - A male character implies a female character's value is tied to sexual usefulness.
- Alcohol use
  - A few of the characters drink socially around a campfire.
  - A female minor (16 years old) references that she no longer drinks alcohol, implying underage drinking previously.
  - A male character mentions being sober.
- Grief, loss, and emotional distress

- A female character and two male characters discuss losing loved ones prior to the story.
    - A male character mentions the death of his girlfriend during the initial outbreak.
    - A male character mentions not knowing where family members are.
  - Infidelity (referenced)
    - A male character mentions his mother having an affair and refers to her in a derogatory nature.
  - Gun violence
    - Gunshots are heard from far away which startles a female character and two male characters.

Chapter 3

- Discussion of weapons and gun use
  - Various firearms and weapons are discussed by multiple characters and specific firearms are mentioned by name.
- References to execution
  - Distant gunfire can still be heard, and the noise is compared to the style of executions by several of the characters.
- Discussion of gun laws
  - A female character and a male character briefly discuss gun regulation in Australia and the United States.
  - A female character makes an off-handed remark about gun control.

Chapter 4

- Graphic violence (storytelling)
    - A male character describes a past gunfight involving many of the characters with references to injury and death, including the death of a "kid" but the age is not referenced as he is referring to a younger male instead of a minor.
- References to rape
    - During the storytelling, the male character references the implied rape of another female character.
    - The female character listening to the story implies that she has been raped.
- Insensitive discussion of sexual violence
    - The male character makes an offensive remark in regards to rape, and the female character chastises him for it (this is quickly rectified and apologised for).

Chapter 5

- Threat with a weapon against a minor
    - A female teenage character (16 years old) is held at gunpoint.
- Post execution (observed)
    - Two male characters witness dead bodies from a distance and mention that it looks like they've been executed.
- Implied sexual assault (observed)
    - Two male characters witness women being mistreated from a distance in a way that suggests sexual violence.
- References to stabbing and death

- A female character mentions that her husband died from being stabbed.

Chapter 6

- Threat with a weapon against a minor
  - A female teenage character (16 years old) is still held at gunpoint from the previous chapter.
- Extreme violence and mutilation
  - A male character violently dismembers and kills another man by cutting off his arm with a machete and then slicing his throat with it.
- Killing in self-defence
  - The act is framed as protecting another person.
- Lack of remorse following violence
  - The character expresses no regret for the act.
- Trauma of a minor
  - The female teenage character (16 years old) is extremely traumatised and distressed from this interaction.
  - During this, she urinates on herself.

Chapter 7

- References to violence, murder and rape
  - A male characters tells a female character (who is unfamiliar with the information) that the group had previously heard of groups along the highway committing various acts of violence.
- Verbal aggression and mistreatment
  - An unknown voice on their radios taunts them.

    ○ A male character speaks harshly and
      aggressively to a female character.

Chapter 8

- Survival violence and societal collapse
  - A male character describes widespread
    violence over resources.
- Dead bodies (referenced)
  - The male character references large numbers
    of corpses in cities.
- Coerced sexual exchange (referenced)
  - A female character recounts her husband
    asking her to exchange sex for protection,
    which she does.
- Alcohol use & smoking
  - A male and female character drink around a
    campfire.
  - They also smoke cigarettes.

Chapter 9

- Dead bodies (hanging)
  - Bodies are discovered hanging outside a house
    and they are described in detail.

Chapter 10

- Animal confrontation
  - A female teenage character (16 years old)
    encounters a black bear at close range though
    neither she nor the bear is harmed.
- Starvation
  - A group of severely malnourished people is
    encountered at a campsite.

- Medical condition
    ○ One of the starving characters also displays
      symptoms of a health condition (orthostatic
      hypotension) and has run out of medication.

Chapter 11

- Animal death (hunting)
    ○ A deer is killed for food (not graphically
      described) but a male character mentions
      needing to tie it up to carry it back.

Chapter 12

- Animal processing (skinning)
    ○ The deer from the previous chapter is skinned
      for food preparation.

Chapter 13

- Abandonment
    ○ A male character considers leaving members of
      the group behind and taking two female
      characters with him (his family members).
- Physical altercation
    ○ Two male characters engage in a fist fight.
- Alcohol misuse
    ○ A male character becomes heavily intoxicated.
- Execution
    ○ An unarmed male is shot and killed by a male
      character in an execution style.

Chapter 14

- Alcohol use
  - A male character is intoxicated from the previous chapter.
- Grief and loss
  - Many of the characters reflect on what they have lost and what they miss.

Chapter 15

- Misogynistic and degrading language
  - A male character makes derogatory comments about and towards women.
- Physical altercation
  - Two male characters fight.
- Coerced sexual exchange (referenced)
  - A female character describes being pressured into sex for survival (the same reference as chapter 8 with a bit more detail).
- Confession of killing a spouse
  - The female character then admits that she was the one who stabbed her husband (the same reference as chapter 5 with a bit more detail)
- Lack of remorse following violence
  - The female character justifies the act without regret.
  - The male character she is speaking with agrees with her.

Chapter 16

- Physical assault
  - A male character attacks a female character.
- Misogynistic and degrading language

- o During the altercation, the male character
    makes derogatory comments about the female
    character.
- Stabbing
  - o The female character stabs the male character
    in the shoulder at the end of the altercation.

Chapter 17

- Dead body with mutilation / branding
  - o A male corpse is found tied to a fence with
    carved markings in his chest.

Chapter 18

- Assisted suicide
  - o An elderly female character requests the help
    of a female character to end her life.
  - o This is not described in detail, as the female
    character assists the elderly character to a
    secluded area and leaves her to end her own
    life alone, at her request.

Chapter 19

- Handling of a dead body
  - o A male character buries the body from the
    aftermath of the previous chapter.

Chapter 20

- Dead body (hanging)
  - o A male body is found suspended from a lamp
    post.
- Insensitive remark about school shootings

- A female character makes an insensitive comment about school shootings, and a male character is offended.
    - He remarks that he lost a cousin to a school shooting, and the female character apologises and they move on from the conversation (he does, however, make a dry joke about it too).
- Forced separation / abandonment
    - A male character is made to leave the group by another male character.

Chapter 21

- Execution (aftermath)
    - Three characters discover bodies that have been executed.
- Accidental physical injury
    - A female character is struck by a male character during fighting training, causing her lip to split.
- Threat with a weapon
    - A male character threatens another male character and holds him at gunpoint.

Chapter 22

- Ongoing threat with a weapon
    - A male character still holds another male character at gunpoint from the previous chapter.

Chapter 23

- Animal death (hunting)
    - A deer is killed for food, but not described in great detail.
- Romantic conflict / perceived infidelity
    - A female character, having previously become close with a male character, shares intimacy with another male character (both of these male characters are close friends).
    - They later share a kiss.
- Emotional & physical distress
    - A male character becomes increasingly distressed and belligerent towards others, and later faints.

Chapter 24

- Near-car accident
    - The characters are all nearly in a car accident when the tyre blows while riding in an RV together.
- Near-injury with a weapon
    - A female character narrowly avoids being impaled by a machete during the accident.
- Threat with weapons
    - Multiple male characters are held at gunpoint by other male characters and a stand-off begins.

Chapter 25

- Ongoing threat with weapons
    - The standoff continues from the previous chapter.

- Reference to poisoning (non-serious)
  - A female character makes a comment about another female character poisoning her (the comment is made in front of her, and she is not offended).

Chapter 26

- Hopelessness and confinement
  - The characters are trapped indoors during extreme winter conditions with little food.
- Consensual sexual content
  - A sexual encounter between a male and female character is described in detail with mild language.

Chapter 27

- Illness
  - A female character becomes unwell (they do not know what it is).
- Emotional mistreatment following intimacy
  - After the previous chapter, the male character behaves harshly towards the female character.

Chapter 28

- Argument and minor physical altercation
  - A disagreement escalates into brief physical contact between two male characters who are close friends.

Chapter 29

- Consensual sexual content (more explicit)
  - A sexual encounter is described between the same male and female characters as in chapter 26, but with greater detail.
  - This interaction is also more physical than the first interaction.
- Ambush and kidnapping
  - The group is attacked during the night and caught off guard, and taken captive.
  - During this, various characters are physically mistreated and forcefully being pushed to the ground.
- Death of a child (off-page, implied)
  - A young child (3 years old) is taken and killed, implied through sound.
  - This scene does not go into detail, and the mother does not witness it as she has been rendered unconscious.
  - Some of the male characters reference that children are not welcome where they are going.

Chapter 30

- Captivity and restraint
  - The characters are bound, gagged, and transported against their will.
- Suggestion of sexual assault
  - A threat of sexual violence towards the females is implied but not carried out.
- Near execution
  - A female character is nearly shot at close range.
- Forced nudity

- The female characters are made to undress in front of others in order to bathe, then forced to wear other plain clothing.
- Physical abuse
  - Some characters are beaten while restrained.
- Grief and trauma
  - A female character reacts to the loss of her child (shown through various moments of violent outbursts, as well as slipping in and out of a catatonic state).
- Death (off-page)
  - The female characters are taken outside to discover a male character has been shot in the head.

Chapter 31

- Psychological torture
  - A male character attempts to mentally and emotionally break others.
- Physical abuse
  - A female character notes that the male characters had previously been beaten.
  - Some of them are continued to be beaten during the psychological torture.
- References to pregnancy and termination
  - A male character (doctor) references that his daughter had fallen pregnant and without the necessary tools for termination, she was killed (as they don't allow children where they are, previously referenced in chapter 29).
- Violent restraint
  - A female character is forcibly subdued after attempting to harm someone with a knife.

Chapter 32

- Emotional & mental instability
  - The male antagonist is extremely unhinged.
- Psychological torture
  - Ongoing attempts to break characters mentally and emotionally.
- Physical torture and branding
  - A female character is branded on her arm with a hot iron.
- Threats with weapons
  - A male character uses a gun to intimidate the other characters.
- Sustained violence
  - Multiple forms of violence occur throughout the chapter.
- Vomit
  - A female character vomits on herself, causing another male character to vomit as well.

This chapter may be extremely distressing for readers, as the group is forced to witness the torture of a female character, with some members also experiencing intermittent physical abuse. The antagonist provides detailed explanations of how the characters will be treated, and mistreated, while in captivity.

Chapter 33

- Intentional infliction of pain
  - A female character deliberately causes another female character pain while treating her injuries (they are arguing during the interaction and she uses antiseptic to cause the pain).
- Isolation and emotional distress

o Characters are separated and left alone for
extended periods.
* Taunting and verbal cruelty
o A female character is repeatedly mocked by
another female character.

Chapter 34

* Explicit rape (graphic) / physical injury
o A prolonged and detailed sexual assault occurs
with a female character.
o During this scene, blood, sweat, and semen are
all referenced, as well as physical injury.
o The male antagonist is described to bite her, as
well as lick her blood.
* Suicide (referenced)
o A male character references the suicide of his
wife following a rape similar to the one
witnessed.
* Dead body (referenced)
o The male character references his wife's body
having been thrown into the bay to dispose
of her.

This chapter may be extremely distressing for readers, as the main female character is violently raped by the primary male antagonist. Another male character is present and forced to witness the event, though his internal experience is not described.

Chapter 35

* Aftermath of sexual assault (minor)
o A female teenage character (16 years old) is
treated for injuries following a sexual assault.

Chapter 36

- Attempted rape (minor)
  - A female teenage character (16 years old) is nearly assaulted by a male teenage character (17 years old).
- Death of a minor
  - A male teenage character (17 years old) is killed.
  - This is an accident which happens quickly and not described in great detail, however, his body and eyes are referenced by the female teenage character.
- Taunting
  - A female character is verbally targeted by another female character, causing a brief physical altercation.
- Physical and psychological abuse
  - A male and female character are restrained, harmed and interrogated.

Chapter 37

- Taunting and verbal abuse
  - Three female characters are verbally degraded by another female character.
- Physical and psychological torture
  - A male and female character continue to be restrained, harmed and interrogated (from the previous chapter).
- Forced removal of medical treatment
  - A female character's stitches are forcibly removed as a form of torture (the male antagonist rips them out with his fingers).

Chapter 38

- Sexual assault (aftermath)
  - Injuries from further assault are described from another attack on the main female character by the same male antagonist.
- Self-inflicted injury (with purpose)
  - A male character intentionally harms himself (though this is established prior to be intentional in order to visit a female character in the infirmary to talk privately).
- Violent intent
  - Some characters discuss killing their captors.
- Psychological abuse
  - A male and female character continue to be restrained and interrogated (from the previous chapters) though this has changed to coersion.

Chapter 39

- Emotional distress and outburst (including a minor)
  - A female teenage character (16 years old) reacts with fear and anger towards another female character she is close with.
  - The female character violently reacts (though not towards the female teenage character).
  - The female teenage character then breaks down emotionally.
- Psychological abuse
  - A male and female character continue to be restrained, interrogated and coersed (from the previous chapters).
- Threat with a weapon

- The male antagonist threatens a male character with a gun.
- Threat of self-harm with a weapon
  - The female character briefly turns a gun on herself before attempting to harm the male antagonist.

Chapter 40

- Discussion of trauma
  - Two female characters speak about their experiences as mental health caregivers.
  - They briefly discuss the wellbeing and mental health of another female character.

Chapter 41

- Intense violence and combat (initially off-page)
  - A large-scale conflict erupts between many characters.
- Graphic injury and death
  - Fatal wounds are described in detail.
- Blood and gore
  - Significant bloodshed is depicted.
- Multiple dead bodies
  - Numerous casualties are present and described.
  - A male character is killed with a gun and his death is described in great detail.
- Betrayal
  - A male character is revealed to have betrayed numerous other characters.
- Revenge killing
  - A male character kills a male antagonist while a female character witnesses it.

- Lack of remorse following violence
  - The characters expresses no regrets for the act.

Chapter 42

- Intense violence and combat
  - Fighting continues between many characters (from the previous chapter).
- Graphic injury
  - A male antagonist stabs a male character in the eye.
  - A male character is discovered to have been shot.
- Death and dead bodies
  - Some characters are killed during the conflict, sustaining woulds from gunshots and stabbings.
- Attempted rape (of a minor)
  - A female teenage character (16 years old) is targeted but saved by a female character.
- Defensive killing
  - A female character kills a male character to protect the female teenage character.
- Abandonment
  - Two female characters are left behind during the escape.

If you feel ready to continue, please return to the beginning of the book. If not, thank you for taking the time to read through this guide. Your wellbeing and mental health matters, and it's completely okay if this journey isn't for you.

Acknowledgments

First, thanks to my chronic connective tissue disorder for rendering me bedridden on and off (mostly on) for two years - without you, this book might not exist (though my joints are still mad at me).

To my partner (who rarely reads) - thank you for being the most incredibly supportive man, reminding me to eat, sleep, and exist outside my hyper-focus on writing. I literally could not have done this without you.

To my mother (who reads NOTHING but biographies) - thank you for actually reading this, for sending me moment-by-moment reactions to book events in the form of unsolicited, hilarious commentary.

To caffeine - without you, this book might still be a very extensively planned spreadsheet.

And to the characters themselves... well, you know who you are. Thanks for making me laugh, cry, and occasionally question my life choices.

Finally, thanks to you, the reader, for picking this book up, for staying awake through the chaos, and for letting this story into your imagination. You're the real MVP.

DYSTOPIA SERIES

In a world decimated by plague and fractured by power, a group of survivors clings to hope in the face of unrelenting darkness. What begins as a desperate search for safety becomes a relentless battle against tyranny, fanaticism, and the ghosts of their own pasts.

Led by fierce loyalty and fragile trust, they navigate captivity, betrayal, and shifting alliances in a brutal landscape where freedom is a fleeting illusion and survival demands impossible choices. As one woman is thrust into the heart of rising regimes and twisted ideologies, her strength becomes the spark of resistance - and the key to reshaping what remains of humanity.

In this emotionally charged, post-apocalyptic epic, resilience is forged in the fire of adversity, and the greatest battles are waged within.

Get updates and follow the journey at

www.ceshorland.com/dystopia-series

DEADWEIGHT

BOOK ONE

In a world shattered by a relentless pandemic, survival comes at a cost few are prepared to pay. As civilisation collapses, the lines between right and wrong blur, and the people left behind are forced to decide who they are when there are no rules left to follow.

A group of survivors fights to stay alive in a landscape shaped by fear, shifting alliances, and ruthless power. Every choice carries weight. Every mistake leaves a mark. And the further they push forward, the more the world demands from them in return.

But when their path leads them into the hands of something far more controlled, and far more dangerous, survival becomes a different kind of battle. One where power is enforced, loyalty is tested, and escape may cost them everything.

As the past refuses to stay buried and the future grows more uncertain, they must confront what they're willing to sacrifice - not just to live, but to hold onto what makes them human.

Because in this world, survival isn't the end goal.

It's only the beginning.

More information can be found at

www.ceshorland.com/dystopia-series/deadweight

DOMINION

BOOK TWO

After a narrow escape from unthinkable captivity, the search for peace leads Beth and her allies to a fragile stronghold deep in the wastelands. But even in a place that promises safety, danger wears many faces - and some threats come not from outside, but from within.

As a deadly force spreads and power shifts into the hands of a rising zealot, tensions boil over into chaos. Bound by loyalty but torn by doubt, Beth must confront the price of survival in a world where faith can become a weapon, and no sanctuary lasts forever.

In this tense continuation of the series, strength is tested, trust is shattered, and the fight for freedom is more treacherous than ever.

More information can be found at:

www.ceshorland.com/dystopia-series/dominion

DEFEAT

BOOK THREE

In a world ruled by fear and fanaticism, one woman's captivity becomes the crucible of a quiet rebellion. Trapped behind gilded walls, Beth faces a cunning tyrant whose vision for humanity is as seductive as it is brutal. To survive, she must become both a weapon and a whisper of resistance.

As secrets fester beneath a crumbling empire and the line between faith and control blurs, Beth risks everything to reclaim her voice - and her future. But freedom, like truth, comes at a cost.

This harrowing chapter in their journey explores the price of defiance in a world where breaking free is only the beginning.

More information can be found at:

www.ceshorland.com/dystopia-series/defeat

STILL TO COME

And this is only the beginning. Over the course of this twelve-book series, our characters' journeys will continue to twist and turn through trials and betrayals, testing the limits of their courage and resolve. Nothing comes easy in their world, and every victory carries its own shadow.

They will face challenges that push them to their breaking points, forcing impossible choices and demanding sacrifices that will leave scars both seen and unseen. Alliances will shift, loyalties will be questioned, and danger will lurk in every corner, reminding them that survival is never guaranteed.

Yet through the darkness and uncertainty, they will grow, evolve, and fight for what they hold most dear. Their stories will be filled with heartbreak, unexpected triumphs, and moments that will leave you breathless, proving that even in a world of chaos and cruelty, resilience and hope endure.

More information can be found at:

www.ceshorland.com/dystopia-series

9 781764 251600